Martyn Whittock was born in Somerset and took a degree in Politics at Bristol University. After graduating he taught history in Dorset and in Buckinghamshire, and has since become Head of Humanities at a Wiltshire school. He has published a number of scholarly articles and is the author of three textbooks, *The Origins of England, AD 410-600*, *The Roman Empire* and *The Reformation*. He has acted as an historical consultant to both the National Trust and BBC Radio and his previous historical novel *The Dice in Flight* (available in paperback from Headline) was praised by *The Times* as an 'accomplished first novel'. Martyn Whittock is in his early thirties and lives in Bradford-on-Avon with his wife and daughter.

Also by Martyn Whittock

The Dice in Flight

The Moon in the Morning

Martyn Whittock

HEADLINE

First published in Great Britain in 1992
by HEADLINE BOOK PUBLISHING PLC

First published in paperback in 1993
by HEADLINE BOOK PUBLISHING PLC

10 9 8 7 6 5 4 3 2 1

ISBN 0 7472 3985 1

Typeset by Keyboard Services, Luton

Printed and bound in Great Britain by
HarperCollins Manufacturing, Glasgow

HEADLINE BOOK PUBLISHING PLC
Headline House
79 Great Titchfield Street
London W1P 7FN

To my wife Christine, with love
and thanks for her advice,
encouragement and support

Author's Note

As with any historical novel *The Moon in the Morning*
is built around a factual framework. For this particular novel there are three main strands within that
framework.

The first is the fact that, despite the inferior legal
and social position of women in the late Middle Ages,
a widow could exercise considerable power. Isabelle
Crosse's struggle to be recognised as having the full
rights of a man was one experienced by many widows,
both noble and in the merchant classes of the towns.
It was a search for respect and power which could
create violent opposition both from those who dis-
agreed with it in principle and from those who felt
that a widow could be intimidated by force. Isabelle's
conflicts are all well attested in the legal documents
which survive from the fourteenth century.

The second strand is that of the lucrative trading
that existed between the east-coast ports of England
and the forest lands of the eastern Baltic and Russia,
or the 'Land of Darkness' as it was known in medieval
chronicles. This trade flourished in the 1380s and
provoked bitter opposition from the Germans who
had previously enjoyed a monopoly in the sale of furs
and beeswax. In Boston, merchants like Isabelle were

in a prime position to exploit this source of enormous wealth.

The third strand is provided by the fen-country itself. To all outsiders who visit it, this land of flat and wet still possesses an unnerving quality even after centuries of drainage have tamed its spreading wildness. In the late Middle Ages it was still a land of fiercely independent people who had never experienced the more demeaning aspects of feudalism. It was, instead, a 'frontier society' with all that that implies of solidarity against the elements and a quick resort to violence where the writ of the king ran weakly, or not at all.

All of these strands combine in *The Moon in the Morning* and reflect something of the vivid and tragic experiences of real people in the late fourteenth century. The medieval records of the fenland manors and the town of Boston itself have provided the raw material for the characters in this fiction. And there still are fenland families who descend from medieval ancestors named Crosse, Curteys, Pexton, Thymelby, Coppledyke and Redman.

For assistance with this fenland research I am grateful to many people, including the curator of the Guildhall Museum in Boston, and Mrs I. Fleetcroft, Lecturer in Archaeology at Boston College, who pointed me in the direction of valuable sources of evidence. The staff of the Lincolnshire Reference Library suggested numerous ideas including details relating to the organisation of customs in Boston in the reign of Richard II. Martin Brown, of the Trust for Lincolnshire Archaeology provided information concerning roads and navigable rivers.

With regard to research on Russia and the eastern Baltic my thanks are owed to the staff of the Novosti Press Agency and to the USSR Institute of Archaeology, Moscow. Another invaluable source was J. Martin's brilliant study of the trade of Novgorod, *Treasure of the Land of Darkness* (Cambridge University Press, 1986).

The fenland places mentioned in this book can still be explored and, on a misty morning or, better still, a windswept winter's evening, the modern visitor can still glimpse something of the threatening landscape that was home to Isabelle Crosse and to the countless people who lived in the medieval towns and villages of the fens.

Dorchester,
St Martin's Day.

Chapter 1

The River Welland, at low tide, expires into the Wash with a drawn-out sigh. It returns, sudden, like a word of anger. And from the bleak drift of grey mud-flats rise the geese flocks. They cry of mist-haunted melancholy. The wind parts the reeds of the salt-fen. The tide draws in: inexorable, relentless, like the providence of God.

From the causeway Richard Pexton drew back on his reins. His mount was nervous and so was he. Both were fen-born. Horse and rider could sense the dark water surging about them, lapping at the causeway, drowning low islands.

'Mistress, we really should not tarry here.' He glanced at the sky; it would soon be dark. 'Mistress Isabelle. The tide will be high on the causeway. We really should not stay . . .'

He stared down the narrow track, raised up from the water and sedge. Flutters of unease unsettled his stomach. The causeway was poorly maintained; its bridges sagged and earth had slipped away into the tidal creek. But it was not that alone which gave rise to his entreaty. In the gathering twilight he stared hard. No human figure broke the dull monotony of flatness drifting into darkness. Nevertheless, he still

1

could not find solace. He felt strangely vulnerable on the narrow causeway.

'Mistress, the night is not long off. We should not tarry . . .'

The object of his concerns seemed completely oblivious to his words. She stood on the sea-dyke, gazing out into the estuary. Her hood was drawn up. The breeze plucked at it. Strands of shining ice-blonde hair escaped her hairnet of gold thread. Like a blizzard, it blew about her face, catching the light. The woman was in her early twenties, with a long slim face and rosebud mouth. Her fine, fair skin was like the smooth marble of a classical statue. Slowly, carefully, she drew back her hood. Eyes shut, she drank in the clinging, wet air. Then, at last, she turned towards her mounted companion. Her own horse stood nearby, bridle hanging down to the wet grass. Her deep blue eyes swam. Was it tears, or just the wind? Pexton could not tell. Yet even the suggestion of sorrow in her eyes pained him.

'Is it true, Richard, that a man was buried alive in this sea-dyke?'

The voice was a little husky. It was more serious than the pretty rosebud lips and clear skin led one to expect. It was deep; strangely sensual when married to her obvious beauty. She had loveliness and depth.

Richard loved her. His emotions betrayed him, whenever he was least prepared. *Oh Isabelle*, he thought, in agony. *You stir me so*.

'Is it true?' she persisted, catching up her bridle and pulling herself up on to her side-saddle. She held her clerk with a frank and open gaze.

Richard smiled inwardly. It was only the wind.

There were no tears in her eyes. He had been betrayed by an evening breeze. He should have known better. Isabelle Crosse did not cry in public.

'So it's said, my lady. But long ago. In King Henry's time. It was a tenant who refused his service on dyke repair.'

'Where? Which part of the dyke?'

Once more her intense eyes swept the great curve of the green sea-bank. Beyond it, curlews called incessantly.

'Which part? I don't know! It's an old tale. I don't suppose anyone knows any more. It was all a long time ago.' He shuddered to think of the event: the desperate struggling, the choking wet earth; then the awful silence. A man entombed.

'We must go, Richard. It will soon be dark!'

Pexton laughed. He did so only rarely. His midnight eyes were strangers to frivolity. But now he laughed. Who could be prepared for such a woman as this?

'Yes, my lady. I think you may be right.'

Together they urged their horses forward. Hooves splashed in the puddle-glistening ruts and pot-holes of the road. Behind them the sea-dyke stood immense and unyielding, its buried watchman standing guard over the sinking day.

For a mile or so the two rode in single file. The state of the causeway would not allow for riding side by side. To the west, the Lincolnshire fens spread away like a patched rug. Marsh and reedbed, creek and island were painted in pastel by the setting sun. To the east, sea and mud-flats were etched in charcoal by the approaching night. Ahead, the incomplete stump of

3

Boston's great church stood like a boundary marker, raised between light and darkness. At last the way widened. The woman slowed her mount to a walk and allowed her companion to join her.

'It's a disgrace!'

'My lady?' Pexton raised a quizzical eyebrow.

'A disgrace. The state of this road.' Isabelle Crosse gestured with her riding crop. 'If my tenants perform repair work, why are others less diligent?'

She cast her clerk an angry glance. Wisely he held his peace. The rhetorical question elicited no reply. He knew as well as she did that virtually every land holding in the fen-country owed customary service: a sea-dyke to repair, a drainage ditch to clear of silt, a causeway to maintain. He also knew how frequently such services were neglected.

'How many bridges have we crossed since we left the manor?'

Pexton's thick eyebrows knitted in concentration. 'It must be upward of twenty, my lady.'

'And over half out of repair. The prior at Bridge End cares little for the fate of travellers to his convent. By Our Lady, I'll warrant that his patron is not St Christopher . . .'

'No – 'tis the Convent of St Saviour . . .'

As soon as he had spoken, he knew his error. Why was he never quick enough to pick up her irony? Why was he always too eager to reply and please?

She tossed her head and light fell on the folds of white-gold. 'I know, Richard.'

Pexton blushed. Then she smiled at him. And at once he was all too well aware of why he fell over himself to please her. Since he had negotiated her

4

wedding to his late master, he had loved the woman. He wondered if it was as obvious to her as it had been to Anthony Crosse. He blushed again to think of the husband's amused smiles.

Seeking to disentangle himself from this morass of emotions, he at last spoke of what was heavy on his mind. 'There will be trouble, I fear.'

'About the causeway? I doubt it, Richard. Can you see the prior of St Saviour's being brought to book for his lack of concern? I doubt it.'

'No, my lady. Not the causeway. I'm speaking of the will. There will be trouble. I can smell it.' He glanced back the way that he had come. It was as if the twilight mist conveyed some secret message of menace. 'I can smell it.'

Isabelle's horse had begun to trot. She slowed it to a walk once more. Her blue eyes showed no hint of emotion. 'Go on, Richard. Tell me what you fear.'

The clerk let out his breath in a hiss. How could he do justice to his fears? Absent-mindedly he ruffled his horse's mane. His dark brows were knotted in concentration, his eyes clouded with thoughts.

'Long before your marriage, my lady, I counselled my master to draw up a full will. After your marriage, I increased my advice. What with the manors at Swineshead, Bicker and Bridge End, the tenements in Boston and the cloth stores, there was more than enough requirement for a clear . . .' He frowned as he framed the words. 'For a clear . . .'

'For a clear method of disposing of his wealth?'

'Yes! I couldn't put it better. But, try as I might, he would not be rushed. I counselled prudence and he laughed at my caution. I mean no disrespect, my lady . . .' Pexton looked inquiringly at his companion. He had learned that frankness was a virtue valued by this woman. However, frankness could go too far.

'There's no disrespect in stating the truth, Richard. My husband thought he was immortal. Men often do. He was wrong.'

The clerk nodded. Back at the creek-side manor of Bicker, Anthony Crosse lay cold in his winding sheet.

They were close to Boston now. The smoke from the tenements mingled with the sea mist. Soon they would be home. When the clerk next spoke, he did so with some urgency. It was as if there were things he had to say before they reached the town; secrets that could not be divulged before casual listeners.

'A death-bed will is often a cause of grief, long after the grave is covered with grass.'

'A proverb, Richard?'

'Perhaps, my lady. Aye – perhaps it should be! For without a document there will always be those to dispute and contest its provisions. I've known too much distress come from such a will. It was that which I sought to avoid. But I have failed.'

'Not you, Richard. The failure was not yours.'

Her voice, usually so cool and confident, was suddenly tender. Pexton wanted to shout out: 'I wanted to protect you. You!' But he did not do so. Instead he merely nodded before he spoke again.

'There will be those who will question the accuracy of the witnesses. For in truth, there were only you and me and the parish priest . . .'

His mistress broke in on him. 'Who will call me a liar, Richard? Can you name them?'

Pexton was all too certain of who would do so. However he was more circumspect about naming names. 'Believe me, they will arise. There are many who would jump at the chance of seizing wealth from a dead man's hands. They will use every trick, madam. They will seize on every area of vagueness; on every uncertainty. Your husband was a very wealthy man. He had enemies in life. They will not have become friends now that he is dead.'

'Name them, Richard.'

Pexton twisted his bridle in embarrassment. How could he lay charges against his social superiors? How could he accuse masters of the Boston guilds? How could he name his late master's bastard son? He clicked his teeth. 'Edward will not accept it!'

At last he had said it. At last he had named Anthony Crosse's bastard son as a rival, even an enemy. Now he swept on. It all had to be said. 'Without a legitimate heir, all of your husband's wealth devolves to you. He said as much. We heard him. And no one can question the legality of such a singular inheritance. Its legality cannot be questioned.'

'Then what do you fear?'

'Men may see that something is so in law, but still hope to take what they can get. Men break the law. Men work around it. They may even seek to change it. Your husband left his bastard son the manor at Swineshead only. It was his to leave and we heard his words. But Edward will not be satisfied with that alone. He was his son – if base-born! And there will be others who will seek to chip away at so singular an inheritance. Because . . .' His voice faded.

'Because that singular inheritance has fallen to a woman?'

'Aye, my lady. Because you are a woman. They will hope to take from you what they would fear to take from a man.'

Isabelle betrayed no emotion. Her eyes were clear. No sea breeze clouded them now. 'Thank you, Richard. I value your frankness.'

The clerk nodded without comment. He was a very worried man.

'But I think you mistake Edward,' she continued with a slight smile. 'For sure, he will not be satisfied with Swineshead alone as his inheritance. For whatever my rights in law he sees himself as his father's male heir. And does that surprise you?'

Pexton mutely shook his head.

'But I have the measure of Edward. No doubt he will test me! But I shall surprise him from the start. I intend to make over to him my fishing rights on the River Witham.'

'But my lady!' Pexton pulled on his horse's bridle. Snickering with annoyance, the palfrey pulled up its head. 'The fish weirs on the river yield good money! All of your tenants now pay "fishsilver", rather than sticks of eels as in the past. 'Tis a reliable income and a handsome one. Why give over your fishsilver to Edward? 'Tis yours by right.'

'And will not Edward be disarmed by such a gesture of goodwill? For in doing so I increase his income to that of at least a minor guildsman.'

'I see your strategy, my lady – but it may be seen as weakness . . .'

Isabelle cast him a frosty glance. 'Listen Richard, I

am not as unaware as you imagine.' He turned crimson at the mild rebuke. 'It may well be that Edward challenges his father's dying wishes. I think that he may do so! But he is a reasonable man and a gesture of goodwill may win his loyalty. Besides, should he ever go to litigation to challenge the will, what jury will fail to be impressed by my generosity and my attempt at conciliation?

'There's more, Richard. My late husband had trouble enough taking his fishsilver from the tenants along the river. You know that his right to do so has been challenged by more than one other manor north of Boston. Well, that worry is now Edward's. My gift is not without barbs. I shall have – how shall I put it? – other fish to fry, and the loss of one worry will be a godsend.' She gave her clerk a thawing smile. 'I shall also give half the fishsilver rights to the abbey at Ely. Part shall endow a chantry to pray for my husband's soul. The remainder shall be at the abbot's disposal.'

'That will win you a powerful friend and put a check on Edward's ambitions – should he have any,' he added hastily, only too well aware of the implications of his words. 'And furthermore, the parish priest who witnessed to the will . . .'

'Holds his living from the abbey at Ely!'

Pexton's dark eyes danced. 'Very good, my lady. To challenge the priest's word is to challenge the abbot. And the abbot will now be a friend . . .'

'Quite so, Richard. So, as you can see, I have not come into my inheritance totally unprepared!'

She kicked her horse's flanks and the jennet sprang forward. She gave it its head and, amidst scattering puddles, she galloped the last half-mile to Boston.

Richard Pexton, not to be outdone, followed her in a flurry of hooves and mud.

They entered the town from the south-west. The suburb of Boston, west of the Witham, was a sprawl of newly laid-out plots and the stone houses of Lincoln merchants. Both slowed their mounts to a walk as they entered the High Street. On either side, flickering candle-light showed through the shutters of shops and tenements. Here and there a scurrying figure glanced up at the approach of the riders. One raised a hand in greeting, recognising Isabelle's unhooded profile. Other than that, the streets were almost deserted this damp Monday evening, 25 March 1381, the Feast of the Annunciation of the Virgin Mary.

Crossing the River Witham by the Town Bridge, they entered the now quiet market-place. Trestles and hurdles were stacked away. West of the market-place the mighty stump of St Botolph's parish church soared away into the darkness. Around it, the builders' scaffolds and ladders hung like cobwebs.

Isabelle and Richard made for the northern end of the market-place. Here, the thoroughfare of Strait Bargate was flanked by the halls and shops of the great trade guilds. One such hall, its leaning jetties smartly whitewashed, had been the home of Anthony Crosse.

A narrow alleyway led off from the road. Behind the hall lay a courtyard lined with store-sheds and stables. Here Richard jumped down from his horse and called loudly for the grooms. Surprised at supper, they came hurrying. Hands wrestled with fastenings of cotte and cloak, the younger ones smoothing out their tousled locks with eager fingers. The mistress had returned and they scurried about her with teenage blushes and self-conscious formality. Richard brushed aside the attentions of the servants and helped down his mistress himself. He would not share her with the stable boys. They watched him, sullen and resentful.

Richard and Isabelle made their way into the house: she cool and distant, apparently unaware of the stares of the servants; he thoughtful, and limping from an old accident. The mistress and her faithful clerk. A great fire was burning in the hall and smoke hung in clouds amongst the lofty rafters. Household servants scattered before their mistress like mice before a cat.

Isabelle was met by a woman in her late forties. The woman nodded at the clerk in a genial way. Pexton, who was pulling off his riding cloak, returned the familiar look. Then, in a gesture which would not have been misplaced between sisters, the older woman kissed Isabelle.

'Your messenger arrived on Saturday night. We all share your grief. Your husband, my master, was a good man. Rest assured he is with God and his saints.'

Isabelle nodded. 'Thank you, Eleanor. I have truly missed you. It has been a hard four days.'

Eleanor de Bamville nodded sympathetically. She was a round-faced brunette, shorter than her mistress and rounded where the younger woman curved. And yet there was something curiously attractive about her. There was something curiously disquieting too about the relationship between the mistress and the older woman. It was as if the elder woman were more confessor than servant.

11

Richard knew that Eleanor had travelled far. On her ample breast she carried a lead brooch in the form of a cockleshell. But Eleanor had gone even further than the Shrine of St James at Compostella in Spain. Once she had spoken of Jerusalem itself and had made light of a shipwreck on the Syrian coast.

Pexton had no idea how she and Isabelle had met. All he knew was that, when the younger woman married Anthony Crosse, the dark-haired pilgrim had come with her – as companion and confidante.

As Eleanor helped Isabelle remove her riding cloak, Richard watched his mistress lovingly. She had that snow-blown hair and fair skin which spoke of a thread of ancestry stretching back to some unknown Viking antecedent. Even the blue eyes were clear, like northern skies. There was something immeasurably cool about her. And yet, when her small mouth opened in laughter, or when her eyes sparkled like sun on ice, there was a rich sensuousness about her which defied description.

Pexton shook his head. He had always been a contented bachelor; so why over these past two years had he given way to these curious evaluations? Never before had he felt the currents of physical desire which now surged through him without warning. He frowned.

'William Curteys is here to see you,' Eleanor informed her mistress. 'He has been here since dusk. I took the liberty of sitting him in the solar with a jug of hot, spiced wine. I thought that you would want to see him.'

Isabelle brushed back her long blonde hair. Her golden hairnet lay crumpled beside her cloak.

'I had thought to find him here. I sent the same messenger to him as to Edward. Anthony's death has repercussions for both of them. I'll go to see him now.'

Richard made to follow her but she shook her head. 'You must be very tired, Richard. You have served me well these past few days. Now you deserve your rest. I will see William Curteys myself. We have much to speak of.'

The clerk felt a little aggrieved at his sudden dismissal but he bowed stiffly and limped away.

Isabelle found William Curteys sitting in the solar. Eleanor had had the servants set up a brazier to heat the wood-panelled room and Curteys was warming himself beside it. The shutters were drawn tight against the fenland air and sea breezes and a mutton-fat candle burnt steadily on a solitary dresser as another cast light from an oak trestle table.

He turned as the door creaked. Crossing the room he embraced the newly widowed Isabelle. 'I am sorry, Isabelle. You know how I share your grief. Besides yourself, none loved Anthony more than I did. We have – had – been partners for over ten years. His father and mine were like brothers. What can I say?'

He raised strong, well-manicured hands in an open gesture of sorrow. The candle-light caught at the gold and silver of his rings. The same light sent waves across the polished oak of his rich, thick hair and luxuriant beard. 'What can I say, Isabelle? We both loved him.'

Isabelle, who had never loved her husband, cross-ed to the trestle table and poured herself a mug of spiced Gascon wine.

'Thank you, William. I know how close you were to Anthony. He valued your advice and support above all others.' She dismissed his polite denial. 'No, William! You know as well as I do that my husband trusted you and loved you.'

As she sipped the fragrant wine, she could have added, 'More than he ever loved me, whom he bedded with such energy. And more than he ever trusted me.' However she did not, for she knew that no husband had any obligation to make his wife partner to his plans; any more than he had to love her as a lover, rather than for her wealth. Instead, she simply sipped her wine, reflecting wryly that she had always wanted more than a wife had a right to.

William Curteys refilled his own cup. 'Tell me how it happened.'

'You received my letter?'

'Of course. But I want to hear it from you.'

Isabelle sat down on a bench and Curteys joined her. For a moment the room was silent. Only the brazier fire crackled on its plinth.

'You know that Anthony had resolved to spend this month on the manor, out at Bicker?'

'There has been a dispute over turf cutting? A dispute with the neighbouring manor?'

'That's right. There are twenty salt pans at Bicker. Eight are on the land of our manor. The salt-rent, paid by tenants of the manor, is a tidy sum.'

Curteys nodded. 'But tenants of a rival manor have cut turf from your land in order to boil salt?'

'Quite. Last year we lost over ten perch blocks of turf to strangers from outside the manor. So this year Anthony resolved to enclose the disputed part of the

Bicker fen. He is – was – determined to keep out trespassers and protect our rights in the fen.'

'He acted early. The turf cutting does not begin until May.'

'True enough, but Anthony was always one to steal a march on his opponents. By the time it came to the cutting, he wanted to have the whole area enclosed.'

'But there was an altercation with the tenants from the rival manor?'

'There was. No violence, you understand, but a lot of shouting. Anthony's horse shied. Richard had warned him often enough that the brute was unstable . . .'

'But Anthony knew better?'

'Yes . . . and now he is dead. It threw him. He landed against a tree. Oh, William, he was in agony. It was last Thursday. We had him carried back to the manor house. Or rather Richard did – I was not out at the enclosing of the turbary, of course.'

William topped up his cup of wine. He went to pour more into Isabelle's cup. She shook her head.

'But in your letter you said he died on Friday.'

The widow was silent for a moment, as if trying to do justice to those agonised hours at the isolated fenland manor. 'He was in great pain. No bones seemed broken but we could not take the edge off his suffering. Richard and I sat with him through the night. There is a leach who lives in the village beyond the fish stews. An old woman who is wise in herbs and wild plants. She made a poultice of porridge and badger's fat. She swore blind it would relieve his torment.' Curteys raised an eyebrow and his deep chestnut eyes narrowed. 'But it had no effect. He died late on Friday afternoon. Just before sunset.'

'And he left no written will.'

'That is so. When it was obvious that he was in his last hours we summoned the priest from the village church. Before the three of us, Anthony declared his intentions for his manors and property. He received the sacraments just before he died, thank God. That, at least, we must be grateful for. He could have died, unprepared and unshriven, out at the turbary.

'The next day – Saturday – I sent messengers to you and to Edward, his son. We returned to Boston, as you have seen, late this afternoon.'

Curteys was very thoughtful. He ran one jewelled index finger through his wavy beard. 'And Anthony left all to you?'

'All except the manor at Swineshead. As you know, it was stewarded by Edward. Anthony confirmed him in it. It is his, and now he has full manorial rights over it. All dues and services owed to the land belong to Edward. The rest was bequeathed to me.'

'The only witnesses being yourself, Pexton and this village cleric?'

Isabelle caught the inflection in Curteys' voice as he pronounced the word 'only'. She remembered her clerk's comments on the causeway. However she betrayed little discernible reaction, though perhaps her lips pursed a fraction and her cheeks tightened.

Curteys seemed to expect some response and was clearly cheated of one. He looked contemplative and nodded his head slowly. 'That means that you will need an inventory of all the Crosse goods imported into our joint warehouse.'

'There is no need, William. Richard has assured me that he has a full account. Down to the last bolt of cloth and the last flagon of Italian wine. I will, of course, require an inspection, but not a detailed inventory. That much I can spare you – in our mutual grief.'

If Curteys was surprised, he did not show it. He merely let a ghost of a smile play across his lips. 'I can assure you that I shall extend to you all the assistance and loyalty that I gave to your late husband. You may rest assured that at all times I will look to your interests.'

Isabelle nodded. 'Thank you. That is as I had assumed.'

This time Curteys did look surprised. It was as if his courteous offer had been expected, as of right. He frowned. Undeterred, he picked up the thread of his previous offer: 'I shall be pleased to represent your interests in the guildhall and at the quayside. Your clerk – Pexton – is familiar with the Crosse side of the enterprise. He is more than capable of the day-to-day . . .'

'William, I am sorry. You do not seem to have understood me. I do not require a representative. Though it is kind of you to offer me your good services.' Isabelle breathed in the herbed fragrance of her wine. 'I intend to practise my late husband's "mystery". I shall represent the house of Crosse at all levels of trade and decision-making. I am more than familiar with the running of the business. I am the daughter of a guildmaster and have been the wife of one. In short, I intend to carry on the work, in the place of my husband.'

She sipped at her wine. Curteys shook his head slightly, a cynical smile playing about his lips.

'Isabelle, you are stricken with grief. The husband that you loved is dead. Small wonder that you are distressed and . . .' He was interrupted.

'It is not distress that commands my thoughts but realistic planning. You know as well as I do that a wife of a town guildsman, if widowed, has full rights before the law to exercise the mystery of her husband . . .'

'But Isabelle this simply will not . . .'

'There are no buts, William. You know the charters and statutes better than anyone. You are familiar with the Common Law and,with the practice of the guilds. I am Anthony Crosse's widow. I have full rights. Even without his last testament, before witnesses, I would have widows' rights . . .'

'You simply do not know what you are saying!'

Curteys was becoming angry now. The cynical smile was overcome with shock; shock was giving way to irritation.

'On the contrary, I know exactly what I am saying. I have taken possession of Anthony's seal and papers. I am now guildmaster of the house of Crosse. Richard has advised me regarding the legality of my actions and my plans.'

'Your plans! What plans do you have, madam?' His handsome dark features were alive with mockery.

'Oh, I have many plans, William. Both with regard to my manors and to the shipping trade. I have plans – as Anthony had plans. And why not? I was aware of all his dealings. I sat and sewed as the two of you talked. I am fully conversant with the state of affairs of the guilds. And what I lack, Richard will provide, from his experience.'

'Pexton!'

William Curteys spat out the name as if he was naming a conspirator in some dastardly plot of betrayal.

'Yes, Pexton. He has been chief clerk for over ten years. He knows the business backwards. You know full well how he has worked with the Gascon vintners and Hanse traders, not to mention the clothmakers and furriers. He is as capable now as ever he was. There will be no discontinuity in the oversight of Crosse affairs.'

'And what are your plans?'

'Since Edward is illegitimate, I am sole heir to Anthony – save in the matter of the manor bequeathed to his son. I may make grants of land, or property, by charter – as well you know. Tomorrow I shall grant my fishing rights on the Witham to Edward and to the Abbot of Ely, jointly. Richard will draw up the charter and I shall fix my seal to it. It will be made public at the shire and wapentake courts of Holland and Kesteven.'

'Does Edward know of this?'

'Not yet.' Her blue eyes sparkled like shattered ice. 'But I dare say it will not displease him! I expect him to come into Boston tomorrow or the day after. When I wrote to him I made it clear that I would be returning from the manor at Bicker today.'

William Curteys stood up. It was a lithe movement for he was strong and fit. Isabelle watched him with some approval. He was a better looking man than her late husband. He was also possessed of a cooler head.

'You really are serious, aren't you? You truly intend to exercise your full guild rights.' Even the experienced Curteys could not hide his amazement. 'And what do you think will be the reactions of the other guild members in the town?' With a gesture of his jewelled hand he turned the matter over to her.

'Oh, I expect they will be outraged. Not because I'm acting outside my rights, but rather because I choose to exercise my rights and be an honorary man!'

Curteys laughed. It was not a very friendly sound.

Isabelle went on regardless. 'They will expect me to mourn quietly while you and Richard manage the affairs of the partnership. Then they will expect me to remarry – quickly – confident in the knowledge that at that point all my goods, estates and movables will revert to my new husband; I will lose my independence in law and my right to use seal and charter and exercise a mystery. Since I am choosing not to do this, they will be outraged. Do you agree?'

'Oh yes – by St John! I agree! The good burgesses of the town will choke on their wine when they hear their own account of tonight's conversation. As you have said, the point is not what is legal, but rather what is sensible, delicate, right before God and man.'

'Surely the guild regulations and the Common Law are right before God and man? I would not dream of infringing either.'

Will Curteys let out his breath in a hiss of exasperation. Isabelle had taken leave of her senses. She was clearly deaf to all reason, ignorant of all propriety. What could he say to such a woman? When Anthony Crosse had married, his partner had thoroughly approved of the move. Already a widower at the age of thirty-five, and without issue, it had only been sensible to settle the inheritance question once and for all. Crosse had sown his wild oats, but both he and Curteys knew that there was no substitute for a son born in wedlock. Only the death of the one he'd chosen had so far frustrated Curteys in the matter. Four bastard daughters in the fens, and a bastard son, were no real consolation to Anthony Crosse either. However well Anthony treated Edward – setting him up at Swineshead – the young man could never make up for the inadequacy of his conception. And Curteys had known, even if Anthony had not, that many of the town's senior guildsmen referred in private to Edward as Moyne, his mother's name, not Crosse. Such a slur and such a possibility for contested inheritance could not be allowed to continue.

Isabelle Bradhon, at twenty years of age and a virgin – of course – had seemed the perfect answer. Her family had been respected Lincoln guildsmen, dealing in the export of Lincolnshire wool. They were well remembered in the town. If the surviving child, Isabelle, was unnaturally bookish and literate, these deficiences were more than made up for by her firm young body, her small pointed breasts and that mane of glacial hair. When Anthony promised to love her 'at bed and at board', there were few at the wedding ceremony who doubted which option most fully occupied his mind.

Now, gazing at his partner's widow, William surveyed the wreckage of those carefully laid plans. He held her father responsible for encouraging book-learning and inquisitiveness in one who clearly had no intention of safely trammelling such tendencies within a nun's vows or the virginal meditations of an anchoress's cell of contemplation.

Isabelle returned his gaze with quiet determination, her mouth set in a practised smile. It had often worked on her husband but it failed to have the desired effect on William. He still looked decidedly pained.

'See here, Will.' She shortened his name with deliberate care. 'The houses of Crosse and Curteys are the most powerful in Boston. Both you and Anthony took the five talents left to you and made them ten! Before God and the good guildsmen, you have proved your skills and integrity. And never has an opportunity passed by but Crosse and Curteys seized it. Where your fathers traded in wool to Calais, you have traded in cloth to all the lands of the North Sea and beyond. Good Lincolnshire cloth rests on many a back in Norway and Iceland through the merchant skills of Crosse and Curteys. No one before you captured such contracts with the abbey sheep farms of Stanfield and the weavers of Lincoln. More Lindsey wool and cloth passes through your hands than through those of any other merchant.'

Curteys nodded. ''Tis true. We have done well. Praise God and His saints. And we have worked hard . . .'

'And fought off all opposition; winning contracts with the Gascon vintners to carry their wine to the Baltic; forcing the Germans to give you trade concessions and carrying rights; importing fur for the furriers and skinners, herring for the guild of fishmongers. You have dismissed all who accused you of serving more than one mystery. For who can resist Crosse and Curteys?'

Her question hung in the smoky air.

William Curteys drained the last drops of his wine. 'And you fully intend to exercise Anthony's side of the work? You are sure you can practise his mystery?'

'I am. I will and I can.' Then, seeing the merest flicker of his eyebrow, she added, 'And Richard has informed me of the extent of our investment in the purchase of this summer's wool clip. That investment is secure. It will not be withdrawn . . .'

Her mention of Curteys' reliance on her newly inherited wealth brought colour to the guildsman's cheeks. 'Aye, madam, it is an investment to which Anthony was bound: by honour and by law.'

He was nettled now. He rose and reached for his cloak.

'You must go, Will? So soon?'

'I must. You are tired, I have no doubt. And I must discuss matters with my clerk and steward.'

He returned the cup to the trestle table, his lips drawn thin with irritation. He kissed Isabelle's fair-skinned cheek. It was done with strict formality; as an unwilling child might kiss an aged aunt. Few men thought to kiss Isabelle Crosse that way, but Curteys looked unrepentant.

'Good night, madam.'

'Good night, William.'

Their parting was terse and tense.

When her guest had gone Isabelle retook her seat by the brazier. Now, at last, she refilled her cup. She leaned back against the wood panel, her heart beating like the wings of a linnet in a cage.

At the manor house of Swineshead the wind and rain hammered upon the walls and roof. In Edward Crosse's cramped and sparsely furnished chamber two candles cast juggling shadows on the exposed timbers.

'Come to bed, husband. Let me soothe you. Come to your bed.'

Ann Crosse – wife to Anthony Crosse's bastard son – sat upright in the boxbed. Only a coverlet covered her nakedness; one full, swelling breast thrust beyond the cloaking sheet. She was strikingly pretty, with a sensuous mouth and cheeks the shade of morning rose. Her sea-green eyes followed every movement of her restless husband.

'He left her all! All but this ragtag of byres and barns. He left her everything. A woman whom he had bedded for less than two years.'

A crumpled letter hung from his clenched fist.

'I know, husband. But you can beat her! You can take back what is rightfully yours. Do not let her fret you so. For all will side with you. All will see the justice of your claim. You were his rightful heir. His only son. Now come to me. I will show you the real skills of a woman. Come to me. Tomorrow you can plan your case against her.'

Edward Crosse nodded vehemently. His lips moved silently behind his fox-red beard, sharp blue eyes striking sparks of fire. He threw the letter to the floor. Crossing the room he threw back the sheet. Ann gasped as he crushed her naked body against his own and his mouth took hers in a passion of desire and anger.

Chapter 2

The guildhall was alive with the murmur of male voices. Beneath the carved oak beams of the roof the sound was constant, like the steady humming of a vast hive of agitated bees. Now and then, one voice – more strident, less controlled – would break out of the anonymous buzzing and for a moment fly free. Then it would return to the corporate identity of the hive.

Along the two sides of the hall great benches had been laid out. Each was covered with a cloth, or 'banker', of rich Lincolnshire cloth. To one side lay the summer forest brightness of Lincoln Green; on the other the splendid sunset richness of Lincoln Scarlet.

On the benches sat the solid, wealthy guildsmen of Boston, the signatures of power and influence clearly written in their confident faces and the richly ornamented clothing. Doublets and gowns, tabards and surcoats were richly patterned and intricately embroidered. On these pillars of Boston society the fine wool of the wolds met and embraced the extravagant brocades of Florence, Genoa and Venice. Here was cloth of Flanders and the dark black-marten pelts of Russia's deepest forests. A world of trade and commerce gathered on the backs of the guildsmen of

Boston. And around these mighty creatures scurried and fluttered the drones. Sharp-eyed clerks and servants – constantly vigilant for signal or message – hovered about their masters, or carried messages about the tapestry-draped hall.

William Curteys and his entourage entered the hall from the shower-sprinkled street outside. Here and there heads craned and the gossip stilled for a moment. Then it burst out anew. It was agitated now and louder. Curteys acknowledged the customary nods of his fellow guildsmen but did not make a point of stopping to talk to anyone. He was well aware of the curiosity, poorly disguised on the turning faces. He was normally not averse to being the object of men's curiosity. Today, however, he felt mildly irritated by it. He knew full well why he was of such interest. That knowledge, too, irritated him.

He finally came to his allotted place amongst the Lincoln Scarlets. By long practice, each guild family had its apportioned position in the guildhall. It was a right, jealously guarded. Sitting down upon his backless bench, Curteys drew himself upright and stared, unfocused, into the middle distance. Beside him, on his right, the bench stood empty. It was the place once occupied by Anthony Crosse. The empty place seemed like a yawning chasm to other eyes in the room but Curteys did not show that he was aware of the gap. He simply looked away, the fine weave of his flowing crimson robe rustling restlessly as he moved. About his square shoulders hung a loose, full cloak, lined with Russian fur. Few present could boast wealth greater than that of William Curteys, merchant of Boston.

stiffly at her elbow. The room fell silent. Isabelle returned the ritual salutation.

'The finest? The purest?'

'The most finely sifted paynemaine.' He unfolded the linen napkin. The soft white rolls lay cradled within, like gulls' eggs.

Isabelle nodded. With practised care the pantler laid out her bread before her, careful at no point to brush against her as he leant across. Isabelle saw that his smooth hands were trembling as he set out her knife and spoon. All eyes were on her. He snapped his fingers. A round-eyed boy scullion raised great trenchers of husky tourte bread. The pantler took the bread plates and the boy vanished into oblivion. Carefully he placed one trencher before her. The others he piled on her right. Others might share a trencher, not so the lady of the house.

The ceremony complete, the pantler retired. His place was taken by a dark-skinned butler who poured Isabelle a frothing goblet of Gascon wine. She raised it to her lips. It was the signal for the others to sit. All at once the rapt silence shattered into a myriad uncountable conversations.

'It went as well as it might, Isabelle.' The speaker was William Curteys, seated on her right.

'Yes,' she agreed softly. 'It went as well as a funeral might.'

Cautiously she looked to her left. There Edward sat with his wife. She was watching Isabelle with those same angry eyes. Edward, tearing at his bread, appeared oblivious to the tension. Then he looked up, a half smile on his lips.

'Thank you for the fishing rights.' His gratitude sounded almost provocative.

Isabelle averted her eyes and reached for her own cup. 'It is as your father would have wanted.'

A spark kindled in Edward's eyes. 'He would have given it as willingly as He gave the manor at Swineshead,' she went on.

'Yes,' Edward agreed flatly, 'he made adequate provision to keep me in my accustomed station.'

Isabelle made no attempt to reply. Instead she looked out into the hall. Pexton was busily engaged in directing the hurrying scullions. Despite his responsibilities he could not keep his eyes from the high table. A visible colour rose in his cheeks when he saw that he had become the object of his mistress' attention.

'He always loved you, Edward,' she said quietly.

'I know. His love was shown in the generosity of his gift.'

Isabelle sank her fingers into the paynemaine. The fine texture parted between her curling fingers. Edward knew as well as she did that Swineshead was scarcely the richest of Anthony Crosse's manors. Overshadowed by the great Cistercian abbey of St Mary's, Anthony's property in the fen there was but a scattered holding of parcels of land, some of which he held as tenant of the abbey. His own land – his demesne – was a ragtag collection of dyke and reedfen which had come into his hands, by various means, over a decade. Nevertheless he had thanked her. Before she could answer his thanks another voice called her attention. It belonged to a distinguished, elderly guildsman who sat to Will Curteys' right. Curteys himself leaned back better to facilitate the exchange.

'Your courage has been widely remarked on, Isabelle. It was a bold move to ride out to the fens yourself. And it seems that your courage has stunned the rogues who had so disturbed the peace of your manor at Bicker.'

Isabelle paused before she replied to the compliment. A retainer, emboldened by her nod, piled pickled salmon and whelks on to the first of her trenchers.

'Thank you, Matthew. It does indeed seem that my presence stilled the rebellion. No sooner had I arrived than the violence ceased. I feel sure that it was due to men's natural respect for a woman in her widowhood and assured of her rights . . .'

Curteys seemed to choke on a whelk. Isabelle spared him a suitably pitiful look, edged with quiet satisfaction.

Matthew Redman nodded. His silver hair was tonsured by age rather than by calling. His movements were slow, deliberate, majesterial. Likewise, his voice was purposeful and heavy with accumulated wisdom. It was he who had nodded support for William at the guildmeeting when Nicholas Coppledyke had launched his diatribe.

'You are a worthy successor to your husband. And in all things you can count on my support. Is that not so, William? Is she not as capable as she is beautiful?'

William Curteys grunted an inaudible reply.

'You are too kind, Matthew,' Isabelle replied

evenly. 'But I shall do my best to uphold the honour of the house of Crosse and of the town.' Isabelle was gratified at Matthew Redman's support. He was a relative and a namesake of one of the founders of the town's Corpus Christi Guild. Like the Guild of the Blessed Mary, it was a meeting point for members of a number of the senior craft and trade guilds. As well as being a focus for alms-giving and other works of charity, it was one of the ways by which power, influence and patronage was limited. Anthony had always had allies within Corpus Christi and the Blessed Mary. It lay with Isabelle to maintain this position. Matthew Redman's fatherly support was a signal that this was more than possible.

'You keep a good table, Isabelle. Even on a Friday fast, you know how to feed a man well.' Curteys' compliment was unexpected. It caught Isabelle unawares.

'Why, thank you, Will,' she replied, a little cautiously. 'But in this town, amidst all this water, it takes little enough skill to provide a choice of fish on Wednesday, Friday and Saturday.' Warmed by, but wary of William's compliment, she turned and flashed a smile at Edward. She was surprised by the apparent warmth of his returned expression.

William regarded the exchange with pursed lips. He knew Edward and did not trust him.

'Now, take this excellent dish of hakade,' William said pleasantly. He lifted a lump of flaking pike, for which he had reserved the dialect word of the fen fishermen. 'So mellow and inviting . . .'

Isabelle smiled a pained smile. It was not like her ex-husband's partner to show such an exact interest in culinary preparation.

'Who would think that some fenslodger had waded through frozen dyke and ditch to find it? With the sea maws crying overhead like lost souls . . .'

Isabelle coughed deliberately. Such poetic eloquence was not the hallmark of Will Curteys' conversation.

Unabashed, he continued: 'He puts out a tempting bait. And when the fish takes it he cannot contain how pleased he is. He draws it in. The fight is over. He has won. Then he reaches out his hand and this fine hakade – bites it off . . . !'

Curteys cast a disarming smile towards Edward, who returned it, unaware of the topic of conversation. Then he gave Isabelle a penetrating look.

'Thank you, Will. I shall remember your advice – when next I go fishing for pike!'

William smiled once more, but his brown eyes were hard and cold. 'See that you do, Isabelle.'

The dark afternoon was drifting towards mist-filled night as the last of the guests departed into the veiled world beyond the firelit hall. Amongst the disturbed rushes, the dogs snarled over discarded food fragments.

Isabelle bid each of the senior guildsmen farewell. Their wives eyed her carefully, warily. Yet one guest was in no hurry to go. The tall, stooping figure of Phillip Spayne made no effort to leave the hall. At last, free from her duties, Isabelle gave him her attention.

'I thank you, father, on behalf of Anthony and myself. You were friend and confessor to my late husband. I know that I can rely on the support of your prayers, as he once did.'

Spayne's deep eyes shifted. 'I will pray for God's guidance on you. As you seek to conform yourself meekly to His will and to that station to which He has called you, in His wise providence . . .'

The blessing had a slight aura of menace about it. Behind the eagle nose the eyes were unfathomable. Still, he made no attempt to go.

'Would you take wine with me? I think you have more to say to me?' Isabelle gestured towards the far end of the hall. Here, beside the dais, wooden stairs led up to the privacy of the solar and her own sleeping chamber.

Phillip Spayne's face was suddenly animated and for a brief moment the cold aloofness vanished. Isabelle divined the cause of his sudden agitation and gestured to Eleanor to accompany her. Spayne nodded, clearly relieved. His vow of chastity had given rise to a morbid fear of isolation with a woman. Momentarily all his repressed anxieties had flooded his marble face with leaping life but now the hook-nosed face returned to stone.

Once in the sparsely furnished solar, Isabelle motioned to the priest to sit. He perched himself on the edge of a dark wooden bench. His stiffness did not diminish. Instead, he studied her like a black-winged bird of prey. His inner tension was infectious and Isabelle found she had to concentrate as she took up her wine. She smiled, careful to hide her wariness, whilst in a corner Eleanor de Bamville took up her sewing, smiling when Spayne glanced at her. He turned away from the full, ripe curve of her body with noticeable discomfort.

'Will you return to your father's hall in Lincoln?' Spayne asked. Although the priest's question was innocent enough, it sounded more like a challenge. For a moment he put Isabelle in mind of Edward when he thanked her for his fishsilver.

'My father is dead. He died last autumn before Martinmas. There was pestilence in Lincoln during the summer.'

'Ahhh . . .' The priest had heard of the pestilence but not of this death. 'And his estate?'

Isabelle ignored the presumption behind the question. She sensed that a deeper need than curiosity was feeding Phillip Spayne's inquiry.

'It passes to his brother in the main. You know my own brother died a year past and without issue. So most now goes to my uncle now I am married. Except for a manor on the wolds, which Father bequeathed to me to add to the fenland fishing rights which he granted to me on my marriage to Anthony.'

'Your marriage portion? Your maritagium?' Spayne was very thoughtful. He spoke as if she was no longer there. It was as if he was conducting some deep debate with himself.

'That is right. My marriage portion, which has reverted to me on Anthony's death . . .'

'Along with the rest of his manors, lands, rights and chattels . . .' Spayne shifted on his perch, running one thin finger along the curved sweep of his nose.

'With the exception of the parcels of land west of Swineshead, in the fen-country. That manor Anthony left to Edward, his bastard.'

Phillip Spayne pursed his lips at the worldly sound

of the last word. 'It is said that you intend to fulfil all Anthony's rights and obligations.'

He said it as if daring her to confirm the truth of such brazen audacity. In the corner Eleanor laid her sewing down. She no longer pretended to divert her attention.

Isabelle reined in her irritation with difficulty. 'As chantry priest of the guild, you are well aware of my rights in this matter. I hold his seal and enjoy all his privileges as a merchant of the Honour of Richmond. My rights of inheritance have been recognised before the Manor Court Leet of Boston and before the masters of the guilds, great and small. Had there been anything improper in my inheritance then the bailiff of the town would have referred my estate to the steward of the Earl of Richmond. No such irregularity has been brought before the Court Leet.'

Spayne flushed, clearly irritated to find himself on the defensive. 'I did not impute impropriety to anyone. I have not accused you of anything improper, Isabelle. It is what is right before God that I am compelled to raise with you.' Spayne fixed her with a hard stare, ignoring Eleanor's cough. 'I was your husband's friend. I care only for your peace, Isabelle. I see dangers before you. Dangers which crowd towards a woman who goes the way that you go.'

Isabelle could feel her skin tightening at the edges of her mouth. She shot a glance at Eleanor, who nodded imperceptibly, and Isabelle relaxed slightly. 'What dangers do you fear for me?'

Phillip Spayne was a long time in replying. His eyes moved slowly from Isabelle to Eleanor and back again. 'What is lawful is not always prudent,' he began slowly. His voice possessed a funereal quality, similar to that of the town's bailiff of St Botolph.

For a moment Isabelle was taken back to the guild assembly, facing the ire of Nicholas Coppledyke. Then her thoughts returned to Phillip Spayne: 'I pray that I may never be imprudent.' Isabelle licked her lips. 'Was it not Hugh of St Victor who said that Man is the image of wisdom and Woman of prudence?'

Spayne seemed to jerk upright although in truth, his body did not move a muscle. It was his deep eyes which suddenly revealed the emotion which gripped him. No woman had ever quoted Hugh of St Victor against him before. Stung by surprise, and a little outrage, he retorted: ' 'Tis true enough, Isabelle. But it was to Man that such wisdom was granted. The wisdom to hold authority in the councils of the world.'

Isabelle felt suddenly calm, despite her pounding heart. It was as if some sleight of hand had severed the link between her emotions and her thinking. And all because Phillip Spayne had lost the tight rein on his temper.

'Yet, Our Lady intercedes for king and pauper, before her Son. Surely that speaks of both wisdom and prudence in a woman?'

'Our Lady – Blessed Mary – was humble and meek. She did not take to herself stations beyond her God-given place. It is in meek submission to God that she pleads the case of Mankind.'

'I would never deny it, father. It is writ plain in the scriptures. I simply meant to say that the wisdom of Man and the prudence of Woman are not irreconcil-able opposites. Rather they differ in intensity, but where they draw near they mesh.' She intertwined her fingers. 'For whilst Man may enjoy the intensity of God's gift of wisdom, there may yet be grains of wisdom in a woman.' Spayne was shaking his head. 'As indeed there may sometimes be prudence in a man's actions.'

The barb drove deep into Spayne. Before he could retort, Isabelle continued: 'As the scripture says, "God made Man and Woman in His own image." So both reveal God's glory.'

'However Augustine, whom it pleased God to grant divine insight, wrote that Woman may only be seen as the image of God when joined to Man. Whereas Man, alone, is God's image.' Spayne straightened up. His deep eyes, behind the hawk's-beak nose, settled back into quiet meditation as he delivered his masterstroke.

'And yet . . .' Isabelle began, very slowly, 'and yet, did he not also say that the full image of God is only seen in the unity of Man and Woman; that their total make-up is the reflection of His nature?'

Spayne's eyes narrowed and his face coloured; a reflection of his shock of red hair. He found great difficulty in containing his anger. 'Your father taught you strangely, girl!'

'In what way, father?' Isabelle was meek. It seemed to nettle him. 'In what way?' Now her voice was cold, like ice water.

'To read! Aye, and to grow puffed up in your pride. To learn to quote scripture against itself. To act like a man, without regard to your God-given station . . .'

'Because I choose to fulfil my legal rights? Is it not God who gives wisdom to those who frame our laws? Does not Holy Church command us to live peacefully under the law?'

'What is legal is not always right.' Spayne stood up, a rising darkness within the light-latticed room of candle-flame and shadows. 'To act like a man goes against all propriety. It speaks against the possession of a meek and a contrite spirit . . . I came to share my concern but have found only pride and . . . and . . . and wilfulness to greet my words . . .' The priest's words came hard and fast. His nostrils flared as he breathed in sharply and glared at Eleanor, discomfited by the silent presence of this other female adversary. He had heard of this woman. He knew all about her travels and her time with hermits and anchoresses. There was something distractingly confident about her. She looked at him levelly. It was that quiet, assertive confidence in a woman which so nettled him. He had no doubt that Isabelle's reckless attitude could be traced back to the unwomanly pilgrim. He felt a disquieting stirring deep within himself. Rarely had his celibacy felt so besieged. How he longed to crush the pride of these women, these temptresses, these daughters of wilful Eve. How he desired to master them, to humiliate their pride.

'Father?' Isabelle's eyes were swimming with concern.

The fury mounted within him. These creatures of arrogance were no better than whores. Phillip Spayne shook his head savagely, turned and passed out of the solar like a thundercloud.

'Go with him, Eleanor . . .' Isabelle gestured towards the swinging door.

Calmly the chaperone stood up, raised an eyebrow in the direction of the pale-faced widow, then followed after the priest.

When she'd gone, Isabelle turned back to her half-empty goblet of wine. She frowned to think of Phillip Spayne's sudden surge of anger, puzzled by the eruption of emotion. Spayne was a dour man, a character draped in sombre moods, like crêpe about a coffin. Yet his moods rarely encompassed sudden or striking emotions and his outburst had, therefore, been unexpected. There was something disturbingly familiar about his behaviour, though. And yet she could not name it; only feel it inexactly, like an object wrapped in woollen cloth.

'Ahh . . .', she sighed deeply. 'I am too tired to worry.' And yet she wondered still. Wearily she removed the richly embroidered band about her head, carelessly tossing the multicoloured fillet on to the trestle table. Slowly – absent-mindedly – she took off her wimple, allowing her hair to fall loose over her shoulders. Standing again, she pulled her sideless surcoat up over her head, the squirrel-fur lining brushing her cheek. Soon the garment lay across the bench in a tumble of soft, fine wool.

Isabelle held a corner of the cloth. Its weave felt flawless between her fingers. It was 'Black Scarlet', top-dyed into midnight shades for her father's funeral the previous November. At the corners, around the hem, she could still discern the traces of the original cochineal dye. It was sad to think how such a splendid colour had succumbed to mourning. She frowned at the thought. She had loved her father. And now she had buried her husband. It was barely a week since he had plunged from his horse. She could still hardly believe it.

Shaking her head free from such melancholy, she

brushed down the pleated skirt which she wore beneath her tight bodice. She flexed the muscles of her back and arched her neck, running her pale hands up the stretched material of the bodice till they rested under the curves of her breasts and closed her eyes wearily.

Suddenly the candles guttered slightly as air moved within the room. 'Eleanor . . . Have you seen Phillip so . . . oh . . .'

Isabelle felt the colour rising in her cheeks as her eyes sprung open. Edward Crosse was standing in the doorway, his sandy hair damp from the sea mist outside. Moisture glistened like dew in his fox-red beard. Tiny drops of silver water stood proud on the fibres of his close-fitting overgarment. The quartered colours of the cotte-hardie borrowed lustre from the flickering candle-flame. The top buttons of the garment were undone and stains of mud streaked his calf-skin boots.

All these details swept through Isabelle's mind as she faced this sudden intruder, as if the intensity of her awkwardness had made her acutely aware of every detail of her observer. She stepped away from the table.

'You startled me. I – I was expecting Eleanor. She has taken the chantry priest out to the street . . .' She stopped, hesitating. What was going on behind those blue eyes?

Edward Crosse turned and closed the door. The latch dropped with a slight 'snick'. He had been watching her for a few moments before the candle-flame had betrayed his presence. In those brief minutes he had devoured the arching back, the upturned sweep of her throat, the raised firmness of her breasts. It was as if he was watching her naked. She seemed so vulnerable and unaware. Once more he had felt the hard, urgent need; the hot desire which had gripped him whilst his men broke her dykes, the shameful wanting which had risen in him as soon as his father had introduced the new bride to his son.

Tight-lipped, Edward turned to face her. He forced himself to smile a careful, practised smile. Beneath the disarming radiance of his even teeth, his mouth and throat were dry with longing.

'I thought you had returned to your manor.' Isabelle poured herself some wine. 'Is your wife here – in the hall?'

Edward looked at her curiously. 'No.'

Isabelle was puzzled. 'Then I don't quite . . .'

'I have rented a tenement on Wormgate. It faces the river quay. Beyond St Botolph's church.'

'Then you've not held it long, Edward. For Anthony – I . . .' she quickly corrected herself, 'hold a tenement on Wormgate. I had no idea that . . .'

'I only took it this week.' He interrupted her sharply. Then he moderated his tone. 'With my father's death, I will need a house in Boston.'

He spoke of Anthony Crosse as if he was a stranger to Isabelle. His implications were clear. Now that his father was dead, he had lost his home base in the town. Before this week he had slept at the Crosse hall when in Boston. Now he had been cut loose. Or was it cast adrift? His tone implied the latter.

'You are always welcome in this house, Edward. You may sleep here whenever you wish. Your father would not have wished it any other way.'

Edward's lips tightened. Too often he had lain awake in the boxbed listening to his father asserting his marriage rights over his nubile young bride only feet away.

'No! Thank you, but no. It is better this way.'

'As you wish.' Secretly Isabelle was relieved. 'As you wish, Edward.'

Anthony Crosse's bastard son wiped his damp beard. His eyes still held her fast. 'I have sent Ann back to the manor. I have business here in Boston.' He paused. 'Is it true that you're sailing with the fleet this summer? To Riga?' His mottled eyes were thoughtful as he switched subjects.

'That is so. I have full responsibility now for Crosse purchasing of the furs, wax and amber. I intend to go in Anthony's stead.'

Edward nodded. 'I want you to know that my men will keep watch on your manors . . .' Then, as if to explain or excuse his consideration, he added: 'I am grateful for the fishing rights. Keeping a watch is the least that I can do. Father would have wished it.' Inside he felt exultant, knowing it was in his power alone to protect her dykes, since it was he who was breaking them down. It gave him pleasure to feel such power over her. Ever since he had watched the flooding of her pasture, plans had spread through his thoughts like weed within an abandoned channel. He felt excitement at the thought of his cunning and as his excitement grew, more secret schemes put out fingers of growth beneath the dark surface of his words.

Isabelle crossed the smoky room. She laid a hand on his arm. 'Thank you, Edward.'

He felt the touch, like an arrow striking home.

'You can rely on me.' His voice was thick as he put a hand to her waist and felt her warm body beneath his fingers.

Suddenly Eleanor de Bamville walked into the room. Edward spun round, like a sheep tormented by warblefly, his eyes wide. Finally he broke the deep silence. With swift, sure fingers he buttoned the damp cotte-hardie to his throat.

'It's late, I must away.' And then, as if to regain the moral high ground, he added, 'And rest assured, Isabelle, you have nothing to fear in the fens. My men have the power to keep your dykes from harm.'

He embraced her in a stiff-armed embrace, and nodded a curt farewell to Eleanor as he left the solar.

Eleanor expelled her breath and the tension was pricked. 'I was waylaid by Richard. Some worry about the cheese supply. That poor man will worry himself into an early grave! I did not even see Edward. What did he . . . er . . . want? He seemed very relaxed with you.' She raised her eyebrows in self-conscious mockery of her own euphemism.

Isabelle made no reply. She was looking intently at the half-open solar door. She had, in a flash of revelation, recognised what had been so familiar about Phillip Spayne's behaviour, yet so odd. She had seen the hard intensity in Spayne's eyes before. Now she knew why she had failed to recognise it sooner. It was the same light that had blazed in Anthony's eyes when he took her on the night of their wedding. The hungry look that had fed on her nakedness and been satisfied. And she could recall it all so clearly now; because it was that same look which had haunted Edward's green-flecked eyes as his strong hand had gripped her waist.

Chapter 4

A bright April had dispersed the heavy hanging mists of winter. Whilst summer was still far off, winter was rapidly becoming a memory. Out in the fen-meadows the first pale petals of fritillaries fluttered and curt-seyed in the spring breezes from the sea. Along the wide estuaries, with their great shoulders of salt marsh and dark lagoons, returning spoonbills danced and courted in a spectacular mummery. And fisher-men noted their return and nodded. It would be a good summer. Spring had come early.

In and around Boston the enforced lethargy of winter was thrown off with alacrity. Boats jostled in the Haven. Merchants made plans and checked their merchandise. Already, stout cogs and sleek galleys had appeared at the Town Quay and accents of Gascony, Flanders and Hamburg could be heard in the inns, churches and weighing houses.

Nowhere in the town was the bustle of commerce more apparent than about the warehouses and halls in the southern quarter of the town. Below the great expanse of Richmond Fee – with St Botolph's Church on its north-west side – the River Witham twisted in a serpent coil. Below the Town Bridge, the river slowly opened out to a wider anchorage. On the left bank lay the wharves and stores of Town Quay. On the right sprawled the satellite suburb of Skirbeck Quarter, with its stone-built houses of the Lincoln merchants. Below a further twist of the river lay the broad reach of the Haven and the sea.

Isabelle came early to the crowded warehouses and tenements which jostled about the east bank of the river. The bell for lauds was ringing out from the Dominican Friary. It was just after six of the clock. As usual she had breakfasted lightly just after dawn. The quick meal of bread soaked in wine had been followed by the daily reports of clerk, pantler and butler. Once Anthony had listened carefully to the needs and requirements of the household, with his wife at his elbow. Now that wife carried the burden of the task on her own. Truth be known, she rather enjoyed these homely discussions about the price of bread and the shortage of coins in the market-place. It was a time as much to glean gossip as manage the household; a time to listen to market-place tales of villeins refusing labour service on their lord's land, of fishmongers pilloried for the sale of foul stock, of archers returning from the war in France with stories of campaigns turned sour.

It was with some reluctance that Isabelle had drawn this morning's meeting to an early close. She had pressing business. Today she could not linger over casual interest. Instead she had heard mass without receiving the sacrament, and hurried on about her tasks. Now, crossing the market-place of Richmond Fee from St Botolph's Church, she paused briefly to watch the rising tide of brightly coloured awnings.

'They'll have a good day for the fair. The weather's set fine now. Nothing will shift it before tomorrow.' It was Eleanor who spoke. She was cloaked against the morning's chill and her cheeks were apple-red with the crisp, clean air.

'Praise God and His saints,' Isabelle replied. 'For we've enough work to do without getting soaked about it. Last year it rained the whole of St George's Day. I've never seen such a miserable fair. Sky and sea met and we swam!'

Eleanor laughed. It had indeed been a most miserable occasion. For the whole of the three days of the fair the weather had been foul. And yet there had been no avoiding a soaking. Three times in the year the world came to Boston and camped in Richmond Fee: the fairs of St George and St James, each lasting three days, and the great mart of 30 November, with its nine days of trading. No merchant could afford to miss such gatherings, whatever the weather.

'I remember it very well. The streets awash and the nave of the church full of merchants striking bargains, where at least it was dry . . .'

'And Phillip Spayne, hovering like a phantom behind Anthony, when he almost came to blows with the Easterling merchant with the cask of stockfish!'

The two women laughed. There had been good times and happy memories.

'And now he hardly speaks to you . . .' Eleanor's casual reminder brought the laughter to an abrupt halt. The dark figure of the chantry priest vanished into the church. He had passed the two women with scarcely a glance.

'Never mind.' Isabelle pulled a wry smile. 'We'll not let the shadow of last month's disputation fall on such a bright day. And we've no time to dawdle either, Eleanor de Bamville. Or Will Curteys will accuse me of neglecting my responsibilities. And it is too fine a morning to be hectored by him. I'll not give him an opportunity to say how far I fall below the standard set by my dead husband.'

It galled her that William was so dismissive of her suitability for the role of journeying merchant. More than that, the attitude troubled her. She had to do it. She had to prove herself capable of holding a man's position. If she showed any weakness there would be opponents – like Phillip Spayne – who would seize on it.

The two women threaded their way through the stalls and trestles and the brightly dyed canvas. It was a short walk, less than a quarter of a mile, from the church to the quay beyond the Witham's curve. Isabelle was silent as she strolled. She was thinking of how the town would watch her actions more critically than those of any man. She thought of Will Curteys and his lack of faith in her. Her eyes narrowed as she considered it.

Anthony Crosse had owned a number of properties within the long, narrow boundaries of Boston. On Strait Bargate lay his hall and his principal stone-built warehouses; on Wormgate he held the tenement block with its disputed alleyway; in the south of the town he leased a stone-and-wood building from the Earl of Richmond, the manorial overlord of the manor of Boston. It was to this building that Isabelle and Eleanor were making their way. In this large, barnlike structure Crosse and Curteys held their stock bound for Riga and beyond.

Before they reached the warehouse they ran into Richard Pexton. He was hovering on the edge of a group of fur-wrapped merchants. Nearby, at the quayside, two sturdy, square-sterned ships were tied up. The merchants were crowded around a great crate which had been lifted from the ship using a heavy-beamed crane and blocks and tackle. Pexton smiled gravely at the approach of his mistress and her companion. His furrowed brow relaxed a little.

'What is going on, Richard?' Isabelle was interested but consciously controlled her curiosity.

'They are Easterlings, from Lübeck.' He jerked his head towards the group around the crate.

Isabelle had guessed as much. She had recognised the familiar squat shape of the cogs tied up at the quay. More than that it was their time of year. The German merchants of the Hanseatic League of the Baltic Coast were familiar Easter migrants to the ports of North Sea England. Hence their common nickname. These were the men who had been Anthony Crosse's rivals for the Baltic trade. Now they were rivals of his widow. Isabelle watched them keenly. These were powerful men. Powerful and dangerous. It was scarcely ten years since the merchants of the Hanse had humbled the King of Denmark when he tried to interfere with their monopoly of the Baltic trade.

'But they are not all Easterlings.' Isabelle nodded towards a handful of men examining the merchandise which had been unloaded from the Hanseatic cog. The faces of the men engaged in the inspection were

familiar. All were senior Boston merchants. All
members of the Guild of Corpus Christi.

'They are Boston men. Customs collectors for the
king. They are assessing the merchandise of the
Easterlings for customs dues.'

Close by, a clerk was scribbling down details of
merchants' and ships' names as well as an inventory of
goods and their quantity.

'They look sour about it . . .' commented Isabelle,
secure in the knowledge that local merchants were
habitually undercharged by the king's appointed
collectors.

'Aye, they're sour, my lady. They pay every year
but it does not get easier with time! And after this,
there's the weighing of the merchandise at Gysors
Hall.'

Despite its size and trading importance, the port of
Boston was not a chartered borough. It lay firmly
within the jurisdiction of the Earl of Richmond and
his steward. And the present earl – John of Gaunt,
uncle to King Richard II – was not one to forgo his
rights. For all the wealth of its merchants, with their
guilds and elected Bailiff of St Botolph, the town was
still subject to the control of the earl and his Court
Leet. Merchants would find they had to pay earl as
well as king.

'Aye, my lady. Gaunt's steward will charge them
for the weighing and stamping of all their merchandise. But they've no need to weep,' Pexton continued,
'for they will earn a fortune with what they have
brought with them . . .'

'Furs?' Isabelle's eyes lit up.

'Furs. And what furs! Come and see what they are

paying dues on. 'Tis a king's ransom in squirrel pelts.'

For once the clerk's face cleared of his customary frown. The wrinkles softened and vanished. His pleasure at being Isabelle's guide to such items of wonder swept away his propensity for worry. Limping, he pushed between the German merchants.

As Isabelle followed him, she was aware of only the most casual interest amongst the Easterlings. She was only a woman. They had more important things on their minds. They kept an assiduous watch on the scribbling scribe of the king's collectors.

Her appearance provided a more appreciated diversion for the busy Boston customs men. They had seen her defend herself before Coppledyke and come so spectacularly to the mist-wrapped church to bury her husband. She interested them. She was a beautiful aberration. That factor made her stance a little more acceptable. But only just.

'Richard says that the Easterlings have brought furs. May I see them?' She flashed even, white teeth. She knew the signals which would gain her a viewing. Phillip Spayne might value the demure woman, but these men could be impressed by boldness. It amazed her how forward she had become since Anthony's death. And yet it did not come easily. She felt slightly ashamed. It angered her but she could not banish it. Spayne had seen to that. But she knew that she must exploit any advantage she might have to gain acceptance in this male preserve; use her femininity even as others sought her downfall through it.

Pexton watched her, troubled to see Isabelle so bold before other men. More than that, he was troubled by the apparent pleasure that her boldness

brought to the faces of the collectors. To the consternation of the Hanse traders the top of the crate was
obediently pushed back. Isabelle reached out and
touched the topmost fur. It was squirrel. She felt the
exquisite soft and silky texture beneath the tips of her
fingers.

'It is the finest miniver,' she almost gasped. The
collectors nodded. 'It is incomparable.'

Isabelle lifted the mantle of fur. The rectangular
length was made up of many pelts, matched and sewn
together. The grey and white marbling in the fur was
beyond anything she had ever seen before. The pelts
imported by Anthony had been single skins. He had
left it to the furriers of Lincoln and London to dress,
cut and finish the presentation. The pelts had passed
swiftly through his hands. Few stayed for long in the
storeroom on Strait Bargate. Yet, for all their worth,
none compared with those sewn into this mantle.

'It is truly magnificent!' Isabelle turned to look at
Pexton. 'The lining of my finest surcoat is rat compared to this!'

The collectors laughed. Pexton frowned and
Isabelle bit her tongue. It was rare for her to be so
outspoken. But the mantle was superb. Never had
she beheld such first-class miniver squirrel.

Seeking to present a less ebullient spirit she asked,
'Where is it from, Richard?'

Pexton looked at the nearer of the two collectors,
who clicked his fingers at the busy scribe.

'Lübeck, sir. And some of the cargo is out of
Königsberg. Where the Teutonic Knights hold sway.'
He added the last piece of information as if to
enhance his own status. He was a man who knew of

far-off places and strange lands although in truth, he had never been further from Boston than Wisbech.

Isabelle's ears pricked at the mention of Teutonic Knights. She recalled William Curteys' words about the lands of the German crusaders in the eastern Baltic. It was a subdivision of those knights who held Riga for Christendom. And who waged war against the heathen on behalf of the True Church. Riga. Her destination. She felt a trembling excitement. The fabulously soft miniver nestled against her cool fingers.

'But where is the fur from? These furs? This squirrel?' She held up a corner of the marbled mantle. 'Where is it from?'

The Easterlings were watching her carefully now. Their earlier indifference had evaporated like early morning mist. They had noted her confidence, a confidence which exceeded that expected of her sex. They had seen how the customs collectors had responded to her presence. Here was an anomaly indeed. A woman who commanded some measure of real respect. The Hanse merchants were interested.

But before either of the two customs officials could answer, Richard Pexton responded to the query. He turned to the nearest of the Easterlings. A giant of a man, with a luxuriant beard streaked with silver. Great bushy eyebrows overhung intelligent, hard eyes. Pexton questioned him in the Low German dialect of the north German plain. He was well aware that all the Easterlings spoke excellent English and French yet he was careful to demonstrate his knowledge before his mistress. It made him feel less vulnerable, less superfluous. Even the collectors, who only ever spoke in English, or French, looked mildly impressed.

Isabelle listened to the half-familiar guttural tones of the *platte deutsch*. She understood not a word.

Pexton frowned as he turned back to his mistress, hesitating.

'Well, man. Spit it out. What did he say?' The collector was not a man who valued silence. And he suspected he knew what lay behind Pexton's hesitancy.

The clerk reddened. He stammered out his reply. His confidence dissipated. 'H-he s-says . . .' He fought to control his wayward tongue. 'He s-says they are from th-the "Land of D-darkness".'

Isabelle glanced at the great Easterling. The collectors laughed. They knew a screen when they saw one. And who could blame the Germans? No sane man gave too much away.

Pexton sought to regain something of the ground which he had lost. 'Th-the "Land of Darkness" is a heathen term, my lady. It is what the heathen saracens called the Russias.'

'The Land of Darkness?' Isabelle's voice was low. There was something menacing about that strange appellation. Something menacing and yet curiously attractive. A mystery, an enigma, which beckoned a traveller on.

'Aye, my lady. They called it thus because it is a w-wild land. A g-great land of danger and yet of riches . . .'

Isabelle was not listening any more. The Land of Darkness. And Riga lay at the gateway to that fabulous and savage land. Her stomach turned in a shivering spasm of fear and of excitement.

Eleanor de Bamville had taken no part in the conversation. But she had watched Isabelle's face as the young widow had touched the miniver and when Richard had conveyed its origins to her. Alone of the company on the quayside, she understood the conflicting emotions playing over Isabelle's face, like the variegated rays of the setting sun; half light and half darkness. Eleanor touched Isabelle's arm, aware of what she was feeling. She had felt such tearing emotions herself when, as a girl, she had boarded ship at Yarmouth in the company of other pilgrims. As if divining the motive behind the touch, the young woman smiled. 'Thank you . . .' she said softly to the two collectors. 'And thank you . . .' she said to the tall German merchant, knowing he would understand her speech. Then she set down the miniver and beckoned Pexton to follow her to their warehouse. The merchants and collectors watched her departure then, shrugging, turned once more to their lists of quantities and valuations.

The Crosse warehouse was half of stone and half of timber. Anthony had ordered the stone in from the quarries at Lincoln. He had paid heavily for its cutting and its transportation down the River Witham, through the fens of Holland. Never one to cast a penny away lightly, he had considered it worth the cost, for the stone-built ground floor not only declared his wealth to all passers-by, it also gave some protection against fire and rodents.

Its position too had been well worth the hours of negotiation with the steward of the Honour of Richmond. It lay only a short distance from the Steel

Yard, where the Easterlings stored their goods. In such a position it afforded easy access to goods shipped into the town. In addition, since 1369, the raw wool exports of Lincolnshire had been channelled through Boston. This monopoly in trading – the Staple – was controlled from the Steel Yard, south of the Crosse warehouse. Close proximity had enabled Anthony Crosse to store his wool sacks close to where they would have to be weighed and sealed.

''Tis a goodly building,' Isabelle remarked to Richard. 'It pleases me every time I see it.'

'Aye, 'tis that, my lady,' Pexton replied warmly. 'There's none better in the town. And the Lincoln merchants may match it, over the river, but none may better it.' He smiled. He took a pride in the house that he served. And he felt better, away from the crowded Town Quay.

Isabelle recognised the easing of her clerk's tension and rewarded him with a smile. As she turned to enter the warehouse, only Eleanor noticed the warmth in Pexton's dark eyes.

The stone-built ground floor was dim, but not dark for spring sunshine filtered in through long, thin, single-splay windows and the shutters had been opened to let in the light. The wide expanse of the room was full of merchandise. Great bales of cloth stood stacked in piles of common colours: 'Lincoln Green', 'Lincoln Scarlet', 'Beverley Blue', 'Bristow Red'. In one corner rough wooden crates stuffed with straw held great flagons and earthenware jars of an expensive Gascon vintage.

Will Curteys was leaning over a bale of cloth, a vellum ledger open before him and a pile of tally sticks notched on one side, each stick coloured to represent a different dye of woollen cloth. From the thin, curling wood shavings on the floor, it seemed that he had only recently finished the computation.

He straightened up as he sensed the approach of the two women and the clerk. When he saw Isabelle he made as if to reach for his cotte, slung carelessly over a nearby bale. Then he checked the movement. Instead, he remained in his state of relaxed undress.

'Will, we have seen the most wonderful furs. The mantles are the most exquisite I have ever seen . . .' It pleased her to have discovered them herself.

'Squirrel pelts. Miniver.' His tone was flat.

For a moment it stifled the words flowing from the slim-faced woman. Then, almost annoyed at his tone, she continued: 'The merchants are from Lübeck but Richard has discovered that . . .'

'The pelts are from Königsberg.'

'Yes, but when he questioned them further, they told him that they came from the "Land of Darkness".'

'As all such pelts do.'

'But you should have seen them. If we could but discover from whence they came we could buy pelts beyond our wildest dreams. Never did Anthony bring back such furs from Riga in the past.' Curteys' flat put-down had angered her.

Curteys still did not look impressed. 'The mantle is from Novgorod. The Hanse have a base there. In their barbaric tongue they call it a *kontore*. They have many such kontores in your Land of Darkness. The one at Novgorod is named the "Peterhof". They buy furs from the Russians, ship them back to Riga and

Königsberg where they are cut and sewn into the mantles that you saw on the quay. From there they are transported from the Baltic in the spring. The ones this year are particularly fine.'

The last point was his only concession to her enthusiasm. It was more than balanced by the dry matter-of-fact delivery of his lecture. His message was clear: 'You think you know this business. But I know much more!' Pexton had understood the hostile message. His mouth was set tight. Isabelle, too, had grasped the gist of Curteys' words. 'Thank you, William. I had thought it might be of some interest to you!' Her voice was frosty. 'It is possible that some further information may be gained from the Easterlings. Richard speaks their language.'

'The Hanse give nothing away,' William replied, crushing her suggestion. 'Whether one speaks their gibberish or not.'

Isabelle's face coloured rose. But before she could speak, Curteys picked up the ledger. 'We've been tallying the last of the finished cloth. I had thought to go over the quantities with you. But you are late. The job is finished.' Before she could defend herself, he continued quickly: 'It is too bad that we have lost one of the Yarmouth ships. But we can make do with the remaining three and the one from Lynn. We have been altering the balance of the stock, to take account of one less ship.' Only this past week, news had reached Boston that one of the ships due to sail to Riga had been taken by the French in the Channel.

'But,' William continued, 'we can take less of the raw wool and woad. It is the finished cloth which will command the best prices. We cannot afford to

84

diminish it.' Then, as a poorly disguised afterthought, he added, 'I trust you approve of this decision?'

Isabelle gave a sharp nod. She longed to disagree with him but she could not. The logic was inescapable.

All too obviously satisfied, he switched the topic of conversation. 'You know Adam, of course.'

Preoccupied by the exchange of cold words, Isabelle had scarcely been aware of the other man by the ledger. Now, at last, she acknowledged him. 'Of course. Good morning, Adam.' She nodded stiffly. 'I trust that you are well?'

Adam Thymelby was one of the party of Boston merchants who intended to sail for Riga before the month was out. He was related to Matthew Redman and there was a matrimonial link to the Curteys family, part of the tight circle of marriage and politics which limited the outflowing of power and patronage within the town. It was his nephew who assisted the collector on Town Quay. The circle was a tight one.

'I am well, Isabelle. And you look well.'

He was a span shorter than Curteys and stockier; more obviously muscular, with almond-shaped eyes. The upper half of his right ear was severed, a permanent reminder of a savage sea-fight with German pirates. His square jaw held tight control on his counsel and beneath his sealed lips a long, thin scar puckered his skin.

Adam Thymelby had a reputation as a hard man, some said a brutal one. It irritated Isabelle that Curteys had made her look foolish in front of him. She too had given much thought to the preparations for the journey. Only two days previously Pexton had been busy in the ale-houses of the town, looking for fighting men to act as guards on the merchandise.

'I have been mindful of our last discussion, William,' she said carefully, aware of Adam Thymelby's stare. 'Of how you spoke of the need for men of war to guide the ships. And our own persons.' Curteys nodded in a perfunctory manner. 'Well, I instructed Richard to seek out such men. He has succeeded. Only two days ago – at the Saturday market in Richmond Fee – he found a group of archers newly returned from the Duke of Buckingham's expedition to France.' She nodded approvingly in the direction of Pexton. He reddened to the roots of his thinning hair. 'They are good men. Men of the Parts of Holland. All local men, fen-dwellers. But highly experienced in the arts of war. They were with the duke at the siege of Nantes last winter.'

She paused to catch any reaction from her partner. There was none, except for a slight wry smile. Determined to ignore his less than encouraging expression, Isabelle continued. 'They were returning home. But glad of any new employment. For their captain had contracted with the duke for the duration of the campaign and now that it has ended miserably they are without employment. Richard gave them ale at the Saracen's Head and they have agreed to six pence a day for the duration of the journey to Riga and back. 'Tis a fair price. No more than the duke paid over the winter.'

Curteys broadened the cynical smile. 'Thank you, Isabelle, but Adam has already made arrangements for our defence. How many men have you contracted, Adam?'

Suddenly a flurry of activity at the door of the hall caught the attention of the guildsmen and their bevy of attendants and the hum of noise rose to a new level. The pitch changed too. It was immediately more troubled, even more animated. The last head to turn belonged to William Curteys. He had no doubts whatsoever as to the cause of this disturbance. His clerk whispered something in his ear and Curteys smiled cynically and nodded slightly. Then he turned towards the commotion.

Isabelle Crosse stood just inside the threshold. Around the slim young figure, liveried retainers spread out like a lapping sea of blue and silver. Blue tabards bore silver crosses on each male breast. Isabelle herself was dressed in elegant simplicity. It was a classic understatement of her new-found wealth. It was all the more striking for not being emblazoned for all to see. Her hair was carefully braided over her ears and she wore a demure head covering of wimple and veil. She acknowledged the stares of her fellow guildsmen with simple nods. The buzz of noise grew louder. With careful dignity she walked the length of the great hall until she came to the space beside William Curteys. Anthony Crosse's space. She nodded to her late husband's partner and sat down.

All eyes were upon her. There was shock etched on many faces: Isabelle Crosse, widow of Anthony Crosse, did not wear black. Neither had she confined herself to her own hall. Instead she had come to the guildhall for all to see. This only four days since her husband's death, with his body still awaiting carriage to Boston. Frowns creased the scrutinising faces and guarded comments gave rise to less guarded looks of disapproval. Some of the younger guildsmen however looked less shocked, judging her according to different sets of standards. The odd smirk revealed a thought more approving but no less patronising.

Sitting at her place, Isabelle Crosse seemed totally unaware of the approval and the disapproval. Only the most astute observer would have noted the white knuckles of the clasped hands, and the odd, sharp glance in the direction of the more hostile of her male appraisers.

After what seemed an eternity of waiting, the town bailiff called the meeting to order. The call did not produce silence but it did reduce the noise to manageable levels. One by one, the craftguilds announced the names of the journeymen who had now graduated to full guild status, each having been initiated by his own guild. As each stood before the full assembly of the guilds, there were nods and grunts from assembled masters. Every fresh new face was known but was now studied with a new intensity, for each man had crossed the invisible line marking the boundary between the seekers after power and the possessors of it. Each could now trade under the guild regulations of the town and was publicly recognised and accepted. Rival guilds, in particular, noted changes in each other's membership with special care.

The presentation over, the bailiff stood in silence before the bejewelled throng. 'It is with great sorrow that we recall the death of Anthony Crosse,' he intoned with intense solemnity. 'His death is a loss to his guild and to all who honour the town of Boston.'

Heads – both grizzled and youthful – nodded at this statement. 'For all will recall his kindness to the poor and his wisdom in counsel. His loss is a loss to the whole town and to our trades.'

Even those who knew that Anthony Crosse had been short on charity and long on impetuosity had to agree with the last point. Without doubt he had done much to further the economic prosperity of his house and the town.

The bailiff went on. 'For it was through his foresight that the Easterlings were made to grant us trade rights in the Baltic. And though they have often tried to restrict our access to the ports of Danzig and Riga, he was as energetic as anyone in resisting their plans . . .'

The reference to 'Easterlings' provoked grunts of approval from around the room. There was bitter rivalry between the Boston merchants and the German Hanseatic traders. It was only with great difficulty that the German monopoly on carrying goods to and from the Baltic had been broken. It was a monopoly that the Germans would reinforce at the earliest opportunity, only they feared the loss of their own trade rights in Lincoln, and in London and at Boston's great annual fair.

'Let no one forget,' the bailiff continued funereally, 'that he contributed more than anyone to the provision of the guild chantry chapel. We may rest assured that, even as I speak, the prayers of the priest are speeding him, through the refining fires, to eternal peace – as befitting his station and righteousness.'

Heads nodded once more. William Curteys glanced

at his silent companion. Isabelle seemed to be carved out of marble and no flicker of emotion passed over her features. Yet her blue eyes followed every movement of the bailiff. Curteys noticed the white knuckles and nodded, almost imperceptibly.

The oration finally drew to a close. The bailiff's gaze passed over the upturned faces. They knew what he would be referring to next. He was clearly uncomfortable. At last his eyes met those of the young widow. She did not look away. He did.

'It is the wish of his widow that she be allowed to practise the mystery of her husband, with full rights, with seal and charter, with training of apprentices and rights in the market-place.'

It was no rarity for the widow of a craftsman to practise her late husband's trade. The town was no stranger to female fullers, or weavers. It was however a considerable rarity for such an inheritance of rights to include the practising of a major mystery. That Isabelle Crosse intended to do so had become common knowledge. All knew that she was fully within her guild rights. Still, there was an upsurge of disapproval. Its intensity could almost be felt in the room. Amongst the craftguildsmen there were looks of sympathy; amongst the wealthy tradesmen only frowns and whispered comments.

Isabelle rose to her feet and the humming throng fell silent. When she spoke, her voice was cool and low. She made no attempt to raise it. It was as if she willed the assembled crowd to crane forward to hear her. Without dominating, she commanded.

'Guildsmen of Boston, you know me full well. For

often have many here present eaten at my husband's board. Often have you experienced the hospitality of the house of Crosse. And as you knew my husband, so you knew his wife . . .'

She paused for a moment. Her clear blue eyes swept the room. She let her gaze linger momentarily on those faces that she knew best. Some were full of genuine interest. Others possessed eyes brimming with ill-disguised hostility. Isabelle Crosse did not waver and when she spoke once more it was with a slightly raised voice.

'As the widow of Anthony Crosse I have full rights in the guild and in the market-place. I have rights to trade within the town and import and export through the port. I share the exemption from tolls enjoyed by all men residing on the Earl of Richmond's estates. I am the voice of the house of Crosse when prices are regulated and fines fixed for the breakers of our regulations. My vote stands alongside yours when our bailiff is elected.' She emphasised the word 'our'. The tone was not missed by her listeners and there were muttered comments. 'As the widow of Anthony Crosse, I claim my full rights within the guild. And until I marry again – should I marry again – I hold all privileges due to my late husband. I look to all present to uphold my rights as I, by God's grace, will seek to uphold yours and those of this town . . .'

'It is declared before all and recognised by all present.' Once more the voice was that of the funereal bailiff. 'The widow, Isabelle Crosse, stands as full inheritor of the lands, tenements and property of her husband. Can any speak against it?'

'Aye, I can speak against it.' A red-faced choleric man almost jumped to his feet. He had small, close-set green eyes, which darted to and fro as he spoke. His speech was obsessively fast, spittle glistening on his lips. 'All here know, full well, that my tenements abut the tenements of Crosse on Wormgate Street. 'Twas there that Anthony Crosse did deny me access to my rear yard. All knew that the alleyway from the street was on the property of my father. Yet Crosse did both deny my rights and refused me access to my own yard.' The green eyes glared at Isabelle.

'Nicholas Coppledyke forgets some trivial matters pertaining to this case!' The speaker was William Curteys. He had slowly risen to his feet while Coppledyke was engaged in his impassioned diatribe.

Coppledyke sneered. 'And of what have I been unmindful, Master Curteys?' he asked with an arrogant upturn of his mole-spotted jaw.

'Unmindful of but two trivial details: one, that whilst the passageway was in dispute, Anthony Crosse allowed you free access. It was you who sought to close off the alleyway to his tenants. Two, this disputation has long been over. The matter was heard before the town council and at the shire court. You know full well that both found in favour of joint use of the alley. These are the details which seem to have slipped your mind.'

William looked about him for confirmation of what he had just stated. One other of the senior guildsmen nodded a head and the agreement was noted. Coppledyke glared as William nodded to the bailiff and sat down and Isabelle cast a glance at her unexpected champion. Curteys did not return the look. His gaze was still fixed on the bristling draper, Nicholas Coppledyke.

'Preposterous . . . It was by lies that Crosse confused the courts. Men bore false witness. But I have a deed that proves my rights. Let the widow now make redress for the wrongs done by her husband.'

Attention switched back to Isabelle. She stood, her carriage and fine beauty seeming out of place in this talk of tenement rights and law suits. At last she spoke.

'Firstly I put my trust in the guild assembly of the town and in the courts of the wapentake and the shire. All such assemblies found in favour of my late husband. Who casts a slur on his name casts it on the judgement of the honest men of this town and shire . . .'

She let her words linger a little. It was a clever move. Coppledyke could hardly accuse all present of being dupes of Anthony Crosse. From the look in his eye, he would dearly have liked to but he checked himself in time.

She went on. 'Secondly, this is not the time to raise such matters. It is my right to practise my husband's mystery that you have been called to recognise, and the legitimacy of my inheritance. Any issues pertaining to the day-to-day use of my lands and tenements are not the subject of this day's consideration . . .'

'That is so.' The bailiff was clearly a little nettled at having Isabelle point out the illegitimacy of Coppledyke's comments. 'This matter of rights to an alleyway should wait for the shire court, or be raised in another meeting of the town.' His irritation lessened as his command of the meeting was re-established.

'Thank you.' Isabelle bowed slightly in the direction

of the bailiff. Then she continued, 'And I trust that I may settle all such disputes fairly, with the law of England as my support and my shield. For the guilds of this town should work for the common good of this town. You all know how well my late husband fought to extend the trade rights of Boston. All the guilds – drapers included – have cause to remember him with gratitude. And I shall endeavour to carry on his work and serve my mystery and this fine town. For this reason, I shall fulfil all his promises and obligations. I shall discharge all debts and support all plans made in his name. I shall sail to Riga this summer, as he would have done . . .'

She did not finish. She could not. The hall exploded in uproar. Voices were raised in astonishment. Others were raised in condemnation. William Curteys turned his chestnut eyes on her. They brimmed with a mixture of shock and disbelief.

'Riga?! Riga?! Have you any idea of what you have said? I can only assume that you have taken leave of your senses!'

William Curteys paced to and fro in the solar of the Crosse house. When the meeting at the guildhall had ended, he had wasted no time in confronting Isabelle. Now he lectured her with ill-concealed annoyance.

'Riga is not Lincoln, you know. It differs somewhat from a day's ride to the shire court!' There was the familiar cynical gloss to his dark eyes. 'I can only assume that you have no comprehension of what is involved in such a journey. On the last trip we lost two, I repeat *two*, ships to German pirates on the outward voyage. Do you know what they do to any women that they capture? After they are raped – by the whole crew . . .'

He stopped his restless pace and looked at Isabelle sitting opposite him. A ledger and a half-sewn sampler lay beside her. The conflicting roles of the woman seemed typified by these two items. Curteys' eyes narrowed as the thought struck him.

'But I'm sure that would not trouble you, Isabelle.' He was almost spiteful in his irritation. 'After all, mass rape is but a trifle! And when you reach Riga, what will you do then? The German merchants loathe us. They have only allowed us concessions under sufferance. They seize every opportunity to oppose us and obstruct us. And what notice do you think that they would take of you – a woman?' He shot the last word at her as if it were his trump card. 'And when they rob you, to whom would you turn? To the Sword Brethren? To the Riga chapter of the Teutonic Knights? Well, when they rest from their labours of slaughtering the rebellious heathen, do you think they will be energetic in defence of your rights?' He laughed at the very thought. 'And then there are the savage natives with savage languages and Russian merchants who would cut your throat for a marten pelt, and the good boyars of Novgorod who . . .'

'Was Anthony committed to this enterprise?' Isabelle interrupted him with her question.

He expelled his breath and frowned. 'Yes! Yes, of course.'

Isabelle studied the man who was so keen to discourage her. Even when he was angry and patronising, he was undeniably handsome. It half amused her that such thoughts filled her mind when she was crossing swords with him.

'And he would have sailed to Riga?' she asked.

'Of course. We did so two years ago. The returns were admirable. Lincolnshire cloth and Gascon wine out; furs, wax and amber home. He would have gone again this year. It was Anthony who contracted with the sea captains . . .'

'And now I am Anthony!'

Curteys snorted in indignation at Isabelle's words.

'I stand in law as his substitute,' she went on firmly. 'If he would have gone, then I must go. I would have thought that you would have understood that, William. You were good enough to defend my interests against Coppledyke.'

Curteys sniffed. 'That was different. Coppledyke was always a conniving troublemaker. Anthony beat him squarely. But this matter of Riga is madness; *your* madness. It is enough that you insist on representing the house of Crosse in Boston, but to go to Riga . . . it is an act of sheer folly. It will bring nought but trouble.'

'I have settled it in my own mind.' Isabelle's tone was quietly determined. 'I shall sail with the fleet from Boston. It is my right and I am as keen as Anthony was to protect the full value of my investment.'

A knowing look crossed Curteys' face. Then he coloured with indignation. 'So that is the meaning of your insistence. You do not trust me! You do not think that I will deal with your investment fairly. This is why you are so committed to this madness. You think that your investment is not safe in my hands!' His voice was raised in pitch. His hands rested on his hips and he stood, legs apart, as if braced against an assault.

Isabelle hesitated a moment, then leapt to her own defence realising as she did so that her hesitation had been a mistake. Curteys had noticed it. By the look on his face he clearly interpreted it as an admission of guilt. He scarcely listened to her.

'You misjudge me sorely, William. My concern for my investment in no way implies distrust of you. It is just that the amount of Crosse money tied up in this enterprise is considerable. Richard Pexton assures me that it amounts to almost four hundred pounds. Such a sum of money demands my attention – my personal attention. Surely you cannot doubt my sincerity in this matter?'

William looked as if he most certainly did doubt her sincerity. He was clearly offended by what he perceived as a slight on his capability and his honour. 'Then I wish you good fortune, madam,' he said curtly. 'You may make your plans for Riga on your own. Anthony would not have required a wet-nurse. You say that you are his substitute? Very well then. You must plan as he would have planned. I had only sought to help you. But that, I now see, is totally unacceptable to you. Since my advice and experience are not required, I shall occupy your time no longer. Perhaps Pexton will be able to assist you. You have this much in common: neither have been to the Baltic.'

'William, I did not mean to imply that . . .'

But it was too late. Curteys had swept up his fur-lined cloak. He stalked from the room.

Isabelle stood in the silence her partner had left behind, her smooth skin creased with a frown. Then she crossed to the open window of the solar. Down in the yard William Curteys was mounting his dapple-grey palfrey, ignoring the offered assistance of one of Isabelle's grooms. He leapt effortlessly into the stirrups and, motioning to his mounted, liveried retainers, he led them out of the yard.

For a moment, Isabelle continued to look down into the near empty yard. The rejected groom glanced up absent-mindedly and his gaze met that of his mistress. Isabelle stepped back from the window, vaguely annoyed that she had been observed watching Curteys' departure.

'He was angry.'

The voice was that of Eleanor de Bamville. Turning, Isabelle motioned for Eleanor to join her on the bench.

'It was that obvious?'

'He had a face like a thunder-storm. Is it about Riga?'

'Yes. It's about Riga. To start with he merely thought that I was mad, like the others do. Now, though, I have wounded his pride. It was offended honour that you saw.' Isabelle shook her head very slightly. She had taken off her veil and wimple and her hair cascaded over her blue shoulders.

'He believes that you do not trust him?' A knowing smile played across Eleanor's lightly weathered face. 'Men always desire to be admired for their honour. Even the worst rogues need to feel that. It is strange . . .'

'William Curteys is not a rogue.'

'I did not say that *he* was!' Isabelle knew her reply had come just a little too quickly. Eleanor licked her lips and grinned.

The almond eyes never moved from Isabelle. 'Sixteen. Four men to a ship. All archers.'

'And at what rate of pay?' Curteys inquired, full knowing the answer. 'How much a day?'

'Five pence.'

Isabelle's mouth twitched slightly. With one hand she very slowly pushed back a stray coil of blonde hair.

'There, Isabelle, so you see that all is in hand. The countryside is full of returning soldiery. As you say, the campaign in France has had little to show in terms of victory and booty. Little enough to show for last year's taxes squandered and the king's crown pawned. Those returning from France are desperate for new employment, for they looted so little, what with Nantes withstanding the duke's siege. It took little persuasion from Adam to reach the price agreed. All have signed a contract and no money needed to be spent buying them ale at the Saracen. They are glad to be taken on. And since we sail shortly, they shall not pay this year's poll tax. They are satisfied and so are we.'

The warehouse sagged under the weight of a heavy silence. The quiet was so oppressive, the timber beams almost creaked under the strain. Richard Pexton shuffled his feet. No other noise broke the stillness.

At last, Isabelle cleared her throat with a sharp, light cough. Her mouth was dry. 'You have done well, Adam.' She nodded graciously in the direction of William Curteys' companion. 'And Will is right, of course, we must watch every penny. Especially now that we will be sailing with one less ship.' She suddenly realised that she was stating the obvious; merely repeating Curteys' words.

She persisted, as if the simple repetition of the facts gave her mastery over them. 'I shall instruct Richard to cease from negotiation with the soldiery.' Her mouth was like sand. 'And since I see that you have completed the business here, I shall leave you. As you can imagine, I have many matters to attend to. There is the matter of final purchases to be made in tomorrow's fair. And my personal possessions. I trust that you will excuse me, sirs . . .' Isabelle summoned up every last reserve of self-control and turned. She gave Pexton and Eleanor the tiniest of nods.

'Be mindful of the lack of space, Isabelle: there is no room for fancy clothes. Others will sleep in what they wear by day. And will live in what they wear for many days.'

'Thank you, Will.' She did not turn. 'I am mindful of such things. And Eleanor has travelled more miles than I – or you!'

Then she passed the last of the cloth bales and reached the door. One more step and she was outside. Outside into the pure April sunshine. A glorious Monday morning.

Back inside the warehouse, Curteys shrugged at his silent companion. 'Can you believe it? A woman? To Riga!'

For a brief moment he glimpsed tossing black waves on a Baltic storm and a ship awash and sinking. As he dismissed it, he realised that he saw Isabelle's hair, like silver threads, in the water. The vision puzzled and disturbed him.

Adam Thymelby grunted. He was thinking of the

'Do not make more of my words than you should, Eleanor de Bamville!' Suddenly both women were laughing. It was rare for Isabelle to laugh and few men would have recognised the sweet, light sound. Anthony Crosse had never heard it.

'But he is a very handsome man!' Eleanor insisted. 'Good thews and an upright bearing. The buttocks of a stud stallion . . .'

'Be silent, Eleanor. Have you no shame? I am burying my husband the day after tomorrow.'

Isabelle was not angry but there was a note of slight disapproval in her voice. Eleanor became serious again. 'Do you trust him?'

Isabelle was thoughtful and her bright eyes clouded. 'He is an honest man,' she said slowly. 'Anthony thought so and I've never heard anyone question his honour. But . . .' She paused.

'But?'

'He is a shrewd one. A sharp one. He can turn one silver penny into two. That is a gift wedded to him, when no woman has been.' She pulled a wry face at Eleanor. 'He would never rob me. But I am not sure that he would work too hard on making my penny two if he could make his penny three!'

Eleanor, who had haggled with merchants from Sleaford to Sidon, nodded. 'And there are a lot of Crosse pennies bound up in the expedition to Riga?'

'As well you know! Anthony bought up bolts of cloth to fill the storehouse before Christmas. And negotiated with the Gascons to carry their wine. Not to mention the contracts with the ship-owners. There are a fair few Crosse pennies in this enterprise. And Will Curteys knows it. But if the last voyage is repeated, the cost will be more than met by the pelts alone, let alone the wax and amber . . .' For a moment, Isabelle's mind lingered on the black-marten pelt that lined William Curteys' opulent cloak. Yes, the furs alone would be worth a fortune. The furs of Riga and of distant Novgorod.

She was called from her daydream by Eleanor. 'I fear that I have bad news for you.' The full, round face was no longer smiling.

The smile died from the younger woman's face. 'What is it?' she asked warily. The two women had been expecting trouble. Ever since Isabelle had returned to Boston two days before, they had been anticipating moves against the newly widowed mistress of the house of Crosse.

Eleanor moved towards the window and gazed down into the yard. It was empty again. 'I did not want to disturb you while he was here.' She referred to Curteys in a casual manner, but there was no disrespect in her voice. 'I thought you would not wish to advertise any problems.'

Isabelle nodded. 'Wisely done. There's little to be gained from telling him every time someone tries to knock me down. He'd only take it as justifying his advice to me. Now what is it? Who is it now? Coppledyke?'

'It's not Coppledyke. Shortly after you returned from the guildhall the steward rode in from Bicker. He says that on Tuesday, the very day after you left the manor, the enclosure about the turbary was destroyed. He had the fences replaced and a guard mounted. Then, last night, one of the dykes on your side of the causeway was broken down. By dawn, over thirty acres of pasture had been flooded. He's moved the cattle back to the manor.'

'Retaliation for Anthony's enclosure of the turbary?'

'He thinks so. He also believes that the attacks are deliberately designed to coincide with your mourning. 'Tis common knowledge that Anthony is dead and a young widow now lord of the manor. They know that tomorrow his body will be returned to Boston. Clearly they think that your mind will be on other things.'

For years Anthony had quarrelled with his neighbours over boundaries and fishing rights. This new chapter of aggression was not totally unexpected. Eleanor and the steward were undoubtedly correct. It had been timed to coincide with the death of the lord of Bicker. Isabelle pursed her lips. 'We shall see about that!'

'I'm sorry?'

'Nothing, Eleanor. Take no heed. I merely thought out loud.' Isabelle paused. She needed to think carefully. 'Has the steward identified any of those responsible?'

'He is sure that the men who broke down the enclosure, about the turf cutting, were from Donington.'

The place name was familiar. Anthony Crosse had long been at odds with the tenants of the manor of Donington. The precious right to exploit the fens was not easily given up by any in that land of sweeping wetness. Only strangers saw the great expanse as a damp desert. To those who lived within it, its wealth in fish and sedge, in turf and salt, in summer pasture, was all too apparent. And the fiercely independent fen smallholders were no strangers to conflict over these customary privileges. They were the descendants of Hereward the Wake and a myriad anonymous rebels over the centuries, who had found in the vast bleakness a home for their hopes and a fortress against outsiders. Isabelle pondered all this carefully. She knew these people well.

'And what of the damage to the dyke? The same men of Donington?'

Eleanor shook her head. 'That is another matter. The destruction of the turbary was done by daylight. That of the dyke was an act of darkness . . .'

'But the men who attacked the enclosure,' Isabelle interrupted, 'they surely did not cry their intentions about the shire.'

'And neither did they hide them! The steward is certain about that. They came and did what they did with arrogance born of . . .'

'Born of knowing they were right? That Anthony enclosed the fen against all customary practice?'

Eleanor's pleasing, round face flushed slightly. It was only the slightest change of colour. Then she smiled. 'Those were not the steward's exact words! But he did intimate that the men of Donington were, how shall I put it, strongly motivated by a sense of their own rightness.'

'Not his exact words either, I'd guess.'

'Miserable curs, who sin without fear for their souls since they are so stiff in their pride that they admit not their sins!'

'That sounds more like the steward,' Isabelle smiled dryly.

'I have omitted the curses. I would not wish to offend your sensibilities, or my own.'

The two women laughed again. It was a refreshing sound. It cleansed the bad news of something of its fearfulness, emasculated the worst and most aggressive threats.

'What would I do without you, Eleanor?' Isabelle placed a hand on her friend's shoulder.

'You would survive. You were born to survive.'

'But you know full well that survival is not enough! One must learn to live . . . and to love.'

Eleanor inclined her head thoughtfully. 'You were but a child when I first came to your father's house and now . . .' She left the sentence unfinished. She could see the willowy eleven-year-old, with the flowing hair and the solemn blue eyes. It all seemed so long ago. Eleanor could still remember the day when the woman she had companioned had died and her bereaved lord had recommended Eleanor as companion to a family with a growing girl-child. Even when the vision passed, she could still make out the form of the child. That child – serious and yet innocent, perceptive and yet vulnerable – was somehow still there, deep within the blue eyes opposite her. The woman had outgrown the child, but only as a tree outgrows its sapling state. Cut down the tree: deep inside it the sapling rings remained, invisible, but the core of the tree itself.

'And you had seen so much,' Isabelle interrupted her friend's reverie. 'You had been everywhere. Jerusalem and Antioch, Byzantium and Rhodes. You were like a tale from a minstrel's hoard of stories . . .'

It was true. To the young girl, Eleanor had been like a vista opening on to another world. And when she had nursed Isabelle's dying mother and befriended the lonely, awkward, yet beautiful girl, that wider world had finally become real: a thing to be explored and not feared. Isabelle's father, always busy, and her brother enmeshed in business, had valued Eleanor's gifts of cooking and herb-lore; scraps of healing knowledge gleaned from pilgrimages amongst the infidel. But it was her words that had entranced an eleven-year-old: her stories of places strange and mysterious; her lack of respect for authorities, which at first had seemed terrifying to Isabelle but in time had become an inspiration. For Eleanor de Bamville was servile to none but God. And Him she served as a friend.

'You will ride to Donington?' Eleanor's question was really a statement.

'You know that I will. I would have gone tomorrow to bring Anthony home. But now I will go today. I will not see my manor despoiled – not by anyone . . . I will need the horses saddled and ready. For it is well past noon already.'

'It is done.'

Isabelle smiled. 'Of course.'

Edward Crosse, known to those who despised his origins as Edward Moyne, surveyed his own handiwork. The sluice was jammed shut. The damming effect was increased by the tree trunks hurled down into the drainage channel. Several of his men were busy shovelling earth on to the blockage. With every sweated effort the heap of debris grew higher, its ability to stop up the channel greater.

Edward sat on the flesh-white stump of a willow. About him, chips of naked wood lay scattered in the coarse grass. He was well pleased with the work. An agonised groan heralded the death of yet another willow. It slumped down the side of the dyke and hit the water with a sharp splash. Immediately men – half-in, half-out of the water – shoved it towards the wrecked sluice. They were already working up to their waists. Green slime hung on faded cotte and hose. The dark, stinking water was rising, slowly but perceptibly.

One of the labourers, a bull-necked man with bulging veins across his throat, splashed his way out of the ditch. Despite the freshness of the spring day he was stripped to the waist. Weed clung to him like some obscene cancerous growth. Cursing, he hauled himself up the slippery bank. Edward Crosse watched him with some detachment. Unlike the labouring man, Edward Crosse's clothes were unmarked by sweat or dirt. No mud or slime sullied his boots or soiled his red beard. He had guided the work of careful destruction without involvement. That was only to be expected. After all, he was the lord of the manor of Swineshead.

'Ha, that'll fix it. It'll take them hours to open up that sluice again. God rot them!' The bull-necked man surveyed the flat sweep of pasture beyond the ditch. 'Look! The water's already backing up down the sewers!' He was right. The labour had not been in vain. Already the dark waters were piling up behind the malicious dam.

'And this was how you fixed the sewer at Donington?' Edward seemed mildly interested in the details of the previous night's destruction. 'Blocked up the sluice? It's flooded a pretty piece of pasture already!'

Bull-neck shook his head. ' 'Twas quicker to smash a hole in the bank. God, but the water poured out.' He spat. 'You should have seen it – like a giant peeing

over their fields.' He laughed again at the memory.
'And now they're working their fat arses off filling it
in again! The whoresons won't do that in a hurry.'

He beamed at his own skill in destruction. He
noted the nod of his master's head and the approval
pleased him. Edward was here in person because he
knew that every man jack of the population of Bicker
would be labouring to close up the breach in the dyke.
Whilst they laboured to the south, he could conduct
his own business to the north of his stepmother's
manor. No one would be expecting it there. And
when it was discovered, the blame would fall on the
'rogues' at Donington.

He tried to picture Isabelle's face when she saw the
extent of the flooding. His wife was right. That bitch
had no right to take what was his. He'd show her that
inheriting was one thing, keeping it all would be quite
another.

Damn her, he thought bitterly, *and damn him for
leaving me nothing but a stinking village*. And yet, as
he thought about *that* woman, there was the familiar
surging in his stomach, the hardness in his loins. For a
moment a fleeting fantasy possessed him: the dyke
was deserted; Isabelle lay naked in the wet grass. In
vain she writhed to escape his determined thrusts. All
about, the floodwater poured in torrents.

'Master?' Bull-neck eyed Edward curiously. He
was not an intelligent man but he could not fail to
notice the glassy stare of his lord. A puzzled look
crowded out the malicious grin.

Edward shook himself free of his anger and lust.
'It's done,' he replied. 'Get those dogs together and
get out of here.' He motioned to the toiling men. 'Get

them out of here. We've done enough.'

He ran his fingers through his beard, his breath coming short and sharp, as if he had been running. As if he had been having her. That thought aroused him again and he clenched his fist in rage. Ever since she had entered his father's house, he had been prey to these conflicting emotions. He had hated her for the threat she posed to his inheritance and, from the moment she had been bedded, he had felt his own future shrink before his eyes. And yet, the desire that had consumed him from the start was loose once more. Torn by his emotions, raging between fury and infatuation, he stared bitterly in the direction of his manor.

'She'll pay,' he muttered. 'She'll learn to respect me. The time will come when she will regret his generosity . . .' He spat again. 'By the saints she'll stumble on his prodigality towards her. She'll wish he'd left all to me. Not wish, but pray for it to be different . . .' As he muttered, a cooler, more careful thought arose out of his desire, and at the bottom of the cooling furnace of his passion lay a refined thought. A fragment of a possibility. He passed one hand through his sandy hair and reflected on his wife's words; her attacks on Isabelle; her fuelling of his anger. A grim determination gripped him. He knew what he would do and he was pleased by the thought.

Outside the whitewashed hall on Strait Bargate, Isabelle Crosse's retainers were mounted, their horses milling in snorting circles. Richard Pexton was with them, a heavy travel cloak slung round his shoulders. All the men were armed.

Isabelle had finished delivering instructions to Eleanor de Bamville and Pexton frowned as he watched the young mistress of the Crosse household being helped to her saddle by a groom. As she pulled up her reins a panting messenger pushed a way through the steaming horses.

Isabelle recognised him. He was a Crosse tenant, from the tenement on Wormgate Street. He approached her carefully; clearly he carried bad news.

'Mistress Crosse.' His voice was strained. 'Coppledyke has blocked the alleyway to the yard . . .' He frowned at the memory of the obstruction. 'He has gated it and bolted the gate. We cannot get to our yards and sheds . . .' His voice trailed off, weakly.

All eyes were on Isabelle. She raised a slim hand, long fingers spread wide. Silence fell.

'A gate, on our alleyway?' The cool voice was now abrim with indignation. 'Then tear it down! Break it off its hinges!'

Her hand fell on the flank of her jennet. The slap was sharp and shocking. The horse leapt forward. Startled, her retainers spurred their mounts to follow her.

The nervous tenant watched in dismay, her words ringing in his head: 'Tear it down. Break it off its hinges!'

He shook his head. The thought of Coppledyke's reaction made him pale. The thought of Isabelle's reaction – if he did not do as bidden – was equally terrifying.

'Tear it down. Break it off its hinges!'

Chapter 3

The mighty nave of the church of St Botolph was mottled by shifting patterns of shadow. The time was full noon yet no spring sunshine played over the stones. Boston's parish church was shrouded in the same sea mist which cloaked the town in a clammy drift of grey.

Inside, the gathered crowd murmured. 'Did you hear? Have you heard?' a blinking merchant asked. The whispers grew all around him.

'About the widow . . . ?' his grinning neighbour queried.

'Aye, and how she rode out like a wild thing!'

A third voice interrupted: 'They say she rode right up to Donington. Stood in the village and dared the men to face her down, right there.'

'And did they?' The merchant was all agog.

'Did they? By Peter's chains they turned like mice. And the very same afternoon her men tore down the door that Coppledyke set up against her.'

'Aye, I heard,' a fourth voice added.

'I saw it,' chipped in a fifth.

'So did I.'

'And I. Right terrible it was.'

The murmurs ran like fire and more were there to

49

view the wild woman Isabelle Crosse than pay respects to her dead husband.

Outside the church, in the broad expanse of Kyrke Lane, Anthony Crosse's funeral cortège stood in the close mist. Moisture glistened on the beards and moustaches of the pall-bearers. William Curteys ran one hand through the dark mass of his thick hair. He stared with narrowed eyes up into the oppressive sky. Then he cast a slow glance towards the woman who headed the solemn procession. It was a look of thoughtful appraisal although what thoughts moved behind those deep brown eyes was impossible to tell.

Isabelle Crosse stood alone, two paces away from Richard Pexton and Eleanor de Bamville who in turn stood only feet away from the long coffin, hoisted on six square shoulders. Despite this, she stood in isolation, her mourning putting her apart: now, at last, she was all in black.

Richard Pexton limped towards her. As usual his features were tense with concentration. 'My lady, the guild torches are lit.'

His comment produced no discernible response in the young widow. He shifted his feet and sighed. One of the pall-bearers coughed. Isabelle turned and faced the cortège. Behind the coffin-bearers the retainers shuffled like rooks. Beyond them the great market-place of Richmond Fee stood deserted, the leaning shops and tenements bordering it almost concealed by the mist. For a moment her eyes rested on Will Curteys. Then she flicked a glance towards his companion. Edward Crosse returned her gaze with a foxy look of quick-eyed concentration. The blue eyes, mottled with green, sparkled intently. She watched the moisture drip from his red beard.

She was glad he was here. It was only right that he should carry Anthony. After all, he knew him better than she had.

She nodded to her stepson. The gesture was slight. For a moment he hesitated. Then with a swifter, surer movement, he nodded back. Contact had been made. Isabelle was satisfied. Back at the hall, Edward's cold distance had been obvious to all. Now at last it was in retreat. As if caught unawares by his response, he blushed. But for her coffined husband, Isabelle would have smiled.

Phillip Spayne, chantry priest of the Guild of the Blessed Mary, left the coffin and approached her. A tall, almost stooping man, his red, rebellious hair was tousled and deep, sunken eyes glowed either side of the great, curving sweep of an aquiline nose. At forty-five he was a year younger than Eleanor. However age, which only added glints to Eleanor's laughing eyes, hung heavy on this priest.

'It is time, Isabelle. The guild torches are alight.' Spayne's voice was pitched low. He spoke to her without deference and yet with a restrained dignity.

Isabelle nodded and stepped briskly back. The suddenness of her movements seemed to animate the assembled mourners. Heads came up. The pall-bearers shifted the weight. Intoning the office for the dead, the chantry priest led the way into the torchlit church.

As the coffin passed, Isabelle fell in behind it, and as she did so caught the look on the face of Edward's wife. Muffled and cowled though she was, Ann Crosse's eyes kindled with hatred. The intensity of the stare caused Isabelle to intake her breath sharply. Pexton glanced at her. Instantly she was composed. She ignored the burning eyes and instead turned to follow the body of her husband. Richard Pexton frowned in puzzlement. Eleanor, who had seen the hot coals set in Ann Crosse's pretty face, clicked her tongue thoughtfully.

The newly lighted nave was quiet once more as the coffin entered. Necks craned and here and there a whisper rustled like a stray leaf. Eyes followed the pall-bearers but more eyes fixed on the crêpe-draped widow. Most of the peering faces held looks of genuine curiosity. Some, however, were more hostile. Around the sneering face of Nicholas Coppledyke, loyal attendants mirrored their master's disdain with careful mimicry. Here were the apprentices who had put up the draper's ill-timed gate. Here too were the journeymen who had seen that barrier reduced to kindling. A dark, stained bandage on a cracked head suggested that some, at least, of Isabelle's tenants had carried out her orders with temerity. Isabelle passed amongst the standing crowd as if unaware of the intense interest. Only Eleanor could guess at the dry mouth and the churning stomach which made such seeming calm possible.

At the chapel of the Guild of the Blessed Mary, Phillip Spayne was met by the second chantry priest. Behind him the great wax candles sputtered on the altar of the Virgin. Like the great torches, they were provided from the silver pennies of the guild's merchant members.

For the next hour Anthony Crosse's funeral was played out before Isabelle like some great pageant, a solemn drama of bowing priests and ancient litany. When, at last, it was done and the funeral party retreated from the altar, Isabelle felt as if she had been a participant in a mystery play. The shadows and the swaying lights, the darkness at noon, all had helped to blur the fine distinction between imagination and reality, life and death. As she turned from the dead and rejoined the living, she was met by the formal kisses and greetings of the guildmasters – her fellow guildmasters. Their solemn faces hid their secret opinions of their new 'fellow' but away in the nave, Nicholas Coppledyke made no attempt to hide his disdain. He, at least, made no secret of his feelings towards the new guildmaster within the Guild of the Blessed Virgin. Despite the formal etiquette which demanded his condolences, the choleric draper strutted from the nave, the crowd parting before his progress and behind him his clerks and apprentices imitated his animosity.

William Curteys, however, came forward and kissed her formally. 'Nick Coppledyke sends his polite regards.'

Isabelle allowed a ghost of a smile to play over her lips. Curteys' cynical humour released a little of her tension.

'Bless him for his thoughtfulness,' she said softly. 'And if he puts a gate across my tenement again I'll . . .'

'Madam, it is the bailiff of the manor of Boston.'

Spayne's interruption stifled Isabelle's whispered

threat. With a careful countenance she turned and accepted the condolences of the town's long-faced bailiff.

When at last the formal church greetings were over, Isabelle, accompanied by Pexton, led the straggling procession of merchants back to Strait Bargate, to the formal meal that, customarily, was held in the dead guildsman's hall. There Isabelle made her way to the top table as Pexton and a little army of retainers directed each guildsman and his wife to their places on the various trestle tables. The most senior men and their wives joined Isabelle on the dais and the rest were placed along two long tables in order of social importance: the most important towards the dais.

Isabelle sat watching her guests arrange themselves, carefully removing her linen veil and tucking it into the long, tongued girdle which fell across her hips. Only the top table was seated. As was the custom, all others present stood; their eyes darted to and from their social superiors on the dais. The busy retainers too kept glancing at the top table, fearful of missing any sign or signal from their mistress. Isabelle could not help but notice the new intensity in her servants' glances. It was as if only Anthony's burial had finally convinced them of his end. Only now could they fully comprehend the change that had taken place and there, on the top table, sat the new focus of their lives. Slowly they took up their social stations about this pivotal point in their universe.

'My lady, your bread . . .' The pantler bowed

young widow's slim figure. He could think of worse people to have as a companion many hundreds of miles from home. His almond eyes clouded slightly. Then he turned to Curteys and his ledger.

'By all God's good martyrs. Can you believe the sheer impudence of the man!'

It had been just over a day since Isabelle had met Curteys and Thymelby. Still the memory of his words riled her. She could feel her face flush with sheer rage.

'It is his intention to unsettle you. You must resist him.' Eleanor's nut-brown eyes exuded sympathy, her full, expressive face set in a firm resolve.

'But, I am ready to burst apart! He has set out to undermine me at every turn. You can see it, can't you? Five-pence-a-day archers! Damn him!'

'Careful, Isabelle. Your words carry. Never let others become party to your anger, until you may profit from it.'

'Yes. Yes. I know that you are right. But he would try the patience of every saint . . . !'

Isabelle took Eleanor's arm and squeezed it. Beyond them the two serving men exchanged pained glances. Like all in the hall by the town's Bargate, they had witnessed their mistress's return home the previous day. Her cold fury had been apparent to all. When she had decided not to take the midday repast with her household, the extent of her displeasure had become clear. Now she was still to be approached only with the utmost delicacy.

Tuesday 23 April 1381 had dawned, full of its speculated splendour. The weather had held, the day was warm and by mid-morning Boston was seething

with activity. Great canopied stalls filled the market-
place and the commercial activity overflowed Richmond Fee. Whilst the Fair of St George was small
compared to the November mart – which even spread
across the river to become the Fair of Holland – it was
still a major event within the town.

Isabelle and Eleanor had spent the morning purchasing stout boots and canvas cottes for the forthcoming journey. After the noon-time meal in the hall
they had returned to the fair, intent on more purchases for the journey. However, there had also been
time to examine the more luxurious wares, brought
from far and wide. Eleanor had purchased a silver
brooch, sold by a silversmith from Wisbech. Isabelle
had bought a fine linen wimple of sheer lawn and a
deep purple cotte of Venetian wool velvet; finely cut
and brocaded with gold thread where it clung over the
breasts. She was determined to find room for it in the
ship.

Tired of the jostling crowds, the two women had, at
last, escaped the late afternoon bustle. They had
come finally to Wormgate, north of the great parish
church. It too was busy but was more tolerable than
the crowds in Richmond Fee. The excursion had
given Isabelle the opportunity to view the disputed
alleyway which her tenement shared with the draper's
shop of Nicholas Coppledyke. All was quiet. The
tenants reported no trouble from their fiery neighbour. After inspecting the outside appearance of the
tenement rented by Edward Crosse, the two women
had followed the street to where it met the river and
the common marsh. With the exception of the mills,
beating the water of the Witham, the area was almost

deserted. Here, at last, Isabelle had given vent to the fury that she felt. It surprised her to realise how little her anger had dissipated since the previous day.

'I have done everything I can to make preparations for the expedition but he has removed each responsibility from me. No sooner do I consult him with regard to a purchase than he has had it done himself.'

'And it is not to assist you?' Eleanor grinned.

'As well you know! He is keeping me away from every responsible decision.' Isabelle laughed bitterly. 'In Boston I can run the hall, train up apprentices, appear before the Court Leet with complaints. Sit in judgement on those who offend the guilds and the bailiff . . .' She clenched one fist. 'But as soon as I come near the expedition, I find that all has been done. I am left with nothing to do but oversee my own personal preparations. There, at least, he does not leap ahead of me. You saw what happened to poor Richard with regard to the archers. Will cut the ground from under his feet.'

'But was careful enough to see to it that the work lay at the door of Adam Thymelby.'

'He is a clever man. But by St John, he drives me to distraction.'

'He is trying to make you doubt your own ability. He is attempting to make you feel worthless. He hopes you will repent of your decision to go on the expedition . . .'

'He is making me angry!'

Eleanor grinned. 'That is better than feeling worthless! Your anger may be turned to your advantage. It is a fierce energy which can fuel action. Like doubt. It only fails you when it turns on itself and feeds on itself, in grief and misery. But you will not let it do that.'

The two serving men had wandered off a little. They were watching a barge of cutstone making its slow way down river, from Lincoln. Eleanor took the opportunity to draw near to the young widow.

'It is hard. For like all men he has little faith in your ability to do this task, which God has laid on you. And should he fail, or the task falter, he will seek to blame you.' Isabelle nodded and Eleanor continued. 'Men always do so. It is their way. But you must bide your time. You must watch and learn. Aye, and accept his actions, though they drive you to madness. For in time you will prove your worth.'

Eleanor lifted a small cloth package. Carefully she opened it. The slight breeze rustled the edges of the cloth and murmured in the marsh grasses. 'You know what this is?'

Isabelle reached out and touched the silver brooch. She nodded and Eleanor looked at her with eyes of such caring and concern that Isabelle glanced away.

'But do you?' The older woman queried. 'Do you truly know what it is?'

Isabelle pulled a face. 'It is the brooch that you bought from the silversmith of Wisbech. The one with the stall in Kyrke Lane. I was there! Mayhap you have forgotten?'

'Ah, but this is more than a piece of pretty metal. For this is time and effort, prayers and fears.' Before Isabelle could query such a strange description, she added: 'How did its maker come by this skill?'

Isabelle sighed. 'His father apprenticed ·him to a silversmith. He served as an apprentice. He learned the trade. Could be, he travelled as a journeyman working with different masters. Until his guild accepted the quality of one of his works – his "masterpiece" – and he became a guildmaster himself. With rights to train others . . .'

Eleanor looked at her and nodded in agreement. 'Indeed. This piece did not spring forth from nothing. Only God may create worlds from nought. Even His own son did not shrink from an apprenticeship at His Father's bench. In the same way you must work out this apprenticeship in the face of all Will Curteys' jibes. And, in time, you shall produce your own masterpiece. Then you will astound him. All of them.'

'Thank you, my dearest friend.' Isabelle was deeply moved. She felt tears in her eyes. 'Thank you.'

The two women embraced: the pilgrim who had travelled to Jerusalem and the widow who had never travelled further from Boston than the Abbey of Ely.

The late afternoon sun was sinking. Drifting down into the horizonless landscape of the fens, it would suddenly plunge the world into darkness. Great writhing ribbons of scarlet suffused the horizon with a drench of blood. Deep in their conversation, Isabelle and Eleanor retraced their steps down Wormgate. Ahead, the rising tower of the church was soaked in the light of the setting sun.

Before Isabelle and Eleanor reached the church they met Edward Crosse and his wife Ann. They had been to the fair and were now returning to the rented house opposite the shop of Nicholas Coppledyke. The four paused awkwardly. Stiff pleasantries were passed. Neither Eleanor nor Isabelle could forget the circumstances of their last meeting with Edward. Since then he had buried himself in his fen manor: his return to Boston was unheralded.

The red-bearded coil of contrary emotions was held tightly in check this day. His wife was as correct but perfunctory in her greetings as usual. She seemed to sense the tension between bastard son and step-mother; a tension which undermined her own con-fidence.

The conversation was short and stilted. Isabelle told Edward that she would soon leave for Riga. He, in turn, wished her well and reiterated his promise of protection for her manors. Ann Crosse just watched, her sea-green eyes as hostile as ever. It was a relief when the chance encounter came to an end. The parting was as awkward as the greeting.

A more welcome encounter was with Matthew Redman. The silver-haired guildsman was leaving the church as they passed, having just concluded a good day's business. In his fatherly way he seemed pleased to see the young widow and her companion. With slow movements of his head he paid grave attention to the plans of Isabelle.

As they talked, Isabelle noticed two household servants on their way back to the hall, laden with merchandise purchased at the fair. In an act of generosity, Isabelle dispatched her accompanying retainers to assist them. It was a sure sign that her equilibrium was returning.

Meanwhile, Matthew Redman, who had lost his first wife when she was Isabelle's age, seemed only too interested in the plans for the summer's trading in the Baltic. With his slow, deliberate movements and encouraging nods, he asked detailed questions about the trip. There was something in the turn of Isabelle's head that stirred a deep memory and he felt a little comfort that a tenuous thread seemed to link him to the long dead. Isabelle – glad to be taken seriously at last – explained her expectations and outlined the personal preparations that she had made. Redman seemed the only man in Boston interested in her choice of strong woollen dresses and cloaks, leather boots – even her extravagance in the form of the Venetian wool velvet; and he chuckled at Eleanor's contribution of an inflatable leather bladder to support a swimmer. Isabelle's thaw of mood continued and soon she had shaken off the last of the manacles of ill humour with which Curteys had bound her.

Darkness had fallen as they conversed. Candlelight glowed in the doorways of shops and tenements. The last traders drifted from the nearby marketplace. The noise of drunken singing echoed from the nearby pot-houses. Finally taking leave of the elderly merchant, Isabelle led the way back home. Aware that she was later getting home than she had planned, Isabelle took them down the narrow alley which led from St Botolph's church through to Strait Bargate. When the two women had almost reached the end of the alley, leaving behind the overhanging houses and the close leaning timber-framed walls of mud and stud, they both heard a sudden movement behind them. Within seconds a series of shapes came upon them like deeper shadows and the stale stink of ale filled the confined space.

'Isabelle – run! Out of here.' Eleanor reacted to the dark presence more swiftly than her companion. But as soon as she shouted, footsteps echoed in the narrow alley and a hand caught at the pilgrim's cloak. The hand pulled tight. Eleaner lashed out. Her fist met an open mouth and she was spattered with warm blood. She slipped out of the cloak, stumbling.

Other hands caught Isabelle from behind. Hands, wild with drunken lechery, but sober enough to possess sense and feeling. She felt herself lifted off her feet. Her head struck a wall and she screamed and screamed, barely aware that the sound she was hearing came from her own mouth. A great hand closed over her face and she could taste sweat and ale. She gagged. She choked. She bit and she felt blood flow: not, she thought, her own.

Suddenly she was on her back, kicking like a mad thing, the hand still clamped on her face. A heaving body crashed down on her and she felt a man hard against her belly, thrusting at her. A hand tore at her dress. Hard, groping fingers reached the smooth flesh of her thigh. The fingers pushed upwards, hungrily, desperately. She could hear the tearing of cloth. The man was gasping; grunting like a rutting animal, as he rammed himself against her.

Her legs were revealed. Naked white flesh flashed. They were forced apart. He was between them. She desperately tried to buck him off but he was too heavy. His hand was tearing at his own chausses whilst her legs were spread in utter vulnerability. He drove himself hard against her. She twisted and arched her back in terror.

Then – over the animal noises of nearly consummated lust – rang the shout of an alerted householder. For a moment it had no impact on the man; then, in a torrent of oaths, he rose from her. She pulled herself upright but a fist smashed her down again.

'Isabelle!' Pexton's voice echoed in the alleyway. Drawing nearer, he crashed through the darkness. 'Isabelle. For God's sake!'

As the frustrated rapist trampled over the prostrate woman, Pexton caught him from behind, digging his fingers into the man's arm.

Suddenly a slim blade struck and Pexton fell heavily. A wooden wall shook with the impact and blood spread out over the clerk's slashed sleeve. The knife jabbed again, this time at his face He parried the blow and it sliced over his hand. Effortlessly. Bloodily. He was unaware of any sensation of pain. He snatched at the blade. It slid through his fingers, razor-sharp. Fresh blood spurted. It sprayed over his face, now contorted with rage beyond words. With a strength fuelled by desperation, Pexton threw himself forward. He hit his assailant like a solid bale of cloth. The two fell across the alley.

Voices rang out from the direction of Strait Bargate. Pexton gripped his enemy, heedless of the knife hilt smashed against his skull. One dark figure – who had been engaged in a brutal wrestle with Eleanor – let off his assault to come to the aid of his fellow.

Richard felt a booted foot hammer into his ribs but he clung on like a terrier. The voices grew louder. The hue and cry had at last been raised. The boot swung like a battering ram. The clerk's fingers slipped. Cloth parted. His fingers closed on air. The two assailants were escaping him. He heard the thud of their feet. He tried to rise but could not catch his breath. Falling to one side he lay against his mistress. With one

bleeding hand he touched the wild drift of her hair.
'Isabelle . . . Isabelle . . .'

He was still shielding her body when Isabelle's two
retainers arrived, wide-eyed with horror. As one
knelt beside the mistress and her clerk, the other ran
after the assailants but by now they were only running
footsteps fading away into the night.

When Isabelle recovered consciousness she was lying
in her own boxbed. Eleanor sat beside her, a bloody
bandage about her head. Pexton hovered nearby, like
an agitated hen. He was pale with anger and anxiety
and he too was bandaged about the head and hand.
His wounded arm hung awkwardly.

The attackers had vanished, he reported. Lost in
the night. There was little hope of identifying them,
with the town so crowded. The bailiff had been
alerted and the earl's soldiers, to no avail.

Isabelle cursed herself for her short-cut. She was
even more angry with herself when Curteys arrived
and chided her sharply for her lack of prudence. She
saw only the anger on his face but Eleanor recognised
fear in his eyes. After a short, sharp conversation he
left her wincing at his hardness. But all night long he
searched the alleyways for her attackers, sword in
hand.

For several days Isabelle was painfully sore, her
thighs a mass of sullen black and purple bruises. She
moved only with difficulty and kept mainly to the
solar. While she lay imprisoned in the hall, Curteys
supervised the loading of the ships, freshly anchored
in the Haven. Bales of cloth and crates of wine were
manhandled into the yawning deck hatches. Leather

bladders of water and the rations of dried biscuits, dried stockfish, hard cheese and salted herring followed the merchandise.

All this time, Pexton was Isabelle's eyes and ears; tireless in her service despite his own injuries. He was at Town Quay from first light until evening and then he reported to her every detail. As he did so he could not hide his grief that he was not to go with her. It had never been possible, that he knew – too much remained behind, in Boston, to be taken care of. And yet he had secretly hoped . . .

One evening Adam Thymelby came to the hall on Strait Bargate to report on the final arrangements. 'We've taken on the archers I spoke of.' The almond eyes flicked towards Pexton. 'And almost all of the stores are together now.' He eyed Isabelle with a hint of amusement. Clearly he could not truly believe that she intended to go through with the journey.

As if she read his thoughts Isabelle replied, 'Richard has told me. But it's good to hear that all is going well.' She shifted her position on the bench. It took a conscious effort not to wince at the ache from her back. 'You have loaded the fine cloth from our warehouse?'

'This morning.'

'I supervised it, my lady.'

Thymelby smiled. 'That's right. He supervised it.' There was a hint of mockery in his voice. 'It was well done.'

'And is William well? I have not seen him for two days. Not since the night . . .'

Isabelle felt the words drain away, like water into sand. The silence that flooded in behind her words embarrassed her. It seemed like a declaration of weakness. Like a cold wind the thought crossed her mind that all her life she had laboured to preserve the cool mask with which she faced men like Thymelby: men who thought her of little worth or of worth in only one way. Such men must never see her fear, or pain. She struggled to maintain the wall of ice which stood between them and it.

'Not since that night,' she continued. 'I am sure he is very busy.'

'He's busy enough.' Thymelby seemed amused by her interest, oblivious to her reference to the night of the attack. 'There's much to be done and many people to see. The Lincoln merchants brought in their scarlet cloth only this morning. Will has completed the negotiations on the purchase. I'm sure he will soon pass on the details to you.'

Isabelle sensed a curious edge in the merchant's voice. As if he were probing for why she had missed Curteys' presence. The thought angered her. As if she cared for William Curteys! Still, she was disappointed that he had not come. The feeling puzzled and also irritated her; like a strand of hair escaping from her golden hairnet. She brushed away the feeling which was so out of place.

Thymelby stirred. 'It's late.' The hour candle had burnt beyond nine o'clock. 'It'll be dark enough in the streets and my men are tired. I wish you a good night.' He bowed toward Isabelle. 'Goodnight, Pexton.' He scarcely glanced at the clerk.

As he descended the stair from the solar, he grinned. It was Curteys who had asked him to convey the latest news to Isabelle and to check on her health.

William had been crisp and clear about why he was too busy to do so. A little too stiff, in Adam's opinion.

The merchant was still grinning as he summoned his men to him. Curteys seemed overly conscious of hiding his concern for Isabelle. It was as if he still hoped to freeze her away from the trip and Thymelby was not convinced that his motives were simply commercial.

On Monday 6 May 1381, five days after the feast of St Philip, Isabelle took ship. She still limped, and William Curteys offered stiff, self-conscious assistance as she climbed the gang-plank. She asked for no more. It did, however, give her some pleasure to point out to her partner that all her personal belongings were crammed into one modest oak trunk although she did not mention the carefully folded Venetian velvet secreted at the bottom. As the sails filled and the small crew of Yarmouth men ran about the deck and climbed the castles, fore and aft, Isabelle watched the shelter of the Haven fall away to port. The rising swell of the open sea surged up against the short, squat cog and swept along the high-sided clinker planking. Gulls cried overhead.

Isabelle meditated on Eleanor's advice and prayed for a safe journey. She would have felt less peaceful had she known that, amongst the archers crowded in the rearing wooden platform of the ship's castle, was one who watched with narrowed eyes. Around one hand was wrapped a grubby bandage. Beneath the dirty covering was a new wound; the teeth marks still clearly recognisable.

Chapter 5

Ned Gosse hurled himself into a dark corner. Outside, beyond the woodyard the sound of his pursuers' voices changed pitch. The hatred and bloodlust gave way to puzzlement and frustration.

Guttural voices questioned one another. Then the pack gave cry again: some clue had been discovered. Invigorated by the fresh scent, the angry mob drew away. Soon all was quiet outside the dark storeroom. The archer could only hear the sharp panting of his breath, freed at last from the constraints of his own terror. Beneath his quilted gambeson his heart beat with a frantic speed. It was as if his body could not yet believe that he had escaped.

At last his curiosity overcame his fear and he pulled himself to his feet. Between him and the door stood a barrier of logs. With grimy fingers he could feel the lazy curls of birch bark. The sharp scent of butchered pine filled his nostrils. He was in a storeroom. Yes, that was it. He nodded to himself as he realised the nature of his sanctuary. With increasing confidence he explored the windowless shed. It was piled high with fresh-cut trunks. Here the pale corpse of birch, there the rough skin of Baltic pine and spruce. In one deep, dark corner the knotted bodies of fallen oaks lay like the victims of some primeval slaughter.

The archer hoisted himself up on to a pile of logs. The ruptured resin was still sticky beneath his fingers, sweet in smell. With irritation he surveyed his battered condition. Even in the half light he could make out the tears in his chausses and the rip in the leather of his gambeson.

He rubbed his face with one hand. His round, heavy face. It was a visage which did not easily give in to laughter and if it did it was a coarse sound, like a crow on a roof. Yet he was not ugly. He had a bull's arrogant hardness that some women might call attractive; others merely brutal. Now it was the brutal anger which burned in his unreflective eyes.

'Bugger them.' He had the slow drawl of the fen-country. 'Bugger the bastards,' he repeated with increasing venom. 'The stinking bastards . . .'

His voice trailed off as he considered the disaster which had nearly befallen him. With slow deliberation he turned and spat. The careful, furious action summed up all his hatred of the Easterlings and their gibbering mobs. With some calmness returning to his racing thoughts he mulled over the violent events of the last half-hour. He spat once more. It was all the fault of that damn woman, he decided. God, how he would punish her if he could get hold of her. That at least gave him some comfort in his enforced hiding-place.

He had hardly been able to believe his good fortune when he had seen her board ship. Until then he had only dealt with Thymelby and Curteys. When he had seen her on the quayside he had at last begun to think that his luck had turned. For when the damned servants had disturbed him on top of her he had been only moments away from triumph. Then, to see her board the same ship as himself . . . his mouth went dry just thinking of that moment.

He grinned to think of how she passed him daily and did not know who he was. In a ship that size it was impossible to avoid him. It had made the voyage less tedious. He had contrived to fetch her her water whenever the older woman had not got in his way. Once or twice he had brushed against her, before Curteys told him to mind himself. And every time she roused that hard masculinity in his loins. And every time she had no understanding of what stirred in him. To her he did not exist. But she would see him soon enough. He licked his swollen grey lips at the thought. He was a patient man. He would wait.

The sweet memory of her firm flesh – in the alley off Strait Bargate – aroused him again. He would get her alone. Then no one would prevent him from having her. No one thwarted him twice. He thought of the screaming French farm-girls and laughed. It would be worth waiting for. And it was more enjoyable when they screamed.

He liked it best when they were fine ladies. Common whores he could have any time. And a ripe village girl could be plucked and deflowered with ease. It was fine ladies that he wanted most. And the opportunity of enjoying one was so rare. Even on the French campaigns a common soldier was fortunate indeed if he got a chance with one.

For a few moments he pondered on their patterned

silks and damasks; on their dismissive comments to one as lowly as himself. He was just a shadow to a woman like Isabelle Crosse. Gosse spat. But that would change. Her fine ways would avail her nothing when he finally got his hands on her.

He bit his lip as he thought of the tearing of her clothes and of the white thighs that were deemed too good for him. He would show her who was the master. He would teach her a lesson she would never forget.

There was movement in the yard outside. He straightened up. His eyes narrowed, cat-like. With swift feline movements he slid from the logs. There were voices, German voices, one heavy and old, the other younger, higher. The younger voice spoke with a strange accent. The archer had only a smattering of Low German but he caught the inflexion.

'Damn her,' he hissed. 'Damn that stupid bitch.' Perhaps after all he would not have the pleasure of assaulting her. Not if the mob had returned. 'The stupid bitch. What does a woman know about anything?'

He thought of how Isabelle Crosse had insisted on going out into the town. All the archers knew there would be hell to pay when Curteys found out. But Curteys had been off busying himself. And she had insisted. The archers had cast each other exasperated glances but followed her instructions with mute resignation.

Then the Easterling mob had sniffed them out. Her in the furriers and the five archers outside. It was only his quick thinking that had saved him. Before the rest could act he had been gone, off to get help from the ships, or so he'd told them. They had probably thought him a hero.

'Like hell,' he muttered, thinking of his own quick-wittedness. 'Like hell. The stupid sots.'

The rest were probably dead by now. He had thought himself out of danger; but then the mob had seen him, damn them. And he had been hunted like a rat. But like a rat he had bolted into a hole. And the hunt had missed him. Until now.

Were some of them returning? He could not be sure. Very carefully he drew the long, sharp blade of his dagger from a boot. It was the only weapon left to him. He had discarded his yew bow and arrows in the chase. The thought still grieved him. He'd lost his kettle helmet too. Silently he cursed the woman and his mates and the German mob. He would willingly exchange all their lives for the return of his precious equipment.

The door of the shed opened. The sudden sunshine sent a volley of light through the dusty air like a flight of golden arrow shafts.

An elderly man entered. He was well dressed. Probably the owner of the wood, and clearly one of the merchants of Riga. He was carrying a ledger, heavy, with leather bindings and a board cover. He came into the store with the quiet confidence of one who was totally at home. He began to examine some of the piled wood, slowly advancing down the aisle, further into the shadows.

The archer shifted almost involuntarily. His sleeve caught a fist-like knot. Too late he realised his error.

The timber slid and the groan seemed to fill the shed.

The Easterling turned. He was surprised but not yet alarmed. The archer rose swiftly.

'*Wer bist du?*'

It was a question, not yet edged with fear. The archer recognised the words. He laughed as he leapt.

'I'll tell you who I am.'

The dagger was raised. In vain the old man turned towards the door, his voice now twisted with terror. The ledger fell heavily to the ground as the archer grabbed the woollen collar of the fleeing man's surcoat. He spun him round and the old man crashed against the wooden panelling of the shed. He opened his mouth to cry out a wild high alarm but the cry was crushed in his throat. The English soldier's padded forearm crashed into the merchant's Adam's apple and the old man's head thudded against the wooden planks.

The archer's knife-arm swung backwards and forward in two hard pumping actions. A convulsion shook the elderly merchant's body. A whistle of breath escaped the stifling forearm pressure and hissed between the parted lips. Just to make sure, the knife struck again. The Easterling's body went limp. The restraining arm removed, it slid down the wall to lie twisted and alone on the wood-shaving-littered floor.

The archer grinned. He had scarcely begun to exert himself. With slow, deliberate movements he began to wipe the blade of the misericord on the good woollen clothing of the dead man. Then he tensed again. Footsteps sounded in the yard.

The young Livonian manservant walked confidently into the woodstore. He had heard the sound of falling wood and assumed that his master would have need of him. As he stepped from light into shadow, he stumbled over the body of his employer. Before he could grasp the significance of his discovery the hilt of the dagger hammered into the base of his skull.

'Careless . . . fool.' The archer bent over the younger body. He lifted up the head by its wavy mouse hair. 'Very careless. And now it's lowsing time . . .'

He grinned as he used the homely fenland term for knocking off after a day's honest toil. The sharp blade nicked the slight folds of skin under the unconscious man's chin. Here was a knocking off that would last for eternity. The rough humour pleased him as he prepared to cut the young servant's throat.

Then he hesitated. A sudden thought bit through the rough laughter which had begun to tumble from his mouth. He let the servant slump on to the floor once more. Then, impulsively, he hauled him off his master. Lifting the flopped head, he punched it full in the temple. The young man fell backwards.

Then, with narrowed eyes, the archer pulled the gold rings from the hands of the dead merchant. He bit his lips as he fought temptation. Instead of pocketing them, he pushed them into a crevice in the disturbed stack of birch trunks. Hidden – but not too carefully. Then, with a sigh, he prised open the fingers of the youth and inserted the handle of the blooded misericord. The job done, he surveyed his handiwork.

'To hell with you. My knife, bow and helmet all lost in one day. And six good goose-feathered arrows.' Looking down on the dead and the doomed he felt real sorrow at the loss of his possessions. But there was no choice. 'To hell with you,' he spat once more. Then, checking that the yard outside was deserted, he darted out through it to the alleyway which connected the yard to the dusty, rutted street.

The day was once more darkening under another storm from the sea. The street had emptied in anticipation of the lowering clouds and the approaching shadow of rain. Keeping his head low he turned on to the thoroughfare. No one was there to see him leave the alley. He passed down the street with the first drift of rain.

Isabelle Crosse lifted the fur pelt. Turning it over she showed it to Eleanor de Bamville.

'It's good. There's no denying it but it does not compare with the ones we saw on Town Quay. What do you think?'

Eleanor pursed her lips as she examined the pelt. It had yet to be stitched into a mantle and hung, still squirrel-like, over her forearm.

'No. It does not compare. You had better hold on to your bolts of cloth. For they'll buy you better than this.'

Isabelle murmured her agreement. 'And I'll not give Will Curteys the pleasure of telling me I've undersold myself. Not until I see the best this Land of Darkness can offer.'

As she handled the pelt she smiled at the thought of William's grudging approval. He'd be less dismissive when she landed a good purchase of furs. For some reason that had come to matter to her. At times it was like a little spur jabbing at her actions.

It was over a month since the party of Boston merchants had arrived in Riga. Already Isabelle was becoming more confident in her own judgement. To the outright astonishment of some of the Hanse authorities she had asserted her own right to buy and sell on behalf of the house of Crosse. The interpreters, taken on by William Curteys, had rarely accompanied such a formidable woman merchant.

'It would indeed be a shame to give him grounds for criticism.' Eleanor winked shamelessly. 'After you struck a better deal for the wax and amber.'

Isabelle's long slim face broke into an equally shameless smile. Who cared if the merchant had been flirting with her, the price had been a good one. A very good one. She could vividly recall Curteys' face when the archers carried in the baskets of amber, as golden as a cat's eye. She could well imagine the look on the faces of the jewellers of Lincoln when they saw it. She was not going to surrender that triumph with the purchase of furs of lower quality than those seen on the eve of the Boston fair.

'I think Will is right, Eleanor,' she conceded. 'The Easterlings bring such furs direct from Russia to be prepared as mantles by their furriers alone.' She sighed. 'I fear that we shall not see such pelts for sale by the furriers here. We shall have to go to where the Hanse go themselves. Into the Land of Darkness . . .'

She could not hide the excitement in her voice. Had such furs been available in Riga she would have been consumed with disappointment. Now they would have to press on. The strange and the exotic beckoned to her. Already William had begun to make plans for leaving Riga and journeying on to Russia, before the rains of autumn and the snows of winter. On into the Land of Darkness.

It seemed an age since Pexton had haltingly framed those words, since the customs men had laughed. Now, an age away, the German interpreter sensed that his client would not be purchasing today. He frowned with disappointment. He had an arrangement with this particular furrier. Now it looked as if he would lose his cut. He cast a despairing glance at the other German, who shrugged.

'Please mistress. Of these furs you will buy none?' There was still a hopeful hint in his voice. 'Or to the ship ourselves should go back?'

Isabelle flashed him a smile. He blushed before her cornflower-blue eyes. 'Yes. I have seen enough. Be sure to thank the merchant on my behalf. But to the ship ourselves should indeed go back.' She laughed as she imitated the stilted language of her interpreter. 'We will go back now.'

Before she could turn away from the pile of pelts the heavy wooden door of the furrier's was flung open and one of the archers fell into the room. The Hanse merchant rose in consternation. Isabelle stepped forward but before she could rebuke her escort he cried out his warning.

'There's a mob, mistress. Coming this way, mistress. Coming for us. We must go. Go right now. The whoresons are after us . . .'

In his panic he forgot himself. He reddened as he

112

realised his error but Isabelle ignored the curse. Signalling to her now-reluctant interpreter to follow she stepped briskly towards the half-open door.

Outside, the four remaining archers stood in a semi-circle, their faces towards the street. Their bows were strung. One of them drew the feathered shaft to his cheek. He grunted at the reassuring feel of the powerful tension in the man-height bow, now flexed and straining.

Down the narrow street rang the baying voices of a mob, voices ragged and untidy. Passers-by stopped to gawp, seemingly well aware of who was in danger. Curious faces turned in the direction of the little English party, as if some primitive spectacle was about to be played out.

'It is for us that they come . . .' The interpreter's face was grey as dead coals. 'Evil men will have sent them. Often they are doing this. Sent by wicked men who are jealous of our English friends.'

Isabelle needed no further enlightenment. Curteys had warned her of the animosity felt towards the English intruders by a good many of the Easterling traders. It was not a unique occurrence. On more than one occasion German merchants had been assaulted by the Boston rough. And as for Flemings, hunting them had become a sport in many an English town.

Spurred on by these reflections, Isabelle ordered an immediate retreat to the ships. She had no intention of emulating the fate of a Flemish weaver and she took a little comfort from the news that one of the archers had bravely taken it upon himself to go for help.

The furrier's shop lay in the shadow of the newly erected cathedral of the Blessed Mary. From here it was but a short walk back to the waterfront with its castle and the stockaded house rented by the merchants of Boston. A little enough walk, but today it seemed of epic proportions. The crowded streets, with their timber houses, pressed in on the hurrying party. Hostile faces watched their progress. Someone jeered. The words were lost but the meaning was plain. There were no friends in the winding lanes of this alien town.

'Mistress, look.' One of the archers pointed, despair edging his voice. 'They are ahead of us. Damn them . . .'

He was right. Two hundred yards ahead a mob had tumbled out of a twisting side-alley. Jubilant shouts heralded the sighting of the English. Isabelle flashed a glance behind. Around the corner of the street angry faces appeared. The way back was cut off. There was no way forward. Encouraging comments flew from one mob to the other.

'See the men behind them,' Eleanor hissed as she drew close to her young companion. 'See them?'

Isabelle nodded. She too had seen the figures at the rear of the two mobs. Behind the sea of patched cottes and faded hose stood richer merchants; well-heeled and with fur-trimmed robes. Little archipelagos of manipulative wealth within the troubled ocean of the poor.

An archer drew his bow and a stone struck a jetty above their heads. It ricocheted into the street. Another was hurled. And another. Isabelle sidestepped one of the missiles. A rock cracked against the kettle helmet of one of the archers and the man staggered.

The mob before them surged forward, like a flood tide through a ruptured dyke. An arrow flew, its pent up energy released with a high vibrating cry. One of the mob pitched backwards, the arrow half out of his back.

Suddenly the street was full of the wind of rushing shafts. The mob fell back, cursing with fury as their dead twitched in the ruts, or hung – transfixed – from log walls.

'Well done, men!' Isabelle could scarcely believe the rapidity of the arrow fire. 'Well done!'

The archers though were less than pleased. They knew full well the limits of the skill they possessed for dealing out rapid death and were also well aware that they had dispatched most of their arrows. The mob sensed it too but was still reluctant to move, its collective mind swept by currents of fear as well as hatred now. But cooler heads had counted the arrows too. The instigating merchants moved back and forth amongst the crowd, urging the men forward.

When at last the rush came, it was irresistible, despite the flights of goose-feathered slaughter. The tide of cursing humanity swept on to and over the little rock of English resistance. Isabelle was thrown backwards. One of her archers threw himself over her, blows raining down upon the falling Lincolnshire men and women.

Eleanor struggled to reach Isabelle but she was hurled to the ground. Greedy fingers clutched at the scrip that she carried, thieving hands pulling open the heavy leather satchel. Eleanor kicked and flailed her fists but, it seemed, to little avail.

Then, at the height of the tempest, the sea parted and ebbed. Horses' hooves pounded in the confined space of the lane. What felt like a herd of towering horseflesh stamped and whinnied about the cowering and bruised English. Terrified, the mob ran, blood streaming down faces now contorted with fear.

Isabelle was aware of clattering hooves beside her and the thud of boots on earth as the rider swiftly dismounted. Isabelle's covering archer was pulled off her and a figure leaned over her. Mail gauntlets were hastily pulled off and strong but manicured hands gripped her about the waist, raising her to her feet.

Dazed, she brushed her loosened hair from her eyes to gaze at her rescuer. Above her was a face deep-tanned from campaigns beneath sun and frost. A curving white scar ran the length of the broad forehead beneath hair the colour of a wide wheatfield. A hard, tight mouth was beginning to relax into a reluctant smile. Eyes as blue as brittle ice bored into her own.

'Who? Who are you?' The question sounded absurdly vulnerable as, half-concussed, Isabelle raised slim fingers to where a crimson sword and cross were emblazoned across the left shoulder of a white surcoat. She felt the coldness of steel plate and mail beneath the concealing softness of the drift of linen. 'Who are you?' she persisted, her fingers gripping the shoulder beneath the surcoat. 'And what are you?'

At that her rescuer laughed. Without pausing to reply, he lifted her into the saddle of his still-snorting destrier as if the effort was as nothing. A grey-robed sergeant handed him the reins. With a shout to his entourage the knight pulled himself up behind Isabelle. One of his arms locked about her waist like a vice. Behind him Eleanor was raised to a saddle in similar fashion.

Twisting about, Isabelle could make out more white-robed horsemen and grey-clad soldiers on foot. But before she could question her fate, the knight who held her drove his horse on up the street, scattering those who had returned to stare.

Along the streets the horses pounded with snorts and flared nostrils. Rain drove in their faces as they rode and Isabelle was forced to turn her head from the wet, burying her face in the white surcoat of her protector.

Light-headed, what seemed like minutes later she was scarcely sensible of being lifted from her mount and carried through a courtyard full of milling servants. Then there was a dark corridor and the homely smell of woodsmoke.

When Isabelle regained her senses she found herself reclining on a long, low bed, the covers strewn this way and that. Something warm and wet splashed on her cheek. As she opened her eyes, a wary servant withdrew at a word of command, putting down his bowl of warm, scented water as he left the room.

When Isabelle looked up she was met once more by those eyes the colour of ice.

'My name is Albrecht von Fellin. Who are you?' The voice was calm but held an iron self-confidence. The man spoke almost faultless English, with only the faintest trace of an accent. Isabelle ran a hand through the tangle of her hair. The knight leant forward. With one tanned hand he brushed away a stray lock and Isabelle felt her heart quicken at the feel of his hand against her cheek. It was many months since she had felt the gentle touch of a man's hand. The very thought quickened her pulse and to her irritation she felt her cheeks redden. The blush deepened.

The strange knight smiled as if he read the meaning behind her discomfort. In an attempt to recover her composure Isabelle answered him while trying to catch her swirling thoughts.

'My name is Isabelle Crosse. I am a merchant of the town of Boston, in England. I am with the party of merchants in the house beside the castle.'

Her interrogator nodded. He had guessed as much.

'But who are you?' she asked. 'Are you one of the Teutonic Knights?'

Try as she might, her inquiry could not shed its coat of girlish curiosity. When he smiled she knew that he was flattered by the awe in her tone. And yet she could not control herself. It was as if a gate had broken within her: emotions long hidden were eddying uncontrollably about her. And all because this knight, with the knowing glance and confident touch, had lifted her from a street brawl. Disconcerted she tried to dam up the unexpected flood of adolescent feelings.

'No, I am not a Teutonic Knight.' He laughed at the hint of disappointment about her blue eyes. 'I am from an order more ancient in these parts. I am of the Sword Brothers. That is the *Schwertbrüder* in my own language. Yes – you have heard of us?'

Isabelle nodded. William had talked of these knights.

'And what have you heard tell of us?'

'That you fight for our faith against the pagans. That you defend the cross against the heathen and the savages.'

That was indeed how Will had put it. And the retelling was clearly to the liking of her attentive companion.

'You have heard truly. For almost two hundred years we have defended the Church against the forces of her enemies. And now the whole of Livonia has turned from darkness to the True Faith. And all those desperate sons of deceit who still oppose us will fall in time to our swords.'

Before Isabelle could reply he crossed to the door and called an order into the corridor. Immediately the servant reappeared with two pewter goblets of wine. As Isabelle sipped at the proffered cup she suddenly remembered her companions. In the presence of this attentive man she had almost forgotten her friends.

'Those who were with me, who were attacked as I was. Are they safe?'

'They are quite safe,' her knight replied quickly. 'The men-at-arms are drinking ale. And your female companion – the one with the sharp eyes and hard fists – is having her cuts attended to. None of your servants was seriously harmed.'

'Eleanor is not my servant. She is my friend,' Isabelle replied curtly, beginning to recover her composure. 'To where have you brought us? It is kind beyond words but our friends will fear for our lives. One of our brave archers went to spread news of our danger.'

'Do not fret yourself. I have sent a messenger to the English party – for I guessed your origins. Your friends will be here shortly.'

He turned and poured himself another mug of wine. Isabelle watched him closely. He must be Will's age, she thought as he poured the deep red wine. Not more than thirty-five and yet with all those years sitting lean on him. He was just like Will, and yet not like him at all. Unlike Curteys he made her feel like a woman. An object of desire. Someone valued. She scolded herself at her romantic extravagance. All he had done was rescue her. He would have done that much for a hag. And yet there was something more. Something about the confident way in which he had touched her cheek.

'You have never been to Riga before?'

Isabelle shook her head.

'It is a fine town. A town carved out of the wilderness.' He came and sat beside her, as a friend might. 'Two centuries ago twenty-three ships of crusaders came to claim this land for the True Faith. My ancestors were with them.' Pride was evident in his voice. 'And though the pagans opposed them with barbaric savagery, they built this town and tamed this land of forest and lake and waste. Tamed it by the sword and by their faith. You know these things?'

Isabelle nodded. 'A little. I know only a little.' And then out of curiosity she asked, 'Are we in your house?'

'I hold estates for my order out in the forest lands. On the march lands of our domain, where the savages have good reason to fear our swords. I have a town house for when I come to Riga in the summer.'

'You choose to spend the winter in the wilds?' Isabelle sounded surprised. 'Is it not better here than in a land so wild and cold?'

'So you have heard tell of our winters! It would be softer here no doubt. But there are tasks which are better done in winter than in summer.' His face was suddenly crossed by a curious look, then he shrugged. 'It was lucky for you that I was in Riga this summer. Had I wintered here your rescue would have come three months too late.'

Isabelle laughed at the truth in this statement. Von Fellin laughed too. It was a clean laugh, a laugh which encouraged laughter. However, there was one thing which puzzled her. 'If you are a crusader of the Sword Brothers, how is it that the Teutonic Knights control the harbour and the customs dues? It is their castle by the waterfront, is it not?'

Von Fellin nodded casually. 'My order was in Riga before them. Protecting Christian settlers. But we paid a heavy price for our bravery. Many heroic knights fell in battle against the heathen, both here and further north. Our Grand Master himself fell in battle. That was why we joined with the Teutonic Knights. They had subdued the pagans of Prussia. They had lands and wealth abroad more than my order could have dreamed of. It was God's will that we should be united in our struggle.' Von Fellin smiled wrily. 'Since 1237 we have been one order of chivalry but out in the wild lands we do not forget that we are Sword Brothers. There we live as our fore-fathers lived: as defenders of Christendom. We are joined but not submerged. Do you understand?'

Isabelle nodded. 'And so the German knights have

civilised this whole country?'

'There are still some who hold out against us, out in the forests. But they are doomed and of no account. And in Lithuania there are enemies of the Faith, but they too will not withstand us.' His eyes flashed a smile. 'More wine?' Isabelle nodded and he attended to her request. 'But no doubt you will have met the Landmeister of the Teutonic Knights. I know he commands acquaintance with all foreign merchants who do business in the province of Livonia. You will have met him in the castle by the waterfront. What did you make of him?'

Isabelle paused before she replied. Von Fellin was correct. The Landmeister of the order had indeed commanded a meeting with the English party. However, on Will Curteys' strong advice, she had not attended. Now she felt embarrassed to admit her absence from the party. It was as if it undermined her right to be taken seriously as a merchant. She flushed a little as she carefully worded her reply.

'I did not go myself. My associate has been to Riga before. He felt it best that he alone should explain our business to the Landmeister.' Von Fellin raised an eyebrow and she hurried on. 'His name is William Curteys. He was a good friend to my husband. And is now my partner in this enterprise.'

'Was? You said he *was* a good friend to your husband. Then your husband is not with you?' Von Fellin looked thoughtful.

'No. My husband is dead. He died in the spring.'

'He was older than you?' The question would have sounded impertinent had anyone else asked it. Yet Albrecht von Fellin possessed such a natural sense of authority that it was as if every detail lay within his brief.

Isabelle nodded. She was surprised but not offended. 'That he was, but he was not an old man when he died. I am twenty-two years old. He was thirty-seven when he died – four years older than William. It was not of age that he died. He was killed in an accident.'

'I am very sorry.' The Sword Brother did not sound very distressed. 'It is a terrible thing to suffer such a loss. And so this William Curteys spoke for you with the Landmeister. I see.'

Isabelle was keen to drive the drift of the conversation away from this particular topic. She swiftly thought of some other avenue to pursue.

'You must pardon my impertinence, good knight, but how did you come to speak my language so perfectly? It is quite faultless.'

She had chosen wisely, for the compliment clearly pleased her companion. Once more the tight mouth broke into a charming smile. 'You should not be surprised, for many of the flower of your English chivalry have crusaded with the order. In my father's day your Henry of Lancaster fought against the pagans in Lithuania. Henry was a brother-in-arms with my own uncle, and a friend of your great king.'

'Our late king.'

'That is so. But a noble knight when he lived. One of the greatest and bravest. And Lancaster was no less brave. I was but a child then. You would not have been born. But you will have heard of him?'

Isabelle smiled. 'His son-in-law is John, the uncle of our young King Richard. John is Earl of Lincoln as well as Duke of Lancaster. He is the manorial overlord of my own town of Boston.'

Von Fellin raised one open hand as if the news was the portent of some great event. 'Then our meeting is destined to be. For see the bands which join us. I was fated to save you. And you were fated to meet me.'

Isabelle broke into laughter and shook her head. It was outrageous flirtation. Silly and foolish. Yet how long had it been since a man had flirted with her? She had fulfilled all of Anthony's physical needs but he had never wasted time in such small talk. William would have snorted at it, Phillip Spayne would have condemned it; but Albrecht von Fellin flirted. It was a mere dalliance but, oh, how welcome!

In this fashion they talked for more than an hour. It was easy to talk to him. There were no deep silences and awkward moments, no furtive glances about for diversions. He listened and laughed. He made room for her comments and yet with consummate ease filled any gaps in the conversation. Here were courtly manners and gentility such as Isabelle had hitherto only heard of in stories of romance. For the first time since she had arrived in Riga she felt herself relax.

Then Eleanor arrived, cleaned and rested. Isabelle felt disappointment; followed almost immediately by a pang of guilt. If von Fellin minded the intrusion it did not show. He was as courteous to the newcomer as to the younger woman. All three were engaged in light-hearted banter when William Curteys was announced.

The Boston merchant was wet from the rain outside, his beard and hair glistening with silver drops of moisture. He flashed one irritated look at Isabelle, clearly embarrassed by the events of the morning. But before he could speak he was forestalled by the German knight.

'Welcome, my friend. I have heard all about you. Come, take a cup of wine with us.'

Von Fellin clapped his hands and attentive servants appeared noiselessly with trays of wine and sweetmeats.

'I am deeply sorry that you have been inconvenienced.' William spoke as if apologising for the actions of a wayward child. He also spoke with deference. 'Your kindness puts us all in your debt.' Isabelle had rarely heard Curteys so wary.

Von Fellin laughed. 'It is I who am in your debt. For I have spent time in the company of such charming and beautiful women. And more than that. Women of such knowledge and learning. You are a fortunate man indeed to travel with such ladies.'

Curteys looked as if he was anything but thrilled by the company he was forced to endure. He held his peace though.

Von Fellin continued: 'And I have learnt that you intend to push on into Russia. On as far as Novgorod itself. For only there will you find the furs that you seek.'

William raised one eyebrow in the direction of Isabelle. He smiled carefully. 'You have spoken truly. We do indeed intend to push on as far as the city of Novgorod the Great. We sail by way of Reval, in Estonia, which the natives call Tallin.'

'Ah yes, the "Danes' Town" in the language of the Ests.' Von Fellin smiled as he interrupted the English merchant. 'Though you will find few enough Danes there now. For upwards of forty years now it has belonged to the Teutonic Knights. And after two centuries of Danish rule! They did not have the stomach for endless rebellions and the creatures of the dark forests, and so they sold it to the order. Reval it is now and Reval it will remain.'

William Curteys knew all this. He had travelled to Reval with Anthony Crosse. However he made no attempt to inform the German that the lesson was unnecessary. Instead he merely nodded his head.

Von Fellin smiled graciously. 'But I interrupted you. You intend to travel to Novgorod by way of Reval? Pray proceed.'

Curteys once more sipped at his wine. The servants hovered around him, watching him like hawks. William cleared his throat. 'We will pick up interpreters there. Finns, who speak Russian as well as the dialects of the tribes in the forest lands. Then from Reval we shall sail eastwards along the Gulf of Finland. We shall leave our ships at the mouth of the River Neva and hire river-craft from the Russians. I have done this before.' He paused as if to emphasise his experience. When von Fellin made no response he continued, a little peeved. 'We shall travel by river-craft into the lake that the Russians call Ladoga and then to Novgorod by way of the River Volkhov . . .'

'I am in a position to assist you.' The German knight interrupted the Boston merchant in mid-flow. 'I am known in Reval. I shall get you interpreters. You are right to employ Finns, for they speak all the barbaric dialects of the savages of the forests. But most of them are thieves and rogues themselves. I shall see you have an honest man – if there is such a one amongst the Finns of Reval.' He smiled at Isabelle.

The smile was not lost on Curteys. 'I do not understand. You will help us? But surely the knights hold Riga and Reval as Hanse towns . . .'

'And so I will not help you!' He smiled at the obvious confusion on the face of the other man. 'You are right of course, in many ways. The order has done much to help and encourage the merchants of the towns. The wealth of the woods flows out through Riga and Reval. And the towns joined the league of the Hanse a century ago.' At this point his smile vanished. 'No doubt this is why some of the merchants of the town sought to turn the scum of the settlers on to your party. There are many amongst the merchants who resent foreigners in the trade of the forest lands. You will find this in Novgorod too. Many Hanse merchants there will not welcome your arrival.' He flung a glance in the direction of the women beside him. 'But I am of the Sword Brothers and we have always had an independent turn of mind. Have no doubts that I will help you. It will be an honour to be of service to one so lovely.' He bowed towards Isabelle, who blushed again. 'Now these ladies will be tired. I shall have a party of my sergeants escort you back to your house.'

He gave a curt order to one of the servants who scurried away. A few moments later an armed sergeant appeared and bowed stiffly before his superior, who issued a series of guttural orders.

'And now I fear that you must excuse me. For I have pressing business in the town. My sergeant speaks no English but he knows where you must go.

And from now on I will post three of the brothers of my order at your gate. Armed, of course.'

He led them to the courtyard where the four archers were waiting. They smelled of ale and looked very cheerful. One of von Fellin's sergeants whispered something to his master, who smiled.

'I have good news for you. It is the archer who risked his life going for aid. My men found him near to your ship. The mob had found him again, but my men rescued him with no harm done. He is here.'

Von Fellin motioned to the sergeant who jogged away. Moments later he returned with the heavy-faced Gosse. Isabelle smiled to see the return of their servant and even Curteys looked pleased. It was as if at least some English bravery had been of note on this day of succour from the German knights. More than this the man was proudly sporting his bow and kettle helmet which had been retrieved by von Fellin's men from louts carousing in a tavern by the harbour.

Reunited and escorted, the English party made a safe return to the stockaded house in the shadow of the order's castle. Curteys seemed oddly subdued, as if he had been caught unawares by the sudden turn of events and felt in danger of losing full control of the enterprise. His only remark to Isabelle was a muttered comment about von Fellin. 'By God, Isabelle,' he grunted as they dismounted, 'he is a powerful man. I have heard of him and how he holds the wildest estates of his order. He has taken the vows of a Cistercian – but did he look like a monk to you?' He glanced darkly at her. 'He lives like a prince and rules his lands like a palatine. I cannot believe that he will aid us . . .' He almost sounded as if he resented

Isabelle's enlistment of such a powerful friend and protector. 'For God's sake watch what you tell him. For he need not know all our plans. And from now on I want to know whenever you leave the stockade. For your own safety.'

Isabelle shook her head at him in patronising reassurance. 'Fret not, William, for I have Albrecht's guards now, as well as our own archers. There will be no more dangers. And I must be about the town if I am to find more godsends like the amber!'

Curteys frowned. It came close to a scowl. Isabelle had never seen her partner so deflated. She smiled sweetly and made the most of it.

Throughout September the English merchants sold their bolts of cloth and haggled with the wary merchants of the Hanse. Overhead the flocks of black storks clattered their beaks and wheeled in great numbers; then drifted south across the endless miles of forest. Summer was flying with them and the evenings drew in slowly. The nights cooled and the days saw the heat drain slowly from the resisting sun. Most days also saw rain blow in from the Baltic and the English merchants began to finalise their plans for the next stage of their journey, before the short autumn gave way to a northern winter.

The decision had been taken to leave three ships at Riga and press on with one alone. This ship would itself return to Riga once it had delivered its passengers to the head of the Gulf of Finland. The small party which pressed on would be led by Curteys and Thymelby, in the company of Isabelle and Eleanor.

There was little enough time to prepare for the next

stage in the journey. From late November onwards, the Gulf of Riga would begin to fill with ice. It would not be free for shipping again until the middle of March. The ship carrying Isabelle and her party would need to complete its travels and return to the port before the winter ice sealed Riga off from the sea.

In the days of preparation each of the merchants hurried to finish transactions started in Riga. The sprawling mass of wooden buildings which made up the town was now safe – Albrecht von Fellin's punishment of both the mob and its merchant instigators had seen to that. And the goods the traders desired were about the town in abundance. The summer's supply of wax had been carted in from the outlying estates and homesteads; the little settlements amidst the rolling forests and the myriad jewelled lakes of Livonia.

Isabelle in particular was concerned to purchase wax for the monastic houses of the fens. In these days of early September she was often in the town haggling with the merchants. William had insisted that she have a personal bodyguard as well as the escort of archers. He had chosen for the task the archer who had risked his life on the day of the mob assault. Curteys had noted how the man was always about Isabelle and had assumed it was due to the natural devotion that she seemed to inspire in the serving men of her household. The choice of escort seemed appropriate and Isabelle humoured her partner.

There was only one major disappointment for Isabelle. After putting into effect his plans to assist her party, von Fellin had left hurriedly for his country estates. Some pressing business had called him back earlier than expected and Isabelle could only hope that she would enjoy the pleasure of his company when she returned to Riga in the spring.

Two days before the time to sail Isabelle went with Eleanor to pray at the cathedral after breakfast, then made her way to a woodworker's shop in the shadow of the castle. The overhung streets were fresh with the misty smells of autumn and the timber tenements leaned over haggling street-sellers peddling the wares of the forests. Isabelle stopped to purchase a basket of hard pears, allowing her interpreter to conduct the haggling.

Pressing the firm curve of the fruit, Isabelle luxuriated in the air of the town. In one sense it was so familiar. Woodsmoke drifted from the roof louvres, damp straw lay about the gutters, a warm smell of bread slipped silently between the fingers of some unseen baker and danced along the street. It could be Boston. And yet it was also strange. From a nearby pot-house came the unfamiliar scent of stew spiced with who-knew-what. Long strings of dark red sausages, of a type she had never seen, hung from the stall of a butcher's shop. Words alien and mysterious called from shops and houses.

Isabelle pointed out the cooked meats nearby to Eleanor. 'Have you ever seen the like?'

Eleanor sniffed the sausage. 'It's spiced with nothing that I know. It smells good though!'

Isabelle waved a small silver coin at the broad-faced butcher. He cut half a string but the interpreter muttered a sharp rebuke. The butcher shrugged and cut some more.

Eleanor bit into the meat. Isabelle did likewise and pulled a face at the flavour of the pepper. It was hotter than anything that she had ever tasted before. The butcher looked surprised. Chewing at her purchase, she strolled down the street.

The woodturner's shop was a well-built structure, its gables freshly painted in a riot of wild colours. All about it the other buildings were also richly painted. The colours were vibrant and ran in broad geometric patterns, quite unlike the solid, sober tenements along Strait Bargate.

Eleanor followed her young companion's gaze. 'I think they must paint them so because the winter is so dark and cold. It gives colour on a winter's day.'

Isabelle nodded. The suggestion made sense. She rather liked the exuberant gaiety of it. Like the smells and tastes of the town, even the colours ensured that the familiar was shot through with the strange. It was as if she had come to another world. A world seemingly modelled on her own and yet, on closer inspection, different in ways she could never have imagined. And would not Russia be even more exotic? She felt a thrill of excitement. A thrill of having gone beyond the boundaries of any other woman in Boston, beyond the boundaries explored even by many of the men, amongst them those who had doubted that she had the courage and determination to exceed their achievements. Isabelle breathed in the Baltic air and was satisfied.

The inside of the woodworker's shop smelt of beeswax polish and of smooth wood. The craftsman lovingly handled his bowls and finely carved boxes, murmuring in German a litany in praise of the wood.

Isabelle had seen fine woodworking before, in Lincolnshire, but never such a profusion of different woods. It was as if all the wonders of the forest lands had passed through the hands of this master craftsman.

'I will take the little box with the inlaid mother-of-pearl,' she said finally.

The German did not understand the words but reached for the piece indicated by Isabelle's long finger. He handed it to her with approval and she felt the glowing wood kindle beneath the shafts of daylight.

'I will keep the palm from Jerusalem in it,' Isabelle murmured. It was one of her most treasured possessions: a piece of palm frond which Eleanor had brought back for her many years ago from the Middle East. Isabelle turned the box so that it once more caught the light in its polished depths. 'I think it is fine enough.'

The box was carefully wrapped in a piece of soft cloth and Isabelle held it to her. 'And now to business!' she announced, enjoying herself.

By mid-morning she was down at the waterfront watching the return of the Easterling summer merchants from Russia. Behind her the escort of archers were none-too-pleased to have exchanged their bows for crates of straw-packed beeswax, and the fact that Gosse, Isabelle's escort, was free from such burdens did nothing to improve their humour. He lolled around making the most of his elevated station.

'You see the barrels of furs?' Isabelle pointed to a nearby ship. 'I'd wager they are of the same quality as those we saw at Town Quay. See how carefully the

133

merchants watch their handling?'

Eleanor nodded. 'You'd think they contained the finest pottery from the way they coddle and caress them.' She laughed provocatively. 'It's been a while since I saw a man give such attention to a woman!' Then she added cheekily, 'Since the German knight poured you your wine, actually!'

Isabelle blushed. 'You exaggerate, Eleanor.' And then, in order to change the subject, she asked her interpreter: 'What are the merchants so animated about?'

On the quay a group of well-dressed Easterlings were engaged in lively discussion. Her interpreter listened to the Hanse traders' noisy exchange with the look of one who was eavesdropping on a private conversation.

'It is the trader in fine timber.' he reported to her. 'You have heard of him?' When Isabelle nodded he continued. 'It is of the servant who killed him that they speak. He who stole his master's rings. Hanging he will be tomorrow. Hanging for sure. He was tried this day, before the Landmeister in the castle. And before that, before all Hanse merchants in the *Rathaus*.' The German paused for dramatic effect. 'They are too angry for words to tell. His master treated him as one treats a son. And he killed the old man for a handful of gold rings. All Hanse merchants are angry. They have many Livonian servants and slaves. Hanse will treat them hard now.'

'Serves the dog right, madam.' It was Isabelle's escort who spoke. 'To murder a kind master in that way. It is the work of a dog. Hanging's too kind . . .'

'That's enough. Speak with more grace, or speak

not at all,' Isabelle chided him.

The archer turned away, scowling slightly, but his scowl melted into the coldest of smiles as he looked out over the crowded quayside.

Moving away from the harbour, Eleanor was suddenly waylaid by the galloping progress of a small child. It was filthy from head to foot, its torn woollen clothes matted with dirt. The hair – as blonde as Isabelle's at the roots – was soiled and greasy. Clutching at Eleanor's dress the child turned great tear-filled eyes to her as little fingers reached for the leather scrip slung from Eleanor's shoulder.

Immediately a mighty hand grasped the child's tiny frame and wrenched it back. Another hand struck the little head with a painful smack. The child wailed, great sobbing cries of deep misery. Guttural curses met the child's distress along with another blow.

The man who administered the punishment held out a begging palm to the two foreign merchants. He was less grubby than the child, although his cotte and chausses were patched and frayed. With the other hand he held the child's arm in a grip that made the little girl's cheeks run with tears.

Pushing in front of the women and their interpreter, Isabelle's archer-bodyguard pushed the man back to be met with guttural shouts which could only contain curses from the foulest reaches of obscenity.

Isabelle forced herself forward. 'Tell him to leave go of the child, or he will break her arm,' she demanded.

Her interpreter shook his head but did as he was bidden. The response was a gale of cracked laughter and a hawking spit. Then a torrent of words.

'He says this child a damn nuisance. Touched in head is the child. She is two years old but is like a baby. An idiot child. He beats her but an idiot she remains.'

'Is she his child?'

Eleanor watched Isabelle carefully as the interpreter interrogated the beggar, beginning to have an inkling of what was coming. She pursed her lips but held her peace.

'Child is his niece. Daughter of his sister. Mother and father both are dead. Like the man, were settlers in the woods. Plague came, killed older ones and this child only survives. Damn nuisance she is. He asks will kind lady give money to a poor German farmer who has no home and this idiot child to look after.'

Isabelle was watching the face of the child. Its intelligent black eyes were a pit of utter misery. Pain dwelt there like some disgusting basilisk in its lair: pain and hurt beyond words.

Isabelle had never borne a living child. In two years of marriage to Anthony she had miscarried twice. As she stared at the tiny scrap of abused humanity she felt something surge within her.

The beggar whined again, only this time the voice was more obsequious. The interpreter frowned. 'This rogue says the child is for sale. To keep her he cannot. Perhaps she will die of cold this winter. He asks will the rich lady buy this child? Good servant she will grow up to be. Beat her if not; then the stick will make her good.' The interpreter shook his head. 'Best we go now. This rogue will only make trouble when you say no. Best now we go.'

'Buy her.'

The interpreter looked as if he had been kicked between the eyes.

'Buy her.' Isabelle's face was grim and determined. 'How much does this son of perdition want for her? Go on . . . ask him, man!'

The reluctant German did as he was bidden. He returned the price in a voice tinged with outrage. 'He says the price of the girl is one silver mark. Price is too high. Rogue this man is. We should beat him. Tell him no, mistress. One silver mark is too much, far too much.'

Isabelle carried very little silver. Most of the transactions were carried out as a barter. But William had insisted that silver be carried by the merchants. At Novgorod the Russians would be more easily swayed by the glimpse of silver coins. She handed one such coin to the beggar. He grinned and shoved the child towards her. The interpreter shook his head at the madness of what he had just been a party to.

On the way back to their rented accommodation neither Eleanor nor Isabelle spoke. The filthy child was carried by Isabelle's bodyguard, his tight-lipped silence speaking volumes. In the courtyard, behind the stockade, Curteys and Thymelby were checking over crates and bales. They straightened up as the archers laid down their burden of wax. Isabelle ignored the astonishment in the eyes of each merchant as the heavy-faced archer handed the silent scrap to Isabelle.

'I have bought this child.' She would have named the girl but could not get her tongue around the strange sound volunteered by the child's seller. Before either of the men could speak, she added: 'I will discuss it after she – I think it is a she – has been washed, fed and put down in my bed. She is hungry and distressed.' There was an authority in her voice which temporarily overcame their incredulity. 'I will be a little while. Eleanor will assist me.'

When at last the child was asleep, Isabelle Crosse came looking for Curteys and Thymelby. The other merchants on the expedition watched her and shook their heads. Once she had passed they fell into outraged conversation.

Isabelle found William and Adam in their shared chamber. In one corner stood the ancient bed that they shared with three other merchants and in the middle of the room Thymelby was taking a bath. Suds of wood-ash soap and grey water lay in pools amidst the scattered rushes and straw.

Curteys was the first to speak. 'Have you taken leave of your senses? In the name of God and all his elect have you gone mad?' His voice was hard.

'The child was in desperate need . . .'

'Desperate need? You will see much desperate need on this journey. Will you buy every child that you see?' The familiar eyebrows raised in cynical condemnation. 'You see the poor every day in Boston. But in God's name do you buy every orphan, or house every beggar down on his luck, every wounded soldier home from France? So why have you done this here?'

Truth be known, Isabelle could not tell him why. Ever since she had been rescued by von Fellin she had felt a breach made in her emotional defences. She was not as she had been in Boston. But how would William understand that, or the mocking Adam

Thymelby? She hardly understood it herself.

'Our Lord Himself told us not to reject the little ones . . .'

'Aye. Aye, He did. But I do not recall that He said to take them to Novgorod in the middle of winter. Or have I forgotten the scriptures? Was I dozing at matins? Did the priest drop his voice as he came to that part of the Gospel? Pray do tell me, Isabelle.'

She ignored his biting sarcasm. Instead she just stood in silence. Thymelby hoisted himself out of the tub. Naked, he padded over to where his clothes lay in a heap, rivulets of water running down his stocky muscular body. His actions were in no way a breach of etiquette but Isabelle felt that he had chosen that moment to humiliate her. As he pulled on his chausses and boots he was grinning.

'This sums up the whole problem, Isabelle.' Curteys stood legs apart, arms akimbo. 'This business of the child is like your being here. Your intentions are excellent but are always misplaced. Not for you the life in Boston; not for you the acceptance of reality on the quayside of Riga. Always your heart rules your head. Always you are at the wrong place at the wrong time. You are like the moon in the morning, Isabelle. Have you not seen it: pale and lost in the lightening sky. Lovely, a thing of beauty, but out of place, out of its God-given station.'

Isabelle breathed deeply. 'It is not for you to lecture me. It is Crosse money which pays for this enterprise.' She saw that the reminder stung him now as it had when she had seen him after Anthony's death. 'I have full rights here. I have authority to act. This is my decision. It is on my own head.'

'Yes! By Our Lady, you speak the truth. This is on your own head. On your head alone!'

He stared at her, half in anger and half in outraged astonishment. Her independence shocked him. Nothing in his experience of women had prepared him for what Isabelle had become since the death of Tony Crosse. Once she had simply been Tony's beautiful wife. Now she had become a force to be faced. Her assertiveness shocked him. This was not how such a woman should be. She was like a wind in a room: she overturned the familiar as she passed. And her success with the German knight and in the market-place seemed to make even his warnings of danger sound hollow. But he knew she might not always be so fortunate and her rashness would bring trouble on him too.

Isabelle said no more but turned and left the room. Behind her back Curteys raised open hands to Thymelby in a gesture of speechless outrage. The bull-like merchant – still half naked – just laughed derisively at the foolishness of women.

The next day William insisted that the whole company witness the hanging of the Livonian servant. It would be a rare distraction for the archers, he insisted. 'God knows,' he had added, 'they'll have little enough to entertain them this coming winter.'

Isabelle felt that the cruel comment was secretly aimed at her. William knew full well how she detested viewing hangings. Her squeamishness was exceptional. Once more she felt taunted and frayed and on top of this she had slept badly. The little girl had cried all night and now Isabelle's eyes were underlined with pale blue shadows.

When at last the young servant hung twitching and gyrating, William gave orders to return to the loading of the ship. At least the archers looked as if they had enjoyed the public spectacle.

'You look tired, Isabelle.' Curteys' concern sounded false. 'Is there something wrong?'

Isabelle shook her head. 'He was so young. So young to die so horribly. And they say that his master treated him like a son . . .'

'Clearly he misjudged him. Sometimes errors of judgement must be paid for in blood.' His voice carried something of the previous day's tone. 'You should heed his example. Think hard about your judgements.'

Before she could reply, he had called the bowmen to order. Motioning to Gosse, the archer, he signalled him to keep close to Isabelle, as a dutiful bodyguard – appointed to the task – should.

They walked back towards their ship, in silence except for Isabelle's bodyguard who whistled a lively ballad, popular with the English armies in France. Behind them the Livonian servant pivoted slowly about the axis of his throttling rope.

Chapter 6

The single Yarmouth cog left Riga on Friday 27 September 1381. For two days it hugged the low coast of the Gulf of Riga as it pushed north through choppy seas, wind freshening from the west and the showers of summer steadily developing into the heavy rains of autumn. Foul weather blanketed the islands to port and the open sea beyond.

For those on board there was no escape from the penetrating dampness. By day and night they huddled in the relative shelter of the castles, while the East Anglian seamen ran to and fro about the glistening timbers of the deck. Isabelle and Eleanor clung together in their glistening canvas capes. Between them they sheltered a bewildered child, whose silent misery and confusion was as emphatic as her tear-wracked weeping had once been.

Slowly the low coast, with its broad beaches and forests beyond, gave way to a littoral of rocky inlets and then a steeply rising wall of limestone cliffs.

On Sunday 29 September their coast-hugging at last put the wind behind them. The sails filled and the pace quickened as the irritable sea rose and slapped at the heavy, rounded bows. Before nightfall they entered the deep bay which sheltered the port and town of Reval. Isabelle clung to the forward decking and watched the town appear from the mist and approaching dark. Above her head the sails strained and the ropes groaned.

Eleanor had volunteered to watch over the child. The blonde girl was even now tightly wrapped in a Lincoln wool blanket and asleep on Eleanor's full bosom. For a few moments Isabelle was free to drink in the cool air and watch the approaching land.

'You see the castle above the town?' The speaker was Will Curteys. He had barely spoken to her since the argument over the girl. Now his voice had its usual matter-of-fact tone. There was little warmth in his words but nevertheless, Isabelle was pleased to hear him speak, even if the conversation was a little stilted.

'Yes. Beside a church. I can just about see a tower, though the sea mist is all about the town itself.'

Together they stared intently to where the Danish castle, perched on Toompea Hill, stood out from the mist as if moated in grey shadows.

'Our friend, von Fellin, has made arrangements for our shelter in the Lower Town.' He spoke the words 'our friend' with a noticeable tone of irony. 'Not that you can see it in this mist. Tomorrow we shall meet his guide at the castle. It seems he is a man who has been of service to the order before. Let us hope it is now us that he serves . . .'

There was a heavy note of suspicion in the last few words, as if William could not bring himself to admit that von Fellin was acting without duplicity.

Isabelle was a little irritated by the implication of Curteys' comment. She too had read Albrecht's written instructions and had no doubt that he acted with their interests at heart. Secretly she hoped that it was her particular interests which concerned the knight. But either way, Curteys' suspicions were ungrateful and unnecessary.

'I think you misjudge him. Mayhap he only thinks of the safety of strangers in his land. I for one am more than happy to accept a kindness as well as give it.'

Curteys grunted as if to say he expected little better. He turned away, to where Thymelby was giving instructions to the assembled archers. Isabelle sighed. So much for her first conversation with William for two days.

The quay at Reval was masked by a mass of bobbing cogs. Each stout little hull rose and fell against the gentle movement of the sea and the sail on each single mast was furled. Nevertheless the evening breeze plucked at the canvas and filled the grey air with the sound of a myriad throaty whispers. Overhead the ravens croaked a hoarse welcome; or was it a warning? There was little in the scene which promised a hearty welcome for aliens far from home.

When at last the Yarmouth men had ground the hull against the wooden pilings, a gangplank was swung out. Curteys and Thymelby were quickly ashore.

'By God, but I'm glad to feel firm ground under me again,' Thymelby muttered as he stretched.

'And I shall be happier to feel a good bed beneath me,' Curteys replied as he flexed his muscles. 'I'll not pine for the stink of the bilges and the slap of the waves all night long.'

Thymelby grunted. 'Or the biscuits stinking of rats' piss. Still, we could have had it worse.' He eyed Isabelle and Eleanor who were still negotiating the gangplank. Then he added: 'And I can think of better things than a mattress to have under me . . .'

William cast him a dark look and then went to offer a hand to Isabelle. She thanked him, though he seemed almost embarrassed by her gratitude.

The newly landed merchants stimulated some interest on the quayside. German sailors laid down their ropes to watch the new arrivals. Whilst fur-coated merchants leaned on their barrels and bales and surveyed their rivals. There were no friendly greetings. It was all a far cry from the Town Quay and the familiar faces of the king's collectors.

Nevertheless, collectors there were. Within half an hour of landing, the Easterling customs men descended on the English ship, happy enough to accept the proffered harbour dues, but making no attempt to hide their animosity.

It was clear that the Germans spoke English: their reactions to comments were too quick to conclude otherwise. Despite this they insisted on conducting all business in their own language. They targeted Curteys for most of their questions, having quickly detected that his grasp of German was not as fluent as that of Thymelby. Clearly they were doing their utmost to be awkward.

'Damn them . . .' William muttered to Thymelby. 'I've told them that we will not trade here but only stop to provision. Yet they insist on checking the cargo of the entire ship.'

A hail of questions cut him off before he could finish. Haltingly he replied. He was aware that Isabelle and Eleanor were watching his efforts. A hint of fluster suffused the edges of his normally detached demeanour.

He was saved from further irritation by the arrival of a new party on the dockside. A grey-cloaked sergeant elbowed his way through the ranks of grinning onlookers. He wore the red sword and cross of the Sword Brothers and his cheeks were sunken and as grey as his surcoat. Sharp words passed between him and the collectors. They did not seem afraid but after confabulation appeared to give ground. The sergeant was accompanied by an interpreter.

'Welcome to Reval. We greet you in the name of Christ and of our Lord Albrecht von Fellin.' The lines were obviously learned by heart. 'It has given him much pleasure to have you shelter here and tomorrow a guide will come for you. One who speaks the languages of the Russians.' The interpreter turned to the sergeant who updated his orders. 'If you please, come with us, we will escort you to lodgings for the night. Tomorrow guide comes to the castle.'

The interpreter bowed slightly. Clearly the invitation had something of an order about it. William Curteys nodded and thanked him curtly. With a glare at the customs collectors he led the way after him and Adam Thymelby followed after, leaving instructions for three of the archers to stay with the sailors at the ship. Food would be sent down to them.

The hospitality of the Sword Brothers was acceptable but not lavish. Even if von Fellin had the power to have his will obeyed in Reval, he could not ensure that his minions did it with enthusiasm. Feelings against the foreigners clearly ran deep.

The guesthouse of the order was a heavy, log-built structure. One room had been set aside containing two beds but the straw-filled mattresses were grubby and stained. Curteys and Thymelby were to share one bed; Isabelle and Eleanor the other. A fire burnt in an iron brazier. That, at least, was cheerful.

Lay brothers brought in a light repast of cold hare and spiced mulled wine. Not for the travellers the traditional roast goose on this evening of the feast of St Michael and All Angels. Even Isabelle, who was gratified by von Fellin's actions, could not escape the conclusion that it was the most miserable Michaelmas she had ever celebrated. When the baby girl – strangely quiet for the past hour – had broken into red-cheeked wails, the desolation of the evening had been complete.

It was with some relief that Isabelle and Eleanor slipped into bed. Curteys and Thymelby were talking to the grey-coated sergeant in another chamber and the child was composed at last, having wolfed down a mash of cold meat and porridge. Now she lay between the two women curled up and snug, the tears and distress smoothed out of her little face.

'Oh Eleanor, this is a cheerless place.' Isabelle gazed up into the darkness as she spoke. 'Do you feel a long way from home?'

There was a tentative nature to her question, as if she dared not give vent to her feelings. As if this tiny scrap of homesickness was a token of a vast store of such feelings. For some reason she had not felt this way in Riga. Now, though, the true nature of their foray into unfriendly lands was creeping up on her. Her fears battled with her well-worn mask of cool repose.

In the darkness Eleanor smiled. 'It is often thus a long way from home. And there is no easy exchange of the unknown for the tried and familiar. Still, one of us sleeps as if she had lived here all her life.' She turned her head slightly. A little head nestled against her cheek. 'And the same stars and the same angels look down on us always. Believe me – we are never as far from home as we feel.'

'Thank you.' Isabelle's voice was low. 'Thank you.' She too could feel the vulnerable little body against her own nakedness. 'By God's grace we shall have better cheer tomorrow.'

She prayed silently that her wish would be answered. For now she felt far from cheer. Something vulnerable had been exposed in her and she could not quite cover it up. Something had been released within her; something dangerously fragile. Only since she had left Riga had she felt this way. Pandora-like she had opened a box long shut and now, try as she might, she could not catch and cage her feelings again.

Long after her two male companions had retired to bed she lay awake. When the cold of the early hours crept over the cooling ashes in the brazier, she was still wide-eyed in the darkness. About her the building groaned and shifted. She heard every sound. She knew it was not a something which had penetrated her defences but a someone, and try as she might she could not dismiss one persistent thought in her mind. In the solitude of the night she could still feel

Albrecht von Fellin's hand against her cheek.

The next morning brought brighter, colder weather.
The merchant party climbed the hill that led from the
port to the old Danish castle. While Curteys and
Thymelby went to meet their Finnish guide the two
women lingered in the nave of the church beside the
fortification. Earlier all of the party had heard mass
said and gained comfort from the familiar Latin
prayers of the eucharist. That at least had not
changed with the distance.

Coming outside at last they sat on the steps and
gazed down the way that they had come. Below them
the walled Lower Town ran down to the sea inlet. The
autumnal sunshine glinted on the sheen of frost still
clinging to the wooden shingles of the jostling roofs.
Beyond the jumbled masts at the quayside, the sea
was a silvered plate of polished metal. A sea-eagle
floated lazily in the crisp air. Then, with slow
wingbeats, it drifted effortlessly out into the gulf.

Isabelle sighed as she watched the progress of the
splendid bird. Never in her life had she seen such a
majestic creature. Something in her longed to follow
it: to move upwards and outwards into the sparkling,
boundless blue of the sky. She was stirred from her
reverie by Eleanor. The older woman was cuddling
the baby girl. For some reason the child had made
herself inseparable from Eleanor who could hardly
move without causing a wail of protest and a clamour
for affection.

'This child starves for love. Have you seen how she
acts with us?'

Isabelle smiled. 'How she acts with you, you mean.

150

She has taken to you with a vengeance. But then you have always had a way with children. I can still remember how as a child you fascinated me. You were one of the few who acted as if I mattered. Saving my father, of course. To all the rest I was just a girl: too tall and awkward with growing up to be anything but a nuisance. Can't you recall it?'

Eleanor surveyed the child in her arms. She shook her head slowly. ''Tis different, Isabelle. You pined for attention and being seen as being of account. This one hungers for love itself.'

'No wonder. I would think that the wretch who sold her to us wasted little love on such a scrap as this.'

Eleanor lifted the little golden head. Great hazel eyes peered at her. 'She is not a fool. You know that?'

Isabelle nodded.

'The only fool was the one who described her thus. She acts like an infant because she has not learned to grow up. I have seen it in the east. An orphan can shrink away without love. Become frozen like a bud in a May frost. By Our Lady, this child is no fool.'

Isabelle took comfort from the tender hopefulness of Eleanor's words. But she was taken aback by what followed. 'Why did you do it?'

'Do what?'

'Buy this child?' Eleanor caressed the curls beneath her fingers.

Isabelle looked pained. She had not expected such a question from this quarter. She had somehow assumed that Eleanor was a party to all her thoughts. She could not hide her disappointment at discovering that she stood alone on this issue.

'Why did you buy her?' Eleanor's voice was gentle

but very insistent. 'Can you not tell me?'

The younger woman paused. Her brow was knitted with rare wrinkles of doubt. 'I thought that you of all people would know the reason!'

'Perhaps I do, but do you?'

Isabelle looked puzzled.

Eleanor continued: 'There will be hard days ahead of us. And fresh recriminations from William. You must know yourself why you did it. Only then will you face the unknown with some measure of fortitude.'

'I bought her because she was a girl. A girl and of no account. Just a foolish wilful daughter of Eve. A thing of no importance. Just as I am. So I bought her to show she had a worth.'

Eleanor clucked softly. 'So speaks Phillip Spayne! And if it had been a boy you would have left it in misery?'

The question was stark. Isabelle frowned. Then she shook her head. 'No. I could not have done so. I suppose I would have bought any child adrift in such a storm of hate and cruelty.'

'So why did you buy this one in particular?'

Isabelle wrestled with her own thoughts. She was not truly sure. Or rather that which she was sure of she could hardly say.

'It is hard to say this.' She ran a hand over the green wool of her dress. 'I think I shall never marry again. I cannot cast away what I have gained at such cost. And I would lose all if I married. I bought the only child I shall have.' The words were strangely cool. Placid and unruffled but also desolate.

'And you would not be the first widow who resolved to remain in her chaste state. For God knows you would pass all your rights to a new husband. But think of this: if you had had a dozen children at home in Boston would you have left this little one on the quay at Riga?'

Isabelle was almost angry now, a rare emotion when Eleanor was the cause. 'By Our Lady, Eleanor, what do you take me for? Didn't your heart break with pity when you saw her? Surely you felt the pity which filled my . . .'

'Enough . . .'

Eleanor was quick to extinguish the fire which she had started, a flame she so rarely saw in this young woman of ice and snow.

'You have said it, Isabelle. It was pity which made you do it. The rest was there too. But it was pity which decided you. And daughter of Eve you are, but none ever said she was bereft of pity when she fell from grace. And many a son of Adam would do well to mimic the pity which still lies in the heart of the daughters of Eve.' Eleanor smiled after her own outburst.

'It was a gracious thing that you did. A foolish thing no doubt. But it was a like foolishness which took Our Lord to the cross. And it is right that you recognise the true motive behind your actions. We will face hard days ahead. And you will be blamed for this action of yours. On such days you might doubt the wisdom of your impulse were it founded solely on love of sex, or pity for self. But, as Peter holds the keys, you will hold fast to your decision each time you recall that it was done at bottom-most for pity and for love.'

Isabelle reached out a hand. With great care she stroked the little head.

'Aye,' she said very quietly. 'I did it for pity and for love . . .'

Eleanor squeezed her hand. 'But still you've shown me that I do not know you as I ought. For I would have never credited you with such impulsiveness. It was that which shook William, you know. For he thought he knew you too. You shook him.'

Isabelle smiled a steady smile which belied her racing heart. For she had thought that she knew herself! And yet no one was more surprised than she had been at the loss of her careful self-possession in Riga. The thought disturbed her deeply.

'A fine view no doubt. But we've work to do.' The arrival of Curteys and Thymelby shattered the moment of heart-searching. The two Englishmen were accompanied by the grey-faced sergeant and a short, bearded fellow with a face like leather and a body like a barrel. He was perhaps in his fifties but had a face which defied accurate estimates of age. It looked as if it had been everywhere and seen everything.

'This is the Finnish guide provided by von Fellin. He has been of service to the order before. The sergeant believes him to be an honest man. Or as honest a Finn as we will find. He has acted as a guide before, for parties of Easterling merchants going on to Novgorod. It looks as if he is as good as we will get in these parts.'

William spoke as if the guide – who clearly understood all that was said – was not present. Despite this the little man beamed with irrepressible bonhomie. With a short step forward he bowed before the two women.

'*Hyvaa paivaa.*' The words were strange but the tone warm. 'Good day, my ladies. My name is Ilmarinen. My honour it is entirely to serve you. You could have found no better guide than I. For I speak the language of the English and the Germans and the Russians too. Bargain for you am I. For I speak the language of all tribes of the forests. Languages more than any other guide speak I.' He beamed at his own genius. 'I speak language of Livonians, of Ests, of Vodians and Ingrians. I speak language of Carelians . . .'

'Enough!' Curteys raised his eyes in irritation. 'We're paying you to speak Russian, that is all.' Turning to the women he added: 'The sergeant says he talks like this all the time. It's going to be a long journey to Novgorod.'

The little guide beamed and bowed again. Eleanor grinned and winked at Isabelle. It was clear from the returned smile that the Finn had found a way to both their hearts. William sighed as he recognised the significance of the exchanged glances.

The rotund guide quickly took the two women under his wing. With a week of preparations ahead of them he made himself responsible for escorting them about the alleyways of Reval, and their little party – Isabelle, Eleanor and the child, escorted by the Finn and the ever-watchful Gosse – soon became a familiar sight in the walled confines of the Lower Town. It was on such a trip that the little girl gained a name that Isabelle was happy with and could freely pronounce.

One rainy day Isabelle's party was searching the market for provisions. Curteys and Thymelby were likewise employed in another part of the town. The women had already bought medicinal herbs to fill Eleanor's leather scrip; now they were engaged in a haggling contest with an old Danish trader in nuts and winter fruits.

'It's worth the price,' Eleanor whispered to Isabelle. 'There's nothing to beat a ration of nuts and beech kernels. I've known of shipwrecked souls who have survived on little else . . . But pay him half of what he is demanding, for the man's a rogue.' She smiled at the trader.

As Isabelle concluded the transaction the child slipped from her arms. Increasingly the little one had become more independent, as if a separate life was reasserting itself after the confusion of the change which had occurred on the quay at Riga.

The Finnish guide scooped her up as she toddled past him, the archer escort watching the scene with mild irritation.

'What is the child called?' the Finn asked. 'She is a lively one, is she not? She is your child?'

Eleanor retrieved the wriggling blonde bundle as Isabelle watched, very thoughtful. The naming of the child was a matter which had been troubling her for some time now. It was clear her present name would not do!

'Her name is Eve.' Eleanor cast her a glance, half of surprise and half of amusement. 'She is called Eve. And she is not my child. I bought her from a cruel rogue in Riga.'

Despite her superior status she sounded a little defensive. She expected to see shock in the eyes of the rotund little Finn, the same look of incredulous scorn which had flashed in William's eyes and which lived in the scornful eyes of Thymelby and the ever-present Gosse.

Instead the Finn beamed. 'It is a good name. And she is a good girl. She has spirit. And the bounding life of a snow hare! It was a kind thing that you did. Yes . . . a kind thing. You are a good woman!'

The younger woman laughed but the Finn just nodded his head. Some bond of loyalty had been forged there. Eleanor saw it and so did Isabelle, though she said nothing. It was as if something in her action had struck a cord in the guide's own experience and despite the autumn rain there was something warm and tender in the guide's nod and smile. Outside this circle of human kindness Gosse looked away into the mist.

A week and a day after their arrival in Reval the party pushed on. Provisioned with portable dried food and furs they faced the last leg of their journey into the Land of Darkness.

Isabelle was not displeased to leave the little town, with its brooding castle and suspicious traders. She had a strong feeling that, had it not been for the invisible presence of Albrecht von Fellin's goodwill, they would have faced the same open hostility as at Riga. It was clear they were not welcome in these parts.

For two days they sailed eastwards into the Gulf of Finland. On the port and starboard bows the forested shores seemed a little closer with each passing hour, at least when the cold drizzle did not blot out any view with its anonymous cloak of corpse-grey.

On the eve of the feast of St Denis, Eve and

Eleanor lay dozing in the relative comfort of the damp forecastle whilst Curteys and Thymelby were drinking water from one of the ship's clay-lined water-butts. Isabelle was once more alone. With narrowed eyes she traced the line of the dark shore.

'It is a strange land to you?'

She turned to find Ilmarinen, the Finnish guide, behind her. He was draped with a battered fur coat for the weather was turning chilly.

'Yes, it is a strange land to me.' Isabelle took no offence at the man's presumption in approaching her in this fashion. 'But not for you?'

The guide sighed. 'I know it well. This is the land of my birth.' He gestured off the port bow. A dark smudge of charcoal was all that remained of the coast of Finland. 'I have travelled these waters more times than any other that I know.'

'And do you love this wild land?'

The Finn laughed. 'Of course, my lady. Do you not love the land of your birth?'

Isabelle considered this question. Lincoln with its narrow streets and the fens around Boston, patterned with creeks and dykes, felt almost beyond the reach of her imagination. The house on Strait Bargate seemed like a trick of the mist, so hard was it to recall its solid stability from such a vast distance. Nevertheless, it was home; regardless of how far away it was.

'Yes, I love it. It is a fine land.' She gave the guide one of her rare smiles. 'There are some in my country who call it a bleak land too. But to those who know it, there is nowhere to compare with it.'

The Finn laughed in appreciation. 'But does your

land freeze like my land?' He spoke with pride, as if
the awful power of the natural world was to the credit
of the humans who were familiar with it, even though
they had no control over it.

'Not as I have heard this land freezes. William
Curteys says that soon the sea will be solid ice. I have
never seen the sea freeze. Can it truly do such a
thing?'

The guide nodded. 'When cold grips the land even
the sea cannot escape. Where we now sail will be ice a
month from now. When my father was a boy he heard
it said that the sea froze so solid that traders could
walk from Germany to the lands of the Danish king!'
He smiled at the look of surprise on the pretty
woman's face. 'I have not seen it so myself. But I have
spoken to old men who saw it so. And the rivers we
shall sail to Novgorod: they too will be frozen soon.
There is no delay possible for us now. We must hurry,
like deer before the storm.'

Isabelle listened, fascinated. Then, cautiously she
ventured a question. 'You have often worked for the
Easterlings and for the order?' The Finn nodded with
the air of one who knew his own worth. 'Have you
served the knight von Fellin? The one who recommended you to us. Or is it your reputation rather than
your person which went before you?'

'I have served with this knight.'

The answer was flat. Its toneless quality was quite
unlike the Finn's normal humorous resonance.

Isabelle was puzzled. Seeking to push the discussion forward, she asked him: 'Did you go with him to
Novgorod?'

The Finn laughed as he shook his head. 'The

knights of the order do not go to Novgorod. The Russians will not allow it. A hundred years ago they tried to subdue the Russians in the way they have crushed the folk of the forests. But they failed to do so. The prince of Novgorod – Alexander Nevsky – defeated them.

'They say it was a terrible battle. Fought on the ice of a lake. Since that day to this, the order has not come against the Russians in battle. No knight goes to Novgorod the Great; only the merchants who do their will. These the Russians allow there. And this Alexander Nevsky, who defeated the order, the Russians revere him almost as a saint . . .'

'Then what work did you do for Albrecht von Fellin?'

An unusual and hard look crept into the once-smiling eyes. A muscle twitched in the full-bearded face. 'It was long ago. So long I can hardly remember. I translated for him. Amongst the tribes of the forests – Livonians and Ests. It was a long time ago.'

'But clearly he remembered you. You must have done him good service, all those years ago?'

The Finn did not reply. He looked out across the dark sea. Towards his homeland, a darker line of shadow, far away. 'It is a strange life, to be a guide. To walk through the languages of tribes and peoples as through a wood of many types of trees.' His voice was distant, enigmatic. 'Do you know how similar are the languages of Finns and Ests? And yet the people are so different. For the Finns are free and the Ests . . .' He pursed his lips. 'And . . . the Ests serve the order as once they served the Danes . . . Did you know that in my language the word for blessing is "*siunata*"? It is a fine word. Yet in the language of the Ests the word is "*siunama*". And it means to curse!' He rubbed his hands together, as if trying to free them of some clinging dirt. 'I have served the order. I have been a blessing to them . . .'

Isabelle was not slow to ask herself the unspoken question of what he had been to the Ests, yet sensed that she should not pursue the matter. There was some secret here which the Finn would not divulge, or at least he would go no further than these tangled hints. It was quite unlike the man; usually so open and jolly. And in some way it touched on Albrecht. She longed to quiz him further but she held her peace.

Silently Isabelle followed the guide's gaze. Together they watched the white-capped waves and the dark shoreline as the wind quickened and then the rain blew in their faces.

The next day brought landfall. The tapering Gulf of Finland at last came to an end and ahead lay the unimaginable vastness of the Russias. The Yarmouth vessel anchored off the mouth of a wide estuary as the day dawned bright and clear with an edge of frost. A thin layer of ice glistened on the ropes and rigging and sheened the single sail.

'It's getting cold early,' Curteys remarked casually as he and Isabelle watched the sailors lowering goods and trunks into an anchored Russian river-boat. 'And there was that other frost the day after we landed at Reval. Mark my words, it will be a severe winter.'

He rubbed his hands as if relishing the prospect of an early shift into ice and snow. Isabelle wondered if he was trying to frighten her. She bit back an angry reply. It would have been all too clearly identified as bravado.

It took most of the morning to load the river-boats with the English merchandise. William had made a contract with the ferrymen the previous year and seemed to know them by name. The work was vigorous and raised a sweat to combat the cold and even the archers were set to work on lowering bales – all of them, bar one.

As the women and their escort prepared to leave the ship the toiling soldiers looked up from their labours.

'Look at Gosse, the bastard,' one hissed. 'Always away when there's work to be done. Always on his fat arse, in spitting distance of her ladyship . . .'

His companion muttered in agreement. Then Thymelby was yelling at them to 'get your eyes back on your work' and their envy was silenced.

While the unloading went ahead, Isabelle, Eleanor and Eve went ashore with the first boat, the Finnish guide and Gosse accompanying them. A little stockaded settlement was situated beside the mouth of the estuary of the River Neva. From the activity going on it was apparent that the native Russians were used to the arrival of merchants from foreign parts. However, there was a stir of interest at the appearance of Isabelle.

'What are they saying?' she asked the grinning Finn. 'They stare so.'

The guide glanced at the Russian boatmen. He thought for a moment before replying. 'They think that you are one of the "*Nemets*", that is to say a

German. Also it is the colour of your hair which interests them. They are used to Germans but your hair is still striking.' When Isabelle raised an eyebrow, he added: 'My lady, you asked what the Russians said.' And he grinned wickedly. 'They also express interest in whose woman you are. Some say you belong to the tall aloof one. Others that you belong to the one with the face of a soldier.'

Isabelle smiled briefly at these portraits of Curteys and Thymelby.

'If you have the opportunity you may inform them that I belong to neither of them.'

'That would not be a good idea, I fear. For it is safer that they think you belong to a man. Safer for you and for us all.'

Isabelle opened her mouth to rebuke the guide's impertinence but thought better of it. She nodded curtly. 'Say I belong to the tall man. To the aloof man.' Eleanor tried to catch her eye but failed. 'So they will be satisfied. And no doubt it will amuse him if he hears of it.' Then she lifted up little Eve to see the water sparkling on either side.

Eleanor pondered the light on the face of the water. She had noticed how Isabelle reddened a little as she gave the guide his outrageous instructions. Perhaps it was due to the fresh sea air. Then again, perhaps it wasn't. Eleanor held Curteys and von Fellin in her mind's eye and wondered.

When the two river-boats had been loaded, teams of muscle-knotted Russians began the slow task of rowing them against the flow of the river. The way forward now lay along a broad stream, between banks dark with spruce and pine. As Curteys had told von Fellin, their route lay along the River Neva as far as Lake Ladoga, then south along the Volkhov to Novgorod. It was a distance of some one hundred and seventy miles from the open sea of the Gulf of Finland, the best part of two-and-a-half weeks' travel.

The coming of an early frost had made any relaxation of pace out of the question. As the guide explained to the attentive merchants, the Volkhov itself would freeze over some time after mid-November. It would not be free of ice again until early April. There was no time to delay.

Long hours on the river by day, and nights under canvas in clearings on the bank, persuaded Isabelle that they had indeed finally entered into a strange land. South of Lake Ladoga the River Volkhov flowed through a low basin bordered by marshes and wet pastures and beyond the reach of its wet fingers the great evergreen forests rolled like the frozen waves of a dark green sea.

One late October morning another cold night had reluctantly given up a frost-laced dawn. The tents of the night's bivouac were silver with ice and the grass at the edge of the camp was stiff with cold but by eleven o'clock the little convoy was warmed by a weak sun. Isabelle was up at the prow of the leading boat, with Eleanor and Eve beside her, like her, swaddled in furs. Curteys was attending to a bale of Lincolnshire cloth which had burst its bonds.

Eleanor had travelled many seas but never on a journey as cold as this one or as far north. With a practised eye she studied the actions of the river-boatmen. She knew the look of competence when she saw it and watched with approval as they manhandled ropes and oars.

Isabelle was attending to Eve. 'She likes this porridge,' she remarked, stirring a grey mix of oatmeal, milk and honey. 'She would help me do it, but I fear she would have it over both of us.' The little girl was trying to claw her way into Isabelle's lap, her quick, dark eyes fixed on the bowl, little fingers grasping at it.

Eleanor turned from her appraisal of the boatmen. 'She grows more confident; have you seen it?' Isabelle nodded in agreement with Eleanor's observation. 'And she sleeps better at night. She knows us both now. And responds to us. I told you that the child was no fool.'

'But her speech is slow. She cannot talk as she should.' Isabelle paused. 'Lord knows I've watched the children play about the Bargate at home. A child of her age should speak.' She stroked the little blonde head; the child really was very pretty and talked with her eyes, if not her tongue.

'I think the problem is that she has rarely been spoken to. Her craving for love shows how little she has received of it. Even now she will not let us leave her. Besides, would you have her speak German?'

Isabelle shook her head. 'By Our Lady, no! I hardly speak a word of it myself.'

'Then be grateful that the Lord has seen fit to start this little one's learning late. Now perhaps she will learn to speak the same tongue as you, or I. Indeed, as if she had barely known another.'

Isabelle was about to ask her older friend whether a child carried its language in its blood, when a cry from behind seized her attention. One of the Russian river-boatmen was leaning over the side. He was gesticulating wildly in the direction of the water. Setting down her bowl of porridge, Isabelle once again lifted Eve up to see what all the excitement was about. Holding the child tightly she leaned out over the edge of the decking.

A great tree was sweeping towards the boat. Like some drowning dragon it flung dark and twisted arms of branches out of the dark water. The current was swollen by rains upstream and with unseen hands it turned and rolled the mighty fallen pine.

Realising her danger, Isabelle began to pull herself back. The Russians were shouting and the voice of the Finnish guide, Ilmarinen, could be heard. Eleanor called out a sudden, sharp warning.

With a brutal crash the tree rammed the surging bows. It was a hammer blow. The whole boat shook, bales fell, men slid as the craft yawed about. Its sail flapped and cracked as oarsmen leapt away from snapping oars.

Suddenly Isabelle found herself spinning into space, her arms open wide with shock. Eve flew out of her grasp in a nightmare whirl of light and dark.

Crash. Isabelle hit the water. The searing cold smashed the breath from her body and she cried out at last. Freezing water filled her mouth as panic snatched at her flailing arms. All was black, a roaring, choking, swirling blackness.

Then daylight. She flung out her arms. Water closed over her head once more. With desperate strokes she clawed at the light. Again she surfaced, her hair spread about her like some fairy weed.

'Help . . . Help . . . Eve . . . Eve . . .'

Her screams were incoherent with terror. The numbing cold was crushing her will to resist. She sank again. The dark waters of the Volkhov closed over her head. One desperate hand clutched at the disappearing daylight.

William Curteys saw the two fall and he sprinted the length of the trembling deck. As he careered he tore off his heavy fur coat, pushing aside the archer bodyguard who was gawping over the side. With one high movement the Boston merchant rose from the deck and flung himself into the river.

Will Curteys had learned to swim in the summer dykes and rivers of the Lincolnshire Fens on slow days of brazen sunshine and amethyst skies. He was a strong and keen swimmer, yet nothing had prepared him for the utter shock of the cold which hit him now. By the time he had towed the limp body of Isabelle towards the arms outstretched over the side of the boat, his legs were growing numb with cramp.

Heedless of the warning cries he threw himself back into the river. Towards the wooded bank a little bundle of cloth was bobbing about. Not until he had reached the child and towed her back to the boat would he give in. By the time he did so he was almost spent himself. Twice he slipped from the grasp of the boatmen. At last, with the Finn clutching his bobbed thatch of chestnut hair, he was hauled aboard. Half-dead himself he choked and retched on the timbers of the deck.

Urged on by the little Finn the Russian boatmen put into the bank. Thymelby and the second boat followed. Leaping ashore the guide began tearing down small branches and twigs. He shouted to the Russians to do likewise. Already some of the English archers were at work at the edge of the surrounding forest.

Eleanor clambered ashore; the semi-conscious Eve in her arms. Thymelby took the dripping body of Isabelle from the arms of Gosse and carried her to where Eleanor had laid down the child, a little way from the river at the very edge of the dark trees; a spot sheltered and overhung with the fresh-scented raft of spruce branches.

The Finn was busy with a flint and tinder. Eleanor knelt beside him and opened the scrip that she carried. From the dark recesses she produced a handful of flaky grey material: travellers' tinder, made from the dried underside of the broad leaves of coltsfoot, scoured with care from the living leaf.

The Finn understood her action before she could speak and piled the fluffy tinder amidst his own broken twigs. Soon a thin and fragile flame responded to his frantic rubbing of flint and metal.

Now Curteys too was beside the growing fire. He almost thrust his hands into the flames as the sweet smell of burning pine resin filled his nostrils. He gulped in the hot air.

While the archers erected the canvas tents, Eleanor, Thymelby and the Finn stripped the three half-drowned survivors of the collision whilst on the edge of the fireglow the boatmen and archers cast a professional eye over Isabelle's naked, slim white body.

It was now essential to restore heat to the frozen limbs. Eleanor roughly pushed Thymelby away;

she would attend to Isabelle. The tough merchant shrugged and began to pummel the dazed Curteys. The Finn massaged the cold chest of the smallest survivor.

It was nightfall before Eleanor was satisfied that all were out of danger. Even so, Isabelle and Eve were exhausted and the child delirious. They piled the daytime fire higher with wood and around the clearing other fires were built against the bitter cold of the dark. All night Eleanor sat up with her three charges, each wrapped in blankets and fur coats. Just before dawn, as if to compound their difficulties, it began to snow.

For three days the party remained in the clearing by the River Volkhov. On the second day Isabelle and William had almost recovered from the shock of their freezing plunge, enough for William to rebuke Isabelle for what he described as 'foolhardiness'.

Now that it was clear that the woman and child would live, the Boston merchant felt a strange and shameful satisfaction at the near disaster. It was as if it justified all his dire warnings. It was strange how his fears of danger had been so utterly fulfilled. Partly it disturbed, partly reinforced him, to consider his prophetic flashes. The feeling of satisfaction shocked him whenever he caught it rising within him. Yet he could not deny it. It was something to set in the scales against Isabelle's confident ignoring of his prudent advice.

At any other time Isabelle would have stoutly defended herself. This time she chose to endure his sharp words. Partly her silence was due to the grudging debt she owed William, partly because she was worried about Eve and felt herself to be to blame. She also felt very foolish. It was an emotion which she did not easily admit to. That Will Curteys had been witness to and rescuer from such foolishness did nothing to lessen the sense of humiliation.

The girl was still listless and fevered and a chesty cough disturbed her sleep. Closeted in one of the rough tents, with Isabelle and Eleanor, she seemed unable to shake off the blow dealt her by the icy river. Outside the snow piled up in sheets of drifting white.

'It's cold, isn't it?' Isabelle held the child against her breast. 'My God, if she dies 'twill be my fault. William is right.'

'Don't fret, she will not die. And Will Curteys is as worried about her as you are. Only he must hide his concerns behind complaints. All men do.' She rummaged in her scrip. 'Now lay her down and pass the kettle of boiling water. I've dried feverfew leaves for the heat in her head.' She pulled out a handful of dried leaves. 'And the leaves of Adam and Eve for the cough on her chest.' With great care she lifted out the white spotted leaves of lungwort. 'And a little poppy syrup to make her sleep . . . Have no fear for the child.' She gave Isabelle's arm a reassuring squeeze. The gesture was returned with one of Isabelle's rare and intimate smiles.

With concentrated care Eleanor placed the leaves in a wooden bowl. Slowly she poured in the boiling water. 'There, we shall let it infuse for a moment or two.' Then, to take Isabelle's mind from the sick child, she added, 'What is William doing?'

Isabelle glanced towards the laced slit that acted as a door. A cold draught blew through the lace holes despite the fire burning constantly outside.

'Oh, he is looking after the mending of the boat. The tree broke in the planking beneath the waterline. Adam and the archers are helping him.'

From outside came the steady, solid sound of axes on tree trunks. Then a creak, groan and crash signalled the death of one of the spruce trees on the edge of the camp.

'The Russian boatmen are not happy,' Isabelle continued. 'They say that only the Easterlings have permission from Novgorod to cut trees beside the rivers. They are not happy at all. They only agreed to help when Adam threatened them with our archers.'

'I see.' Eleanor sniffed at the herb-water. 'Hold her nearer. Yes, that's right . . .'

Isabelle lifted Eve's reluctant head. Brow creased with concentration, Eleanor poured the herb drink into the open mouth. Despite a large quantity splashing on to the two women, Eve managed to drink some of the medicine.

'Lay her down now. She should sleep a little easier. The poppy syrup should see to that.'

Isabelle drew a fur coat over the sleepy child. A well-sucked thumb found its way to a familiar mouth. Soon Eve had drifted into a light sleep.

Outside, in the snow, Adam Thymelby was inspecting the axe work of his archers. The snow was deep, well up his calves, and his fur coat held the flakes in little clots of ice. He looked like some cave bear.

Suddenly he straightened up, pulling back the ear flaps of his squirrel-fur hat. Wet flakes slapped against his mutilated ear as he turned to face the wind. His almond eyes narrowed. He had not been mistaken. He called to the archers to leave their work and, when they were slow to respond, he cursed them roundly. 'Move, you whoresons. Get your bows.'

His face, puckered by the scar beneath the lips, was animated with anger. He cursed the archers and cursed himself. How could he have missed the sound?

He had only covered half the distance to the tents and his sword when the first dogs broke from the light cover of a screen of spruce. Snow rose behind them like wood smoke. The Russian boatmen dropped their axes. The English archers fumbled with their bows. Some had damp bow strings and they struggled and spat. Gosse moved off in the direction of his charge's tent, away from the likely scene of action.

Three sledge teams swept towards the camp. Already some had discharged their cargo of men-at-arms. Four men to a sledge; Thymelby quickly counted some twelve armed men.

The Finn was at Thymelby's elbow. 'Your men must lay their weapons down. They cannot help us now. I will speak for you. With words not arrows.'

Thymelby did not look happy at the prospect of taking orders from his interpreter but he was too practical a man to let social status get in the way of his judgement. He waved to the archers to lower their goose-feathered shafts.

By now the lead sledge was only yards away. It veered to the left and swung to a halt in a veil of snow and a cacophony of yapping. One of its occupants leapt down and strode towards Thymelby. From the cut of his ankle-length coat and the sheen of the pelt, he clearly occupied a higher station than his fellows.

Stopping an arm's length from the Boston merchant he barked out a series of short, sharp sounds. Thymelby stood his ground and his narrow eyes did not so much as blink.

The Finn stepped forward and bowed answering the Russian who snapped back at him. 'He says he is "*Voevoda*" – that is "commander" – of the forts of Novgorod beside the River Volkhov. He holds a commission from the military commander of the Republic of Novogrod – the *tysiatskii* himself.' Then the Finn added, as an afterthought: 'I think we are meant to be frightened.'

The Russian barked out once more. This time, though, a raised intonation indicated the presence of a question.

'He thinks that we are *Nemets* – Germans – and he wants to know why he has not had word of our coming.'

'Tell him who we are.' Thymelby's mouth was thin with controlled violence. 'Remind him also that we are merchants who travel freely and should be spared interference.'

Choosing his words with care the little Finn ironed out the more jagged edges of Thymelby's assertion. For good measure he bowed at the end of his speech and called the Russian '*gosudar*', or lord.

His efforts seemed to avail him little. The Russian's voice now took on a tone of measured craft.

The Finn sighed. 'He asks: if we are not *Nemets*, why are we cutting trees? Only the Germans have the right to cut living trees on the banks of the Volkhov.'

'Tell him it is because we hold a charter from the Archbishop of Novgorod to act as the Easterlings do!'

The voice was that of William Curteys. He had come over from the moored boats during the course of the altercation. In his hand he carried a tightly bound roll of vellum which had been in his possession for over a year.

The Finn passed on the news to the Russian commander. The effect was almost comic. He twitched as if stung. The mention of the archbishop had clearly taken him unawares. He stamped his foot in the snow.

As Curteys knew all too well, it would be a very brave man indeed who flouted the wishes of the mighty Archbishop of Novgorod. Even a representative of the *tysiatskii* himself would think twice before crossing travellers who went under the peace of the most powerful man in Novgorod.

After a moment of hesitation the commander came to a decision. With lowered brows he muttered to the Finn. 'He says you must come with him. He will take you himself to Novgorod.' Then the guide whispered: 'He is angry that you have thwarted him. He does this to show he still has authority.'

'That is quite impossible,' William replied. 'We cannot leave our merchandise here. Tell him we cannot do it.'

When the guide retold his message it was met with a sharp laugh. Now the Russian had a reason to assert his authority. 'He is being difficult. He says you come under his jurisdiction and he is answerable to the *tysiatskii* for all traffic on the river. And since he knows nothing of your coming, you must go with him.'

William hissed angrily. Thymelby spat. Both were

thinking of the bales of good English wool cloth and the flagons of sweet wine on the two river-boats.

The Russian spoke again and the Finn nodded. 'The commander says you may leave your archers to guard the boats. He will leave some of his men too. Our boats will be under the protection of the *tysiatskii* as well as the archbishop. None will dare lay hands on them.

'He also says that the boats must leave today. The Volkhov is already freezing above Novgorod. Soon the river will be impassable.'

Recognising the inevitable, Curteys nodded a reluctant agreement. There was no other option. He could not afford to get embroiled in a conflict with the Novgorod militia. There was only so much protection afforded by his charter. If he pushed his luck he would lose the goodwill of the city authorities and then the Hanse would gain from such a situation.

Reluctantly he turned towards Isabelle's tent. At that moment she herself emerged. There were audible noises from the direction of the Russians, as if a vision had appeared in their midst. They were clearly taken aback.

'We must pack our personal possessions. We will travel with these Russians . . .'

'But the child. She cannot . . .'

'There is no debate, Isabelle. And this is not my idea. Wrap her warmly. Tell Eleanor too.'

'But William, she is too ill to . . .'

'I cannot and I will not enter into an altercation with you.' William's voice was low but hard. 'We have no choice in this matter. We are in your Land of Darkness now. Things here are different. Now gather your possessions and wrap the child well.'

Within the hour the sledges were ready to go.
Isabelle clutched the sleeping Eve and William the
heavy, locked box containing the precious hoard of
silver pieces.

As they clambered aboard, a grim-faced Gosse
pushed his way towards the sledge. It had been with
mounting dismay that he had watched his privileged
position evaporating. 'Where my mistress goes – I
go,' he grunted.

The Russians rose angrily.

'Hold your peace, Gosse,' William commanded
sharply. Turning to the Finn he rapped: 'Tell the
commander this man comes with us.'

The Russian shrugged and the archer climbed up
behind William and Isabelle. William twisted about.
'Your courage does you credit, man, but for God's
sake do your speaking through me.'

The command, softened by the compliment, caused
the archer to bow obediently. As the sledges pulled
away he looked back to where his mates toiled over
the fallen trees. He felt well satisfied with his success.

For the duration of the snow-sprayed journey
Isabelle sat hunched amidst her furs, Eve lay warm
against her body. All about was a spume of snow, the
cries of the drivers and the sharp barks of the sledge
dogs. Between the spaced trees the sledges rushed as
if the dogs followed well-marked trails. The snow-
storm had abated and a pale sun was sinking when
they cleared the last regiment of ordered pines. They
were atop a slight rise and below them the silver coil
of the Volkhov lay – half water, half crystal.

'See . . .' The Finnish guide leant forward and

pointed. The gesture was unnecessary. The sight could not be missed.

A bridge spanned the broad river, both ends guarded by massive towers. Joined by the bridge two towns gripped the river in a firm grasp. Both settlements were girded with high timber stockades. At regular distances along the line of each wall, tall turrets stood proud and alert. From within the wooden walls, columns of thin smoke rose from countless hearth fires as the light of the sun played across the silver aspen shingles on the onion domes of many churches.

'See . . . ,' the Finn whispered. 'It is the city itself: "Lord Novgorod the Great".'

Chapter 7

If persistence in prayer could be equated with piety, then the Orthodox believers of Novgorod stockpiled spiritual merit, as if they held a monopoly in the commodity. The services – great pageants of earth-bound glory – went on for hours.

Within the tall, onion-domed, central vault of the cathedral of St Sophia, clouds of incense rose with the prayers of the faithful in vast drifts of heavy-scented mist. The interior of the church was heaven-bright and earth-cold on Sunday 8 December 1381, the eve of the Orthodox Feast of the Conception of the Mother of God.

In the midst of the congregation Isabelle Crosse shifted the weight on her feet. No one was a more regular attender at mass in the church of St Botolph, but even she was beginning to feel the strain. 'These Russians,' she whispered to Eleanor, 'must have iron feet.'

Her companion chuckled: 'Iron feet and beards enough for two men apiece.' She smiled at the child asleep in her arms.

It was true, Isabelle agreed in her own mind. These strange people were not only remarkable for their devotion to a liturgy that lasted hours; they even looked unearthly. Peering through the incense she had to admit that she had never seen such beards. Much as she took it for granted that all men wore them, she had not seen the like of those in the wide and roomy nave. Curteys with his full growth and Thymelby and von Fellin with their close-trimmed jaws could not compete with the rolling folds of dark shadow adorning the chins of the men about her.

'Quite amazing,' she muttered to herself. 'Really quite amazing.'

She shook her head in wonderment. Truly she was in a strange and contrary land; a land a thousand leagues beyond her experience. And beards were the least of the strangeness in the church. Every act of worship had astonished her with its outlandishness: children receiving their host at mass, fasting from mid-November until Christmas, clanging bells at startling points in the worship and, most of all, the prayers.

At home Isabelle came to mass to compose her private prayers as the priest conducted the solemn rites. Here, everyone seemed to join in. It was most alarming; such a noise of prayer and chanting. It was as if the priest and people celebrated together. Even now that she had grown used to it, she found it hard to meditate against the rising and falling eight tones of Byzantine plain chant.

Near where the wooden screen closed off the holy space of the sanctuary, a group of richly-robed merchants were bowing and genuflecting. One looked back down the frescoed narthex of the church, peering intently. Isabelle recognised him as the wax merchant she had come to see after the mass and as their eyes met he nodded. He had recognised the exotic foreign trader.

'The candle . . .' Eleanor hissed. 'Light your candle . . .'

Isabelle blinked out of her concentration. Eleanor was right, of course. She had forgotten to light her candle. Some of the crowd were watching her as if she was a poorly trained lap dog.

With care she leant towards the sparkling tiers of candles before a side altar. Then, in imitation of their Finnish guide, she carefully crossed herself, kissed the icon and lit her own candle. The flame sputtered and the beeswax smelled oily and sweet. It was a physical symbol of her prayers; in her case a heartfelt thanks to God that Eve had at last recovered from her persistent fever.

She was careful not to kneel. At her first service she had been hauled to her feet by the embarrassed Finn. Apparently no Orthodox knelt on Sundays. Isabelle had been as scandalised as she had been humiliated but she had learnt her lesson. Now she imitated the inhabitants of this Land of Darkness, these people who worshipped her God in a manner disconcerting and bizarre; in their city on the marchlands of Christendom.

For a moment her gaze met the frank, green eyes of the icon gazing from a background of brilliant cinnabar flames; a dazzling face of a martyr as alien to the Boston merchant woman as he was handsome: the Grand Martyr Nikita. It stretched her faith to its limits to allow such peculiarity within that which she held to be so familiar and so dear. However, the ritual completed, she turned to face the front once more. Her wax merchant was smiling. The crowd no longer viewed her with interest.

'Well done!' Eleanor smiled faintly. She winked over the head of Eve, snuggled into her shoulder. 'Well done.'

'Thank you, I almost forgot.'

In billows of smoke a priest had emerged from the great doors in the icon screen. Behind him a glittering altar was suddenly ablaze with light. Bells swung and rang in the outside belfries. All about the tiny English party the crowds were crossing themselves and bowing. Alarmed lest they appear heathen in this great gathering of the faithful, Isabelle and Eleanor began crossing themselves.

Their Finnish guide grinned to himself. He would make Orthodox of these well-meaning but uncivilised Latins yet. Then, still smiling, he bowed in time with the chanting and added his own responses: '*Gospodi polilui . . . Gospodi polilui . . .*'

And because he had instructed them well the two English women also bowed and repeated the words in their own barbaric tongue: 'Lord have mercy . . . Lord have mercy . . .'

Adam Thymelby grimaced as he held up yet another pelt. 'He's an imbecile; the man is an imbecile.'

William Curteys shook his head in response to Thymelby's intemperate speech. 'Mind your tongue, Adam.' He nodded in the direction of the peering Russian merchant. 'We'll gain little advantage from the *tysiatskii* learning your opinion of one of the commanders.'

Thymelby shrugged. 'He speaks no English, as you well know.' He turned to face the merchant and false lines of laughter spread about his cold almond eyes. 'Do you, you whoreson?' The Russian smiled encouragingly. 'That's right, you savage, you don't understand a word of English. Do you?'

The Russian merchant continued to smile politely. Behind his smile he wondered why these two barbarians had come to him without an interpreter. Try as they might they were unable to communicate in a civilised tongue. The futility of the exercise was not ameliorated by his own hunger. He was three weeks into the Orthodox Christmas fast; three weeks without even a sniff of salted meat. And over a fortnight to go to the feast. His belly rumbled as he nodded at their obvious efforts to settle on a price for the pelt in question.

'Told you!' Thymelby grinned in a malicious fashion. 'Hardly any of these savages can speak English. And anyway, the *tysiatskii* is an imbecile too.'

Curteys shrugged. Perhaps Thymelby was right. Ever since the altercation on the frozen banks of the Volkhov their endeavours had been hamstrung by the prince-commander of the Novgorod militia. Had it not been for the charter gained from the archbishop it was doubtful whether they would have made any progress at all. Without it, their goods probably would never have reached the city. Clearly it had rankled to have the aliens back-chat one of the commanders of the *tysiatskii* of Novgorod. Nevertheless Thymelby could push the situation too far. Nothing would be gained from an outright conflict with one of the most powerful men in the city. Even Isabelle had listened attentively while he explained the delicate nature of their position. Not so Adam!

'I know that he's a thorn in our flesh, Adam, but keep a rein on your tongue. He's a powerful man and while we've the goodwill of the archbishop and the boyars he could still be a dangerous enemy. And he is a prince, man! From the Ryurikid family itself.'

'And an arsehole!' Thymelby gave a mocking laugh. 'And don't trust the boyars either. There are too many of those good merchants of this city who have their palms greased by the slimy silver of the Easterlings . . .'

Curteys grunted and lifted up the pelt. He was tired of the conversation. The whole situation was beginning to irritate him. That unsettled him too. He was not a man to allow things to get to him. However, things were different on this trip. Everything had been out of joint since the start. And he knew who was to blame for that. This thought only served to deepen his irritation. He shook his head slightly as he gazed at the dangling fur.

Thymelby mistook the gesture. 'Bloody rubbish, isn't it? I'd not insult the guildsmen of Boston by hanging it in the latrine!'

Curteys was happy to be misinterpreted this time. 'It's a poor quality pelt all right. He must have better than this . . . Even Isabelle would not have fallen for this rat skin . . .'

While the women had gone to mass at the cathedral, the two male merchants had set out to verify Isabelle's claim that she had found fine quality furs. It had been the previous day that she had returned from a search advised by the Finn, who had personal contacts with a Russian who owed him a favour. Even so, it was only a careful watch of the premises, planned by Isabelle, which had detected good furs going in. The men of the English party could not believe it. How could a woman have ferreted out the best pelts? It was as disquieting as it was unbelievable.

Intent on their quest the men had gone without the Finnish interpreter, only a group of archers trailing behind them. As a result much of the conversation so far had consisted of signs, grunts, and a few garbled phrases in Russian. Indeed it was probably a travesty to call the inept rag-bag of sounds and symbols a conversation at all.

Already William was beginning to doubt the wisdom of going out so unprepared. It was not normal for him to act in such a fashion. Yet he had been possessed by an insatiable curiosity to check on Isabelle's claim. He should have hoped that indeed she had discovered a fine store of furs. Instead he found he was almost willing himself to go away empty-handed.

Her single-mindedness troubled him though he could not think why. What was she to him anyway? Simply a business partner? He pondered this as he handled the pelt. What did it matter if she had shown herself to be undisciplined and unpredictable. What did he care if she behaved in such a way? And yet he did care.

'It's an early summer pelt,' Curteys continued

drily. He turned the white-marbled grey fur this way and that. 'The type that the Germans call "*poppelen*".' At the sound of the German term the Russian's face twitched. William noted the involuntary action. 'And this cunning bastard knows that they will not buy any summer fur. The quality is too poor . . .'

'So he thinks he might sell this whore's mantle to us.'

'That he does, the rogue.' William tossed the pelt down on to the hessian sack from which it had come. '*Niet* . . .'

As he had once proudly told Pexton and so embarrassingly displayed on the quay at Reval, he took little delight in foreign languages. Still, there was a time and a place for everything; he could get by when it suited him.

'*Niet . . . na rybyem mekhu.*'

The Russian boyar snorted with indignation. The accusation that the pelt was 'fish-fur' had pierced his pride. Before he could defend his product the English merchant struck again.

'You give us *schoenewerke*, not this rag. You understand me: *schoenewerke*.'

To make the point Curteys picked up the pelt and spat on the cold boards of the floor. He had communicated. The Russian understood the German word and, more to the point, he had sacks of fine quality pelts in his storerooms. He pulled a face as he turned to get them. He'd sell the summer pelts some time but not today.

Thymelby was impressed. 'Well, well . . . quite a diplomat, Will.'

He ignored Curteys' raised eyebrows. 'And more surprisingly, she really must have found something here. Not just a pretty face . . .' His puckered lip curled in a lustful grimace. 'You can't beat a woman with brains. A more refined hump . . .'

'That's enough, Adam.' Curteys' voice was cold. It displeased him to hear Isabelle spoken of in such a fashion. 'That is quite enough . . .'

'You're getting old, Will. All these months away from home and you've not got to her once! And you her partner too . . .' He turned the last word on his tongue as if it were a confession of intimate indecency. 'You'd better leave her to a firmer hand.' His almond eyes narrowed. 'She must be dying for it. It's been almost a year since Tony Crosse did it with her . . .'

'Enough!' Curteys turned on his partner. 'I'll not have you talking about her that way . . .'

'It's all right, Will. I was only joking.' The cold eyes danced with a cruel light. 'Fond of her, are you?'

'For God's sake, Adam, she was Anthony Crosse's wife. He was my friend . . .'

'Of course, of course . . . It's only right that you should defend her honour. Her being the widow of your friend.'

William pursed his lips in annoyance at the way in which Thymelby had so easily nettled him. Fortunately, at that moment the boyar returned with a servant bowed beneath a sack. It saved him from further consideration of why Thymelby's remarks had so offended him.

With some relief William pulled the fresh furs from the bag and spread them out on the table before him.

'That's better,' he muttered, as if the previous conversation with Thymelby had not occurred. 'That's much better.' He nodded in the direction of the Russian. '*Schoenewerke* . . . much better.' The boyar nodded with a look of resignation.

The English merchants made arrangements for a barrel of the same quality pelts to be conveyed to their lodgings for the night. It was recognised practice; any experienced merchant knew the dangers of low quality fur being hidden beneath the best pelts. The Easterlings had long established the right to inspect a consignment overnight. Curteys and Thymelby had no intention of accepting any lesser treatment. With some five thousand pelts in a barrel, it would be a long night's work that lay ahead of them.

William knew he should have been rejoicing. The pelts were good: some of the very best he had ever seen. And yet he felt disturbed. It was as if Isabelle did not need the advice of her male companions. As if she competed with them. The thought jarred.

Never in his life had William Curteys had to compete with a woman. Never had he had to acknowledge female proficiency in his own trade. The thought of such a woman being so independent was alien. Far more natural that a woman should depend on a man. On a man like William Curteys, for example . . .

Outside the Russian merchant's shop it was still snowing. The whole city lay under a shifting veil of white. Here and there the darkness of frozen planking stood out from the ice-sheened walls of the buildings. The city was strangely quiet, despite the movement of sledges and the hurrying, fur-wrapped citizens. The snow subdued all, melding all into one and snuffing out sound. It was as if it had frozen out one of the senses of humankind.

On their way back through the thick snow to their rented house, the two men called at the church of St John. As with the other churches of the city this one was the centre of its residential district. However, this aspen-shingled place of worship was a little different. It was the organisational heart of the wax merchants' guild.

Lights were burning within to offset the shadows of winter which lay across the city. They cast a pale glow wherever oiled linen cloth had failed to stop up a gap in the shutters. Heavy swags of snow hung down from the wooden roofs of the buildings in the street and now and then a slide of snow fell with a sound like muffled thunder. Curteys and Thymelby entered through the narrow porch of the church.

Before the English could partake of the lucrative trade in forest beeswax they had to gain admittance to the guild. Already they had delivered the customary bolt of wool cloth to the archbishop and the *tysiatskii*. Today they handed over the additional fee of fifty silver coins to the merchant elders of the guild. Only then could Isabelle's merchant at the cathedral deliver the wax she had contracted for the previous week.

Already, though, the business had cost the English party dear. To make payment in the silver roubles of Novgorod they had been obliged to change almost one hundred and eighty of their glistening Prussian marks. For this service the Russian money-changer had charged a hefty fee. It was consequently a mildly aggrieved pair of merchants who left the church at the end of the transaction.

'It had better be bloody good wax,' Thymelby hissed. He resented paying customary dues as much as every merchant. 'Or those sodding Russian money-changers will regret the fee that they charged.'

'It's a good wax,' William announced. 'Isabelle has seen it. And she vouches for its quality. She says it's as good as the cases we bought at Riga.'

The thought of how she had secured such a competitive price for the wax at Riga caused him to frown. Von Fellin had ordered merchants to approach her directly – luck was smiling on the woman. He frowned again and did not know why he did so. Perhaps it was because she had managed to reduce even the fair price that von Fellin had pressurised the merchants to accept!

At the church of the wax guild the two Englishmen had met their Finnish translator, fresh from having escorted his charges back to the English quarter. He had informed Curteys and Thymelby of the fair price agreed with the Russian wax merchant in the cathedral and been surprised at their lack of jubilation. Now they set off on their next item of business: a serious matter indeed.

'You know that the bastards are behind it. I know that the bastards are behind it and those sods know that the bastards are behind it,' grumbled Thymelby as they trudged through the falling snow.

He spat in disgust. 'So why are we wasting our bloody time . . . just tell me that?'

'You know damn well why, Adam. Because we've no choice.' William Curteys brushed the snow from his beard. 'And if we don't play this their way we really will know it. Mark my words.'

Thymelby seemed far from convinced. 'It's a waste of time. Everyone knows that the Hanse have been spreading it around that we are Tartar spies – God rot the lot of them – and it's not our job to sort it out. The bloody Russians should be doing it. It's not a matter for the Hanse to investigate themselves. The lying sods should be answering before the council of the city for their lies.'

Curteys did not answer him; he knew that Adam Thymelby was right but it did no good to go over it all again. Ever since they had arrived in the city someone had been slipping the word to the ignorant and the stupid that the English merchants were spying for the Tartar khan.

The previous summer the Tartars of the Golden Horde – the overlords of the Russias – had set out to crush the Russian cities who, for two years, had asserted independence and refused to pay tribute to the Tartar tax collectors. Allied with the pagan Lithuanians – those objects of von Fellin's contempt – they seemed set to come against the rebellious Russian princes as soon as the next campaigning season began. It was not a prospect which sat easily upon the hearts of the citizens of Novgorod. Any suspected of treating with the Tartars risked destruction.

It was nonsense to accuse the English, but just the thing to appeal to the idle and the paranoid. And as an accompaniment to the rumours, there had been acts of vandalism against English property.

Curteys had taken the matter before the ruling

merchants of the Novgorod council: the *Posadniki*. He had had high hopes that such a move would squash the nasty little accusations. His hopes had been reasonable.

Under the overall rule of the archbishop, the web of power within the city was stretched between the council and the jealous prince, the *tysiatskii*. Possessing a trade charter from the ruling ecclesiastic and a faith in the rightness of their cause, it had seemed a mere formality to have the alderman of the Hanseatic community in Novgorod summoned to the council and warned off.

'And a lot of bloody good those whoresons on the council were,' Thymelby hissed menacingly, as if he had been reading the thoughts of his companion. 'What the hell did they say?' He spat once more before supplying his own answer: '"Lay the accusation before the Germans at their own headquarters; just run along to the 'Peterhouse'. The Germans will sort the matter out themselves." And what the hell will that avail us? It's no better than appointing the poacher as the reeve . . .'

His narrow eyes tightened. He knew full well how he would like to lay his accusation before the Easterlings. His fingers played over the hilt of his dagger.

Curteys recognised the gesture and smiled his cynical smile. He sympathised with Thymelby. It was indeed a waste of time to leave the matter in the hands of the Germans. Whilst the city had accorded the Hanse merchants the right to jurisdiction over their own affairs, an accusation such as the one the English made should have been settled by the council.

It was all too obvious that someone spiteful towards the English cause had influenced the decision. It was with some regret that William remembered the altercation with the fort commander on the banks of the Volkhov. For, whilst the Germans had been in Novgorod long enough to gain powerful friends, the English seemed to have been resident just long enough to make powerful enemies.

The compound of the German community in Novgorod lay, along with all the wooden houses and sheds of the merchant population of the city, on the trade side of the Volkhov bridge; the other half of this twin city being dominated by the cathedral, the archbishop's palace and court and the assembly hall of the free citizens of Novgorod.

For more than two hundred years the German traders had come in either summer or winter to the great capital of the northern forests. There they had established a trading settlement; in their own language a *kontore*.

Into the great nerve centre flowed the produce of all the outposts of Novgorod, scattered throughout the sprawling forest lands. And from it the Hanse distributed this northern treasure in return for salt and fish; in return for Flemish cloth and sweet wine and shining Prussian silver. And in two centuries of residence the Hanseatic traders had become a force in the Land of Darkness.

The complex of buildings, known from the dedication of its church as the 'Peterhouse', lay under the same heavy mantle of white which swaddled the whole of the city. In the drifting snow it was easy to suppose that all its inhabitants were safely closeted within its timber-walled buildings. But eyes were always watching from the stockade of the Peterhouse.

Before Curteys and Thymelby reached the gate they were met by fur-swathed, armed guards. It was obvious that they were expected. The Finn consulted with the Germans.

'They say that they will take our message to the alderman. We are to wait here for his reply.'

The two Boston merchants were not used to being kept waiting at the best of times. To be kept outside in the freezing air and by the Easterlings of all people was galling. They stamped their feet in annoyance and the English archers cast aggressive and insolent looks at the Hanseatic soldiers. They were met with expressions no less belligerent and mocking eyes peered over the tops of cloths tied across the cold faces of the German guards.

At last the reply came. 'We are invited to attend on the alderman.' The Finn gestured in the direction of the open gates.

'About bloody time too,' Thymelby muttered through frozen lips. 'About bloody time . . .'

Inside the stockade were crammed an odd assortment of buildings: stables, warehouses, huts and church. From the bars across the tightly shuttered windows of one log cabin it was clear that one of the buildings also served as a gaol. A drunken voice crooned from within; some hesitant carol in the rolling accent of the north German plains.

The alderman – heavily built and bearded like a Russian – was waiting for them in a sparsely furnished room. Birch-bark account rolls lay scattered over a wide table. From the styli beside them it was obvious that he had been disturbed in the middle of transcribing accounts.

A great fire burnt on fire-dogs in the centre of the room and the air was thick with woodsmoke as it reluctantly meandered upwards towards the louvre, fractionally open in the roof. Still the room was cold. Breath made a pale mist; a physical symbol of their host's intangible speech. Great baskets of logs stood against one wall. Beside them a wolfhound lay sprawled in elongated repose. It opened its yellow eyes to take in the strangers.

'You know why we have come?' Curteys was unusually blunt.

The Finn began his translation but the alderman waved him aside. 'I speak English good enough. Often I am coming to London. It is a fine city. As fine as my native Lübeck.'

Neither Curteys nor Thymelby seemed impressed by what was obviously meant as a compliment.

'We have reason to believe that some of your men are stirring up the mob against us.' Curteys ignored the deliberate look of horror which slowly spread over the Lübeck merchant's face. 'They say that we are spies for the Tartars. They incite the rough against our property and our lives . . .'

'Evidence you have?' The German licked his heavy lips. 'Evidence you have laid before the city council?'

'We have and they instructed us to lay the matter before you.'

'Ahh . . .' The alderman sighed as if to say: not enough evidence, eh? Well, what a pity . . .

Thymelby took up the case gruffly. 'And we

demand that you take action against these dogs. If you don't, we will . . .'

'Ahh . . .' the alderman sighed again. 'But the city authorities would disapprove of such an action. It would be . . . so regrettable.' He smiled and stroked the beard which rolled down on to his chest. 'Most regrettable, I am thinking.'

Curteys bit down on an angry reply to match Thymelby's irritation. 'We come to you as honourable men, seeking redress. There is more than enough trade in this city for all of us. We do not threaten you. The archbishop himself told me you shipped out over two hundred thousand pelts last year alone. Nothing that we do threatens you. We do not intimidate and do not expect to be intimidated.'

The representative of Lübeck refused to be nettled by this semi-accusation. 'Of course not, of course not.' His voice had a hollow note. 'If any of our men are being found guilty of such a crime we would of course take action. We will take action.' He smiled and raised open hands in a gesture of transparent honesty. 'You may trust me; as one honest man may trust another. For it is wickedness to accuse fellow members of Holy Church of duplicity with the Tartar sons of Satan.'

'Quite.' William's voice was toneless.

The alderman picked up a stylus and began to scratch figures on a strip of bark. He glanced up. 'You want more of me, brothers?' The dismissal was so obvious it belied all the fellow-feeling central to his speech so far. 'For I must complete these accounts before dark. You know how it is . . .'

Curteys nodded stiffly. Thymelby made as if to say something then at the last moment changed his mind.

Outside where the swaddled archers were shivering in the snow he was more forthright.

'You know that that bugger is behind it all! All that shit about "one honest man to another". The bastard was laughing in our faces. We can't let him get away with it. You know that?'

Curteys nodded. 'I have no intention of letting him off the hook. But we've done all that the council told us to do. Now it's up to him. If he can't – or rather will not – control his men, we will have to.'

'Meaning what?' Thymelby's hand was clenching and unclenching. Snowflakes froze on his cheeks. 'Meaning what?'

'Meaning whatever is necessary to protect our lives, reputation and property . . .'

William was deliberately vague. He was not yet sure what they could do. He was all too well aware that an angry move on the part of the English would place them in jeopardy before the city authorities. He would have to think this out very carefully.

And Thymelby would have to watch his temper. As for the women and the child: they were useless in such a situation. Their presence only gave more things to worry about. He gazed upwards into the white canopy of sky. Why was providence testing his patience so? He wished that he knew.

As they bent their backs and lowered their heads against the driving snow the German guards watched them from the closing gates of the Peterhouse. One said something coarse and the other pulled down his face-cloth and laughed crudely. But the sound only swept away in the streaming white air. The objects of their humour vanished into the snow and night of early afternoon; vanished like the mocking laughter.

The Christmas feast passed in bitter frost and heavy snow. The New Year brought little respite from the aching cold and beneath layer on layer of fur the English shivered within their compound.

Yet the work went on. Wax and pelts were checked and purchased and on more than one occasion Isabelle repeated her success with the fine quality furs and the well-priced wax. She was beginning to feel quite confident again, despite the irritatingly grudging praise of her male companions. Time and again she met the wax merchants after mass in the cathedral and haggled and flirted in a strangely detached way through the person of her Finnish interpreter. And if once she had felt shame at such brazen confidence she felt it no longer.

It gave her particular pleasure to prove herself after the near disaster on the river. The embarrassment of that had hung over her all winter: she had told Curteys that she was not a liability and yet the plunge into the Volkhov had seemed to underscore all of his doubts. Often when she was alone her mind would return to the incident. Always the memory left her feeling foolish and vulnerable. It would have surprised her companions if they had been able to read her thoughts. She never came across as a person who dwelt on her failures. They would never have guessed at the cross-currents which eddied beneath the smooth surface of her outward appearance.

It was with special energy that she threw herself into the purchases of the goods they so desired. It was something to set in the balance against her supposed weakness, something to make William Curteys sit up and take notice, to reassure her that she really was up to the great task that she had taken on.

And with each little triumph, Isabelle became more and more convinced that she could succeed in this world of male merchants. But her doubts she kept to herself. All were entrenched behind the mask she had spent a lifetime manufacturing to hide her emotions from the eyes of men.

On one particularly bright morning she found herself before the towering wooden stockade of the kremlin of Novgorod. She gazed in wonder at the great trunks bound together in the fortification. Never in her life had she seen anything to match the mighty defences of the city. Beside the large planks of Novgorod the boundaries of Boston appeared pathetic in the extreme.

It had not snowed for some days. What snow there was on the ground was now firmly packed underfoot. In places the passing of sledges had pressed and polished the surface of the ice. Isabelle trod carefully to avoid sliding on the treacherous surface.

'I have never seen so much snow,' she confided to the Finn. 'The winters at home are a child's play compared to this. How long will the snow last?'

'Until March – and then mud everywhere . . .'

'The roads at home turn to mud about then too.'

'But are these roads of yours rivers of mud? Oceans of mud?' The Finn smiled. 'For here it is mud by the river. You have never seen the like.'

Isabelle was willing to believe him. There was much here the like of which she had never seen. In fact the whole city was a source of constant wonder to her. Its sounds and smells excited her and at times unnerved her. Never though was she unmoved by them. When she had time to think about it she rejoiced that she had come to this place. She would never forget it. It had repaid all her hopes. Just to say that she had been there would silence many who doubted her abilities. She took strength from that thought.

For a few moments she stopped and watched a group of people who had come in from the country. They were unloading a reindeer sledge, a beast strange to Isabelle. With interest she watched as it stood patiently in the harness. The street here was wider than most in the city. The plank-built houses stood a little further back from one another. It was a space which spoke of affluence. The extra room had given the reindeer leeway to turn before an open gateway into a stockade.

'It is a beautiful animal,' she remarked. The reindeer tossed its antlered head. 'Very lovely.'

'You should try such a sledge!' The Finn laughed at the thought. 'When two beast pull they need a strong hand.' He parted his hands as a demonstration. 'They pull wherever they want, by God. A strong hand is needed. Strong indeed.'

One of the country people – a lad of about twelve – smiled readily at Isabelle. Like the others by the sledge he was blond with green eyes. He could have been Isabelle's child. The thought struck her, as she smiled back at him, rather sadly.

'Where are they from?' She was curious.

The Finn reeled off a string of Russian words and the lad answered him in a clear and musical voice.

Isabelle would have loved to have heard him sing.

'They are from a village far to the north. Deep in the forests. Many Novgorod merchants own estates in the forests. They live on one, around a great lake. They are far from home today . . .'

'Why are they here?' Isabelle asked. 'What are they carrying in the bales?'

The Finn relayed her question. The boy laughed and pointed to a pile of nets on the rear of the sledge.

'Ahh, *bobrovaia lovishcha*?' the Finn asked.

When the boy nodded, he replied to Isabelle, 'The nets are beaver traps. These bring in the year's rent to the boyar who is lord of their village. The rent is beaver pelts.'

'What is it like living in the forests?' Isabelle's appetite was whetted.

'Wild it is there. They are many miles from nearest village. The forest spreads like an ocean. It is trackless and beyond count. In it live many things so strange.' He paused as he recalled the stories. 'Men who serve their children as feasts to strangers . . .'

'No!'

'And stranger too. Others without mouths and others with no heads. Mouths only between their shoulders and eyes on chests.'

Isabelle had heard tales of monsters before. 'And have you seen them, these men without heads?'

The guide frowned. 'Not I, but I know men who say they have.' When Isabelle looked disappointed he added: 'The forest holds many things. Many strange things. Many terrible things.'

Suddenly Isabelle was glad to be within the walls of the city. Beyond, the dark forest pressed close, but within, the sounds of human voices drowned out the echoing cries of beasts beyond description. It was good to be about the business that she understood, a fragment of the familiar amidst a land strange and dark.

The kremlin, near which Isabelle Crosse stood, was the heart of the cathedral side of the city. Within it the mighty cathedral of St Sophia rose in incense and praise to God. Once more Isabelle had come to meet her wax merchant near this great house of litany and light. Around the kremlin ran a moat, now hidden in snow. Between the walls of the kremlin and the outer defences, residential areas of close-packed wooden houses clustered around the onion-domed churches.

It was at a crowd of houses about a little courtyard that she stopped. Bearded retainers met her at the gateway. She was expected and as she entered the house an elderly women rose and blessed her. A servant came bearing little flat cakes of bread and salt. Behind him the bearded merchant bowed before the guest from across the sea.

At once they got down to business. The room was full of noise and smoke but over the platter of radishes and boiled eggs the two merchants haggled. Midway through their deliberations the bearded Russian called for thimbles of a fiery liquid which burnt Isabelle's throat with its alien heat.

'Ahh . . .' she spluttered. 'If only Nicholas Coppledyke could see me now . . .'

'Please?' The guide heard her words and did not understand them. 'Who is this "couple deck"?'

Isabelle laughed. 'Someone in another world . . .' She raised her thimble cup to the Russian who beamed approvingly and raised his in return. A thimbleful of this man's hospitality would swamp all the warmth that wretch Coppledyke could muster in his mean lifetime, Isabelle thought as she toasted the Russian.

There was something so immediate and spontaneous about the people of Novgorod. An uncontained warmth, quite unlike anything she had previously experienced in Boston. It won her over and at times she found her mask was slipping. She suddenly did not care.

The business was soon concluded to the mutual satisfaction of both parties. It was left to Isabelle's attendants to convey the straw-packed boxes back over the Volkhov bridge to the trade side of the city on the understanding that Isabelle would follow a little later. Before she left, the merchant insisted that she eat a more substantial meal. In the hall the retainers danced: a folkdance which the Finn told her was known in Russian as *ksenovia*. It was full of simple steps and Isabelle was invited to join in. At first hesitant, she at last succumbed to the insistent cries. To the amusement of all present the heavy-bearded merchant took his guest through the unfamiliar steps of the quadrille.

It was something she would normally never have done; but so disarming was the charm and warmth of her Russian hosts Isabelle could only enjoy the sensation of no longer being on her guard. It was with some regret that she finally took her leave.

When she arrived back at the English lodging she found William Curteys inspecting the crates. Straw was tumbled on to the cold clay floor of the storage shed and he was kneeling and handling the wax. In the weak sunshine his well-formed profile reminded Isabelle of why the servant girls became tongue-tied in his presence. He was a good-looking man; there was no denying it. Better looking than her husband had been. William looked up and she blushed. Could he read her thoughts? The very possibility made her cheeks taut.

'What do you think?' She quoted the price and her voice was controlled and cool. He could not stifle the look of approval. 'I think it is a good price,' she asserted.

'It is good,' was all he would say in reply.

Isabelle sighed. It seemed that the more she proved herself the more he resented it. She left him and went to warm herself in the house. She could not deny that she felt a twinge of disappointment. She had hoped for more from him and it angered her that she had wanted more. Had she not been so foolish, his attitude would not have nettled her.

Behind, in the shed, William replaced the cakes of wax within the straw. As he shut the lid he could not but feel respect for her judgement. It had been a good price for top quality merchandise. He could not have done better. Yet he could not admit it to her. He frowned as he stood up. If he did so there would be no stopping her.

Something troubled him whenever she appeared nowadays. He could not put his finger on it but neither could he deny it. Whatever it was it disconcerted him. It had never happened before, when Tony was alive. So what was it now? He rubbed his beard with annoyance. William Curteys was not used to being disconcerted.

As January gave way to February, news filtered into the city of Tartar preparations for the coming campaigning season. Already the Grand Dukes of Riazan and Suzdal had made grovelling approaches to their Tartar overlords in order to fend off destruction.

In the English quarter the merchants discussed the likely implications of the coming war. A Tartar success was sure to result in heavy taxation of the city. Traditionally Novgorod paid the tax known as the 'Black Collection', levied on top quality pelts. The seizure of pelts by the city authorities would inflate prices. More than this the whisperers were once again at work. In the streets and market-places it was said that the English were the agents of the khan himself.

The matter came to a head through the unlikely offices of Gosse, the archer. It was Tuesday 11 February 1382. The fact that the day was the feast of the Blessed Saint and Martyr Vlasij of Sebaste was totally lost on the archer. The animal sacrifices associated with the saint excited no curiosity in Gosse's mind, only his usual disgust and contempt for the alien and unknown. He ignored the bleating and mooing and kicked his way through the drifts. At least the snow had stopped.

He was on his way from a visit to a whore, a very compliant teenager with – to Gosse – an unpronounceable name. But Gosse never was interested in their names, only in what tricks they would perform for half a silver Prussian mark.

This obedient teenager was now nursing her bruises and a bloody lip in a dirty little hut beside the bridge over the Volkhov, and trying to decide if the humping had been worth the silver. Gosse had some disturbing tastes. One of them was violent rape. When he could not do it for free he was prepared to expend a little of his earnings in order to gratify his lusts. In his opinion the whore had been worth the money. He would patronise her services again – soon.

In his frenzied bursts of sexual activity Gosse was aware of a persistent fantasy which dominated his thoughts at the moment of sexual climax. While the writhing whore squirmed and cried beneath him, he was back in the alleyway off Strait Bargate. The Boston night was close about him like a dark gauntlet. And Isabelle Crosse was pierced and entered beneath him.

It was unusual for the archer's thoughts to be dominated by one woman. He pondered the emergence of this new phenomenon as he stepped out of the way of a heavily loaded dog sledge. The central role of Isabelle in his contrived rapes of the prostitutes took him a little by surprise. He mused on the matter. It was strange. Perhaps he was falling in love, he thought.

The Russian prostitutes were not the only ones left ruing the acts of sexual violence perpetrated by the Englishman. Their pimps were beside themselves with fury: the archer's peculiarities were leaving the merchandise badly used and well worn and they had decided to teach the English archer a lesson he would not forget. As Gosse walked down the street he was tailed by a shadowy figure.

Already he was late, as he had been instructed to meet Curteys and Thymelby just after twelve. Then the two merchants were due to meet Isabelle at the northern end of the Volkhov bridge in the early afternoon. Ostensibly Gosse was out on an errand for his mistress but whenever he was able, he stretched out these little perks to cover his other activities.

Luckily for him the two Boston merchants had been delayed in their business. The party of English archers were still standing in the snow when Gosse arrived at the appointed rendezvous: a honey merchant's house nestled up against the high wooden walls of the city. At least the close proximity of the stockade kept off the worst of the biting northern wind.

'Where've you been, Gosse? Nicked anything nice?' one of the others asked.

'Yeh, Gosse. Where 'ave you been? You're a soddin' waste as a soldier.'

Gosse sneered. 'Had a good morning, lads? Carried any interesting bales of cloth?' He laughed at their bitterness. 'Done any good "soldiering"?' He smirked at the second fellow who had cast aspersions on his activities.

Before the argument could develop, the Boston merchants and their Finnish translator re-emerged from the relative warmth of the Russian hall. From within came the twang of the gusli – the stringed musical instrument beloved of the tellers of Russian epic poetry.

Both merchants smelled of sweet German wine and appeared in good humour. Obviously the transaction had gone well. The archers stamped their feet and breathed misty life into cupped and frozen hands. At last it was time to get going.

The snow had begun to fall once more. As Curteys and Thymelby led the way towards the cathedral half of the city the trouble started. A group of well-wrapped Russians began to call names after them. Their tone spelled trouble and the Finn fought to catch the drift of their words. Finally Curteys turned to face them. He was sick and tired of the damned Easterlings and their stirring up of the Novgorod rough. By his side Thymelby was struggling with his furs; reaching for his dagger.

Hard, iced snowballs were pelted at them. They stung as they struck against the face and head. Thymelby was cursing; he pulled on his weapon. The archers moved forward to shield their masters. More toughs were emerging from dim side-alleys. Some were holding knives. The situation was beginning to get very ugly.

Kicking open the gate of a roadside building the English poured into the sanctuary, slamming the broken door behind them. Inside was the familiar smell of dampness and animal urine: two scrawny milking cows occupied stalls along the far wall, casting great liquid eyes at the intruders.

'Watch out.' Thymelby shouted the warning as a head appeared through a swinging shutter. 'Watch that bastard.'

A heavy Finnish fist slammed against the skull and it dropped back out of sight. The archers were holding the door shut. It whined and creaked on its hinges as bodies cannoned against it from the outside. The badly rusted hinges groaned terminally.

Curteys examined the byre for a back exit. There was another door but it obviously led into the house and it was heavily barred on the inside. Try as he might he could not shift the thing.

'No good, no good,' the Finn insisted. 'Locked . . .'

Outside the mob was howling like a pack of wolves. *En masse* they fell upon the door in a frenzy.

'I'll kill that damned alderman,' Thymelby promised his companion. 'I'll ram that pen up his arse, the treacherous pig.'

A heavy plank was smashed through a shuttered window. The remains of the shutter swung in white gashed tatters. A body attempted to enter. A broken lump of wood was thrust into the howling face. Blood poured from the shattered nose and with screams the broken face fell outside.

'We'll not hold this door much longer,' one of the archers called.

Thymelby stood facing the splintering door and jutted out his close-clipped chin. 'Let the buggers in. I'm ready for them . . .'

A single, low-pitched note hummed instantly in the air. An animal shriek rose in a desperate throat; a throat beyond the door. More screams ripped from panicked mouths as the air was full of the familiar sound of goose-feathered shafts. The pressure on the door was gone. The assault had collapsed, apparently in a rout.

The archers clambered up to the shutters to peer outside.

'Well I'll be damned . . .'

'Yes, Gosse. You undoubtedly will.'

Curteys elbowed the heavy-faced archer out of the way. He hissed as he saw the scene in the street. At least five bodies lay huddled. Startling crimson blood stained the snow. He raised his eyebrows at the figure who stood behind the dead at the head of the remainder of the English archers.

'It's all right now, Will. They have gone.'

It would be a long time before he would forget those words of Isabelle Crosse. They were more chilling than the wind which sought to carry them away. He had been rescued by a woman; the very woman whom he had been on his way to meet. Behind him Thymelby swore. This would take a lot of living down. Will Curteys swallowed very hard. Behind Curteys the barrel-bodied Finn was grinning at the unexpected sight.

Isabelle's cool rescue of her partner notwithstanding, the situation in Novgorod was getting more uncomfortable. The slaughter caused by the English archers was hardly popular amongst the citizens of the city and it had provided support for the more discreet antagonistic policies of the Militia Commander which otherwise would have been above the heads of most Novgorodites!

At a lengthy confabulation the Boston merchants agreed that it would be wise to leave the city before the snows melted. The stores of merchandise bought over the winter could be shipped out by Russian carriers when the rivers unfroze. Boyars, en route to Visby and Gotland, were happy to be paid for the transportation of the English merchandise to Riga.

'There should be no problem,' Curteys rubbed his cold hands as his companions crowded about a flaming fire. 'For whilst the Easterlings handle most of the carrying trade, there are still trustworthy

Russians who go with their goods to the towns of the Hanse.' He smiled before he concluded. 'And there is a sweet irony: I have contracted with Isabelle's wax merchant. He goes this summer with the ambassador of Novgorod to Lübeck on a trade delegation. They will travel on German ships . . .'

'But surely—' Eleanor made as if to interrupt him.

He anticipated her concern. 'They'll not harm our goods. Nor will they refuse to carry them. They do not have the right.' He gave a slight smile at the thought of how much this would irritate the alderman from Lübeck and all at the Peterhouse. 'Since our King Henry's time the Easterlings have been bound by treaty to carry the ambassador of Novgorod and his merchants and their goods. It's a rule well-founded, more than a century old now.'

'And if they refuse?' Isabelle was intrigued.

'If they refuse, then Novgorod will deny all responsibility for their safety as they travel the route between the Gulf of Finland and here. You see, they have no choice! And the boyars of Novgorod may pay to carry as much merchandise as there is room. It suits this one to make a little extra money from the journey by carrying our goods as far as Riga.'

The two of them grinned, united by their pleasure at the thought. It was a very satisfying turn of events indeed.

'While we return overland?' This time Isabelle's voice was more thoughtful. Outside a cold wind howled about the house.

'That is so.' William nodded to Thymelby who rolled out a thin scroll of birch bark under the watchful gaze of the Finn who had helped him compile its contents. 'Adam has the details.'

Thymelby gestured to the guide to hold down one end of the bark. Isabelle and Eleanor looked with interest at the ink squiggles painted on the smooth surface.

Thymelby traced one scarred finger over the map. 'We travel by sledge, of course. I have contracted for a total of four dog sledges for the journey. There are always plenty of dog teams to choose from. They regularly carry the Easterlings: as many of them come and go in the winter by dog, as do in the summer by ship. Travel by dog also frees us from the tolls we would have to pay if we travelled out by river-boat.'

The Finn coughed; he had in fact done all the work. Thymelby ignored him and continued: 'We shall travel through Novgorod territory as far as Pskov.' He touched an ochre dot somewhere to the south-west of Novgorod. 'There is food and shelter there. The Easterlings – God rot them – have a minor base there. Then—' his finger carried them westward over crudely represented low hills – 'we shall cross the Livonian Heights – ignore the lakes on this map as they will all be frozen – and so to Riga. And from Riga we will be under protection of the order once more. Your province, Isabelle . . .' He smirked at her but she ignored the blatant reference to her relationship with von Fellin.

It all sounded very easy. Thymelby's finger had completed the journey in under a minute. The Finn looked less complacent: it was he who had compiled the map and, where Thymelby's finger glided over empty spaces, the guide's experienced eyes saw two hundred miles of forest dark at noon and frozen clearings haunted by the cries of the night-running wolves.

Eleanor too was looking at the map thoughtfully. She was the veteran of many journeys and was not impressed by Thymelby's confidence. She had seen enough gaps on maps transform themselves into heart-stopping obstacles in real life. She noted the serious look on the face of the Finn and concluded that her misgivings had foundation. Nevertheless she held her peace.

'And we should leave soon?' Isabelle queried.

Thymelby nodded at the Finn who answered her: 'Before this week ends, for cold as the weather is, come late March and the land now frozen will turn to mud. No good for sledges.' As the day was Tuesday 11 February, there was little time left.

William Curteys read the thoughts of his companions. 'We shall eat Valentine's feast on Friday and go this coming Saturday. We shall leave the carrying of our merchandise as a love token for the Easterlings!'

All present laughed at Will Curteys' little joke, though Eleanor's eyes reflected troubled thoughts. Only the Finn did not join in the laughter. He was looking intently at the birch-bark map; gazing with concern at the gaps over which Thymelby had travelled with such ease.

The weather held and Curteys' predicted departure date was met without incident. All the furs and boxes of wax were left in the secure care of the boyar contracted to the English, a deposit of Prussian silver marks, with more to follow when the goods had been safely transported to Riga, ensuring their safety.

Along with the trade goods all superfluous items were left behind. There was little room for luxuries on a dog sledge. Isabelle however had been careful to pack some changes of clothing in a large leather scrip bought in Novgorod market from one of the Lübeck Easterlings. It was larger than the one owned by Eleanor, and Isabelle had taken care to secure it with a criss-cross of stout twine. She kept the bulky parcel close to her breast and personally supervised its lashing on to the sledge. She had not brought the cotte of Venetian wool velvet all these miles to leave it in a Russian storehouse. It lay within the pack in folds of deepest purple and within its heart was hidden the sheer lawn wimple of milk pale linen.

Curious, William Curteys watched Isabelle's scrutiny of the parcel. He wondered how a woman could take such an inordinate interest in a travellers' pack: his own personal collection of leather beaker, knife, flat cakes of bread and hard grey cheese was strapped under the tents and the bundle of leather milk flasks. But before he could ask her why she was so concerned, his attention was seized by more pressing matters.

The Engish party left Novgorod in the grey light of mid-morning. The *furka*, or dog sledge, was cramped to put it mildly. Isabelle, Eleanor and Eve travelled with the Finnish guide; Curteys and Thymelby shared their transport with Isabelle's guardian archer and one other of the bowmen. The remaining four soldiers cursed and froze on the third sledge; the fourth vehicle was reserved for bulky packs and the tents. Ahead of each sledge the thirteen dogs raced in a pink-tongued, yapping fan; each secured to the sledge by a separate trace. Behind them a thin spray of fine snow coated passengers and packs in a veil of freezing white.

From the city the route lay to the south-west, through deep-piled woods of winter conifers interspersed with the occasional thicket of beech and oak. The shadowy cloak of trees stretched away into white-rimmed shadows, which allowed no glimpse of any horizon. From the dark branches icicles hung in convoluted shapes; inverted castellated battlements and silver turrets which tinkled and broke as the barking dogs passed. And as the sledges vanished the forest once more smothered the sound in a suffocating silence of crushing cold.

Isabelle and Eve sat swaddled on their sledge. As the young woman gazed into the black depths of the woods she could not help but remember the tales told by the guide. How different this journey was from ones undertaken in Lincolnshire. Where was the vast, beautiful horizon and the sweep of the sky? Where were the little villages on the islands at the fen edge? Here there was only mile on mile of shadows beneath the suffocating trees. No human voice broke the stillness; at night wolves bayed beyond the firelight. It was a terrible place.

To keep up their spirits, Eleanor recounted tales of storm-tossed sea voyages to the Holy Land and blistering hot miles of desert. Isabelle felt encouraged by the thought that her friend had come through such in the past; it was not too much to expect their own deliverance from the dark woods. Even so there were hours before dawn – as the forest pressed close, like a cold hand – when she could not ignore her own fears.

It took just over a week for the party to reach the Russian trading city of Pskov. Along the way they camped in the shelter of the woods and once took refuge in a tiny hamlet known to their guide. At Pskov they rested in a cramped inn. The fur rugs on the communal beds were greasy and the great mattresses stank of sweat and urine. The beds, sleeping ten apiece, were crowded into one ill-lit and unventilated room over the stables. For the sake of propriety one was for the use of males, the other for females. Each contained a motley crew of naked travellers.

There was nothing in Pskov to tempt the English merchants to extend their stay. Only Gosse and one other of the archers succeeded in slipping away long enough to get a little physical exercise in a hole of a brothel. Even there the facilities were sparse; Gosse and his mate had to share the same fat Russian whore. The experience only served to heighten, rather than assuage his lust for his mistress.

On Sunday 23 February, the English fasted in honour of St Matthias and in support of their prayers for a safe journey on to Riga. The next day – the feast day of the saint – they continued their journey. The sky was lead-grey. Despite the lateness of the season it looked as if more snow was coming. The Finn sniffed the air and frowned.

After Pskov the land rose slightly on to the range of low hills marked on Thymelby's birch-bark map: the Livonian Heights, a rolling countryside of pine and birch dotted with numerous small lakes, now frozen over.

Two days out of Pskov they dropped down to the flank of one of the frozen sheets of water. It was late afternoon and night was closing in. From the distance came the otherworldly howls of a wolf pack. Set back from the lakeside was a little settlement. It was made up of a battered collection of buildings. Each *izba*, or log-house, was half covered by drifts of snow. One of the houses looked a little more prosperous than the rest, its dove-tailed wooden walls set on a brick-built storage floor.

The sledges arrived with the usual herald of barking, yet no one appeared to greet the arrival with bread and salt. No smoke drifted from the wadding-clad timber roofs. No human sound broke the crystal silence; only the dogs barked. The settlement seemed quite deserted.

Led by the Finn, who knew this village of forest people, each house was searched. Some were stripped bare. In others were personal possessions laid neatly on the meagre furniture. But of the occupants there was no sign. The place was as silent as the grave. It was, Isabelle concluded with fear in her heart, as if it had been evacuated in a tremendous hurry, as if a terror had driven the people away.

It was getting dark, so the party took up residence in the larger of the log-houses. Outside, in the space between the buildings, the sledge drivers were feeding handfuls of frozen fish to their canine companions. The dogs gulped them down: head, backbone, tail and all. Then they all sat back on their haunches, little pink tongues licking black lips. The Finn watched them, oblivious of Isabelle's approach.

'Why is this place deserted? You did not expect it to be, did you?'

The guide turned. 'I do not know why . . .' He was

very pensive. 'This is a village of southern Ests.' Isabelle nodded, she recalled how he had referred to the Ests as they had sailed into the Gulf of Finland. 'They hunt for furs and collect wax and honey and fish the lake.' He gestured to where the expanse of ice was fast receding into darkness. 'I have been here before, many times. Both with Hanse merchants and with the order. I know these people . . .'

'So where are they now?'

He shrugged. 'Where are they?' The watching dogs gave no reply. 'I do not know.'

For a few moments he watched as the last of the dogs were untied from the tangled leather traces. He scratched at his beard. There was a pricking on his thumbs that he did not like. 'I saw this once before. It is possible that . . .'

But Isabelle had slipped away and was already ascending the steps into the log-house. The Finn shrugged; perhaps it was all for the best. He had no real evidence to substantiate his fears. Yet, he still pondered and stood watching the lake as night fell.

Gosse slept badly that night. He was consumed with lust. The whore at Pskov had done nothing to reduce the throbbing fire within him. He wanted Isabelle and he could wait no longer. When at last he got up he was sweat-streaked with frustration.

The next morning it became apparent that some stranger had returned to the settlement during the night. The lower storeroom had been broken into and a large quantity of the dried cheese, hazel-nuts and beech kernels stolen. William was furious. He ordered the archers to get their bows; to follow the trail leading off into the forest. Curteys, Thymelby and the guide pulled on their long fur coats. Leaving Gosse and another of the archers behind with the Russian dog-men, the muffled party set off in pursuit of the thieves.

Gosse was delighted: here, he saw, was an opportunity too good to miss. Away from the village lay a small barn, on the very edge of the cleared ground of the village. It was the usual arrangement with a loft above the stalls for animals on the ground floor. He had checked it out well. His only problem lay in getting Isabelle there unobserved. Eleanor was busy checking items in the plundered storeroom while Eve pottered on the threshold catching up handfuls of soft snow. Isabelle was with Eleanor. Sauntering over to the doorway Gosse smiled at the child. He hated children but his plan hung on the goodwill of this one. Raising hands to his head he waggled extended ears. 'Rabby . . . rabby . . .'

Eve was delighted at the archer's imitation of one of the white hares they had glimpsed in the woods. Gosse grinned at the little girl's response. He had watched the two women teaching the girl the name of the animal, planning for an opportunity such as this. Silently he beckoned to her to come with him. She hesitated then tottered forward and he began to hope.

'Come on you little bastard.' The sound escaped his lips. Eve looked thoughtful. Biting back on his disgust he changed his tone: 'Rabbit . . . rabbit. You come with me. I'll show you rabbit.'

It took a long time to gain the child's trust and at

any moment he expected to be discovered. Rage, fear, hope and lust boiled within him. At last she consented to follow him slowly, very slowly. He struggled to master his gnawing impatience.

Across the yard they hopped in between the buildings. No longer could they be seen from the storeroom door. Eve hesitated and looked back.

'Rabbit . . . rabbit . . . this way.' Gosse hopped and the movement excited the hardness between his legs. 'Rabbit . . . rabbit . . . this way, you bastard.'

Slowly but surely they made their way to the barn but once inside Eve became unsure, turning to go back. Gosse grabbed her and she cried. He struck her on the head: she screamed. He hit her harder – silence. Then he threw her into one of the stalls.

Now all depended on Isabelle. Gosse could scarcely contain his excitement. Soon enough, as he had planned she missed the child. He could hear the sounds of the search within the storeroom becoming more urgent. Soon the two women were hunting about the yard, in the snow, but Gosse had taken care to criss-cross it with trampled footprints. They found no clues there as he sauntered towards them, carrying his bow and quiver.

'Gosse, have you seen the child?' Isabelle was already worried. He could sense the tension in her voice.

'By Our Lady, no. Is she lost?'

Isabelle nodded.

'I'll help you look, madam.' She was really grateful, he could see that.

Together they searched the nearest house. Eleanor was exploring elsewhere. This was Gosse's chance.

'Have you tried the barn? She could be in the barn,' he suggested.

Together they hurried towards the edge of the forest. Gosse could hardly believe his luck as he fingered the long blade of the knife in his pocket. When he had finished with her she would not be talking, and they would blame the thieves who had raided the storeroom. More than that he could not plan. He only knew that he wanted one thing and it was within his grasp.

Inside the barn the air was scented with the smell of crushed straw and cattle. Isabelle moved anxiously from stall to stall, halting to strain at the tiny sound of the whimpering child. Gosse lay down his bow and gripped his knife. So he had not hit her hard enough. He would have to use his knife on both of them. He pushed the door shut and wedged it with a piece of wood he had brought for the purpose.

He came on Isabelle from behind, clamping one hand over her opening mouth, stifling her cry of surprise. The other hand clutching the knife, swung round her waist like a vice. He wrestled her to the floor.

She struggled and writhed but his hand stayed clamped over her mouth. Releasing the knife he tore at her clothes with wild fury. He felt his hardness pushed against her thigh. So did she and she bit down on his hand as she had in the alley off Strait Bargate.

Blood coursed over his fingers but it only fuelled his savage energy. His free hand was inside her robe thrusting towards her breasts. He felt her nipple against the palm of his hand and kneaded her breasts as he pumped himself against her thigh.

'Very nice!' he hissed in her ear. 'Very nice!' He dug his fingers into her breasts with exultation. 'And soon you'll get it – harder than you've ever had it . . .'

Outside, the snow was falling. Curteys and Thymelby had returned from two hours of fruitless searching. The tracks led deeper into the forest and threatened pursuers with an ambush. Both men were angry. When Eleanor ran to meet them and told them the news about Eve it did nothing to calm their annoyance.

As Curteys accompanied Eleanor, the archer who had been left with Gosse informed Thymelby that he had seen Isabelle and her bodyguard going in the direction of the barn. Thymelby nodded curtly and went after them. As he approached the door he heard strange noises from inside: panting and groaning laid over the sounds of a struggle. He was perplexed but not yet alarmed.

He tried the door. It would not move. He put his shoulder to it. It creaked but did not open. From within came the sound of a sharp slap and a hurried movement. His shoulder hit the wood and the wedge sprang out. He almost tumbled inside. He picked himself up and swore, taking a moment to adjust his eyes from the glare of the snow. Gosse stood in one corner, fumbling with his bow.

'What the bloody hell are you up to, Gosse?'

Then Thymelby saw the woman in the straw. Her clothing was in disarray; her breasts, red from Gosse's nails and teeth, exposed. She tried to pull herself up. Her cheek was marked by a weal.

Thymelby fumbled for his knife. The bastard was raping Isabelle. The blade swung forward and only then did he realise what the archer was doing – he had strung his bow. For an instant the Boston merchant hesitated. 'Curteys! Curteys!' he howled, then he sprang.

The arrow struck him square in the chest. The full force of the taut bow and the trained muscles of Gosse lay behind its flash of light. The iron head passed clean through Thymelby's body. He somersaulted backwards, his body scudding across the beaten earth floor. He was dead before he collided with the logs of the wall.

Gosse pulled another arrow from his quiver. Curteys' voice could be heard at the door. Gosse panted as he laid the bowstring along the notch in the end of the arrow. Blood dripped from his wrist. Fired without a leather guard the slap of the string had torn skin from his arm.

Curteys was through the door. Eve was wailing. Gosse raised his bow and as he did so a searing pain hacked open his left leg. The arrow missed Curteys and thudded into the wall. Gosse screamed like a wounded pig. His own blade was sunk haft-deep in his thigh and blood was pumping over the straw. Isabelle released the handle and spat into his contorted face.

Then Curteys reached him, knife in hand. The two rolled on the floor in a chaos of blood and dirty straw. Gosse bit William's hand and seized the released knife. The merchant grunted as the blade pierced his side but managed to butt the archer who jerked backwards, nose broken. Will butted him again. Gosse howled and fell on his wounded leg; the protruding knife twisted and he squealed. William Curteys linked his hands, bringing the combined fists down on the archer's jaw. Gosse's head snapped to one side and his body twitched and then lay still. His neck was broken.

By the time help arrived it was all over; William Curteys lay across Isabelle in a pool of his own blood; Eve was wailing as she fought to get over him to reach the crying woman.

Curteys had been stabbed in the side. He could be moved but only carefully. Despite his pain he gave orders for the women to go on with the three sledges. He and the guide would follow on the fourth sledge with two of the archers, when he was able.

A grateful Isabelle beseeched Curteys to let them stay with him but Curteys, weak but very lucid, would hear none of it. He had talked to the guide about the deserted village and wanted the women away as quickly as possible. Despite her concern for Curteys, Isabelle could have wept for joy when he insisted that she go. Every particle of her being screamed for escape from the village and the horror of the barn.

With great reluctance the rest of the party left while there was still afternoon light. They would have over an hour's travelling before the night's camp. The Finn gave orders to the sledge drivers to make for an estate of the order three days' travel away. There they would be reunited.

Isabelle felt desperately cold. She burrowed into the piled furs but found no consolation. It was as if part of her deepest being had been torn open, as if all her hopes to prove herself had been shattered. If she had ever felt vulnerable before, it was nothing compared to now. 'Oh my God,' she whispered softly to herself. 'Oh my God.'

Throughout her life she had striven to prove herself. Against all William's advice she had maintained her ability to face the unknown. Now two men lay dead and William was wounded. And all her confidence lay scattered over the bloody straw of the silent barn, scattered beside the body of the disgusting animal who had tried to violate her. She felt totally alone.

With one hand she reached for Eleanor. Over the bumping of the sledge, her companion felt the movement. Their hands locked and as the snow flew behind them, Isabelle closed her eyes. Curteys' pained face floated before her. Guilt as well as helplessness flooded over her and a tear froze on her cheek. Each bitterly cold yard, each snowy mile, took her away from the place of horror. Yet its miasma of fear followed her. When they at last stopped for the night it was a cheerless camp. Isabelle watched the archers gather wood for a fire and suddenly loathed them. Who else amongst them lusted for her like a beast?

That night the little sleep she gained was splintered into loose fragments by nightmares. Eve was frightened by the anguish of Isabelle and would not sleep. By dawn Eleanor was cradling both in her arms.

The next day they travelled until a snowy noontime break. Isabelle and Eve hunched by the fire as the Russians checked the leather traces of their dogs and threw them frozen fish to chew. Away from the clearing, shadows shifted amongst the watching trees.

Will Curteys had been shocked by the deathly pale face of Isabelle as the sledges pulled away. Inwardly he cursed the twisted corpse still sprawled in the bloodied barn. The speed of departure had left him almost no time to speak with Isabelle. He had surrendered her, battered and shivering, to the arms of Eleanor.

He felt a sense of guilt that he had not seen the danger that had stalked her. Within him boiled a mixture of anger and distress: anger that she had ignored all his advice and had thrown herself into a man's world of violence; distress that he had not protected her.

It was a new feeling for him. He felt responsible for her. He cursed the ridiculousness of it but could not quite dismiss it. And now she was gone. There was nothing he could do to protect any of them. The new-found feeling of helplessness depressed his spirit.

For another two days William rested and the guide attended to his wound. Together they discussed their fears.

'So it seems certain then: the forest people are in arms against the order?' William lay on his side as a bloody bandage was peeled off.

The Finn swabbed at the scar tissue already beginning to form around the thin, deep wound. 'It is what I fear. This village is deserted because they fear reprisals for something that they have done. I think they have gone deeper into the forests. And the anger of the order will be terrible. I have seen it.' He remembered scenes of butchery and shook his head. 'Believe me they will have reason to have fled.'

Curteys winced. 'And no more than they deserve for being ungrateful savages.'

The Finn's eyes narrowed at William's words. He

slapped on the replacement wad of cloth.

Curteys winced. 'For God's sake, go easy, man.'

The Finn repented of his anger. How could this foreigner know the truth? How the forest folk were hunted through the snow like mere hares, game to be slaughtered and hung up. The Finn had guided the order too many times. There was blood on his hands too. The horrible thought made him pause. With greater care he finished the dressing of the wound.

A week after they first arrived in the deserted village the last sledge left. That night they rested after a bare ten miles' travel, erecting their tent behind a screen of birch trees. William accepted the constraint imposed by darkness and his wounds with ill grace. He would not be content till they had joined the rest of the party.

That night the air was rank with the smell of wolves and none of the group slept well. They huddled about their fire and stared out into the night listening to the dogs barking at the moving shadows. In the snow the Finn traced out the way in which a wolf pack attacked a sledge; showing the party how they would come up on it from the front and flanks.

'And will they come against us?' William was pale from the short journey.

'Who knows. They may, unless they can find easier prey . . .'

Until the first reluctant light of dawn they crouched, eyes straining with the desperate fear of what lay behind the savage howls beyond the fire-light.

By the end of the next morning they knew why the wolves had not attacked. Some five miles further on, mutilated bodies lay over the snow-bound trail. The wreckage of two sledges lay smashed against the trees. Scattered clothing was stiff with frost.

Horrified, William recognised the face of one of the fenland archers, his teeth ground together in a mask of agony. A feathered shaft from a short bow protruded from his chest. Near him a knot of Russian sledge drivers lay in the twisted contortions of ice-sheened death. More arrows festooned their corpses.

The wolves had been active, for all the bodies bore the marks of their teeth and some frozen limbs were gnawed to the bone.

'Where are the women?' William's voice barely veiled his rage. 'Where are they?'

The Finn was busy amongst the trees. 'They took them this way. Two people struggling.' He pointed to a pattern of confused footprints leading off into the forest. 'There were maybe twenty who attacked them. But the trail is old; days old. Soon fresh snow will cover it entirely.'

A light snow was once again falling as they followed the trail. William thanked God that there had been no snow since the two women had left, or their trail would have vanished. Deeper into the forest they went, fearfully. The afternoon was twilight here and soon would succumb to night. The Russian sledge driver and the two archers were clearly afraid, following them reluctantly, starting at shadows.

The trail led through the trees to a simple crossing of paths in the wood. Beside the crossroad a stake was set up. What looked like a goat's skull was jammed on to the top and the stake was black with old blood.

'Jesus God, what is it?' asked Curteys, appalled.

'It is a sacrifice in honour of the wolf-god. The Ests also kill beasts to protect them from the anger of Mezavirs, the "Woodman" spirit who stalks the forest by night. This is a sacred place.' The guide peered about as if expecting some apparition to emerge from the close-crowding forest. 'You must wait here . . .'

Without a word the Finn lunged into the trees, deep-set in snow. He was gone some time. Curteys stamped his feet as he waited, aware of the soldiers' muttering. The sacrifice and the terrifying forest had quite unnerved them and the Russian kept crossing himself, Orthodox fashion. At last William could wait no longer. He went after the Finn.

From the track the ground sloped downhill. Soon it formed a natural and sheltered amphitheatre. The snow here was less deep. After a few minutes searching in the half-light, William broke into a clearing. In the centre a vast oak tree reared into the evening sky. It had obviously survived numerous lightning strikes and at its blackened foot the guide was leaning over a pile of rags.

'What is it?'

The Finn straightened up. His face was white. 'We must go back. Go back now.'

Curteys pushed passed him. The bundle of rags was tied to the tree and was blackened with fire.

'Good God . . .'

It was not a bundle but a person. Rusted links of mail and plate armour fused together by the heat of a conflagration. On top of the human debris sat a visored bascinet helmet.

'This is a sacred grove; sacred to their god Perkun, the lightning god. None may come here but the Ests.

229

And to this place they bring sacrifices . . .' His voice trailed away.

Curteys was levering up the rusted visor. 'Sweet Mary . . .' He stumbled backwards.

A grotesque face, half contorted skin and half white bone, stared from within the soot-crusted helmet.

'It's a knight. It's one of the order.'

Curteys could not wrench his gaze from the nightmare vision which leered at him in a mocking grimace of long-passed agony; yet suffering was still etched on the decomposed face as if pain had transcended the frailty of the crumbling flesh.

'Do not move. Keep absolutely still.' The Finn's visage was expressionless. 'The Woodman comes, with the dark . . .' His eyes flickered up towards the trees on the edge of the clearing, up to where half-seen shapes hovered in the gathering gloom.

Chapter 8

Within the log-built outhouse it was always semi-darkness. The heavy shutters were rarely moved and the occasional opening and shutting of the one door scarcely allowed the weak sunshine to penetrate the cold shadows. Inside, the room was piled with pelts in various stages of preparation and wooden barrels of beeswax.

William Curteys lay against one of the rough-hewn log walls. The dull pain in his side was there again; throbbing and pulsating. He felt sick. He moved a little to shift his weight but his movements were hampered by the iron chain which bound him to a wall-ring as surely as a draught animal within its stall.

He sighed and lay back once more. From the barrel behind his head came the familiar aroma of wax. It made him think of home. When he closed his eyes he could see the high altar of St Botolph's shimmering with light, its candles fluttering.

From outside the hut came the voices of women engaging in the preparation of the wax. Already the combs of last summer had been scraped and melted in hot water and now the women were engaged in straining off the wax from the last cask of melted comb and pressing the residue to extract every drop of the precious substance.

'They are busy today.'

William turned to where the Finn was chained in another corner of the room. 'And happy with it from the sound of it. Do you know what I was just thinking?'

The Finn shook his head. The movement could just be seen in the half light.

'These people probably produced the wax that we bought in Riga last September. By God, I'd wager that half the churches in the Parts of Holland and Kesteven have wax from here . . . Perhaps in Boston itself.'

'I do not know these places but it may be true.'

William paused to consider the situation. He leaned towards his companion. 'These people provide wax for the worship of Christendom while burning knights to death in honour of the devil. Now do you think that is ironic?'

The Finn grunted.

'And while Phillip Spayne prays for the soul of Tony Crosse I lie here beside the very wax that will light his prayers. And with that thing in the corner . . .'

The guide did not follow the sense of all that was said but he understood the last reference. 'They believe that it will tell them if we plan to escape. It is their eyes and ears in here.'

Both men looked to where a large green snake lay asleep on a cushion of hay in one corner. At dawn and dusk one of their captors came to feed the reptile on tit-bits and curds. The presence of the heathen beast disgusted William but in the weeks since his capture he had come reluctantly to accept its presence. More to the point he could do nothing about it even if he had wished to do so. The sacred snake possessed more freedom than he did.

'What will they do with us?' It was not the first time that he had asked this question. 'They have held us for almost three weeks now.'

For a few moments his companion considered the question. 'I think that they mean to hold us hostage against reprisals by the order. It has been more than four generations since the Danes and Germans crushed the Ests but still hatred for the order burns fiercely in the forests. That is why the Germans burn and destroy all the pagans who will not bow their necks. These people hold us to keep back the fury of the knights.'

'That is why we have not been killed?'

'I think so. They killed the soldiers and the Russians because they thought them of no account, but us they spared. They see that you are a wealthy man and me they spared to speak for them. All others they killed . . .'

'But you don't think they killed the women?'

'No, not the women, for they too are worth a ransom. They did not kill the women.' This was not the first time that he had reassured Curteys. It was clear that he cared more for his female companions than he had shown in the past. 'I think you need not fear for the women,' he reiterated. And then to shift the argument away he added, 'They hold dark-haired beasts sacred to their gods, so you they would kill first, not the mistress with the silver hair.'

'Thanks.' William's voice was rueful but he smiled. 'Thanks a lot.'

He could not bear it if Isabelle was dead. The realisation cut him open. She had to be alive, somewhere – the desperate hope flared within him and his pulse thumped wildly in his temples.

Later that day, when they were led out for their daily exercise, the Est women had gone and so had much of the snow. The sun was shining weakly and the earth was turning from white to a muddy slush. Here and there a brave frond of green ventured out from the receding snow.

William scratched at his untrimmed beard. 'It must be almost April,' he muttered to himself, 'I've lost track of the days . . .' Suddenly an Est, armed with a crude spear, was poking him, rudely ending his calculations.

Before nightfall the headman of the village came to see his prisoners. He was flanked by two of his young men, one of them wearing a torn English gambeson, the other proudly sporting a dented kettle-helmet. As usual William took the opportunity to complain about his still delicate wound and make an appeal for more water.

'*Haige . . . haige . . .*' he mumbled as he pressed his hand to his side. He had picked up the Estonian word for 'sick' from the guide. Now he redoubled his theatrical efforts. '*Haige . . . haige . . .*'

The grey-bearded headman ignored him totally and addressed himself to the Finn. A torrent of words passed between the two, all of which was lost on William Curteys. At last it was clear that the audience was over and the elderly Estonian turned to go. As he left he bent and whispered to the sentry snake which guarded the threshold. He also placed a morsel of bread on a little flat stone beside the door; a customary offering to the earth spirits. Then he was gone and the door was locked.

'He told the snake to guard us well. And he believes that the earth spirits will also assist him in gaining victory over the knights,' said the Finn.

William sighed. 'But the rest of it, man. What was all the talk about?'

'You saw he was agitated?'

Curteys nodded.

'Well, it seems that the order have burnt and totally destroyed two Estonian villages. Many women and children were killed. Crucified and burnt alive. The order have attacked before the snow goes. This way they can hunt the survivors and track them like hares.' The Finn paused to watch the effect of his story on his hearer. 'And they have seized two women and a child captured by the Ests. Yes – it must be our women.'

William could not have pronounced the word 'our' with more feeling himself. 'Thanks be to God,' he breathed.

'There is more. The headman says that his people will not surrender. They know the ways of the order with those who revolt. And believe me he speaks the truth – for on my life I have witnessed it too. He says that we will die before we are recaptured. He will kill us with his own hands for what the order have done to his people. This he will do if the order attacks his village.'

At that moment they were interrupted by one of the headman's guards who carried a bowl of cool water for William. Curteys took it with amazement. 'The old bastard . . .'

'They are strange and wild people but they know the meaning of kindness; though they have seen little of it shown to themselves.'

The Boston merchant splashed the refreshing water on to his grimy face and nodded.

Isabelle Crosse stood still to listen to the bird whistling in the topmost branches of a silver birch. As she watched, a flash of vivid black and yellow signalled the flight of the oriole. From further away an early cuckoo was sounding. The familiar two notes floated over the pleasant meadows which broke up the woodland into parcels of bottle-green on a sea of new grass.

She stretched and breathed in the fresh moist smell of new vegetation. There was no season to compare with spring and this year it was more wonderful than ever. It was as if her spirit was being liberated along with the caged and cowed earth. Life was budding and bursting about her and in her soul.

She was at last free of the hell which sought to drag her from the ladder of life, in the barn by the frozen lake. For long days afterwards she had found herself locked into a private prison of shock. In that dark personal cell she had been haunted by the vision of a church wall she had seen as a child. On the clammy plaster an unknown artist had drawn, in vivid colours, demons clawing the damned into hell. In her mental confinement she had felt soiled with the filth and squalor of the groping assault and the death of Thymelby. It was as if she had been drawn into a pit of the damned.

Her dreams had been nightmare-ridden and even in daylight she had found herself once more in the reeking straw; had felt Gosse's lust all over her, like a sea of sewage. And more disturbing of all she felt that she was to blame.

Phillip Spayne's words floated into her kaleidoscopic thoughts like a litany of damnation. How else could she explain her situation but by reference to her own refusal to accept the place ordained for her? Ever since she had stepped from the ordinary she had excited men's hatred. And in her blackest moments of guilt and despair the chantry priest of St Botolph reminded her that she was a daughter of the temptress and a weak vessel of sin. Once, in Boston, she had refused to heed such condemnations; since Gosse's attack she could scarcely summon up the will even to think of a defence.

She had indeed been in such a state of mental anguish that the disaster which befell her party had seemed almost acceptable. What disaster would be withheld from a woman who so disturbed the natural order of the universe? Her temporary imprisonment had passed as one more vale of shadows against the rest.

She thought back over the events of the recent past. The attack had swept over them. She had been struck on the head and her escort had died whilst she lay oblivious. The next she was aware of was the stinking smokiness of a sod-walled hut, where light and air rarely disturbed the fetid darkness. That and thin ropes which held fast her arms and legs. It was like a continuation of her nightmare; a waking dream.

She paused from her recollections and picked a flower from amongst the spring grass that had sprung up at the edge of the courtyard. 'Beautiful,' she murmured as she lifted it to her face. There was little scent but she cherished it like the most richly perfumed rose. 'Quite beautiful . . .'

For days her world had been restricted to the packed-earth floor of the hut of an Est village elder. William, the most solid link she had with her old life in Boston, was certainly dead and she felt devastated. It was as if a blizzard had fallen upon a field of summer flowers; as if devouring locusts had come with sun-blackening wings on a scene of harvest. All was lost and destroyed. Only Eleanor and Eve were left to her. All the rest had been swept away. No bitter tears, no desperate sense of loss could restore them.

Even the curiosity and slight acts of kindness shown by the village women seemed meaningless. There was no more hope left in the world. Her vision was clouded with bereavement and pain. It was as if all her optimism had gone down before a hail of cruelty.

She recalled the events as if in a distant dream. Only at eventide had she been allowed out of her imprisoning hut; only when the woodsmoke of the village fires mingled with the cold gloom of the forest edge. And then she had drunk in the chill air as if it was the purest wine.

At all other times she had been forced to endure the rancid air, thick with ammonia and the sour smell of fat and grease. The darkness too had been almost overwhelming. Confined to the corner of a room, amongst the domestic animals, she had found it hard to mark the passage of the hours. Had it not been for Eleanor's patience and presence of mind she would have lost track of the passage of the days.

'Three weeks . . .' she murmured to herself. 'Three dark weeks . . .'

According to Eleanor that was how long it had been. And during that time Isabelle had slowly come to notice how the village women were fascinated by her hair; how they even tried to communicate with her. Gradually she began to measure her own life by the slow rhythm of the village. It was as if she was being passively and inexorably absorbed into their routine. Without being able to influence it, the life of the Ests had come to dominate her own existence. Yet it was a dark absorption, for behind the village life lay the images of the men butchered in the snow. Every change of routine seemed to signal a change in their chances of survival. For three weeks they did not know if they would live or die; had no way of knowing if the routine of the hut would suddenly be fractured by the men of violence, finally resolved to destroy the strangers in their midst. It was like living on the very edge of the precipice of death and in the end they were sapped and exhausted by its very presence.

Then the darkness had been shattered and from the grave new life had blossomed. Phoenix-like she had been lifted from the ashes of her own self-destruction, for Albrecht's men had laid siege to the village of forest rebels and, shielding her from the fighting, had rescued her. It was in that act that she had passed, as it were, from darkness to light. A personal Easter after her abandonment in a Gethsemane of loneliness. Now she felt liberated and the fibres of her being were slowly feeling the return of life and hope. Only the nightmares remained, deep down inside her where she had buried her grieving for William Curteys; in a dark spot where she did not dare go any more. She simply could not face it.

Now in the meadow Eve was running free. Eleanor de Bamville was pursuing her in a way designed to let her escape and peals of little-girl laughter rose from the chase. It was as if Eve too was being liberated from a winter confinement of sterility and death.

The sound of a horse's hooves drew Isabelle's attention back within the stockaded manor-house complex. In the courtyard a roan palfrey was tossing its aristocratic head. Grooms ran to take the bridle from their master as Albrecht von Fellin dismounted, still keeping the gyr falcon strapped to his wrist. He stroked the soft feathers of the majestic bird's black-flecked breast and the falcon ran its short, hooked beak along the familiar fingers, all the time its eyes taking in every movement in the courtyard.

'You must come hunting with me tomorrow,' he called to Isabelle. 'We can ride along the lakeside.' He smiled at her obvious pleasure at the suggestion. 'I have a merlin that you can fly. Will you come with me?'

Isabelle stood by the stairs from the first-floor wooden-planked hall. She walked over to where Albrecht was waiting for her by the doorway into the stone-built undercroft. A little gingerly she ruffled the breast feathers of the large hawk perched on Albrecht's heavy leather gauntlet. The bird twitched one yellow leg but otherwise accepted her touch.

'I would love to.'

She was touched by the offer and gratified as well. In England royalty alone could hunt with the coveted gyr falcon and none below the rank of noblewoman could hold the jesses of a merlin. Yet Albrecht carried one and offered the other with total assurance; a prince indeed amongst knights.

'And I should love to carry the merlin.' Isabelle smiled to think how proud Anthony Crosse had been of a mere goshawk in his mews at Bicker. 'It will be splendid.'

His offer accepted, Albrecht at last consented to give the falcon to a hovering servant. In his hands the approaching boy carried the bird's leather hood; in his eyes he carried a frightened look, Isabelle noticed, though the knight seemed quite unaware of the disquiet of his attendant. 'Come, we must take a little wine together,' he said.

As the trembling youngster carried the falcon back to its wooden block in the darkened mews, von Fellin escorted Isabelle back up the stair she had so recently descended. The way he took her arm made her feel valued, even precious. It was balm to her wounds.

As they entered the hall, grey-robed sergeants rose from their benches and bowed and a quick-stepping butler snapped fingers at two buttery servants who offered goblets of wine.

'Do you like Auxerre?' Albrecht gestured to one of the goblets. 'It is a good vintage, of course.'

Isabelle nodded. What with the interminable war between England and France, it was very difficult getting a good vintage of fine French wine in Boston.

It took Richard Pexton at his most astute to trade successfully with the king's French enemies. And then one had to be satisfied with what one could get. Holding up the brimming goblet, Isabelle allowed herself a moment of delight. It was a pleasure to savour the wine breath alone.

'We have news of your friends.' Von Fellin was watching her carefully and noticed how she trembled; how the wine spilt on to her hand. 'It must be the merchant named Curteys . . .'

Isabelle could not disguise her astonishment. 'How? What news do you have of him? Is he alive?' She felt a flicker of wild, eager hope.

It had shamed Isabelle that, so engrossed had she been in her own liberation, she had not grieved for William as publicly as she ought. It was as if she could not allow anything to darken her new-found happiness, as if she would be drawn down into the pit once more by ghosts.

'I have many men who hold the marchlands of the order's estates. Good Christian knights who hold land from the order and who guard the German colonists in the forests. It is such God-fearing men that the savages sought to drive out and to replace with their own heathen abominations.

'One such of these knights has sent me word. He has heard that deeper in the forest the Ests hold two prisoners. This same knight first heard news of your whereabouts. These are the very same barbarians who ambushed and seized one of my sergeants last winter. But we feel sure that the stories do not refer to him.'

'You think that one of the men is Will Curteys?'

Isabelle ventured, scarcely daring to frame the question.

'I do.' He smiled gently. It pleased him to carry good news to her. 'I have sent twenty of my men-at-arms this very morning to search the woods and rescue him. Believe me, they can do it.' He had recognised the look of doubt that stood clear in her blue eyes. 'More than once they have rooted out these pillaging butchers and driven them further back into the woods. This time they will make an end of these robbers and murderers.'

The German knight took Isabelle by the arm and led her towards a window-seat. He signalled to the butler to refill her goblet.

'I can hardly believe it,' she said softly. 'Will Curteys is alive. And I had given him up for dead.' The she turned to her rescuer. 'Thank you, Albrecht, for doing this thing for him . . . and for me. It is an act of kindness and surely heaven will smile upon your goodness.'

Von Fellin touched her hand. It seemed neither too forward nor misplaced. 'I only do my duty. My duty to the Holy Church. And to you.'

Isabelle glanced down and a rare blush coloured her cheeks.

The Estonian village headman sniffed the air of dawn. The last of the snow was fast disappearing. It only lingered in the shadows that lay longest on the northern side of the log-houses and in the cold hollows amongst the pine and birch trees. He had risen early, as was his habit, and it was only just light. The reluctant sun had not yet risen above the branches and night still clung tenaciously to the earth. The forest smelled damp and cold. Mist hung in pockets about the stream which watered the village and somewhere the last of the night birds was calling. Nevertheless the streaked sky and the pink glow between the serried black trunks held the promise of day.

As usual he strolled to the byre at the edge of the clearing. From within came the lowing of the precious milk cows and the jostling of penned calves. He laid down a morsel of cheese on the flat stone by the doorway; an offering to Moschel, the cattle spirit, to ensure the longevity of the beasts who provided the poor village with its supply of milk, butter and cheese.

As he squatted he pondered on the return of yet another spring. He had witnessed the cycle of sixty years and never had he felt so fearful for the future. Since his grandfather's day the village had given tribute to the foreigners, firstly to the Danish of Tallinn, which the foreigners misnamed Reval; then, after he had seen twenty-four summers, to the German knights who had advanced eastward from Riga. And every year it had been given reluctantly and mindful of days long passed when the Ests had met these invaders in battle and when the forest folk had been free.

The headman reflected on the campfire tales of battles that were legendary and of suffering and slaughter which had reduced his people to a remnant. He sighed, for with every passing year the German farmers bit deeper into the forest lands. With each turning of the seasons the forest folk were either subjugated or destroyed.

He rose from his haunches with a feeling of burdensome sadness. Now he no longer withstood the young men of his village who burned for revenge and for freedom. Yet what would it bring them? He wished that he knew. With creased forehead he looked to where the two strangers were locked away. And what of them? He shook his head slowly. Sad days had come upon the forest folk and he was heart-sick for his people. Still shaking his head he retraced his steps towards his own hut.

The crossbow bolt hit him in the small of his back. Wordlessly he lurched forward on to his face. Then, mouth open in astonishment, he made as if to rise. His legs would not function. In dazed confusion he raised his head – face black with mud, slush and dung. His numb hands thrust at the yielding ground as he sought to push himself up. Another bolt – fired from closer range – smashed into the base of his skull. This time he made no attempt to get up.

A bird was singing, far away in the forest. Around the village clearing, though, there hung a deadly silence. A spider's web of terror seemed to grip time and space in its sticky embrace. Light came clowly to the world and the headman lay motionless in the slush; a slow lake of blood mingling with the water and mud.

Then a cry ripped the stillness. A cry like a wolf howl. The dawn air was shattered by the baying of an entire 'pack' of white-robed, mailed riders, splashing through the mud. Grey-coated crossbow men ducked and darted behind them, their bolts singing through the air. Men and women appeared sleepily at door-ways to be shot down immediately.

Kneeling in the mud the foot soldiers excitedly cranked the windlasses of their crossbows and inserted fresh bolts, vying with one another to fire into the backs of the retreating villagers. One turned to his fellows waving fingers to denote his score so far. All about the settlement the churned earth was littered with corpses.

Behind the handful of knights and the crossbowmen a pressed band of free German farmers, armed with knives and boar spears, moved methodically from house to house. While their compatriots crushed the resistance of the bolder Ests, they carried out the more mundane tasks of cutting the throats of the weak and the infirm. In the darkness of each loghouse there was pitiless butchery.

The first house was burning. Exuberant flames sprang from doors and windows. The fire seemed to excite the soldiers and they ran from house to house clutching brands, incinerating those who had taken shelter within. The sweet air was profaned with howls of human agony.

One soldier ventured too close and was seized by the doomed hands of a young man. Held in a deadly embrace he was dragged inside the house he had fired. Soon his screams were lost in the collapsing crash of blazing timbers. After this the soldiers kept their distance, firing bolts into the gaping windows at any sign of life within the infernos.

Eventually one of the horsemen located William Curteys and dragged him from his place of imprisonment. Curteys blinked at the light and gasped at the corpses which littered the village. Men, women and children were being systematically slaughtered. A group of villagers had tried to make off into the forest but had been pursued by two mounted men and a handful of blood-stained German farmers. From the cover of the trees screams revealed that they had not escaped.

Smoke hung over the village. Beside the body of the headman two grey-robed sergeants were directing the throat-cutting of the precious cows. The calves had been left inside the burning byre: bloodlust had blotted out any thoughts of theft.

As clarity of thought returned at last to William, his dismay gained voice. 'My God, what are you doing?' he shouted.

A grinning German settler was firing the barn from which Curteys had been freed.

'There's a man in there.' No one understood him, and his cries grew more frantic. 'Holy Mary, you stupid bastards, there's a man in there! My guide . . . for God's sake . . . !'

The Boston merchant tried to drag himself free from the hands which gripped him. He could not and they held him fast. He screamed at his rescuers who were now his captors. 'There's a man in there. In there, you damned whoresons. In there, you murdering bastards . . .'

The Germans shrugged. They had been given a description of the man they had to rescue. That man they had found. Their master had given them no instructions to save anyone else and so they felt under no obligation to do so. Despite the inane thrashing about of the man they had rescued he could not escape their grip.

The roof of the barn fell in and flames belched up in

a flash of hideous orange. William tried to raise his hands to block his ears. But his guards held his wrists and so he could not even shut out the agonised cries of the man that he had failed to save.

Tears, more painful for being rare, tracked down Curteys' grimy cheeks. He slumped in the vice-like grip of the Germans. And then came the sudden bitter realisation – that in all the months of travelling he had never taken the time to find out the name of the place that was home to the good-humoured Finn who was even now burning to death.

Monday 20 April 1382 was mild for early spring. Isabelle and Albrecht von Fellin had once more elected to go hunting through the woods and meadows which so pleasantly surrounded the fortified manor house.

As usual Isabelle carried the light little male merlin. As she removed its hood with one hand, she stroked the slate-blue back with the other to steady the bird. As she lifted the hood the little falcon hissed and blinked at the sudden light. No bigger than a blackbird, it sat easily on her gloved hand. Growing more aware of its surroundings the brown-eyed tiercel flexed its wing muscles and pulled at the jesses that held fast its strong yellow legs.

'We should move down to the meadows beside the lake. The merlin and the gyr will prefer the open country there,' Albrecht suggested.

Isabelle nodded and slowly they walked their horses away from the scattering of birch trees that shielded them from the manor house atop the lightly wooded rise. Behind them trailed a little band of mounted retainers led by one of the sergeants. The sunshine glittered on the surface of the lake and the slight breeze touched and ruffled the surface of the water playfully. The disturbed water made the light flash.

Riding through the thickening grass, Isabelle released the tiercel. It flew close to the ground, above the budding bushes and at last flushed out a meadow pipit too nervous to remain still. Twisting and turning it followed every desperate move of the terrified bird until, overtaking it, the talons struck the prey with killing force.

For a moment the merlin turned out over the lake, then it returned to the outstretched hand with a reluctant cry. 'Quik-ik-ik,' it scolded Isabelle as she summoned one of the servants to remove the prey from its talons.

Albrecht was lifting the hood from the gyr falcon, talking casually as he did so. 'What was the name of the saint whom you and Eleanor honoured yesterday?' he asked.

'It was St Alphege.' Isabelle smiled. 'I do not think he is treated with such reverence by the Germans...' There was a merry growth of lines at the edge of her mouth.

'And you say that he was killed by Danes who pelted him with meat bones?'

Isabelle nodded.

'Well, my dear, we Germans tend to celebrate saints who are a little more fortunate in the table manners of their companions.'

At any other time Isabelle would have been a little shocked, but today she only tutted in mock condemnation at the knight's dismissal of the English martyr. It was difficult to be offended by anything that this man did.

'Now,' he whispered as he changed the subject, 'let us see how the gyr falcon flies.' And as he lifted his gloved hand, the great bird rose in flight, beating the air with rapid movements of its great white wings.

Isabelle and her knight spent most of the day out along the lake; the merlin taking small songbirds and the gyr two water-fowl which rose in its path. It was well into the afternoon when they turned their horses back towards the manor and saw as they entered the courtyard that a number of horsemen had arrived briefly before them. Servants were watering the dusty horses and mailed riders were stretching cramped muscles but one man remained on his horse. He wore clothes several sizes too large for him and appeared to be viewing the throng with some detachment.

'It's William!' Isabelle was not given to sudden bursts of emotion but her pleasure was real enough. 'Thank God – it's William.'

She reined in her horse and handed the hooded tiercel to one of the mews attendants, wrestling impatiently with the jesses and the gauntlet. Von Fellin watched her thoughtfully.

Helped down from her jennet she ran across to the man she had not seen for weeks. 'William, William!' she cried and he seemed to awaken at her call. He swung down from his mount and she embraced him. Laughing in joy, Eleanor and Eve had run up from the meadow and now Eleanor held up Eve to see all the excited movement. The little girl giggled with glee at the infectious happiness of Isabelle Crosse.

'This is God's providence, surely,' Isabelle said to her battered-looking partner. 'That you should be alive and well and rescued by our most Christian Brothers of the Sword.'

At last Curteys seemed to show emotion. A cracked laugh escaped his lips. 'Aye, it was our most Christian brothers who did rescue me.'

There was a cynical spread of lines about his lips. The look was familiar to Isabelle and she was puzzled. Before she could say anything though, von Fellin passed through the parting crowd, handing the now hooded gyr falcon to the frightened mews servant. Fumbling, the boy almost dropped the bird and the falcon flapped its wings as it hung for a moment from the jesses. Its blindfolded head snapped to and fro but the panic-stricken boy at last gained control of the situation. He backed away under the cold glance of his master.

Removing his glove von Fellin greeted his guest. 'Welcome, it is once again my honour to do you service.'

For a moment he and Curteys locked eyes in a startling confrontation. Isabelle glanced at Eleanor who was as puzzled as she was.

'Thank you.' William's reply was almost grudging when he at last allowed it passage. 'Your men were most efficient in carrying out their orders. Unfortunately they burned my guide to death . . .' His voice was ironic in tone.

Von Fellin nodded with magisterial sorrow. 'What can I say? It is the terrible nature of war. The barbarians who took you hostage must bear the blame for this tragic death. Had my men understood who he was they would have saved him.' Then, seeing that Curteys appeared unconvinced, he added: 'I know how much you will have tried to save him but you did not speak German. That is so, is it not?'

He said it very softly as if to imply that the failure to save the Finn stemmed from Curteys' intransigence in learning a foreign language.

William shook his head slowly. 'No, I do not speak good German.' For a moment he looked as if he meant to say more. Then he just shook his head again.

Von Fellin broke the silence. 'We must not dwell upon this sorrow now. Today is a day for celebrating and tomorrow we shall hold a feast in your honour. When you have recovered from your trials.' Then the knight led the way towards the hall. He took Isabelle's arm and bowed graciously to Curteys as a perfect host would.

Isabelle was outraged by the behaviour of her partner but it was only later that night, as she and Eleanor joined Eve in bed, that she at last let out her irritation.

'I do not know what Will thought he was doing,' she fumed. 'I have never seen such ingratitude. And after all that Albrecht has done for him. It really is appalling.'

Eve stirred between them as Eleanor blew out the mutton-fat candle. In the darkness both women contemplated the meaning of William's strange behaviour.

Eleanor turned to Isabelle. 'It is clear that Will has

taken the death of the guide very hard. Truth be known, it surprises me, for Will never showed him much regard before. The death saddens me but Will's grief is unexpected.'

'And there you have it, Eleanor. Will feels bad that he treated the man poorly now that he is dead. But instead of taking the blame on himself he is seeking to put it on to Albrecht. And how can he be blamed for that terrible accident? And after his men risked their lives in battle against those armed tribesmen.' She paused as she recalled Albrecht's words. 'It seems that the Ests lived deep in the forests and the German knights took no heed of the danger themselves in facing them in open combat. Albrecht himself told me so. I really do think that Will Curteys is jealous of Albrecht.'

'Mayhap he is . . .' Eleanor was considering this option. 'Mayhap he is . . .'

'For you saw how Will resented our friendship with him at Riga and even then he was doing us nothing but good. It seems clear to me that Will Curteys is jealous because he owes so much of our good fortune to Albrecht. And because Albrecht is my friend: it is too much for him to accept that I have won us a good ally! I hope that tomorrow he will have recovered some of his courtesy . . .'

So the joy at William's rescue was spoiled by the manner of his homecoming. It hurt Isabelle to see Albrecht's kindness treated in so offhand a manner. Her anger at William's mood almost eclipsed the tenderness that she had felt when it seemed that he was lost for ever.

However, whatever William's feelings towards von

Fellin he seemed to heed Isabelle's quiet hope. When the household broke fast at dawn he was civil if restrained. By the end of the light repast he even shared a little of his experiences as a prisoner. It seemed that he was thawing.

That evening the household met together in the hall for the promised celebratory feast. As with everything that he did, von Fellin succeeded in making the occasion memorable for the quality of the food and drink, and the light multi-faceted nature of his own conversation. At table they were joined by the knights who held land from the order and who had supervised the rescue of the Englishman. They were more taciturn than their host and failed to display even a fraction of his wit and humour. Against such a dull backcloth Albrecht von Fellin shone like Gabriel in a Mystery Play. He was so witty, so well-read, so utterly urbane. Even William was finding it hard to maintain his wall of silence. There was something about the German knight which made others relax and talk freely. Isabelle smiled to see the improvement in relationships.

But even had von Fellin himself not been the sweetener, the meal itself would certainly have startled palates jaded by a winter of salted meat and the privations of being the prisoners of impoverished people. The manor cooks, pantler and butler had obviously been set the task of captivating the appetites of their guests. All who sat on the top table found soft wheat-bread before them in abundance. Given the vagaries of the Baltic climate it was apparent that the wheat flour must have been imported at considerable expense. On the lower tables the household ate the coarser breads compounded from the hardier rye, barley and oats, which could survive the damp weather.

On the trestle table lay the abundant riches of the land: pickled salmon and trout from the lake; suckling boar for the privileged and umbles pie for the lower tables, as well as roast swan and ducks brought down by the gyr falcon. It was a table fit for a prince. And, as if to trumpet his power and influence, von Fellin had the servants carry a closely guarded loaf of sugar through the hall. What was more, he even allowed his favoured guests to pare away crumbling shavings of the precious spice. Even William Curteys could not hide his approval of this tremendous generosity.

At the end of the meal, as the guests departed for their communal beds, Eleanor decided she needed to take the fresh evening air. Although it was late – well past nine of the clock – she was too full to sleep. As a consequence she slipped out of the hall after explaining her whereabouts to Isabelle.

For a moment she stood next to the door of the external stone-built kitchen. A rich aroma wafted from the now cooling ovens; a rich olfactory conjunction of cinnamon, nutmeg, galingale and a host of mingling spices.

Eleanor was still too full to enjoy the wonderful scent. Instead she passed down the darkened yard. On her right the long, low bulk of the mews lay against the timber stockade. As she passed it she heard a strange sound. In quality it lay half-way between a whimper and a series of barely concealed sobs. It sounded like a badly thrashed puppy.

Eleanor had a soft spot for domestic animals. She began to search for the pup, imagining it to be one of the young wolfhounds punished for some misdemeanour. However the noise seemed to come from within the mews itself. Puzzled, she traced it to its source.

As she walked along the wooden planks of the wall she saw that there was a light burning inside. Now she was deeply intrigued. This was not common practice. By rights the hawks and falcons should be asleep in darkness, their rest made all the more certain by their leather hoods.

Eleanor sidled up to the door. There were gaps between it and the door-frame. With some difficulty she could manage a view into the shed. Isolated by wickerwork partitions a goshawk was perched on a bow perch. Further down the mews Eleanor could dimly perceive the shape of Isabelle's merlin. However it was not this which astonished her. Directly in front of the door the mighty gyr falcon stood on its wooden block. Over three spans tall, it dominated her view. A low candle was burning on a shelf and, as the falcon shifted its claws, the light flashed on the steel swivel which secured the leg jesses to the block.

Beside the falcon – less than a span from its beak – sat the figure of a boy. He was securely tied to a tall upright chair. There were few chairs in the manor and Eleanor recognised it as the one which usually stood in von Fellin's chamber. She recognised the boy, too, as the clumsy servant who had distressed von Fellin's falcon the previous day. The boy had been skilfully trussed so that he could move his head only a very little.

Eleanor hissed an exhalation of breath when she peered again at the falcon. It was unhooded. Its imperious eyes blinked in the light and its hooked beak seemed to transmit a terrible menace. Every time the boy moved his head the falcon snapped its own head towards him. The jet eyes of the bird were deep and cold. Had it wished it could have torn open the face of the sweating boy whose cheek muscles were twitching with terror.

For a moment she drew back from the door. Her first instinct was to break the boy free. The second was to confront von Fellin with the outrage that she had discovered. As she thought about it she began to doubt whether either was the wisest move for the child within the shed, or for herself and her friends. The realisation sickened her and she fought it for long, tense minutes.

At last she was reconciled to the dreadfulness of her decision. She turned away from the door. Slowly, with heavy feet, she went back to the hall. Behind her a shallow light flickered within the mews until, just before dawn, it stumbled on its own wax and turned into a wisp of greasy smoke.

The next day, as they ate the noon-time dinner, William Curteys made the first mention of their leaving. His words were quietly spoken but they seemed to have a sudden effect on von Fellin.

'We are grateful for your help,' William said, 'but we must soon be on our way. The Gulf of Finland will be free from ice by now and our goods will be on their way to Riga. We must soon rejoin our party there and set sail for England.'

It was as if von Fellin did not hear him. He smiled at

Isabelle and instead remarked: 'I had thought we should go riding this afternoon. We should go now to make the most of the sunshine.'

Curteys looked as if he had been slapped. He even reddened. When von Fellin rose from the table he almost interrupted him but instead bit back his annoyance. Isabelle looked a little perturbed at the curious exchange of words but accompanied her attentive host. Behind her William broke off a lump of wheat-bread with obvious anger. Eleanor watched the two leaving the room with a look of deep concentration.

A few minutes later William rose to take the air out in the courtyard. He could not deny his jealousy. The German knight had clearly captivated Isabelle. The realisation of his own resentment had come as an unexpected blow: William was not a man who allowed himself to be moved by a woman.

The last one to have touched such chords in the guildsman was long-dead. It was a rare enough happening that a man should love the woman chosen for him since he was a child, but such had been the case with William Curteys. His betrothed had been the daughter of a guildsman of Boston, a slight girl with hair the colour of beech leaves in autumn. The sickness that had stolen her from him before they could reach the altar had wasted her away, her fair cheeks had been hollowed by death and the promises made at plighting of troth had gone to dust.

Since then William had never been moved by a woman, at least not until Isabelle Crosse had risen from the quiet obscurity of being his partner's wife. Now Tony Crosse's transformed widow was stirring feelings that had laid dormant in his heart for so long. The first sign had been anger. But even that had been strange in the normally detached merchant. Then latterly his feelings had touched on desire. And who could deny her beauty?

Since his arrival at the manor of von Fellin another feeling had disturbed him. He had first felt it in Riga but now it was getting harder to ignore it. It was stirring in him every time he saw Isabelle looking at the knight. As he considered the situation, William was determined that they should all return to Riga as soon as possible.

On Friday, over the fast-day fish, William raised the matter once again. It was again dismissed but this time with the confident assertion that no boatload of Russian merchants had docked at Riga and so there was no need to leave the manor.

When William asked how his host could possibly know such a thing he was met with a thin smile, a dangerous smile which cut through all the charm like a misericord blade through chinks in the armour of a fallen knight.

That afternoon, while Isabelle and von Fellin were out riding, Eleanor told William about the boy tied up in the mews. Sitting on one of the benches in the hall he at last recounted the tale of the death of the Finn and the slaughter at the village.

The two sat in silence for a while. At last Eleanor broke the spell. 'You think he means to keep Isabelle here?' she asked in her usual level tone.

'Yes.'

Neither of them had previously alluded to this topic of conversation but it was as if both could now declare their thoughts as they unpacked their separate news concerning the secret brutality of their host.

'It is possible that he had not previously given it much thought.' William did not sound very convinced. 'But he is thinking about it now – now that I have talked of leaving. You can wager all our bolts of Lincoln cloth that he is thinking about it now.'

'Do you think that he loves her?'

'No.' Curteys laughed derisively. 'Do you?' He dared not contemplate the thought.

'No, but I was asking you . . .'

Eleanor's male companion leaned back against the panel of the wall. He had never before spoken so openly to Eleanor. Truth be known he resented her presence and her shrewd appraisal of events. Now, with Thymelby dead, he thanked God that Eleanor was with him. He smiled at the turnabout in his thoughts.

'I think that our knight is a man who gets whatever he wants,' he said. 'He is as absolute as a prince in these lands and we are strangers far from home.' He paused as he reflected on the dismal picture that he had just painted. 'He is charm itself and yet I believe that he is the angel of death to those who oppose his will. Does that sound hysterical to you?' He half expected the woman to be shocked by his words. After all, he did not have a reputation for theatrical language.

Instead she merely nodded, then confirmed his worst fears. 'He is such. And he would add Isabelle to his possessions. And I doubt that any have thwarted his will, though perhaps he has never felt this way for a woman before.'

When Curteys looked interested she added: 'He does not have a reputation as a womaniser, only an uncorrupted crusader against the heathen. He would not be the first man who bent all his energies to the absolute destruction of his enemies only to be suddenly startled out of his single-mindedness by a beautiful woman. And such a man might then devote all his cold cunning to keeping hold of such a rare treasure and never letting it pass from his grasp.'

William felt his stomach turn within him at such a prospect. He dared not explain the feeling and he did not like it. All he knew was that he felt consumed with a bitter hatred of von Fellin and that it was a hatred which exceeded any attempt to rationalise it. He looked at the situation from this side and that and yet he could not understand it. The reason for this failure was a simple one: William Curteys had never before felt jealousy concerning a woman.

However if Isabelle was aware of the tension within her party she did not show it. She had not once mentioned the matter to Eleanor and Eleanor had not raised the issue with her. That was a measure of the seriousness of the situation, for they usually confided everything in each other. And had Isabelle spoken, what would Eleanor have said? That her liberation from her own hell was developing into yet another twisted obsession, less brutal but as suffocating as the obscene craving of Gosse himself? Isabelle would not be able to face it, that her companion sensed. Not so soon after her Easter rebirth.

The matter came to a head exactly one month after Isabelle had so jubilantly welcomed the rescued William. Wednesday 20 May was another feast day of an English martyr, this time St Ethelred of East Anglia. However there was no jubilation or celebration this time, no joking about obscure English saints, for the atmosphere between Curteys and von Fellin had become distinct enough to cut with a knife.

Isabelle watched the budding of the trees turn into full leaf and felt a deepening disquiet. By now even she was beginning to feel like a chaffinch in a cage. She was well fed, cherished and coddled, yet carefully imprisoned. At first she had not even noticed it. Then she had denied it. Now she was desperately sad and not a little frightened. Worse than that she hated Curteys for being the agent who had revealed her imprisonment to her.

At supper William faced their host squarely: 'It is well into May. We must sail before the end of the month if we are to find landfall in England before August. Our goods must have landed at Riga now.'

Von Fellin seemed less cool than usual. 'There is plenty of time. You will not rush away . . .'

'We have been here a full month.' Curteys' voice was level and calm. 'You have been good to us but we must go tomorrow.'

The knight glanced across at Isabelle. She was wearing the purple dress of Venetian velvet which had been rescued with her from her imprisonment amongst the forest folk. She looked very pale.

'And what do you say, Isabelle. Would you run away?'

Isabelle toyed with her fork. Her self-assurance seemed to drain away. 'We must go,' she answered softly. 'We must go home . . .'

William was watching her intently but not as keenly

or as coldly as von Fellin. He watched her the way that the gyr falcon watched the face of the wretched servant. Under the table Eleanor reached out and touched the hand of her friend. It was trembling.

'So, you would play the ingrate too.' Von Fellin's eyes were savage, as if he could not express the raging emotions which surged beneath his usually controlled features.

'By Our Lord, Albrecht, you know that I shall never forget you; but we must return to Boston and our homes.' Isabelle Crosse had not cried in public since she was a very small child but now she could feel the prickling about her eyes. The faces around her began to swim. She clenched and unclenched her fists.

'You think perhaps that you may treat a German knight differently to an Englishman?' His eyes followed the movements of Eve as she ran about the hall chasing the dogs. 'But the child is not English. She is German.'

Isabelle looked up, startled. She could not understand what he was getting at but a nameless fear turned her stomach.

'Yes,' he continued. 'I have made inquiries. She is the child of a tenant of the order. Free German farmers who perished from the pestilence. And as such her overlord is her legal guardian.' He paused as the inevitable message sank in. Isabelle's eyes showed the depth of her pain. 'I am the feudal overlord of the knight on whose land her parents farmed. She is my ward and was sold without my agreement. You may go as you wish but she stays here.'

The knight's voice had lost all its veneer of civility. Now it was brimful only of an implacable will and a cold energy which the forest folk would have recognised and which the boy in the mews would have known all too well. More than this, it had the bitter edge of one who is hurting because he is being hurt. That was a tone unheard before in this man's voice and his own realisation of its presence only served to make him more deadly.

'Oh my God, Albrecht. You cannot mean to do such a thing?' Isabelle's voice broke with anger and betrayal. 'You cannot make war on a child. For the sake of your soul, you cannot do such a thing . . .'

Curteys stiffened. 'Oh, he can make war on children, have no fear. I saw them burning and with their throats cut. He can make war on little children.' He was very angry and that was rare too. 'Go and get your things Isabelle, and Eleanor too.' He waved a hand curtly. 'And pick up the child.'

Von Fellin had never been crossed before. He began to rise. Half-way up he froze and his face turned purple. With fists tightly clenched he sat down once more. Confused, Isabelle looked at William who nodded to her to go.

Unbeknown to her the razor-sharp blade of Curteys' dagger lay pressed through von Fellin's robe, sharp and cold against his groin. For a few moments both men sat in silence. It was as if they had been petrified; as if some spell bound their movements. At last Curteys spoke. 'Tell the servants we wish to be left alone . . .'

Von Fellin turned eyes cold with hatred on him.

'Do it. I've nothing to lose. You, on the contrary

have . . .' Curteys pressed the blade forward and the knight ordered off the attendants who fluttered a short distance away.

'Now,' William continued, 'we are going to talk.' He ignored the murder in his opponent's glance. 'Because both our lives hang on it.' He pressed the dagger into the German's groin once more to emphasise the point. 'You will let the women go and the child . . .'

'My men-at-arms will destroy you. They will crush you like vermin. You know that, don't you?' There was no longer a cloak of chivalry about his words. Each syllable dripped with venom. 'You cannot escape by taking me as hostage.'

Curteys smiled a grim little smile. 'I have no intention of taking you hostage.' He did not allow von Fellin to interrupt; ignored the look of surprise. 'Because you will let us go.' He nodded as if to support his assertion. 'Because at the heart of it, you are a man of honour.' Will tried to suppress the vision of slaughter at the village of the Ests. 'You have offended your very honour today in what you have threatened. You know that you want Isabelle and in your desire you have trampled on every code dear to your order and to any knight. Before Christ you cannot deny it, even if you will not admit it. Before your own soul you cannot deny it . . . You attacked a woman through a little child . . .'

His words hung naked and blunt in the air. Von Fellin's face was without expression. Only a muscle twitched in his cheek as a sign of the emotions which tore like a rip-tide within him. No one had ever spoken to him this way; no one, ever. The cheek twitched and a pulse beat in his temple. His face was as white as the forest snows.

Very slowly Curteys moved the dagger away from the knight, lifting it with minute care as if he feared that it might break. He laid the weapon on the trestle table before von Fellin where it nestled up against one of the trenchers still laden with food. The German gazed down at the blade, his face drained of blood.

'I give you back your honour,' William said softly. 'For now we are in your hands once more, to kill or to let go. You can choose life or death. And our lives are bound to the life of your honour as truly as Our Lord was bound to the cross.' It was not often that the cynical Boston merchant had spoken thus. He could feel his own stomach churning, fully aware that death and life stood before him, like actors on a stage. Both reached for him. Both wished to embrace him. He held his breath.

At last von Fellin spoke. His voice was drained of feeling. 'I will provide you with horses. You will go straightaway. And if you tarry, I will kill you.' He met Curteys' eyes. 'You I will kill . . . by inches I will kill you . . .' As the Englishman stood up he added, with a flood of bitterness, 'And since you have stood conscience to me, do no less for yourself.'

William's eyes narrowed.

'Do not pretend that you do not want her for yourself,' von Fellin hissed.

The Boston merchant clamped his lips together as if he did not trust what might escape them. In silence he turned from the face chiselled with jealous hatred. Then, as if in answer to some summons, he turned back. His question was so absurd and unexpected von Fellin almost laughed.

'The Finn who travelled with us; what was his name?'

The German's face was a mask of incredulity. 'I do not know,' he replied dismissively.

Curteys was not so easily rebuffed. 'He served you well, long ago. He served the order. He told me that he led your men in their raids against the forest folk. What was his name?'

'You are a fool. He was nothing and I do not take the trouble to learn the names of the creatures who do such tasks. I do not know what his name was. He was of use to us and nothing more. What does it matter?'

William Curteys nodded his head. It was as if one last lingering doubt had been dispatched. Von Fellin's total lack of value for the Finn who had served him assured the Lincolnshire merchant that he had not misjudged the character of the German knight.

William's eyes were clear when he looked up. They disconcerted von Fellin; it was as if the Englishman had proved something of vital importance.

'You are a fool, Englishman. A fool,' he spat angrily.

Curteys smiled grimly and said enigmatically, 'There was a moment when I thought I was, but you have shown me that I am not. You have shown me what you are and who you are – and what I am. I have discovered the value that you put on men and have learnt a new value myself. For that I thank you.' Then he turned and left.

Out in the fresh air William felt terribly weak. He cast a glance back towards the doorway. There was no sign of pursuit. Now they must get away. He owed that to the women and to the child. He owed that much to the little Finn. The man too inconsequential to the Sword Brethren even to have a name.

The English merchants were reunited with their friends in Riga before the end of May. Their merchandise had arrived from Novgorod a month before. With no virtue in delay the Yarmouth boats sailed on Monday 1 June.

Isabelle stood in the rear castle of the ship. She had hardly spoken to William since the flight from von Fellin's manor. Inside she was pulled by conflicting emotions of anger and gratitude towards the man who had precipitated the appalling explosion from her knight and yet who had saved her from it.

Most of all she felt stupid. Von Fellin had ensnared her heart as if she were a child. The bitter realisation crushed her pride and, what was worse, she could not begin to explain how it had happened. Anger rose within her at the thought but more than that it confused and embarrassed her. She did not know how to face William Curteys. Her humiliation seemed complete.

She was sure that her partner now took her for a total fool. He must despise her, for she almost despised herself. How would he ever look at her without thinking of her naïvety? The handsome guildsman with the sharp tongue would not forget the manner in which she had allowed herself to be duped.

All her hopes of gaining value in his eyes were now meaningless. She could scarcely talk to him without the realisation choking off her words in deep shame. Hurt welled up within her too, for she had thought that Albrecht had cared and in that caring she had thought she had found the value which Will Curteys would clearly never give her.

William was watching her. He could not grasp why she was so cold to him. After all, he had saved her. He despaired of ever finding common ground with this beautiful woman. She was impossible to understand. He could only assume that she truly had loved von Fellin and now hated the merchant partner for exposing the twisted nature of the knight's desire. The thought made him feel vulnerable and alone. He wished with all his heart that she had stayed at home.

He walked up to where she was standing and coughed awkwardly. 'Isabelle . . .' He leaned towards her, trying to dredge up words that would reach out to her shielded misery. 'I am very sorry . . .'

She nodded and her voice was low. 'Thank you, Will.' And then, before he could say any more, she turned and left the castle.

Curteys leaned against the rail and looked back across the foaming wake, back to where the seagulls wheeled and cried over the heaving dark water, to where a solitary figure stood motionless atop the seaward battlements of Riga castle.

William watched until the town and castle and lonely sentinel were lost in the greyness of the sea and only the gulls remained, rising and dipping through the spray.

Chapter 9

Richard Pexton, Isabelle Crosse's clerk, was alone in the warehouse by the Town Quay in Boston. He was glad of the brief solitude: privacy was a rare experience in the hall off Boston's Strait Bargate. What with the fussing butler and the chattering servants, it was like living in the complex interior of a wood-ant nest. And then there were the innumerable ledgers and the accounts, all demanding attention. Solitude was not part of the daily round and common task of Richard Pexton's life.

For that reason alone it was something of an escape when he had to attend to business here. This day of all days he was glad of the cool shadows within the stone walls. The close confines shut out the light and the noise from the ships at the wharves. He had a lot to get clear in his mind.

'One . . . two . . . three . . .' he muttered softly as he checked off bales of cloth against his tally sticks. For a moment he clucked his tongue as he scanned the merchandise. 'Four, five . . .' He found the bales he was looking for, misplaced by some inattentive servant; the error unnoticed by the journeyman.

He sat down and checked his calculations. All was present and correct. The stock was accumulating well in time for the great autumn market only two months away. He had personally supervised the build-up over the summer. Yet he had risen long before the late August dawn and come down to check once more.

He allowed himself a rare smile. He knew full well why he had come to the warehouse to ensure that all was in perfect order. Only the previous evening, word had reached the hall that ships lay off the coast; anchored in the deeper water west of the Toft Sands. Swinging slowly in the Boston Channel they would surely ride into the Haven at the first swelling of the incoming tide. There was little doubt over which party was carried in the ships. Pexton had spent a restless night.

It was over a year since he had seen Isabelle. Over a year since she had gone painfully up the ladder on to the ship and into the unknown. And for that year Richard Pexton had carried the burden of the Crosse household. Now, like the steward in the parable, his mistress had returned. It was the time for giving account.

'Damn!' Pexton twisted his hands until the knuckles whitened like a sea-washed corpse. 'Damn, damn, damn . . .' This was not going to be easy. In the silence of the warehouse he pieced together his thoughts and, most carefully of all, the words that he would have to use . . .

An hour after dawn the Yarmouth cogs entered the Haven. They rode a wave of shimmering grey; ahead lay home. Soon the blur of morning mist below the great stump of St Botolph cleared to reveal solid blocks: the familiar shapes of the friaries at the southern tip of the town, then the sheds and tenements about Town Quay, with the stone-built houses of Skirbeck Quarter lifting from the west bank of the Witham.

Isabelle and Eleanor stood in the forecastle of the leading vessel, the cool breeze tugging at the wimple holding Isabelle's hair. A little hand encouraged the action of the breeze. Laughing, Isabelle lifted Eve to see the town emerging from the mist.

'It's home, sweeting.' Eve seemed more intent on wriggling and giggling. Isabelle smiled at Eleanor. 'And God knows, I never thought I would be so glad to see it. It's been far too long.'

Eleanor chuckled. 'You'd think you'd journeyed to far Cathay, to hear you speak. You wait until you've done some real journeying. Then you'll know what a homecoming is like.'

Behind the tease was a warm smile but Isabelle refused to be roused. 'I know you, Eleanor de Bamville. And how you long for a soft mattress as much as I do. For all your bold talk!'

The two peered through the lifting veil of grey, each eager to recognise the familiar shapes and name them.

'There's Gysors Hall. There, where the river bends.' Isabelle pointed.

'Now we know we are home. Close enough to be taxed,' said a gruff voice. William Curteys had come upon them silently. His cynical humour reminded them of all that would have to be done once they had docked.

'You are a kill-joy, William,' Isabelle pronounced.

'Fancy spoiling such a view with the thought of the king's collectors.'

The brief moment of warmth hung awkwardly between them. They had talked but little on the homeward journey. Neither seemed sure what to say to the other and the issue was hidden away in silence. As if aware of the sudden tension both looked away towards the quayside.

Richard Pexton was waiting there with a gaggle of carrying men and retainers. There was also a sizeable crowd of onlookers, including, of course, the merchants who had bought into the venture, as well as many others who seemed to be inordinately interested in the returning vessels.

As Isabelle descended from the ship she could not help but notice that she seemed once more to be the centre of attention. She nodded to the onlookers and there was an excited babble of conversation which rippled along the quayside.

'They cannot believe that you have returned alive from the Land of Darkness,' Eleanor whispered, as she too noticed the attention Isabelle was getting.

'Quite. And I but a daughter of Eve.'

Isabelle's voice kept something of the boldness that had once shocked her fellow guildsmen. This time though it took some effort, even with Eleanor.

'Now don't let Phillip Spayne hear you talk like that!' Eleanor leaned close to her companion. 'Actually I expect they are trying to work out how you conceived and gave birth to a two-year-old child – and all in a twelve-month!'

Isabelle had quite forgotten the impact Eve would

have on the idle. She shook her head to think of Eleanor's jibe at the onlookers' curiosity. Stroking the child's head she inclined her cheek to accept the kiss of welcome offered by the perplexed Richard Pexton.

'It is good to see you, mistress.' There was something rather formal and practised in Pexton's welcome. 'We heard last night that your ships were off the Haven. I have assumed you will have eaten but little. A meal is ready for you in the hall. Fresh bread and meats and cheeses . . .'

'Well done, Richard.' Isabelle touched his arm as she interrupted him. 'You could not have anticipated our needs more perfectly. As soon as all is sorted here we will be glad to be feasted. But first you must see what we have purchased with our cloth, wine and silver. You have never seen such furs, or such fine beeswax.'

'I can attend to it all, mistress. You must be tired . . .'

'No, no. We slept better for being close to home last night. And besides, you have not met Eve.'

And so, although it was clear that Pexton would dearly have loved to have whisked them away, he had to accompany Isabelle as she supervised the start, at least, of the unloading of the cargo. While the barrels of furs and crates of wax were manhandled ashore, she explained how she had come to purchase Eve and how the child was now her own. Pexton seemed puzzled but not shocked: it was as if there were other things on his mind. All the while the crowds milled about, pointing and gawping.

After about an hour, a good half of the cargo was unloaded, with Crosse retainers keeping a close eye on the valuable merchandise.

Some of the goods had been purchased on behalf of Lincoln merchants who, unlike the Boston guildsmen, were not exempt the payment of toll for using the port. Their crates and barrels were hauled along to the Gysors Hall where the manorial officials weighed and stamped the merchandise and charged the poker-faced merchants for the honour. The king's collectors had already made their charges.

Isabelle beckoned to Pexton. 'Some of the furs in our store are bought by Lincoln silver. We have only paid the king's taxes and none of Gaunt's tolls on them, as they are reckoned to be Boston goods. I'll show you which ones I mean another time. For a consideration we have agreed this with the men of Lincoln. Come the great market in November we will put those furs across the river to the Fair of Holland. Then the Lincoln merchants living in Skirbeck Quarter will relieve you of them. But we will talk of this anon . . .'

She gave her shocked clerk a nod. In just over a year she had become as sharp as her dead husband. She would have loved to have been able to read Pexton's thoughts. Was he impressed with her business acumen? She felt sure he was.

Suddenly she felt very comfortable in the company of her clerk. It was as if his absence from the journey to the Baltic meant that she could relax when he was there. None of her ghosts seemed to haunt about him. Finally she allowed him to escort her back to the hall,

Curteys, almost to Isabelle's relief, having declined the invitation to breakfast. As the Crosse retainers marched up through Richmond Fee they found themselves surrounded by the swelling numbers of the crowd. At last they reached the hall by the town's Bargate.

In the hall the servants were turned out in good order although there was a rather muted cheer when Isabelle entered the rush-strewn space before the dais and high table. From the fragrance rising from her feet, she knew that Richard had ordered armfuls of meadowsweet brought in from the fen dykes and ditches for its dried flowers crushed at her passing like brittle yellow foam, their perfume rising from the rushes like a cleansing.

To Isabelle's surprise the top table was not laid. Instead Pexton led the way to the first-floor solar. Behind them the servants broke into sharp shards of chatter. More meadowsweet had been strewn amongst the rushes and a meal was laid on the solid table. Pexton dismissed the butler and poured the wine himself whilst Isabelle and Eleanor took window seats to make the most of the clear sunshine and Eve played amongst the rushes. When Pexton had served the women with wine and they had assuaged their thirst, he spoke very quietly.

'Edward has seized your manors in the fens.' His news was met with a stunned silence. 'He took them at Martinmas last year. It was six months after you sailed.'

Isabelle stood up abruptly and, moving slowly to the table, she poured herself more wine. Then she turned to face her clerk. 'So that was why you were so keen to whisk me away from the quay? And why we are not eating with the household in the hall?' She nodded slowly as she answered her own questions. Now she understood the attention she had commanded beside the ships and in Richmond Fee. She could once again hear the nervous cheers of her own household. She was pale but her eyes glittered with a rising fury.

'I think you should sit down, mistress.'

'What's wrong, Richard? Do you think that I will fall away in a swoon? Are you afraid that I am not strong enough to hear the truth? I am guildmaster of this house, Richard. Never forget that.'

For a moment her anger focused on her clerk, but he seemed unflustered. When he spoke it was without the stammer of nerves. 'I honestly think that you should sit, my lady. God alone knows that I have not yet told you the half of it.'

For a few moments Isabelle defied his advice. Then, alerted by something in his voice, she returned to her window seat. 'Go on, Richard. Give me an account of the fortunes of the house of Crosse in Boston since I have been away.'

Richard Pexton stood before her, the morning sun on his black hair, the strands of grey in his beard shining like threads of silver. There was a quiet dignity about him which she had scarcely noticed before.

'For a while all was well after you left,' he began. 'There were no more assaults on the manor at Bicker; no more interference with the enclosed turbary in

Bicker Fen. However, there was much trouble elsewhere. Attacks on the young king's ministers. They say a mob killed hundreds of Gaunt's friends in London. All over East Anglia and the south fenlands there were attacks on landlords and the like. There were revolts in Norfolk and Cambridgeshire. Lawless men were loose all over, until Bishop Despenser of Norwich crushed them with his knights. But we had no trouble. I lay awake at night waiting for it but the fires burned elsewhere, thank God.'

Pexton paused, drawing himself up tall. 'Then last November it happened. I should have smelled trouble. Edward was in Boston more than usual. He must have been planning it then. But all the time he was as quiet as a lamb.' He shook his head, angrily. 'Gentle as if he had been gelded.'

Isabelle tapped her hand against the sill. 'I'll geld him, by God. Just you wait. Or see him exposed as the thief that he is.'

Eleanor frowned anxiously at the thinly concealed edge to her friend's anger. 'Go on, Richard,' she suggested. 'I take it you have a lot more to tell?'

'Too much. It was Monday 11 November. I will never forget the day. St Martin's Day, it was. Our men rode in from Bicker with bloody heads. Apparently Edward and a small army crashed into the manor at dawn. They drove out all our people and took the place.'

'And what did you do?' Isabelle said, her voice cold.

Pexton was stung. 'I armed our retainers and rode out to Bicker. God, it was an armed camp. He had men there in gambesons and helmets, with bills and halberds: an army of them. He must have been planning it for months. Well, we rode straight in. I demanded by what right he had taken control of Crosse property, him being Edward Moyne and a bastard. No Crosse at all in law!' Pexton allowed himself a grim smile at the memory of his own raw courage. 'And he replied that it was his birthright and I was the trespasser.'

'He said what?' Isabelle brought down her goblet with a crack. Whimpering, Eve got up from the rushes and toddled over to Eleanor. The older woman picked her up and whispered something in her ear but the little girl still looked frightened.

'Oh, he told me much more,' Pexton went on. 'He said that his men now held Swineshead and Bicker as his rightful possessions. They had also taken over the turbaries, salt pans, the pastureland and the islands of meadow in the fen. All this he has added to the fishing rights you granted to him on the River Witham.'

'Ah yes, my grand strategy.' There was a rare bitterness in Isabelle's voice. 'The fishing rights which I so freely granted him.' Then something that Pexton had said hit her. 'What did he mean it was all his "birthright"? He knows the law as well as I do. And he knows his father's will . . . Is he questioning the validity of the will?'

'He is questioning much more than that, I fear. He is claiming that he is Anthony Crosse's true heir . . .'

'That is ridiculous. He will be laughed at before every court in the land from the shire court to the king's court at Westminster.'

'That he may . . .'

Pexton sounded as if there was a fragment of a possibility that this might not happen. Isabelle was first flushed with anger, then puzzled.

'Why do you say that? The man is a publicly acknowledged bastard.'

'He claims that he is not and never was a bastard. He claims that only this past year he discovered the truth concerning his own status.' Pexton paused. Neither of the women interrupted him. It was clear that the bolt was about to earth. 'He claims that Anthony, your late husband, married his mother before she gave birth.'

'Good God.' The goblet fell from Isabelle's fingers, its contents splashing on to the meadowsweet. 'Holy Mary, this cannot be true.'

Pexton knelt beside his mistress. 'I did not relish telling you this sordid tale. But better I than one who does not love you.' For one second he touched her hand with his own. 'Edward claims that when Anthony was fifteen years old he entered into a relationship with a girl from Bicker. She was the child of a small freeholder who also rented pasture from Anthony's father in the fen of Gosberton Marsh. Anthony lay with her. That much we all know since, much as his nature argues to the contrary, Edward was not sired by an incubus.'

Isabelle frowned at her dead husband's indiscretion.

'But, he claims the girl had no desire to be a mere plaything of her lord's son. She only allowed Anthony to continue lying with her on the condition that he make her his wife.'

'I presume that he has witnesses to all of this?'

281

Eleanor sounded deeply sceptical. 'Or is it all from his own head?'

Richard raised his eyebrows. 'I will come to that in a moment. Well, as you know, Anthony lay with her often enough for her to quicken with a child. But before her breeding turned to birth the plighting of troths took place. In the end she died in the breeding – God rest her. And Anthony repented of a secret marriage with no end in it. No end, save getting a maiden on her back in the sedges and seeing to it she went home a maiden no more!'

Pexton's tone was judgemental. Clearly he felt that whatever the truth to the story, Anthony Crosse was the one to blame for the present crisis. No one rebuked him.

'You said he has a witness to all of this?' Eleanor probed insistently. 'Who is the witness?'

'Well, only three people knew of the secret promises. And one of them died on the birthing stool. The other was bound to Anthony by close friendship. When Anthony took Edward in as a bastard son, this other witness went along with the ruse. For he too knew that Anthony had been foolish. A marriage to a poor girl would do nothing for the eldest son of a Boston guildmaster. So he remained silent. Silent that is until his conscience could allow it no longer.' Richard said the word 'conscience' as if it was tainted. He took a swig from his wine goblet.

Eleanor seized his arm. 'Who was the witness?'

'Well it was some twenty-one years ago. Anthony was just seventeen, I was a mere child. And Phillip Spayne was twenty-five and had just been priested.'

'Phillip Spayne.' Isabelle's voice was low. 'Phillip Spayne . . . I don't believe it.'

Richard Pexton rose from his knees. Without a glance at his mistress he walked to the table and poured more wine. Then he stepped to the window and gazed down into the street. Outside, the rutted road was alive with many-coloured carts and merchandise. Chickens and pigs rooted amidst dusty feet. Inside the solar the atmosphere was mid-winter. Even little Eve sat motionless; frozen like the rest of them by the tension.

'Where does this leave me, Richard?' Isabelle did not even look at her clerk.

'According to Edward you are his father's true widow but he is the heir. As such you are entitled to all that you brought to the marriage. Which of course consists of the fishing rights in the southern part of Kirton Meeres. All else belongs to him as sole heir of the estate.

'As a widow you would have "dower rights". That is you may keep any gifts made on your wedding day and you may, of course, claim up to one-third of those lands which Anthony held in free tenure on the day of your marriage. Consequently you cannot enjoy any of the income from the lands around Swineshead which he held from the abbey there. Nor can you take from any of the pastures, meadowland, cuttings and salt pans about Donnington and Bicker which Anthony purchased since your marriage. Some of course he did hold at your marriage. Those you may take income from.

'All the stocks held in the warehouses were gained

since your marriage and revert to Edward. You may however enjoy one-third of any rents gained by the letting out of any of the Crosse tenements. All money owed to the house of Crosse is owed to Edward unless we have seal and charter to prove that it was owed before your marriage.'

'Well . . . is that all then?' Isabelle was shaken to the core. Her hands trembled and she sensed tears welling up in her eyes. She could feel the brittle façade she had rebuilt since the attack in the barn fracturing, and she was powerless to stop it. The feeling of helplessness frightened her.

'Not quite. You would lose the right to act as a guildsman in the town. Your place in the Guild of the Blessed Mary would go to Edward. Though one-third of the utensils in the hall here are yours so long as we . . .'

'As long as we can prove that Anthony Crosse owned them on the day that I was foolish enough to marry him.'

Pexton nodded.

'One more thing, Richard.' She was fighting her tears now. 'How have the other guildsmen taken this news?'

'Some were openly exultant. Edward has his friends, you know: the less savoury amongst the guilds, for example, and those who disapproved of a man disinherited by a woman. But others were hostile and believe he cannot be trusted.'

'But where do the majority lie?' She felt the first full tear trickle down her cheek, and tried, without success, to blink back the next.

'The majority are watching and waiting. They want to see what you will do. They are still sniffing for the winning side and don't want to commit themselves too soon. But they smell blood and it is not Edward who has been wounded . . .' Pexton peered at her. 'You understand me?'

Isabelle nodded. Scooping up Eve with one arm, Eleanor leant over to embrace the younger woman, and the little girl reached out hands to touch the sorrow coursing down Isabelle's cheeks.

'But you don't understand.' Pexton's voice was raised. Isabelle looked up, shocked. 'This isn't the end. We can fight this bastard. Believe me we can fight him: he's a bastard by nature *and* by birth. Why do you think that we are still in possession of the hall? Because I was resident here. I promised that bastard steel in the gut if he stepped in here. And I told him I'd geld him if he put one hand on the warehouse!'

Pexton hopped on one leg and gave a swift demonstration of gelding, using an imaginary knife. Isabelle laughed through her tears. She had never seen her clerk indulge in such antics.

'So you see, it's not all over yet. By the Virgin he has not seen half of it yet. We will challenge Spayne, fight Edward in every court, drive out his thugs if they come near the hall. But you must believe that it can be done. If you do not, then we are lost. Now you must eat,' he ordered, desperate not to lose the impetus of his determination. 'All of you must eat.'

To begin with it was a fairly subdued breakfast, despite the clerk's rousing words. Nevertheless it was a welcome meal. As the shock of the news passed, so appetites quickened. Soon the cold meats and hard cheeses were cleared.

With the private discussions over, Richard once more summoned the waiting servants. Now it was time for them to pass back the word that the mistress was in fine form. As long as they were in the room, Isabelle concentrated on keeping up the confident, cool exterior that she had cultivated for so long.

Before the meal was over William Curteys appeared. He had changed clothing, unlike the members of the Crosse party. It was as if he had shaken off the rigours of the Baltic as he shook off his soiled cotte. Clearly he had enjoyed a little rest before the momentous news had been launched upon him.

'What in the name of all that's holy is Edward up to?' He had scarcely been announced before he was in the solar. 'He must have taken leave of his senses. What do you mean to do?'

Isabelle had managed to regain something of her usual outward composure, though inside she felt far from confident. 'I have talked the matter over with Richard. We intend to fight this absurdity. We will attend tomorrow's meeting of the town guilds. It will give me an opportunity to declare publicly that we accept nothing of these absurd allegations.'

'A point he will fiercely contest.'

'As we will, no less fiercely. The next step will be to challenge him before the wapentake and shire courts. Before we do that I shall send a letter under seal to the sheriff at Lincoln to swear in juries for the wapentakes of Kirton and Skirbeck. The jury for Kirton will have jurisdiction over all the fen manors; that for Skirbeck over the town of Boston. We shall see what can be remembered about what was being whispered twenty-one years ago. There will be many living who still recall Edward's mother. The fen folk are no fools. I dare say that we will hear some interesting stories.'

'What of establishing your dower rights? You must establish exactly which third makes up your rights.'

'No! Even to consider that could be taken as an acceptance that Edward might win. I shall not fight that battle yet. By God's grace I shall never have to fight it if I show his illegitimacy to be beyond question.'

William grunted. It was a tacit agreement. He rubbed his beard as he thought. 'I was going to ask you to accompany me to the guild chantry after noon to discuss prayers for the soul of Adam. Perhaps now it would be better if I did it. The masses for his soul will need be said by Phillip Spayne.'

Isabelle laid down her knife. Her eyes narrowed. 'I will go with you. I too have things to say to Phillip Spayne.' She was determined not to show weakness again, not now, with everyone watching her. She wanted all to see that she could face Spayne and not be daunted by his support for Edward. Besides which, perhaps an offering might yet win the priest's approval.

William pulled a pained face but could see there was no hope in diverting her from her errand. 'Very well. We shall go together. It should at least make for entertainment for the townsfolk. Though whether it is the best place to meet him I leave to your judgement, Isabelle.'

The matter settled, William left to attend to

customs business back on Town Quay. He seemed
rather subdued. Perhaps, like for Isabelle, the news
awaiting them in Boston had struck home harder than
he would tell. Rising from the table, Isabelle instructed Pexton to have a tub of warm water sent to
her chamber. She had no intention of remaining in
her soiled clothes a moment longer than was necessary.

Eve was tired and ready for a nap and Eleanor laid
her in a nest of plump pillows in one corner of the
solar. Soon she was asleep, thumb in mouth. Isabelle
knelt beside her, watching the wayward curls on the
little blonde head. Very carefully she brushed her
own lips with the tips of her fingers. She lightly
touched Eve's face with the offered kiss. The child
stirred a little but did not wake. There was a hint of
deep sadness in Isabelle's eyes. Then she roused
herself.

'You are as travel-stained as I,' she whispered to
Eleanor. 'Come, we can talk as we change.'

In the panelled room off the solar, scullery maids
had placed a huge iron-hooped tub, filled thigh-deep
with warm water. Soft cakes of ash-and-fat soap lay in
a shallow wooden platter laid on the rushes. Nearby
the trail of little puddles betrayed the route taken by
the bucket-carrying servants. With a sigh of relief
Isabelle stripped, carelessly throwing her clothes to
one side. Stepping into the tub she gave a moan of
pleasure as the water swept up about her thighs.
Kneeling forward she lowered her aching body into
the embracing tide. It surged up over her belly and
foamed about her firm breasts. Water cascaded on to

the rushes and she closed her eyes. Her breath came slow and deep.

Eleanor took the cakes of soap and raised a weak grey lather on Isabelle's back, noting the red lines that still ran faintly across her companion's shoulders, lines scored by the nails of the archer in the Livonian barn.

'You might do well to heed Will Curteys' advice,' Eleanor said. 'If Edward has done you this much hurt he might do you more. It could do no harm to establish what exactly should make up your widow's third. Edward is more than . . .'

'No.' Isabelle did not move. Her eyes remained shut, but Eleanor could feel the slight tension in the muscles of her neck as she gently massaged her companion. 'No. And you should know better.'

'Isabelle, there is no virtue in being unbending. Listen to advice. There's no fault in listening to someone else. You don't diminish yourself by showing that you are not all-knowing.' It was rare for Eleanor to scold, but it seemed to have little effect on the mood of her companion.

'No. I'll not let him sniff blood. I'll not do it.' This time the words were choked with emotion.

Eleanor quickly changed the subject. 'What will you wear this afternoon when you go to the church?'

Isabelle was silent for a few moments as she considered the question. When she replied her words were pitched so low that Eleanor had to strain to catch them.

'I shall wear the surcoat of pale blue. The one with the silver lilies. But without the mantle.'

Eleanor nodded and understood. It was the dress Isabelle had worn when she came before the assembled guildsmen the week after Anthony's death. On the day that she shocked her enemies and astonished her friends. The day that she declared she would be guildmaster of the house of Crosse.

Isabelle stood beneath the star-burst vaulting of the tower of the church of St Botolph, on the spot where Anthony's coffin had rested before its final passage to the guild chapel. It all seemed so long ago.

Out in Richmond Fee the sun was shining. The stall-holders were still dismantling their booths from the previous day's market and a small group of merchants were haggling in the cool shadows of the porch. Their talk had been stilled as Isabelle passed. Now it resumed in earnest.

'Wait here,' she instructed Pexton and the four armed retainers. 'I want to pray a little before Will comes.'

Leaving them she crossed the nave to where a wooden bench lay up against the wall. It was near the entrance to the chapel of the Guild of Corpus Christi. As she passed the entrance she could not fail to see the arms of the Coppledyke family over one of the doorways. She paused, taking in the three red Jerusalem crosses on their sea of gold.

She pursed her lips at the thought of God and her enemies all about her. Here was the place where her battle would be fought. Somewhere nearby Phillip Spayne's stooped body was bending before an altar. She felt her hands tremble.

'God, how I hate him.' The words escaped her lips

and hung before her. Stunned at her own passion she sat down, feeling faint and frightened. She had cursed a man in the house of God. Perhaps William was right; perhaps it was madness for her to see Edward's witness in this place. Yet she could not go back now. She would not.

She leaned her head against the cool marble of a tomb set into the wall. It was a woman's tomb and Isabelle knew it well: it belonged to Margaret Tilney, the woman who laid the foundation stone of the steeple, in the days of the first King Edward. There was some reassurance in that. Perhaps that woman was praying for her now? Trembling, she ran her index finger over the wings of the angel holding the stiff stone pillow.

'Mary, mother of God,' she prayed softly. 'Intercede for me. St Botolph pray for me . . .' The cool of the marble calmed her a little. 'You know what I have been through and the cost. You know the traps laid by my enemies. Help me . . . help me . . .' She could feel the tears again. She breathed deeply to master them. 'Help me to be strong. Help me to be good. Oh, Christ on the cross help me to win. Free me from this darkness that will not let me go.'

'Mistress, William Curteys is in the porch.' Pexton's warning gave her time to compose herself but she knew he had seen the tears and the pale cheeks. He offered her his arm and she took it gladly. Somehow it did not seem so bad that Richard had seen her tears. She could not bear it if William saw them.

Phillip Spayne was waiting for them in the guild chapel of the Blessed Virgin Mary, attending to a box of new wax candles. One already lay on the altar trimmed and ready, next to the reliquary containing the finger of St Anne in a silver and gilt hand. His sunken eyes glittered at Curteys' approach.

'Welcome back, William. I hear you have had a good trip. God in His mercy has been good to you.' The Roman nose twitched a little as he turned to Isabelle. 'Good day to you, Isabelle.' He sniffed again.

Isabelle did not reply. She fixed him with clear eyes and the effort made her face look frozen and haughty. Spayne's cheeks reddened as he turned back to the altar.

William let out his breath in a hiss. 'We have come to arrange requiem masses to be said for the soul of Adam Thymelby.'

'Ah yes, dead in the Russias.' Spayne seemed very well informed. 'Should this not be the work of the alderman of the guild, or one of the guild chamberlains?'

'The guild will make its own arrangements as is proper. We are here to make an offering from the trip. A gift to Our Lady and her sister.' William held out a heavy bag. 'It is our wish that the money contained here should buy candles for the altar on the anniversary of Adam's death and that this should be in addition to the masses purchased by the guild itself.'

Phillip reached out a blue-veined hand and took the money. He seemed unmoved. Before he could turn, Isabelle spoke.

'And have you no word for me? No word for one whom you have set your heart on destroying?'

'Isabelle!' William raised a hand as if warding off the words. 'Not here. Not now.'

'It is as good a place as any. Here before the altar of Our Lady. What stirred your memory after all these years? Was it the fact that I was away, or did Edward offer you more . . . ?'

'Isabelle, that is enough.'

'It is all right, William. I have nothing to fear from the slanders of this woman. I have seen her haughtiness before and her pride. Her words are not unexpected. They are rooted in a heart that is not meek and contrite. I had expected no different when she was confronted with the truth.'

'The truth? You have always set yourself against me. You are pleading in your own cause now! What know you of truth? Who are you to lecture me in the finer points of truth? You who now act as a false witness against me.'

'Jezebel! Do not accuse me of lying. You only fear the truth because it pricks your pride.'

'That's enough, Isabelle.' William took her firmly by the arm. He knew he had to stop her. He was convinced that she would achieve nothing by this. The only thing that seemed assured was her distress. William could not bear to watch it. For a moment he felt her resist him; then the wave of passion passed and she allowed him to escort her from the furious presence of the gaunt priest out to where Pexton was waiting for them in Richmond Fee. William berated Isabelle as if the clerk had not been there! Richard grew pale as Curteys spoke.

'And what by Anne and the Virgin do you think you achieved by that mummers' play, Isabelle, that pantomime?' he demanded as they stepped into the sunlight. 'If this is your strategy, you had better think again. For this will win few friends when the guilds meet tomorrow to hear the first words in the suit between you and Edward.'

Isabelle heard only the tone of his condemnation, not the concern behind it. She went pale and her eyes swam. She was hardly listening to exactly what he had said. Her attack on Spayne had not been commanded by any strategy at all. Her mind was adrift in a storm of anger, outrage and pain. She could not defend herself, for William was surely right. Yet she could not stop herself either. Her tightly clenched fists were tokens of her battle to hold herself together. For, to all intents and purposes, her world appeared to be falling apart. And once again William Curteys was witness and critic. It stabbed at her heart. Crossing the market-place she was oblivious of the critical gaze of the men and women on Richmond Fee. 'I am alone,' she murmured softly to herself. 'William thinks I have lost and am a fool. Even Eleanor thinks I have lost. Spayne will turn all hearts against me. I am lost, lost, lost . . .' While beside her limped Richard Pexton, glaring defiance at all who stared, friend and foe alike. He could only guess at what had passed between Isabelle and Spayne but, unlike Curteys, he did not rationally examine the issue. His first response was loyalty to his besieged mistress.

Back in the hall, Isabelle insisted on a full inspection of the household. She toured pantry and buttery, quizzing the butler on the wine stock and the grooms on the state of the horses. She handled the new rushes and cases of eels ready for salting, determinedly stamping her authority on the household once more. Then, exhausted and confused, she retired.

She slept through dinner and did not wake again until the seagulls were mawing and crying above the Haven and the light of a new day painted the tower of Botolph's church.

The Bailiff of St Botolph watched the guildmasters as they assembled in the hall near the river, Matthew Redman by his side. While the bailiff nodded to each arriving merchant and master craftsman, he kept up a low conversation with his silver-tonsured companion. Across the hall William Curteys was sat, with his retainers, on one of the long, low benches.

'It's all most unfortunate. God alone knows why Anthony did not name the boy as legitimate when he was alive. He set him up at Swineshead, didn't he? Let him carry on all the Crosse business with the abbey? It would all have been a lot tidier if he had acknowledged the lad.'

Matthew Redman adjusted one gold and garnet ring. 'You are assuming of course that the boy was not a bastard . . .' He did not like Edward. On the other hand he was fond of Isabelle.

'Phillip Spayne, man . . . What about Phillip Spayne? He's chantry priest. Knew Anthony well. Comes from a respected guild family. If he says it's true . . .'

'Quite so. However, she is bound to challenge it. You know that. She has to.'

The funereal bailiff pondered that. 'Humph. Don't see why she should. The matter's clear to me. Must be clear to her. It was all messy anyway. Running the guilds by the letter and not the spirit.'

Redman sighed. 'You know she had the right. Many women exercise it. More so than ever.'

'And many don't.'

'True, many don't, which is also their right. But she was legally entitled to act as guildmaster, and still is until the courts finally decide the matter.'

'And that's worse. You know we've spent long enough working for independence from the Honour of Richmond and from the sheriff . . . For almost two centuries now the freemen have elected the bailiff to account independently to the king for all pleas and dues to the crown. And it took us long enough to win that. It was a long struggle to keep the sheriff's nose out of the business of Boston. Nor did it come cheap.'

'I know, I know.' Redman's voice was soothing. 'A good weight of gold and two proud thoroughbreds to the king's majesty. These things never come cheap.'

The bailiff paused to acknowledge the arrival of the puffing Nicholas Coppledyke. Then he replied, 'It's not an independence lightly won or kept, Matthew. Without a charter we must guard our rights every day. You've seen what John of Gaunt has done to the Londoners to humble their pride, and they with their charter and mayor. It's a game we must play softly. We don't want to give the sheriff, or Gaunt, opportunity to pry into our business. Gaunt still has fingers in too many of our pies. The tolls on aliens at Gysors Hall are ours by right but he holds them. His manor court pinches our rights to hang and pillory. And he still controls the Assize on Bread and Beer. And it's not only Gaunt. The sheriff still holds jurisdiction over the running of the great November fair.'

A group of fishmongers entered the hall and Redman rose to greet them. Back beside the bailiff he murmured as he smoothed his robe, 'What has this to do with Isabelle Crosse?'

'It has everything to do with Isabelle Crosse. This business of a disputed inheritance must go before the local courts if she pushes it. Try as we might we can influence but not control those courts. And it will be their decision which binds us; not our decision which binds them. Not when it comes to inheritance of land. The sheriff will be overjoyed to interfere in our affairs. And Gaunt will be close behind.'

There was a commotion at the door. Edward Crosse entered, accompanied by his wife and by armed retainers. Some of the town's craft guildsmen entered with him, as if members of his party. The bailiff noted this, as did Redman.

'You see,' the bailiff moaned, 'how she is dividing the town against itself? Others will see this too. They will relish it. If she loves the liberties of this town she will go quietly away. No good will come from washing our dirty linen before all the world. And no good will come from giving outsiders power to decide between disputants in such a matter as this. If she loves the independence of Boston she will go quietly away . . .'

'Ahh . . .' Matthew Redman sighed. 'I do not think that Isabelle Crosse will go quietly away.' In his heart he hoped that she had the will to fight.

As he spoke a slim figure entered the room, dressed in flowing blue. Where the dress met the ground lilies were picked out in fine silver thread. She wore a wimple of sheer lawn. Beside her limped a dark-haired man decked out in the surcoat of the house of

Crosse. Together they sat to one side of Curteys and opposite Redman and the bailiff.

The opening discussions of the meeting seemed mundane. Those who had triumphed at gaining the hearing of the town so early in the meeting must have been cursing the affairs of the Crosse family, for few of the listeners seemed interested in what would otherwise have been regular business.

A baker was accused of selling light loaves and his case assigned to the Assize on Bread and Beer. A fishmonger brought a request that the town petition the young king on the matter of stranded whales. 'Surely,' he demanded with passion, 'it should be as in the first King Edward's days, namely that the king take the head, the queen the tail and we keep the rest of all such wreck of the sea. 'Tis a shame that all should go to His Majesty when our forefathers enjoyed a greater right . . .'

Nicholas Coppledyke yawned loudly. The bailiff frowned and the fishmonger glared. However, Coppledyke had reflected the feelings of all those present. Who was interested in fish when a gladiatorial combat was forthcoming? And one to titillate the palate of the most jaded. Lips were being licked at the prospect. Word had it that money had changed hands in bets.

The bailiff communicated the mood of the meeting to the fishmonger, that it would consider the implications of his request at a future date. The aggrieved fishmonger glowered as he retired.

Then Edward Crosse was invited forward. He was tanned most unfashionably with the August sun, but his clothes were the height of taste. He wore one of the new houppelande robes which opened down the front and fell in voluminous scarlet folds from the fitted shoulders as far as his muscled thighs; and his close-fitting yellow stockings ended in pointed Burgundian shoes. His pretty, rose-cheeked wife was similarly well dressed in a turquoise, silk pleated gown, a high collar giving way to a V-shaped neckline which plunged to reveal full breasts.

At her bench Isabelle turned to Richard Pexton. 'I can see where the revenues from my estates went last year.'

Quietly and confidently Edward made his case before the assembled guildsmen. He had made it before in Isabelle's absence but now he made it to her face. He gave no sign of being disconcerted by her presence, speaking openly and clearly. As he concluded he turned to face his stepmother.

'I know the shock that this news must have brought you. But truth must prevail. All these years I was labelled a bastard when my lineage was secure. In your pain I ask that you remember that. For as Phillip Spayne will swear, I am my father's true-born son. I am not base-born; no bastard.'

Isabelle made no reply, but she saw the look that the bailiff gave Edward and she stiffened.

Next Phillip Spayne was called to give his account. The assembled merchants and craftsmen heard the tale that Isabelle had heard herself the day before: a tale of secret trysts and promises made on nights buried in time for over twenty years; of how the young Spayne had heard the vows of the youthful lovers and been sworn to secrecy for fear of the anger of Anthony Crosse's father; a tale of a secret broken when conscience would allow it to be kept no longer. As Spayne spoke there was rapt attention from all. Only Isabelle's eyes strayed from the face of the chantry priest. Instead she looked at the faces of her fellow citizens, judging her as they listened.

When Spayne finished, the bailiff spoke briefly of the great difficulties of the situation but also of the clear implications of the words that all had heard.

'Well, that's it then,' Isabelle muttered angrily to Pexton. 'The bailiff has made up his mind. It just remains for me to say goodbye and thanks for all the feasts over the last year. Do you think that they have a particular convent that they would like me to retire to?' Her whispers were attracting attention but she ignored the glances. Instead she stood up. The bailiff had just finished speaking. He looked in her direction as she arose. Without further direction she began to speak.

'I am grateful that Edward Moyne and Phillip Spayne have so kindly outlined their claims before this body.' Isabelle paused to see the effect the use of Edward's bastard name would have on him. When he scowled she smiled grimly.

William Curteys turned to the man next to him. 'She's going to play it rough,' he muttered.

'Oh, I do hope so,' his companion replied, his eyes avidly taking in every curve of Isabelle's form. 'Oh, I do hope so!'

She gestured towards her stepson. 'No one here can fail to remember with what bitterness Edward met the news of his father's will. And there were others who agreed with him.' She scanned the assembled faces. 'But Tony Crosse's will was his own affair and he left no legitimate heir.'

At this point there was an uproar in the room. It emanated from the direction of the benches occupied by Edward and his friends. The bailiff took a few moments to restore order.

'It is the truth as Tony saw it on his deathbed. Before God he made no different confession. He set no other train of events in motion. He bequeathed all his goods and lands to me. Now you know how well Edward hated this. And you know how my lands were harried by those who sought to intimidate a young widow. You know all these things.'

Isabelle paused as these assertions sank in. Coppledyke was smirking. He knew that this changed nothing. Isabelle returned his smile. He grimaced and looked away.

'Then no sooner do I leave than secrets which have lain hidden for nigh on twenty years pop out. Pop out like coneys out of a warren. Is that not a surprise? Does that not make you wonder? Suddenly this fen harlot who fornicated with my husband becomes a virtuous madonna who could only breed legitimate children. And all this hidden for twenty years . . .'

Edward was on his feet now, being restrained by his friends. Phillip Spayne was calling to the bailiff to silence 'that brazen Jezebel'.

Isabelle caught his words. 'Jezebel? Jezebel?' she demanded, her voice dangerously high. There was a wild note in it, not heard before. 'If there was a Jezebel, it was her. And if a false prophet of Baal, it was you for all your lies against me . . .'

There was uproar amongst the guildsmen as her accusation rang out. Whilst there were those who were moved by her courage, more seemed shocked at the passion of her outburst. It was unheard of for a woman to speak so to a priest. Coppledyke was yelling at the bailiff whilst Redman whispered urgently in his ear. Will Curteys elbowed his way over to Isabelle. She stood shaking amidst the carnage which she had wrought.

'St Peter's chains, Isabelle, you will lose everything.'

He put his arm around her but she shrugged him off. He stepped back, a hurt look in his eyes. He made to speak but thought better of it. Shaking his head he walked away.

Richard Pexton stood beside his mistress. 'Do not fear, Isabelle. The bastards had it coming to them. They are sons of whores both of them.' The last sentence he whispered, for there were other Spaynes present in the room. He touched her trembling arm and she did not flinch away.

Slowly the emotion died away. The bailiff who had failed to control it himself was humiliated and angry as he brought Isabelle to book.

'As long as you hold seal in this town you will not talk thus to a priest of the guilds,' he thundered. 'Nor speak thus in the hearing of the Bailiff of St Botolph. Now have you aught to say before we consider rights?'

The bailiff had picked up the mood of most of those assembled. Isabelle had just gone too far, even for her supporters.

Isabelle was still defiant. 'Aye, I have.' The bailiff nodded reluctantly. 'Edward Moyne and Phillip Spayne assert that my husband secretly married in the fens at Bicker. By night as if doing something shameful.'

Edward snarled.

'Then whilst this matter has great bearing on what takes place in this town today, its roots lie elsewhere. They lie in the fens some twenty years ago. This body is not empowered to investigate it. It lies not within its jurisdiction. For this body can only deal with the rules and ordinances of the guilds within the confines of the manor of Boston.'

Isabelle looked to the bailiff who nodded unhappily. Satisfied she went on, speaking briskly as if fearful that the power of speech might suddenly elude her.

'I have sent a letter under seal to the sheriff of this shire. In it I have explained all that pertains to this case. I have asked him to summon a jury of the wapentake of Kirton. As you all know, Bicker and our manors lie within that wapentake. I have asked the sheriff to inquire as to the truth of what happened there all those years ago. For there will be many now living who will recall the manner of the relationship between Anthony and his mistress. When all the truth which survives there has been found, I shall take my case to the manorial court of the Honour of Richmond which meets in this town and to the shire court. These courts alone may decide whether my claim to land and property is true. And only then may I be ruled ineligible to hold the rank of guildsman in this town. And I will also demand the sheriff inquire as to why Edward seized these manors before due process of the law. For he took them like a robber – a thief.'

Edward was on his feet. 'This is folly!' He appealed

angrily to the bailiff. 'She but wastes the time of the town. You have heard the truth. Make judgement now! She holds the hall and stores and tenements here which are rightly mine. Make judgement!'

'No!' The bailiff clasped his hands and rested his chin on them. Sunlight burned on an emerald ring. 'Isabelle Crosse has spoken and none can gainsay it. If she insists on this course of action this body can do nothing until the wapentake court and manor court – aye, and shire court too – have examined the matter of the inheritance. For all this business of hall and stores and use of the seal rest upon her right, or yours, to claim legitimate inheritance.'

'But you know it is but the action of a desperate woman,' protested Edward. 'She can think of nothing else to do.'

The bailiff shrugged, a heavy and reluctant movement. He was not a happy man. 'Isabelle Crosse has appealed to Caesar,' he replied finally. 'So to Caesar she must go.' With a movement of his hand he signalled that the meeting was over.

As the meeting broke up the bailiff turned to Matthew Redman. 'Well, Matthew, what think you now?' Redman was silent. The bailiff turned away muttering, 'Nothing good will come of it, nothing at all. She should have gone quietly away.'

Matthew Redman watched as Edward and Isabelle left the room, his eyes thoughtfully hooded. To the bailiff he made no reply.

Outside in Kyrke Lane the meeting continued in a less orderly fashion. Voices were raised in shrill disagreement. Edward was waiting for Isabelle, his green mottled eyes narrow, his emotions a coiled spring. As Isabelle met the full force of the sunshine she was assaulted by a stream of abuse from Edward's advancing wife.

'This whore tried to seduce my good husband . . .'

'What?' Isabelle blinked and stared at the pretty face twisted with jealousy. 'What are you saying, woman?'

Ann Crosse, or Moyne depending on partisanship, ignored the question. Her accusations were to the street not to Isabelle. 'On the night after her husband's funeral this harlot invited my husband to her chamber,' she declared. 'There she tried to seduce him. She would have lain with her dead husband's son. And that husband scarcely cold in the ground.'

The crowd were loving this. Hordes, fresh from the Friday fishmarkets beside Town Bridge, immediately flocked to hear this fresh scandal.

Ann's indignation seemed real enough. Her chest was heaving with the effort of her accusation and a long tress of hair had escaped her net, only increasing the wild aspect of her over-ripe beauty. 'This whore dares to pass judgement on my husband's mother, yet is a sink-hole of lust and perversion. She would have whored with my husband in his own father's bed. Whored in her very widow's weeds,' she screamed.

The images were getting more and more lurid. The crowd was jeering, making the most of it. 'She can whore with me wearing a suit of armour if she wants,' someone yelled.

A Crosse retainer punched the man in the mouth and initiated a brief scuffle. But most of the crowd lacked interest in fighting. They were more interested in the spectacle being played out before them. Ann

Moyne was still defiant but Isabelle looked utterly bemused by this fresh attack.

Pushing forward, Pexton tried to come between them. 'Do your own work, Edward,' he yelled. 'No need to send your wife on a man's work.'

Edward had stood by while his wife acted. Now he shrugged off the accusation by Isabelle's clerk.

'Probably scared to come himself – after last time!'

The quip from the faceless crowd caused Richard to wheel to catch a glimpse of the eyes behind the joke. A sea of leers met him.

'Must have been awful for him. Ravished by her and forced to do her bidding!'

It was impossible to detect who said what. The affair was turning into a crude peepshow.

'Do you deny it? Do you then?' Ann pushed towards Isabelle. 'Do you dare deny it? You were only thwarted when your old servant came upon you.'

'Of course I deny it.' Isabelle stared deep into the eyes of her adversary. There was something strange there, a hint of something just beyond reach. 'You are not a fool.' Isabelle dropped her voice to a tiny whisper. 'You know that all you are doing is trumpeting his lies.'

Pexton finally came between them and escorted Isabelle away. The crowd waited agog for the reaction of Edward's wife. When she said nothing they turned away, cheated of their sport. A few shouted out half-hearted lewd calls in the hope that it might flare up once more. They too were disappointed.

William Curteys caught up with the Crosse party in the thoroughfare of Strait Bargate, deeply worried. He had watched the way that the crowd was taking sides. He was sure that Edward could only be served by Isabelle losing control. Somehow he had to help her but he was at a loss as to what to say to her. He despaired of knowing what would move her. None of his admonitions seemed to have effect.

By the time he'd reached the house Isabelle had gone inside and Pexton was dismissing the crowd.

'You must talk to her, Pexton,' William demanded. 'God knows but I have tried. These emotional outbursts will get her nowhere. I'd have thought after what she had been through that she . . .'

Pexton faced the merchant squarely. 'Emotional? You don't understand anything, do you? You have not got the slightest insight into what is happening to her.'

Curteys was stung. 'Damn you, Pexton. You'll not talk to me that way. You've no right to . . .'

Richard Pexton turned his back and limped into the yard, ordering as he did so the Crosse retainers to close the gates. William gasped at the blatant snub then, snarling at his own gawping retainers, he made off up the street. Soon only a solitary stray dog hung about the doorway. One of the servants threw a stone at it and it too sidled off, looking offended.

A little distance away Nicholas Coppledyke was on his way home. He had stopped to watch the sport in Kyrke Lane and had enjoyed it immensely. With him was one of the undecided guildmasters.

'But what if they're wrong? What if it is some terrible mistake?'

The red-faced draper dismissed the concern. 'Pah! Spayne says he married them and that's the end of it.

She's finished. Did you see them laughing at her outside the church? That will teach her to throw her weight around.'

'But surely that was because she was accused of . . .'

'Oh, yes, yes!' Coppledyke put in impatiently. 'But it's all the same thing. It's all due to her arrogance – and those uncontrollable emotions which are so typical of her sex. Think: did God create women to act like Isabelle Crosse?'

His companion looked thoughtful.

'Of course not. The woman is unbalanced. Now she's finished. And you take some advice from me. When Edward Crosse has her place he will be a force to be recognised in this town. Then it will do you no good to have been slow in recognising his legitimate rights.'

There was a flavour of menace about the words. Coppledyke's companion sighed. 'I see what you mean . . .'

'Anyway, I must get back to Wormgate. I've a fine new gate I intend to put up there. A fine strong one.' The green eyes sparkled. 'Now you listen to my advice. The woman is finished. She belongs to yesterday, and the wise are recognising that today. Only the fools will wait until tomorrow.' Nicholas Coppledyke clicked his fingers at his escort and strode on, whistling tunelessly, through the afternoon sunshine.

Chapter 10

Edward had determined to enjoy all the fruits of being lord of all the Crosse manors. He had spent without consideration. He had even bought a new bed which stood incongruously in the middle of the cramped private chamber at Bicker. About it sprawled three dogs dozing on the dusty floor. The bed, which Edward had recently brought his friends to admire, almost filled the room. Although it was way past dawn, his wife still lounged beneath the covers. The morning air was fresh and Edward had drawn back the shutters.

A faintly silvered late-September mist blurred the stockade and the thatch of the cottages beyond, and across the yard the servants were restacking hay from the valuable islands of fen meadow.

'Edward, come back to bed.'

For a few moments Edward ignored his wife's entreaty. He was enjoying the pleasures of his property.

'Come back to bed . . . please . . .'

She had that mock pleading in her voice. Edward knew it well and although it held no surprises for him it always managed to quicken his desire. He knew that she desired loving him as much as he enjoyed loving her. He had come to accept it as a matter of fact. Never had he used force on her. She had always come willingly to his demands.

He turned and in his nakedness showed his desire. She called to him again and he recrossed the chamber. Pulling back the cover he gazed at her, relishing her curled whiteness. Somehow she had preserved herself from the tan that so disfigured the common girls. He ran a hand over her firm belly. She moaned instantly. It took so little. He marvelled at her responsiveness. She was more lustful than he was. He quickened the rhythm of his massage. She came to him, mouth wide and eyes hungry.

He came down on top of her. He could feel her beneath him, folding her legs about his thighs. Her wide hips were spread beneath him. Now he wanted her badly. His mouth closed over one nipple and he kissed her heavy breast with force. She cried out and her fingers ran through his hair.

She was keen. She was always very keen. He thought of how she had denounced Isabelle outside the church. As he rose above his groaning wife he remembered how she had reacted when first he had told her of Isabelle's attempted 'seduction'. Her green eyes, now wide with excitement, had clouded with jealousy.

Edward was thinking of Isabelle now and of the scene before the bailiff. His wife was far from his thoughts as he rhythmically rose and fell against her. His father must have made love to Isabelle in this very room. The thought sat on him like a dark shadow. Was that why he had discarded the old bed? He snarled. His father might have had his own mother in this very room. No, that was ludicrous . . .

Suddenly he rolled off his wife. Ann pulled herself up, panting. Edward was off the bed. He was pulling on his chausses and shoes.

'What is it?' Her eyes were full of disappointment. 'What is it?'

Edward glanced over his shoulder. 'What? Oh, I've just thought of something.'

He turned to the door without another word of explanation. Pushing it open he yelled. The bull-necked henchman, who had wrecked the dykes of this very manor, came running.

'Come in here,' ordered Edward.

Bull-neck came in. He leered at Ann as she swept beneath the covers swifter than a grass-snake. Edward cuffed him.

'You pay attention to me, mullet breath.' The heavy man nodded. 'You know the villages around here well, don't you? You've been to a fair few by night, as I recall.' The man grinned lopsidedly. 'Tough. You're not going out beating up the farmers tonight. And don't look so sad, the good times will come again. I want you to get some names for me.'

The man looked worried by the intellectual immensity of the task. 'Names? What names?' He looked suspicious. Was this all a trap? 'What names?' he repeated.

'Calm down, you fool. Even you can manage this. Although it will take a bit more concentration than knocking a hole in a dyke side. I want the names of people who knew my mother well. It's twenty years since she snuffed it so some will be getting on. I want their names. The names of the kind of people who might get called on to a wapentake jury.'

He gazed at his henchman. 'Do you follow so far? This isn't too demanding for you is it?' The sarcasm was wasted on the man. 'You can start this morning. Well? Is there a problem?'

'Can I take a couple of the lads?'

'They're getting a bit restless, are they? Not as much fire and blood as they were used to in France. Is that it? Well you tell them they can damn well be patient. They've got as good pay as their captains gave them and a bed for the night. And they can have whichever village women they want.' He shook his head. 'No, this time you go on your own. You get me those names. Then maybe you can go out for the night . . . very soon. And then you can take one or two of the lads with you.'

The retainer grinned. Behind her coverlet, Ann watched in silence. She knew that as far as Edward was concerned other, more important things had crossed his mind, and she was forgotten. More than anything else she wanted to be important to him. Yet try as she might he never seemed to value her. As so often happened Edward left the room without so much as a word to her, leaving Ann full of disappointment mixed with burning envy. She thought of the Crosse woman in Boston. She could see that Edward lusted after her and for a moment she recalled her bitter words in the market-place of Richmond Fee. Doubts gnawed at her like rats. She had to believe that Edward had told her the truth. Yet she could not truly convince herself.

She fell back against her pillow and, unbidden, tears poured down her cheeks. She cried for herself and for all her disappointments. And then at last she cried for all the things that she had said to Isabelle Crosse.

About nine miles away William Curteys sat uncomfortably in the solar of the hall on Strait Bargate. Since his altercation with Isabelle at the town meeting, his relationship with the Crosse household had been strained. The only person who gave him much of a greeting nowadays was Eleanor. Pexton was as distant as his mistress.

It had been over three weeks since their return to Boston. In that time Isabelle had been seen only rarely about the streets and the traders in the Wednesday market had remarked on the absence of the flash of blonde hair. Not everyone disapproved of her. Indeed there were some who had first judged her but now felt a growing sympathy for her. But many others were still undecided.

She was hardly seen at guild meetings either. The trade of the Crosse household seemed to be entirely in the hands of Richard Pexton. Only in the nave of the church was she seen with regularity and then she did not linger to talk with the other merchants in the porch. The only official news was her decision to adopt the little girl Eve. On all other fronts silence reigned.

At last Curteys had tired of such a situation. Whilst it was not in his nature readily to make the first move, he had decided to come bearing an olive branch. Somehow he had to convince her that disappearing was as harmful as her uncontrolled fury. Yet in his heart he was torn. Part of him almost wanted Isabelle to give up and be like other women.

His peace offering, a heavy leather pouch full of silver coins, stood on the trestle table at his side. At Isabelle's instruction Pexton poured out the chinking money.

'It's a good sum. I told you that the Lincoln merchants would pay fairly in exchange for the tolls we have saved them. Even including this payment, they have still saved a pretty penny.' Will prodded the coins. 'The arrangements are as previously stated. We hold their furs and wax until the autumn and then cart them over the river during the November fair. As long as we keep a weather-eye open for the king's men we shall be in the clear.'

Isabelle picked up one of the pile of silver groat and half-groat pieces. It glittered in the sunlight.

'They wanted to exchange the service offered for wool cloth.' William smiled knowingly. 'But I knew you wanted it in silver. They were not best pleased. You know there's been a shortfall in ready coin in Lincolnshire for months now. But I insisted and they gave way. I thought you would be happy.'

Isabelle smiled a small smile. It was less than Curteys felt he had earned and he frowned. The familiar eyebrows assumed their questioning arch. 'Don't say you would have preferred it in kind?'

'No.' Isabelle put down the coins. 'No. You have done well, Will. I am grateful for your help, as always. Richard, more wine?'

The clerk poured the guest a brimming goblet full of red wine. Curteys drained it in silence, before looking up at Isabelle. 'So, what are your plans?'

'Other than a convent, you mean?'

William ignored the remark. 'For the autumn trading. Clearly there is a good deal to do before the November mart. The fair is only nine weeks away. It starts on 30 November . . .'

'Thank you, Will, but I do know what day the feast of St Andrew is on.'

'Quite.' William was getting irritable. Nevertheless he persevered. 'But you have plans?'

'We have a heavy consignment of wax and cloth to go to the abbey and cathedral at Ely.' It was Richard who answered William's question. 'We have contracted for boats to come up from Lynn next week and carry the goods to Ely.'

William ignored Pexton. 'And what of your personal plans? What has come of your letter to the sheriff of Lincoln?'

Isabelle unfolded a piece of vellum. It carried a heavy red seal. From the easy way it unfolded it had obviously been read and re-read many times.

'This came a few days ago.' She flicked her eyes across the page as if to remind herself of its contents. 'The sheriff is not free to act in this matter as quickly as he would like.' She looked up. 'It seems that the king's council has issued an ordinance ordering all sheriffs to arrest unlicensed preachers. The Bishop of Lincoln has published a certificate naming those who are preaching dissent and heresy in the diocese of Lincoln. The sheriff is enforcing the ordinance in the Parts of Lindsay. He has little enough time at present to arrange the calling of juries in Kirton and the Parts of Holland. The deputy sheriff is making the annual round of the wapentake courts this autumn. He will begin getting the beadle of Kirton wapentake to start empanelling a jury. There will be many villages and farmsteads for him to consider.' Isabelle folded the letter once more and put it away in a heavy box on the table.

'The matter of heretic preachers is related to the unrest of last year,' Richard said eagerly. 'Many who rebelled against the king and their landlords were said to be encouraged by unfrocked priests and other lawless men.'

'Thank you, Richard.' William was civil but more concerned with Isabelle. 'So this matter delays the calling of the jury. And until it is called there is no way of discovering more about Tony and his woman in the fens.'

'And in the meantime, Edward holds my manors and enjoys the profits of my land.'

'Though he too cannot move against you in Boston until the matter of the jury has been cleared up . . .'

'Quite.'

'So it's a stalemate. That is, until the evidence is examined out in the fens?'

'It is and that is why I shall be going with the goods to Ely. I have rarely been as far as Ely before.' She stopped as she thought of the incongruity of the statement. She had travelled to Novgorod but rarely as far as Ely. 'Anthony's fishing rights on the Witham are shared between Edward and Ely. So it will be a good opportunity to strengthen the relationship with the abbey.'

William looked concerned. 'You think that it is wise to leave Boston at this time? You'll be away a fair few days. And if the weather turns foul . . .'

'Edward will not move against my property in the town. Not before the meeting of the wapentake jury. That would look very bad. He'll have trouble enough explaining why he used force at Bicker and Donington. To use it here would be unthinkable. It would embarrass the other guildmasters and bring down the fury of the Honour of Richmond and the sheriff.'

William was aware that many of those who had been shocked by Isabelle's outbursts still felt that Edward was far more dangerous, more calculated and cruel.

'I agree, but it's not that which concerns me.' William motioned to Pexton to refill his goblet. The wine splashed like blood against the planished pewter. 'It's not a violent Edward that concerns me.' For once William chose his words with real care. 'It's the other guildmasters.'

Isabelle flashed. 'What do you mean?' She was suddenly back in the town meeting, with the bailiff abandoning her cause. 'What do you mean?'

William tightened his lips. 'Look at it from their position. What does it look like if they see you run away to Ely? How can those who favour you show themselves if they think you are going to throw in your hand?'

'For the sake of God, William, I am not running away to Ely. How can you say that to me?'

'I'm not saying it. It's how it will appear.'

Isabelle glared at him. 'You *are* saying it. I heard you say it. You said that I am running away. And I'm not.' She could feel that irritating pricking behind her eyes again and hated herself for it. Fighting back her tears she carried on, 'I am not running away. I am a guildmaster and I shall do what I see fit.'

William Curteys dismissed her response with a wave of his hand. He had had enough. He swung up from the bench, so that he stood less than six inches away from her. 'I've tried to tell you, Isabelle, but you won't listen to me any more. You rarely did before but now you seem bent on your own destruction. Good day to you.'

As he left the solar Eleanor, who had sat and watched the entire performance, spoke for the first time. 'It's a mistake to treat him so, Isabelle. You cannot afford to throw away his friendship.'

'It will not be my doing. You heard what he said to me. After all of this!' Isabelle's voice was charged with emotion. 'You heard what he said.' Eleanor bowed her head slightly and did not reply. 'Well, didn't you?'

'Yes,' she said finally, without raising her head. 'I heard what he said – but did you?'

William did not break his stride until he had left the hall. Outside in the street his men were waiting for him and his favourite roan palfrey was pulling at the bridle. He clicked his fingers and the stirrup was held out for his booted foot. Angrily he mounted.

His fury had not abated when he reached Matthew Redman's hall down towards Town Quay. Redman was busy in the sheds at the back, his apprentices laying out bolts of new cloth, fresh from the Lincolnshire Wolds. The older man gave Curteys a fatherly smile but when he saw the look on his face he quickly dismissed the apprentices.

'What has happened? The king's customs collectors have surely not discovered the Lincoln goods hidden in your warehouse?'

Curteys started. 'Bloody hell, Matthew, how did you . . . ?'

His question faded as the elderly guildsman tapped his distinguished nose. 'Well, if it's more serious than money you really must be worried!' Redman smiled. 'What is it? Speak up, Will. I knew your father and have seen you grow from boy to man. I think I can keep a confidence.'

William hesitated. He was not sure exactly how to put it. It was only when Matthew inquired that he realised just how worried he was. It was no easy matter to explain. All he knew was that Isabelle Crosse was destroying herself and that he longed to help her but she would not let him.

Slowly and deliberately he spoke of Isabelle's erratic manner and of her decision to go on to Ely. Redman listened intently. Every now and then he nodded his silver balding head. When William had finished he pondered for a few moments.

'How much will the Commission of Sewers fine you if you neglect the maintenance of the drainage ditches on your fen manors?'

William looked a little nonplussed.

'Bear with an old man. How much?'

'If I neglected all three summonses to repair the damage I would have to pay a "woepenny" fine of sixteen pence.'

'No mean fine, were you less than a wealthy merchant of this fine town.'

William grinned. 'No mean fine, I agree.'

'But what if you kept unringed pigs at the dyke-side?'

William raised open hands, puzzled.

'Well?'

'You know as well as I do that the fine could be enormous. It's one silver penny for every unringed pig. And with good reason. Too many dykes have been weakened by rooting pigs. Then, come the winter spate, the dyke bursts. Pigs have killed men that way – and lost good acres to the sea and swollen rivers. A large herd of unringed pigs could cost a man very dear.

'That is how it is with Isabelle. Surely you can see that? All these attacks are hurting her. They are like pigs attacking the dyke of her plans. One at a time and she could ward them off. But all together and she is being undermined. It is as if every enemy she could have has tried to put her down since she took Tony's place. All together they are pushing her to the brink. Like pigs on the dyke they are rooting into her. You should not be surprised if the dam is breaking. After a while even the strongest dyke will give way. Is it any wonder that she can take no more? She is a woman alone and under attack. She needs protection not criticism . . .'

William did not reply. Instead he just tapped one white tooth thoughtfully with his thumb nail. There was much about Isabelle Crosse that he did not understand but one thing was undeniable – he was attracted to her.

It was ridiculous considering the way that she angered him at times, but it could not be denied. Matthew was right; she needed protection. William wanted to be the one to give it but he could not begin to think how he could ever convey such a message to Isabelle. She paid no heed to what he thought, or said. For, to be fair, until this point, only Pexton had unreservedly shown her his support. All William's analysis and comment had glanced off the surface of the pain. Only now did Curteys begin to fathom the terrible depth of that darkness to which Pexton had responded with emotion, he with logic.

The wherries from Lynn arrived on the last day of September. The shallow-draughted, lightly masted vessels lay against the wharf of Town Quay at high tide. From the warehouse on the bend of the Witham the crates of wax and the bolts of fine-spun broadcloth were carried to the open holds. The wherrymen sauntered off to explore the sights of a place as foreign from their native Norfolk as Lincolnshire.

The weather was fresh the next day and so it was not until Friday 2 October that the sea was still enough for the short sail across the grey waters of the mouth of the Wash. It was a good day for the start of a journey: the feast day of the guardian angels.

Despite William's misgivings, Isabelle sailed with her cargo. She went in the company of Richard Pexton, her chief clerk, whilst Eleanor remained behind with Eve.

With the full tide the vast flats of sand were invisible beneath the endless sweep of sea beyond the Haven. The breeze was light and the flocks of incoming geese skeined across the plain of slightly shifting grey. Already though the breeze was freshening and the wherrymen were keen to make Lynn as quickly as possible.

To the south a low, olive-green smudge marked where the sea and salt marsh merged with the silt fens of southern Holland. Somewhere in that intermediate land of mudflats and eelgrass the rivers Welland and Nene poured their heavy waters into the Wash through myriad channels. Beyond that there was no other horizon. Just a low dark line and an aching flatness under a vast mackerel sky.

Isabelle leaned out from the sharp prow of the wherry. Only a little distance below her the grey waters parted before the movement of the loaded vessel. She could not help but look to the south-west. There she knew that the sea penetrated almost as far as Bicker. There along the creeks of the Bicker Haven were her saltpans, amidst the bright islands of spreading cord grass. There were her manors now occupied and raped. As she looked towards what she had lost, the tears coursed down her cheeks and fell to be lost in the unyielding sea.

Richard Pexton watched her from the open deck-hatch of the vessel. He sat on a canvas-bound bale of cloth. Since they had pulled away from the quay he had watched her. Watched her in the way that he had studied her looks and moods ever since she had left the Yarmouth boat, out of Riga.

Blow on blow had been rained on her since then. Although he was far from the trials of the Baltic journey, he had been all too close to the assault before she had sailed the previous summer. He was as aware as anyone of the price that Isabelle Crosse had paid for her independence.

Watching her stand alone was too much. He could not view her anguish from a distance; nor ignore her emotional turmoil. Warily he joined her at the prow and together they looked out over the Wash.

'We'll be at Lynn before you know it.' The words sounded tame and tired. He ached to choose better. 'Look there . . .' He pointed to where a flight of waders curled over the sea. 'See how the water shines there?' Isabelle nodded. ''Tis the Gat Sand. And there . . .' He pointed ahead of them. 'The darker water is the Lynn Channel. We'll follow that ribbon of deep water almost parallel with the coast for a while.'

Isabelle shielded her eyes as she looked south-eastward. 'You know it well, Richard.'

'I've been out here a fair few times. Both with your late husband and over the past year.'

Together now they viewed the monotony of grey. There was an understanding between them: Richard felt it as surely as if she had turned to him and said it. If he had not felt it he would not have said what he did next.

'It hurts deep, betrayal.'

Isabelle considered the statement. 'Yes.' She nodded once but the vehemence of the movement underscored a dozen times the simple word. 'Yes.'

She felt herself fighting to release all the tension within her. Here at last was a man who tried to understand. No one else seemed to any more. Only Richard seemed to share both her blind determination to resist and something of her own hurt. She longed to tell him everything. Yet she could not. There was too much between them. He was her clerk. He had been unassuming for so long and now to make him privy to her thoughts was too arduous a task. She could not do it. It was simply one more difficulty and she could not face it even if it offered release. She was so tired.

'I think I shall sleep a little, Richard. There's some shelter under the awning. I'm exhausted.'

She repaid his openness with a smile which had become increasingly rare. He returned it. For a moment she read in his eyes all the pain that she felt. Then she turned away.

The wherries put in at Lynn in the late afternoon. They had other cargo to take on board for the monks at Ely. With the light fading, Isabelle, Richard and the Crosse retainers took shelter at an inn down by the waterfront, where the narrowing estuary became the river Great Ouse. The place was comfortable and a clean painted mud-and-stud exterior seemed to indicate a landlord who took a pride in his premises.

Richard and Isabelle took a supper of roast fish with the landlord in his private apartment whilst the men took their ale and salted herrings in the straw-floored common hall. The conversation with the landlord was predictable: the state of the war in France; the assizes following last year's disturbances; a row between the Bishop of Norwich and the king over the tolls due from the Lynn market. At any other time Isabelle would have delighted in the local flavour of the news. She would have questioned and inquired. This time, however, she listened politely enough as she picked at her food but her heart was not in the conversation. Once more she felt inordinately tired.

The inn had a series of common bedrooms with large beds catering for up to a dozen customers. It also boasted a handful of smaller rooms, available for additional silver pennies. One of these was taken by a couple of women pilgrims en route to the shrine of the holy house of Nazareth at Walsingham. Pexton took a bed shared with two Norfolk cloth merchants on their way home to Norwich from Lincoln whilst Isabelle parted with more pennies to buy a bed and a room for herself.

The innkeeper called it a room but it was more of a cupboard. A tiny boxbed almost filled what space existed within it, yet it offered what she craved most and what few ever enjoyed: privacy.

Isabelle was alone at last. It was a strange sensation and one that she would have found difficult to endure for long. Yet, now she needed it like a sleep-inducing drug. As she lay down she realised that she could not recall the last time when she had slept alone. Always someone had shared her bed, or her room. But despite her tiredness she could not sleep. This was how it had been since the return to Boston. She seemed always to feel tired and yet unable to smother it in restful sleep. Lately she had taken to drinking a little poppy syrup with her evening wine. It helped but did not cure the insomnia.

In the dark Isabelle lay restless. The hours passed. Events span past her in a mad gallop. She dozed off to sleep but then the nightmares turned the corner and came past again. Each time they were more vivid. She saw Adam Thymelby transfixed in the barn. She felt the lecher's hands tear at her smooth flesh, watched as Albrecht metamorphosised from a knight in armour into a threatening beast, breathing hatred over her and Eve. She felt the gulf that lay between her and William Curteys. Felt only his criticism and despaired of ever gaining his respect. She heard rather than saw the tunnelling of Edward under the foundations of all her work. She was smothered by him. Felt his hot weight on top of her, boring into her, making hate rather than love to her. And when she looked up it was the face of Phillip Spayne panting in a climax of guilt-haunted fury. And as he had her, she felt William and Eleanor and Eve drifting away from her. Leaving her alone.

'No . . . no . . . damn you.' Isabelle dug her fingers into Spayne's face. She gouged his deep-sunk eyes. Her nails broke and raked over his arrogant eagle's nose. 'No, you bastard. No, no . . .'

She woke and lay gasping in the dark room. Her hands gripped the smooth edges of the boxbed. Her nails had scored white grooves into the wood and blood trickled from her hands. Desperately she smothered her face in the goosedown pillow. For although she was awake the images still seemed to haunt her.

'Oh, Richard,' she sobbed, 'help me. For God's sake help me, Richard. Please. *Please* . . .' For only Richard seemed to understand. Then, as she had done for nights on end she wept and wept and wept.

From Lynn, on the Wash, the slow serpentine coils of

the Great Ouse carried all river traffic to the great cathedral and abbey of Ely. The route lay through the fens and levels of west Norfolk and northern Cambridgeshire. It was some thirty-five miles of unrelenting flatness. A desert of green, broken by the twisting flash of sunlight on myriad channels and the slow wing-beats of the herons at sunset.

During the journey there was little to do but watch the turning of the water and listen to the crack of the canvas as the changing wind caught the sail. The weather turned damp a day from Ely and the grey marsh mist soon enveloped what little low scenery there had once been to look at.

Isabelle hunched up in the prow again. A heavy cloak about her shoulders shielded her body from the damp grey air as Richard sat beside her whittling at a stick with a knife. The wherrymen kept clear of their gloomy passengers. It was as if the autumnal weather found its origin in their mood rather than in the season of the year.

'What is it, Richard?' Isabelle turned from the misty prospect. 'What are you carving?'

It was the first full sentence she had shared with him that morning. He looked up, cheered by the sound of her voice. He held up the stick. The moisture clung to his beard and he wiped it with the back of one hand. 'I'd rather hoped it might have been obvious.' He gave it to his mistress for her to examine. 'What do you think?'

'Is it a man's face?'

'It is not!' The two laughed like children. The boatmen looked up at the unexpected sound. 'It is not!' Richard pulled himself towards her. 'It's the tower of Botolph's church. Isn't it obvious?'

Isabelle scrutinised the model. 'It is dreadful, Richard. Eve could have done better.' They both laughed again.

She handed it to him. His fingers closed about it and her hand. For a moment they remained so. She could feel the warmth of his grip, the first masculine touch she had felt since Albrecht. She made no attempt to pull away.

'Who betrayed you, Richard?'

'Ah, it's so obvious is it?' He pulled a face. 'It was a long time ago.'

'Tell me.'

He looked doubtful. But still he held her hand.

'Tell me. I want to know. I know so little about you. Save that you are different from what you were.'

'Different?'

'You are more distinct now. Very much so. A year ago you were not as you are now. Now you are . . .' She paused.

'Angrier?'

'Perhaps. Yes – angrier. And through that more distinct. You are also bolder.' She looked to where his fingers gripped her.

'Yes. I am bolder.' It was an assertion. A statement of territory. 'When I finally told Edward that he was a bastard a cloud lifted from me. I don't know why. It just did.'

He shrugged and toyed with the knife. He did not add that he felt the same way when he had dismissed William's comments outside the house on Strait Bargate. That thought was his alone.

'But we digress. Who betrayed you? I could tell

from your voice the day we sailed. You know how it is because you have been there.'

Richard tapped his leg. 'I broke this damned thing when I was fifteen years old. My father had bought me a place with the companies in France. The old Black Prince was governing Aquitaine and fishing for advantage in Castile at the time. Did you not know that I was so intended? No – obviously not.'

He went on, 'My father had made some money fighting in France; from loot and the like. He saw the same for me. Oh, not that he could afford much. Just enough to scrape together a mail hauberk and a kettle hat. He sold a little land down on Kirton Meeres and bought me a light horse. I was to go as a sergeant, you see, like he had done. With one of the companies shipping out from Yarmouth for the wars.

'I had a sweetheart. Redhead she was.' His mouth grew tight as he recalled the girl. 'I loved her and she said she loved me. Well, to cut a very long story short I never got to France, let alone Castile. The bloody horse put its foot in a hole. I was out exercising it. Smashed itself up and me. It killed the horse and it was months before I could walk again. My father broke himself on the price of a surgeon from Lincoln.'

'And the girl?'

'The girl? Didn't fancy life with a cripple. Wanted a hero fresh from the king's wars. She had her heart set on some French pewter and a stolen bedspread. And cripples are not renowned for the amount of loot they can carry.' His voice was very bitter. It was obvious that he concealed a deep well of anguish and betrayal.

'When was this?'

Richard thought for a moment. 'Would have been

in the spring of '65. That was the year after old King Edward, God rest him, had his treaty rejected by the Scots. Not that you'll recall it. You must have been scarce six years old.'

'Yes, I was just a little girl. My mother died about then. That mattered to me more than a treaty with Scotland, or the crown of Castile.'

'Quite right too. Well, as you can imagine my days of glory were over. The girl married someone from Donington way. She might be a tenant of ours for all I know.' He gave a half laugh. 'Actually, she isn't. I checked once. Damn silly thing to do. People do stupid things don't they?'

'It wasn't stupid.'

'Yes it was. What good would come from knowing she was happily married and breeding children. She belongs to the past.'

'So what did you do?'

'My father did some silversmithing for the church in Boston and for the Cistercians at Swineshead. I already had some letters. They gave me more – for silver of course. That and the possibility that I might take minor orders. You know that I have passable Latin?' Isabelle nodded. 'Well I'm no schoolman but I have enough. Enough in fact to claim benefit of clergy if anyone tried to hang me! I could sing a nice little rendition of psalm fifty-one to save my neck from a secular court.'

The dark eyes laughed. There was something cynically reminiscent of Curteys about that look, as if depths of Richard Pexton were welling to the surface.

'So it was from Swineshead that you came to work for Tony?'

'That's right. He inherited a mixed bag of tenancies there. Some he held freehold with just work owed on dykes and sewers. Others he held as a tenant of St Mary's abbey. He was looking for a clerk who knew the fens well. I was looking for something other than the cloister. We were a convenient match were we not?'

'And you have been his clerk ever since.'

'Clerk and steward rolled into one. A far cry from the glories of war. The limp is my battle wound. But I was grateful to Tony.' Richard gave a sudden grin. It was all the more captivating for being uncharacteristic. 'I still have the hauberk of mail. I keep it in a stout box in my accounts room. You never know when someone will require a crippled sergeant for the wars . . .'

Isabelle squeezed his hand. 'I cannot remember when I last talked to someone this way.'

'But you have hardly said anything. I have gone on and on.'

Isabelle shook her head. Sometimes it was in listening to another's disappointment that one released one's own. She did not say this; not yet. She simply squeezed his hand.

The boat moored for a midday meal. The wherrymen were keen to light a fire and dry out their damp clothes. Isabelle and Richard walked off a little way together and the boatmen exchanged knowing glances.

A cloaking mist curled about them, and they were on their own. A little way along the bank a wide drainage channel flowed into the river. In years gone by, some trespassing local had built a fish weir on it but long since a forgotten Commission of Sewers had wrecked the offending obstacle and cleared the drainage. Now only the stout timber uprights jutted out from the bank. The rotting wood was overgrown with a tangle of spearwort and the pale pink petals of watermint.

Richard bent and picked a stem of the late-flowering plant. Without a word he gave it to Isabelle. She raised it to her nostrils to savour the strangely sharp, sweet smell. From a patch of damp woodland a snipe called 'chee, wick . . . chee, wick . . .' No other noise penetrated the mist.

The clerk hesitated for a moment. Then he closed his hands about hers, drawing her to him, crushing the little sprig of mint against his wet cloak. Then he released her fingers. His hands were about her shoulders and it was her crushed to him now. His mouth was on her mouth and she melted into his embrace with a little sigh. He kissed her mouth and throat as all the time she clutched the mint in hands folded like the madonna's on the guild altar.

As he kissed her Richard ran his hands through the loosening folds of her hair. Her wimple fell away and he cradled the back of her head in his cupped hands. He kissed her with the passion born of intense longing suppressed for years, weeping with the joy of it. Then his arms were around her shoulders, pressing his cheek against hers. For a long time he simply held her in his arms as she shuddered, her slim, slight body racked with sobbing.

By the time they returned to the wherry the boatmen had finished their meal. They eyed the returning couple with poorly disguised curiosity but Isabelle and Richard ignored their looks, settling into the bows as before. Away, up the bank, all that remained of their moment of intimacy was a crushed lawn wimple which lay in a snowy fold beside a twisted sprig of watermint.

The Benedictine abbey and cathedral church of Ely dominated the low marshland countryside. The sheer bulk of its houses of prayer loomed over the market town. Aptly named the 'island of eels' this slight rise of well-drained land had attracted settlement over the centuries, a place of refuge amidst the streaming wetness of the fens. Not by accident had Saxon monks seeking solitude founded this outpost of the church of God. And here, years later, Hereward the Wake had defied the Norman might from his reed-girdled fort.

' 'Tis like a fortress amidst the marshes.' Richard peered at the dark shapes materialising from the mist. 'In the days of King Stephen the rebel Baron de Mandeville held Ely against the king. He spread terror right across the southern fens. His men seized honest men from their beds by night and harried and destroyed the land.' Then, seeing her wonder at his knowledge, he shrugged. 'I did my learning at a monastic house. I have copied more than one chronicle in the scriptorium at Swineshead.'

The afternoon was well gone and the service of nones ended. Hooded figures were about the cloisters between the afternoon service and the sunset office of vespers. At the river wharf the boatmen were unloading the cargo, assisted by a group of lay brothers and a handful of Crosse retainers. From somewhere unseen wafted the distinctive smell of broiling fish.

At the abbey gatehouse Richard announced their arrival to a dozing lay brother acting as porter. 'There is always good food in the abbey guesthouse here,' he assured Isabelle. 'I've been before and, believe me, they know how to live well.'

It was not long before the abbey hosteller appeared. He was a well-built man in his early fifties. The guests from Boston were expected, he assured them, and rooms had been set aside. Fires were being lit in them even as they spoke. More than this, the prior would be pleased if they would eat with him in his chamber after vespers and before collations in the chapter house. He was eager to meet the merchants who brought beeswax personally from the Russias to Ely. Isabelle was pleased to accept the invitation.

Two cosy panelled rooms had been prepared. As the hosteller promised, fires were burning. Tubs of hot water were also to hand and Isabelle took the opportunity to dry her clothes before the fire and wash.

Isabelle's room and bed were shared with an elderly pilgrim to the shrines of Saints Etheldreda and Withburga in the abbey. Since the other guest was attending vespers Isabelle once more had a room to herself. As she scooped the grey foam over her shoulders she could not help but think of Richard Pexton in his own room nearby. She longed to go to him and once more experience the embrace of one who understood. Yet something prevented her from seeking the solace she craved. There was something about her sudden intimacy with Richard which deeply troubled her. She wanted him but her heart fought the desire for comfort, and she did not know why.

The prior's chamber was warm from a brazier full of live coals. The table was spread with an impressive array of goose and lamprey in sharp sauces, fine brawn and the sliced breast meat of fresh pullets. Such an entertainment was by no means unusual. It provided a ready source of intelligence from the world and extended the patronage of the abbey and cathedral. In addition there were always allies to be gained in the Lincolnshire fens where the rival Cistercians held large tracts of land.

As he welcomed his guests the prior seemed particularly taken with the fact that his wax had been personally escorted from the Russias by his guest. He insisted that Isabelle regale the company with the story of the Baltic expedition. However, impressive as the wax consignment was, it soon became apparent that the prior had other interests in the Crosse family.

Also invited to the prior's table was the abbey sacrist and one of the lay stewards of the sprawling lands of the abbey. Alone of the abbey representatives the steward did not wear the black-hooded habit of the Benedictines. A good-looking man in his early forties, he was, like his monastic companions, clean-shaven although this unfashionable aspect was ameliorated somewhat by his drooping black moustache and a generous smile. But, Isabelle noticed, hard eyes suggested that there was steel behind the smile.

'My name is Ralph Kymes,' the steward volunteered quietly as they sat down to eat. 'Father prior was eager that I should meet you. I am from Boston and my family are still active in the town guilds.'

Isabelle knew the family, as did Pexton. For a few moments they exchanged pleasantries about the town and its neighbourhood. Then Kymes came to the point. 'We have been through the records of the abbey. There is a longstanding relationship between this house and the Crosses of Boston. In the days of King Henry, Crosses were freehold tenants of the house here. Your late husband was a descendant of that good family.'

Pexton put down his trencher. He too knew the roots which linked his old master's family to the black monks. He also knew that Tony Crosse had been shrewd enough to pick up tenancies from the white-robed Cistercians as well.

Kymes continued: 'When your husband died, you left fishing rights on the Witham to this house, in memory of his soul and for requiem mass on the anniversary of his death.'

'That is right.' Isabelle too had stopped eating. 'I divided the rights equally between Ely and my stepson.'

'You have been away some while. Did you know that this stepson has trespassed on these rights of ours?'

'Little that Edward does surprises me. I did not know it but I can believe it.'

The prior interrupted. 'You must be as deeply troubled as we are. For these rights bought candles and prayers to ease your husband's soul.'

'It distresses me much, father. I would do all that I could to re-establish the rights of God's house in this matter but I fear I cannot. My stepson is in rebellion against me. He threatens all that I have.'

Richard noticed the confirming glance that the steward cast the prior and pondered its significance.

'This same Edward is the one who now holds the manor of Bicker as its lord?' asked Kymes, stroking his moustache. 'This stepson who does not honour his father's wife?'

Isabelle sighed deeply and inclined her head.

'The manor of Bicker holds a rich piece of land from this abbey,' said the prior, pouring out more wine. 'It is east of the Holland Causeway . . .'

'Between the raised road and the sea.' Richard Pexton knew it well. 'My late master held much freehold land in the fens thereabouts but that holding he had from this house.'

'You know it, obviously.' Kymes was interested.

'Aye, it is well known to me. It is some fifty acres of meadow. A very valuable spot. As well as the rent due on Lammas Day, the tenancy is responsible for the repair of three hundred feet of sea-dyke facing Bicker Haven. In the past that duty was paid as "acre silver", but Tony Crosse took to keeping the silver and repairing the dyke himself.'

Kymes smiled. 'Only now it is over two months past Lammas Day and the silver has not been paid, nor the dyke repaired.'

'That is the work of Edward, the stepson of my mistress,' said Pexton, glancing at Isabelle. 'He has seized the manor and now denies you your due as he denies her what he owes her.'

The bell for collations was ringing and the meal ended. The prior promised to pray for both the soul of Anthony Crosse and for peace within the Crosse family and as he left he said something quietly to his lay steward. Kymes nodded.

A thin rain was falling as Richard escorted Isabelle back to her room, her head bare for want of a covering wimple of sheer lawn. At her door she paused. 'I cannot thank you enough for what you have done for me. You have supported me in all things. And there may be things you must yet do for me which will seem very strange.'

Richard frowned. 'What are you telling me, Isabelle?' he asked gently.

'Not now, Richard.' She shook her head and he drew her to himself and kissed her.

'Just hold me, Richard,' she asked. His arms enfolded her. 'Just hold me.' She buried her face in his shoulder and would not raise her head. It was as if she could not look him full in the face. Richard held her tightly but then she pulled gently away from him and was gone.

He would have lifted her head and kissed her. Afterwards as he lay abed he was on fire to have done it. But something had prevented him. It was something about her open vulnerability. It would have been like seducing a child. He stared open-eyed into the night. This was an Isabelle he had never known before. The change had opened her to him and yet he feared it. It was as if her open rawness was almost too much for him to deal with.

The next morning Isabelle and Richard attended the service of parish mass at 10 o'clock and afterwards Isabelle asked to walk alone in the gardens. Richard was surprised but she insisted.

The damp weather had lifted and there was still

some warmth in the sunlight as Isabelle sat beneath the tangled spiny branches of a crab-apple tree. The bitter little fruits above her head were flushed with ripening redness, the grass, she could feel through the layers of her woollen skirt, was still damp. Unmindful of the moisture she leaned her head back against the twisted trunk. Away across the deserted garth a young novice was running, late for chapter. Otherwise the enclosure was deserted. From without the enclosing walls filtered the street sounds of home and market. Within those close enfolding stones was tranquillity and order.

Isabelle thought of the elderly pilgrim who shared her room. She had come to pray at the shrine and find peace on the death of a husband. That much Isabelle had learned over breakfast in the common refectory of the guest hall. It was a strange thing, this search for peace. As she thought of it the panic began to beat in her once more. With difficulty she mastered it and, breathing deep, finally controlled her racing heart. But still the memories of all the accusations, the images of violence filled her.

Then there was Richard. Dear, dear Richard. She bowed her head. Had she led him on? Had she encouraged him? She needed him like a brother but it was not a sister that he sought. The realisation twisted the blade of guilt within her. It also twisted a shaft of longing, for she too needed a lover's touch more than that of a brother. Richard could never be that to her; she could not deny what, deep-down, she knew she felt.

Before she knew it she was crying again. It was not like her, but the consideration of the reality of her lonely existence made her feel utterly desolate. To what bleak calling had she been summoned? At one time it seemed so certain: to carry the house of Crosse forward. To confound everyone who sneered. But now, she no longer knew. Words of Phillip Spayne came to haunt her: words like 'pride' and 'arrogance'; words that spoke of twisted motives that would be judged wanting by God.

The grass which had beckoned with its coolness was now cold. She had found no peace in meditation. Wearily she returned to the church. Inside, the older solid Romanesque pillars blended with the soaring vaulting of the new church. It was as if an imprisoned spirit had struggled to flight and recorded its transformation in the stones.

The building was quiet. The monks were at chapter and the service of sext was still an hour away. Isabelle knelt beneath the octagonal lantern, through whose traceried windows the heart of the church was flooded with light. 'Sweet, merciful Jesus,' she prayed. 'I am so tired and so bruised. I long to surrender myself to You. I no longer know what to do . . .' She sighed and the dyke broke . . . 'Christ I am broken. Help me . . . help me . . .'

Above her the mighty hammerbeam trusses seemed to hold heaven and earth together, whilst Isabelle's last attempts to hold her own world together collapsed. Her desperate pleas flooded upward to where her swimming eyes fixed on the far ceiling; where the vault of the choir twinkled like the stars on a winter's night.

Lost in her own despair, Isabelle was only gradually aware that someone was sitting beside her. It was the lay steward, Ralph Kymes. He did not seem particularly surprised at her distress and nonchalantly waved away her protestations of shame. Instead he asked her to tell him what troubled her.

He made an unusual confessor, this moustached man with the generous smile and the hard eyes and even as Isabelle poured out her heart she wondered why she was doing so. No tonsure assured her of his sworn secrecy. No priesting gave him the power to absolve her with prayer and penance. But despite this she told him all.

When she was done he was quiet for a long time. Then he pointed to where the light fell in sheets from the lantern. 'Before I was born the whole of that central tower collapsed.' He paused to give his hearer time to consider the extent of the chaos of such a catastrophe. 'It was when the brethren were building the Lady Chapel. They were devastated, as you can imagine. On one hand they were engaged in a work to glorify God and honour the Virgin. On the other it seemed that the whole judgement of God had fallen on them.'

'They must have felt God had rejected their prayers . . .'

'Some felt it. There's no doubt about that.' He paused before continuing. 'But in the midst of their disaster they started the work all over again. They called in a master mason to remedy the loss. However, they could not replace the tower as it had been. It was impossible to turn the shadow of the sundial back. It had to be different.

'Instead they built the lantern that you see. There is none like it anywhere else in the realm. Indeed, the prior once told me that there is nothing like it in all of Christendom.'

For a moment the two studied the craftsmanship of the work that launched itself over their heads. Then Kymes added: 'It was a hard job. For a long time many said it could not be done. You see, the vault is too wide to span with stone. In the end they brought in the king's own master-carpenter. And he did not come cheap! The timber vault you see is his work. It took twenty years to finish it. Twenty years of hard work . . .'

Isabelle considered his words, understanding that he was talking of more than architects' plans and builders' scaffolds. 'Thank you, Master Kymes.' She looked once more at the hammerbeams above her head. 'To be struck down in the midst of what seems right; to have the courage to build again; to pay the price of that rebuilding in labour, money, time . . .' She twisted her hands as she considered the demands of such a project. 'And to have the faith to see it through and not give up . . . I am not sure if I have such faith, Master Kymes.' Isabelle stood up suddenly. She left her place and with the steward behind her went over the cool flags to the Lady Chapel. Under its traceried roof arcaded niches were filled with a glittering multitude of statues portraying the life of the Virgin.

She took one of the small candles and lit it, placing it before the gilded sculptured stone. Then she knelt in silent prayer. Kymes picked up a candle himself and lit it too. As he did so he was watching the kneeling woman. He murmured her name as he lit the wick and watched it sputter into blue life.

By the time Isabelle had finished praying, the monks were beginning to file into the choir. She spoke quickly but calmly to the abbey steward. He nodded and said simply, 'I think that you are right. I shall do as you have bidden me and I shall also convey the message to the prior.' Then the two walked out into the abbey garth with its lawns and clumps of burgeoning crab-apple trees. The sun was shining and greylag geese honked as they passed high overhead.

When Ralph Kymes finally found Richard Pexton it was obvious that the clerk had been looking all over for his mistress: they were due to travel back to Lynn on a wherry leaving Ely that afternoon. The lay steward handed the suspicious clerk a carefully folded piece of vellum. Quickly Pexton opened it and devoured the contents. His breath escaped in a deep sigh as he read Isabelle's words.

Dear Richard,
You must forgive me what I am doing. I have not planned it. God knows if I had I would have told you. I will not come back with you to Boston. I need time.

Pexton looked suspiciously at Kymes. There was poorly disguised animosity in the glance. Biting back his distress he finished the letter.

I need time to heal the wounds that are crippling me. If I do not see them healed I will never face what lies ahead of me. Only here in the house of God will I find the healing. I know I can trust you to guard my affairs in Boston and to explain what I am doing to Eleanor. William will not understand.

I will not be long. I need time.

Isabelle Crosse

There was something else in the bottom fold of the vellum. Richard held it between his trembling fingers. 'And she would not give me this herself? She thought it best to leave it to a stranger?'

Ralph Kymes shook his head. 'You put it too harshly and so mistake the sentiment. This is difficult for her. You alone must know that. It was a mark of her affection for you that made her act thus. She could not find the strength to tell you so herself, for fear she would not go through with it.' The hard eyes softened. 'Believe me, she trusts you enough to understand. Do not betray her now . . .'

'I would never betray her.'

Richard turned jerkily away. In his hand he clutched a tiny sprig of watermint. It had been recently picked and with great care. The tiny pink petals were pressed against his heart.

The goldfinch hopped habitually from perch to perch. At the highest perch it raised its red face and poured out its liquid, twittering song. Then it shook its yellow barred wings and resumed its solitary movement.

'Very nice.' Edward Crosse poked a finger against the wooden slats of the cage. 'Very pretty.' Then he turned to his companion. 'Very nice indeed.'

Matthew Redman leaned on the polished wood of the table. A pewter platter of grey goosemeat lay before him, alongside a broken fist of paynemaine bread. The white heart of the bread was revealed through the torn tawny crust.

'You'll take a little food, no doubt?' The elderly guildsman gestured to a neat pile of coarser bread trenchers. 'It's a good lamprey pie.'

'I hear that Isabelle decided to go with that clerk to Ely.'

'Really.' Redman's reply was noncommittal.

'Unusual, for her to go I mean. I would have thought that Pexton would have gone alone. He seems more than usually efficient. And they say that he's very fond of her.'

This last he said with just a hint of suggestion. It was ignored by Redman who instead helped himself to another slice of cold pie. 'But I doubt that you called to see me in order to discuss the travels of your stepmother, however unusual they may be.'

'That's right.' Edward gave an approving nod. 'I admire your frankness, Matthew. Especially as we shall soon be close neighbours in the town.'

'I hear that the sheriff is getting a jury called to cover the whole wapentake of Kirton.'

It was a casual comment but from anyone other than Redman it would have sounded like mischief-making. The significance of the topic was not wasted on Edward. His fingers tightened about the goblet that the butler had just filled for him. Otherwise he hid his reaction.

'I believe 'tis true. It seems a lot of work for the sheriff and the beadle of the wapentake. Drawing up lists of true men with local knowledge. Setting a date for the jury. Dragging people on pain of fine from their fishing and fowling to sit on the jury. Writing down the statements. A lot of work that could be saved them, I fear.' Edward sounded as if he was really concerned at the labours of the agents of shire and local government. It was a civic concern which sat a little awkwardly on his shoulders.

If Redman noted the irony he said nothing to reinforce it. 'Still, I'm sure that the sheriff thinks that the matter is worthwhile. He, or his deputy, would have had to visit the local court this Michaelmas anyhow and the beadle will no doubt enjoy ordering about his fellows. Such men usually do. Besides, should the matter eventually go before the shire court, or even the king's court at Westminster, the sheriff will be keen for all to have been done in good order at the first stage.' Matthew Redman swilled his wine about his mouth. For the first time he let a ghost of a smile haunt his face.

Edward's green-mottled eyes narrowed with displeasure. Nevertheless he controlled his response. 'I do not think it will go as far as Lincoln, let alone the Court of Common Pleas. No other guildsman with whom I have spoken thinks it will last so long. Nick Coppledyke believes 'twill be settled before the spring.' He let the name fall casually. Although he as yet did not enjoy any status within the town, he spoke as one familiar with those who did.

'But it was not of that either that I came to speak with you,' Edward continued as he put down his goblet. 'I believe that the winter after the old king died, your manors suffered considerable loss through the flooding. Though it was near-on five years ago, the tenants on my manors still speak of that winter. Mayhap you still recall it?'

'It was a bad one,' Matthew Redman answered carefully. 'The winter rivers broke the embankments and a wind from the north-east followed it and brought floods from the sea.'

'A bad time. And at that time my late father advanced you a considerable sum to make good the damage that you had suffered.'

It was a bald statement and Redman did not answer it. He was not used to discussing his financial affairs in this manner. Edward seemed unconcerned. 'Then there was that business two years ago when the damned French took those vessels in mid-channel. I believe one of the Yarmouth vessels taken was carrying merchandise dispatched from your warehouses.' He paused, then added: 'A poor business and all lost to them. Nothing to be saved.'

'Is this leading somewhere, Edward?'

The fox-bearded young man picked at the lamprey. 'Once again Tony loaned you money. Almost five hundred marks. And lastly there was that trouble only this spring when those fools up in Holland Fen dug illegal ditches and caused the banks on the river to collapse and flooded the land as far as Wainfleet. Again it was your land which suffered.'

Matthew had stopped chewing his food. He put down his knife and watched the younger man. With a gesture he dismissed the hovering servants from the solar. He did not like Edward, with that torrent of crude force rushing just below the surface of his pretended civility. More than that he liked Isabelle Crosse. He admired her courage and she stirred the old, tender memories.

'What is this to you, Edward?'

'You owe the house of Crosse some large sums of money. And I know that it will be repaid.' Edward smiled as one would to an old friend. 'But it may not be necessary. Soon I will come into my full inheritance. I have much to be grateful to the good men of Boston for: many have declared their aid to me in my search for justice. It is only fair that I should show my gratitude. All who owe the house of Crosse can look to me to halve their debts.'

It was a staggering offer. Redman glanced down at the table. It was a truly staggering offer.

'You are very generous,' he replied choosing his words carefully. 'There must be many who are grateful for such an offer.'

'Enough, let us put it that way. But it is a small thing between guildsmen.' Edward rose from his bench. 'A small thing between friends and allies.'

Matthew Redman gazed across the room in contemplation of the offer. For one thing was clear enough. The only thing that was not small was the sum that he had owed Tony and, if she were to win her battle against Edward, would owe Isabelle Crosse.

Chapter 11

The St Andrew's Fair, or Mart, at Boston was the high spot of the town's calendar. Lasting for nine days from 30 November it was like a great commercial heart beating at the centre of the community's life.

So important was it that merchants attended from all over western Europe: wool merchants from Florence, vintners from Gascony, dealers in fur and fish from the Baltic. And to the fair were drawn the traders and entrepreneurs of the whole east coast. The wealthy abbeys of Fountains, Jervaux and Ely would be represented. The merchants of Lincoln would once more descend on the west bank of the Witham where the mart spread to become the Fair of Holland. It was as if the world came to Boston for nine hectic days.

Richard Pexton was always glad when the November mart was over. It was the most exhausting time of the whole year – and the most crucial to the prosperity of the Crosse household. This year the burden hung all the heavier, for he felt as if the familiar universe was disintegrating about him. Worse still he suspected, with good reason, that the town was watching the slow collapse of the fortunes of his world; watching and enjoying the spectacle with the cruel interest that so often attends the destruction of another human being.

It was five weeks since Richard had returned from Ely. Five weeks in which he had heard nothing from Isabelle at all. Long weeks in which he had endured the constant gossip of the neighbours and the staring in the market-place. As the bearer of the news he had begun to feel responsible for it. It was as if he had instigated it.

Eleanor's silent distress and William's ill-concealed amazement had fallen alike on him. He carried the burden unhappily. For he did not understand why Isabelle had given up. The very thought cut him like a narrow blade. All he knew was that once more he shouldered the weight of the hall and all its concerns. He also felt that whatever he had achieved with her on the journey had been cast aside and lost.

'Ichar . . . Ichar . . .' The little voice called him from his dark contemplations. 'Ichar . . . dogh, woof-woof . . .' Eve struggled into his lap. Try as she might she could not pronounce his name. Instead, the mangled version of 'Richard' was a familiar sound within the hall.

'Dogh . . . woof-woof.' The little girl pointed towards a couple of squirming puppies rolling before the dais. 'Dogh, woof-woof.'

Since her arrival in Boston, Eve had picked up rudiments of English speech with remarkable speed. Now she was willing to have a stab at any word spoken in her hearing. She would wander about the hall and yard to find the 'orses' and the 'dogh woof-woofs'. The disappearance of Isabelle had hit her hard. She had cried and cried for hours after their departure for Ely and in the weeks since his return she had attached herself to Pexton.

No one was more surprised than the bachelor clerk.

At first he had ignored her cries of 'Ichar' and the little hand which slipped into his whenever Eleanor was busy elsewhere. But, like it or not, Richard had been elected into that narrow and exclusive club which had previously only had Eleanor and Isabelle as its members, and after a while he had been forced to stop ignoring her persistent attentions. Instead he had taken to talking to her, and sometimes even played with her. Though he would have been hard-pushed to find words for it, Richard was growing strangely fond of the little blonde scrap.

'I'm busy, you can see that, can't you?'

If Eve understood she showed no signs of being repressed. Instead she showed the clerk a stone she had found in the yard.

'Ichar rock . . . Ichar rock . . .'

Pexton took the gift and examined it gravely. If he had one of these stones in his pocket he had a hundred. Eve was fascinated by stones. She would fiddle with the gravel of the yard for hours. The best stones she brought to Richard and to Eleanor.

'It's a very pretty stone, isn't it?' He turned it over. It seemed identical to every other piece of gravel in the yard. 'A very pretty one indeed.'

The little blonde head leant against his as Eve concentrated on the gift that she had brought. Richard felt a curious sense of warmth within himself. Then the wide eyes were smiling at him and the little fingers were pulling at his beard.

'Good to see you have time on your hands, Pexton.' William Curteys had entered the hall unannounced. 'God rested on one day in seven but obviously you keep to a somewhat lighter work schedule . . .'

Pexton stood up. Eve clung around his neck like a little monkey. He put his arms about her and tried to put her down but she hung on all the more.

'You seem to have made a friend there, Pexton.' Curteys seemed amused at the clerk's predicament. 'But I'm afraid you'll have to leave off the game. I passed the sheriff in Richmond Fee and he seems to be headed this way.'

Richard paled and firmly disentangled the child. The passing servants sighed. Now it was their turn to be pestered.

'How do you know that he is coming here?'

'I don't. But he looked like a man with a mission and I can't think of many other places on Strait Bargate which could be of interest to him. Can you?'

Richard tried to persuade himself that William's assumption need not be correct. The High Sheriff of Lincolnshire – much to the chagrin of the local guildsmen – had overall responsibility for the good order of the November mart, and as a result could be in Boston for any one of a number of reasons. Nevertheless Richard frowned. He could smell bad news.

There was a bustle at the door and one of the journeymen came running into the hall. 'Sir, sir . . .' He panted at Pexton. 'It's the sheriff, sir. The sheriff. He calls to be admitted.'

Richard glanced at William before replying curtly, 'Then let him in. And tell the butler to bring wine to the solar. Hurry up . . .'

Richard smoothed his hair and straightened the clothing disturbed by Eve. He tried to swallow his nervousness, all the while aware that Curteys was watching him.

As the sheriff entered servants scurried out of the way. He was accompanied by two sergeants, wearing heavy quilted gambesons under their cloaks and carrying broadswords. Their scabbards swung against their legs as they walked.

A short man, the High Sheriff of Lincolnshire had the air of one who really should be somewhere else and who was giving up a minute at great cost to himself. His tone communicated itself in his swift nods of the head and staccato speech. No one could have been better designed to discomfit Isabelle's clerk.

'C-c-can I help you, my lord?' Richard bit on his stammer.

The sheriff looked about him as if expecting to find someone of higher standing. His eyes lit up when he saw the more expensive cut of William's clothes.

'I received a petition. A request to call a jury in the wapentake of Kirton. A matter of disputed legitimacy. Where is Isabelle Crosse?'

The irritated request was directed at William. Instead, it was Richard who replied. 'Mistress Crosse is n-not here. She is at Ely . . .'

The sheriff regarded him coldly. 'Still? I was told she had gone to Ely over a month ago. Is she still there?'

Pexton looked very uncomfortable. 'Yes, my lord. She is still there. I am not . . .'

'I have come to speak of the evidence being presented to the beadle in the fens,' the sheriff interrupted aggressively.

'W-would you care for wine, my lord? We may take it s-somewhere more comfortable. I am clerk and act as steward also. I have r-responsibility for the running of the household while my mistress is away.'

'I have not time to idle in pleasantries, man. I have come on urgent business and your mistress is not available.' He gave Richard a glance as if to imply that Isabelle's absence was an admission of some kind of guilt. 'I have no time to waste.' He was obviously enjoying his impact on the guild household. 'I am in Boston to establish which of the Lincoln merchants will preside over the weighing and stamping of wool this year. And as usual there is not a merchant here who accepts the choice.'

It was a comment designed to provoke the Bostonians. The fact that it was a Lincoln merchant who for thirteen years had held the office of Mayor of the Staple, was not lost on the local merchants.

William bit on his indignation and steered the conversation back to what seemed the safer topic of the empanelling of the jury. 'Perhaps you could advise us as to the progress in the matter of the jury.' William was polite but his tone was firm. 'I am Isabelle's partner,' he added as if to explain his interest in the matter. 'What affects her touches me also.'

'There is little to say. I empowered the beadle to call a jury, but he says that the matter is clear enough. The woman in question was virtuous and respected by all.'

He stared hard at Curteys. He seemed to expect some kind of collapse. When it was not forthcoming he added, 'All who knew her say she was a pure maiden. It seems I have been asked to cast doubt on a good soul. Of the question of marriage I have no reason to doubt the word of a priest. And all that I have heard of the matter supports his witness. There seems no reason to challenge the legitimacy of your mistress' stepson.'

'And the beadle has summoned all who knew Edward's mother . . . ?'

The sheriff withered Richard with a glance. 'I am not a fool, nor are those appointed to uphold law and order under me through the wapentake courts. Of course he has empanelled all who knew her! And threatened with a fine any who claim that they cannot attend.' The sheriff snorted. 'I came here to tell your mistress that from what I have learned to date there is nothing to be gained from taking the matter further. In the circumstances I shall trouble the good people of Kirton no further. To go ahead and summon the jury will only be a waste of everyone's time. There is clearly no reason to do so. Unless you çan think of one – in the absence of your mistress?'

'It seems that you have been zealous in your duty, my lord.' William took it upon himself to answer. 'The matter came as a shock to us all. We felt bound to know more of it. You have enabled us to do so. It seems that our concerns were unfounded.'

'Yet I feel sure that my mistress will wish to speak with you about this matter.' Richard felt wretched. Alone he held fast to the cause. 'For there is still much that troubles us. For this matter has appeared from nowhere and we fear there may be enemies who are working against her . . .'

'Then she had better find me more than mere protests. I shall not act again until I am persuaded that my time will not be wasted. I have much to do this autumn in the king's service. I will not be side-tracked by ill-will towards a legitimate heir. And no court will look kindly at such a waste of its time. You may convey that to her wherever she now is.'

Pexton nodded. He blushed before the sharp words of the royal officer. Curteys also looked embarrassed.

The sheriff signalled to his sergeants to go. 'If your mistress has evidence that a wrong has been committed she may present it to me at the shire court. It can then be decided whether the matter should go before the king's judges.'

'I know that she will soon return, my lord. She may bring her complaint to the shire court in December? Or perhaps January?'

The sheriff seemed little interested in Richard's words, but nodded abruptly before turning to go. William watched the departing sheriff. 'Well, so now we know. There seems little enough that can be done now. To think that all these years Tony Crosse had a true-born son.'

'You don't honestly believe that, do you?'

'For God's sake, Pexton, what other choice do we have? You surely don't think that Edward has the sheriff in his pocket?'

'Of course not . . .'

'Then what other choice do we have? Tell me, man.' When Richard did not reply, William shrugged. 'I like it no more than you do. I'll not deny that I thought Isabelle was foolhardy, but she has acted with a brave heart this past year. And for it to end this way . . . Well, I like Edward Crosse no more than you do. But we cannot deny it any longer. The truth is the truth. And Isabelle must face it sooner or later. It will do her no good running from it. She'll not be ruined by it. She will have her widow's third after all. What's more, there will be no shortage of men who would ask for her hand in marriage. She is young and will make a fine wife.'

William spoke the words just a little too casually, and Richard felt a surge of unease. He had never once considered that William Curteys had any marital designs upon Isabelle, but now it seemed that his matter-of-fact tone concealed deeper feelings. As for Isabelle, he felt sure that she felt nothing for the cynical merchant. Nevertheless the possibility that she might now surfaced in his thoughts and his heart lurched. He looked at the guildsman darkly. 'This will destroy her. I have seen how wounded she is. This is no mere disappointment to her. This has gone to her heart.'

'All things pass,' Curteys said with the air of one who might be expected to help in such a situation – a trusted friend. 'It seems the end now but given time and a good husband . . .' He paused, unsure quite of how his own thoughts were running. Was he fearful that a victory for Isabelle might secure her in a single state? He could not deny it.

Pexton, unaware, continued. 'And what of Edward? Can you stand by and watch him win? Can Isabelle live in this town and see him day in, day out? Could you do that if you were her?'

'It will be hard, I grant you.' His eyes narrowed as he considered Edward. 'But she will not be alone. I will vouch for that.'

'It will be more than hard. It will break her. And when Edward has won, will he be content? I think not. He is a lawless man. There will be guildsmen who back him now but who will regret it when he is a power in the town. He may not, for instance, look so kindly on the Curteys' house as Tony and Isabelle have done. You may be about to exchange one good friend for a bitter rival.'

Few people had ever spoken to William this way.

The passion in Pexton's words swept away all impediments and nervousness. It was as if the anger gave him an eloquence that he had lacked when the sheriff had been present.

'For example,' Richard continued. 'Has the rogue offered to cut any money you owe to Isabelle?' He laughed bitterly. 'Don't look surprised. I have heard all about Edward's little deals. Well, has he?' Matthew Redman, in a gesture of support which masked his own terrible dilemma, had spoken to Richard of the offer made by Edward.

'As it happens, he has not.'

'So perhaps he has already decided that you are not a useful ally. And if not an ally perhaps he regards you as an enemy!'

Curteys looked thoughtful. Obviously the idea had occurred to him too. It seemed to him that he was bound to Isabelle by cords not always of his own making. It was disturbing to a man who had always prized his independence.

'So what do you suggest? You have a plan, I suspect.'

'I have no plan at all. I simply know that we cannot give in. While Isabelle is away we can work on her behalf. She has little time left. Once Edward hears of the sheriff's decision he will move on Isabelle's property in Boston. We must act quickly. Isabelle is relying on us . . .'

'It is a pity that she is not here.' William raised his hands to fend off Richard's indignation. 'But I agree that that is done now and we must live with it.'

'So you will help me?'

Curteys raised his cynical eyebrows. 'In what? You have not given me an inkling of your conspiracy yet. So far all I hear is indignation. You saw how much ice that cut with the sheriff. We'll need more than anger . . .'

William was no less suspicious than Pexton. But as yet he was not at all sure that the clerk was going about challenging Edward in the right way. Not that William himself had yet decided what was the most effective strategy for Isabelle, or for himself.

'I know.' Richard smarted under William's criticism. 'We need time to think.'

'Over that wine perhaps.'

Richard nodded. There was something about Curteys that angered him, yet he dared not examine what exactly it was. It had flared when he had talked so matter-of-factly about someone taking Isabelle as wife. The concept made Richard's stomach turn. He still clung on to the moment by the broken fish weir. It was his talisman against the vision of loss that had been opened up by Curteys' casual comments.

'Yes, we will take the wine. We have much to talk over.'

In the privacy of the solar the two men fenced warily about their options. Neither seemed relaxed in the presence of the other. Isabelle both linked them and stood between them.

'I don't believe Spayne's story.' Pexton made the assertion as his opening gambit.

'Why would he lie?' William glanced over his brimming goblet. 'What possible motive could he have? The man is beyond bribery. I know him. What reason do we have for disbelieving him other than we don't want to believe him?'

'I don't know why he would lie. But it all fits too easily. For twenty years he has kept his silence. Then he breaks it the moment Isabelle cannot defend herself. Doesn't that sound suspicious to you?'

'I agree it is disturbing but I still cannot see why he would lie. And if he did, how could we ever prove it?'

'Damn it, are you for her or not?'

Curteys was ruffled by the clerk's anger. 'I want the truth. I thought that was what you wanted too. And we'll not get it without thinking about it. No one cares for Isabelle's safety more than I do.' He dared the clerk to contradict him. 'But we must know the truth . . .'

'But what is the truth?' Both men looked up as Eleanor, carrying Eve, entered the room.

Richard appealed directly to her. 'You don't believe Spayne's story, do you?'

'I don't know what to believe.' When Richard sighed with exasperation she added, 'I mean it, Richard. I don't know what is true. I know what I want to be true but the two things are not the same, are they?'

'One, for example will not stand up in a court of law,' said William, offering a goblet to Eleanor. 'I'm trying to explain to Pexton that passion is not enough. We will not serve Isabelle's interests by just being angry. We have got to use our minds.'

'Ichar . . . Ichar . . .'

Eve struggled from Eleanor and ran over to the clerk. He picked her up and cuddled her. The action seemed to free something from his mind.

'Let's assume that Spayne is lying.' He stifled criticism with a jerk of his head. 'We'll assume it because we want to. No other reason; just because we want to.' He patted Eve's head. 'Now, what can we do to undermine his story? We assume of course that he will not retract it voluntarily.'

'Well, I suppose that you could show that Edward's mother was not the paragon of virtue she has been made out to be,' Eleanor suggested. 'It would not prove him a liar but it might raise doubts.'

'I fear that the sheriff has just shut the window to us.'

'I disagree.' Richard was resolute in the face of Curteys' concern. 'I want to speak to some of those witnesses myself.'

'Oh, for God's sake, Pexton. What is the point?'

'The point is that I don't trust anyone. You know full well how a jury can be tampered with. And the sheriff did not even allow the full empanelling. He made his decision on what the beadle had told him. I want to talk to the beadle.'

Curteys shrugged. 'It can do no harm. Unless the sheriff takes it into his head that you are exerting pressure yourself.'

'That won't happen if you accompany me as a witness.'

William grunted but did not dismiss the idea.

'Then you will ride there with me?'

Curteys nodded.

'Thank you.'

'You realise that none of this refutes Spayne's statement that he was present at the wedding of two people who are now dead?' Eleanor pointed out.

'I know,' Richard conceded, 'but it is a start.'

Eleanor smiled supportively. 'And it is better than doing nothing. I think you are right, Richard. It is a start and when Isabelle returns she will see that we have not been idle in her absence.'

The clerk nodded vehemently. William Curteys looked less impressed with the conclusion but for once held his peace. The decision made, William left for his warehouse.

Despite his intention he did not go straight there. Instead he found himself down on the southernmost reaches of the town, where the autumn mist blew in from the Haven. He stared out over the lapping water, considering all that Pexton had said. It was possible of course that Spayne was lying. However, it was not that which exercised his thoughts. It was Isabelle herself who occupied most of his thinking.

Richard had been right to suspect the nature of William's observation. Whilst he hated what was happening, William secretly almost wished that Isabelle would give up her battle in the town. He could not deny the physical attraction that he now felt for her. It had grown during the trip to Riga, despite all his attempts to dispel the feelings. Neither could he deny his own hope that from this crisis Isabelle might emerge as a woman less wedded to her widowhood. For as long as she held by her guild rights she would never remarry. Only if she was diverted from such a course might she go the way of other women.

'Damn . . .' The normally controlled merchant stamped his feet. His hopes almost made him an ally with Edward. The very thought shamed him.

William turned from the seascape, his thoughts still in flux. Isabelle had always been a beautiful woman, and he puzzled again as to why he had never had these thoughts about her while Tony had been alive. Was it just because she had been his partner's wife? It was possible but he was not convinced. And, he thought despairingly, that were he ever to articulate his feelings for her, he would by no means be secure that Isabelle would respond favourably to his suit. There had been much friction between them. She seemed to pay little heed to him and his advice. He would have been happier if he felt that she respected him more. Instead she just seemed to strike sparks off him.

The thought unsettled him. He felt a pit of unease open up in his stomach. The more he thought of her the more he wanted Isabelle. It was dangerous to feel so for anyone. He had learned that once before. It made a man vulnerable.

Yet he knew he had no choice. In no way could his desire for Isabelle justify watching her ruin; even if her success undermined her need of him. His first loyalty was to her and not to himself. To that end he must work to expose the truth and clear her. And yet such action could destroy his hopes. His brow creased with concentration, he at last walked on to his warehouse and the business of the day. Yet how he would ever concentrate on work was beyond him.

The embanked road ran south-west from Boston through the spreading sedge and reed beds of Kirton Meeres. It was the very road that Isabelle and Richard had ridden the weekend that Anthony Crosse met his death. This morning, though, Richard rode in the company of William Curteys and six armed retainers, three riding with Richard and three with William.

The morning was damp and cold. To the west there was no horizon save the blur where a grey sky met the endless olive green of the fen. To the east the creeks broadened until cord grass gave way to plains of mud and lead-grey water beyond. As the horses splashed through the puddles on the causeway, reed buntings rose in the black-and-white flash of their jerky flight.

The road ran through the villages of Kirton and Sutterton before it kinked inland for three miles to where Bicker stood at the head of the reed-fringed arm of the sea. Then the causeway crossed the top of Bicker Haven to Donnington before twisting back along the south side of the sea-reach until it dived south once more and followed the estuary of the River Welland to Spalding. The eight riders slowed their horses to a walk as they neared the first great deviation in the routeway. The air was fresh with the unmistakable smell of salt water.

'The beadle's manor is on the north side of the sea-reach. This side of Bicker.' Richard had pulled his mount close to William's. The two horses snorted as they touched. 'I know it and I know him, though not as well as I might,' Richard continued. 'We hold fishing rights in the creeks north of the road. These alone of our lands in the fens Edward has left alone. Isabelle brought them to the marriage as a dowry: even Edward would not seize them.'

'What manner of man is the beadle?' William asked as he glanced back over the reed beds. 'And how will he meet our interest?'

'He's a fiercely independent man. But then aren't they all hereabouts?'

Curteys laughed in agreement.

''Tis no easy thing to act as beadle for a fenland wapentake. He's a man who carries his authority less obviously than the sheriff. But then, if he carried it in such a lordly manner in these parts he might end up in a dyke one dark night.'

'That must be the manor there.' William pointed his riding crop towards a group of buildings which lay off to one side of the road. 'Is it not?'

'That's it. Let's see what kind of reception we get.'

Within the stockade lay a mixed group of buildings: barns, animal pens and a wooden hall. One of the barns had suffered a terrible fire. Only two blackened crucks remained to show where the roof had once reared. Much of the debris had been removed but still there was a damp smell of burning about the yard. An elderly man came out of the hall. He was flanked by two teenage boys. One of them had the top of his head swathed in a bandage and both lads looked at the strangers with ill-concealed distrust.

Richard swung down from his saddle. 'God be with you this morning. I am Richard Pexton . . .'

'Aye, I know who you are.' The old man's tone was flat and suspicious.

'It has been a while since I last met you. I am sorry to see your barn. What happened?'

'What does it look like?' The speaker was the uninjured teenager. 'We had a fire.' His father laid a hand on his arm.

Richard waited, but no invitation inside was forthcoming and he realised he would have to conduct his interview in the open air. The atmosphere of hostility was intense as Richard spoke.

'I am sorry to disturb you,' he began apologetically, 'but I must ask about the woman who gave birth to Edward . . .'

'I have given a full account of the life and death of the girl Moyne to the sheriff's men. What more do you want?'

'It is important to us to learn as much as we can about her. Could you please tell us the names of the men that you empanelled to act on the jury? We would talk with them about her if we can.'

The old man spat. 'There is nothing more to be said. She was a good maid and she died in childbirth. We never knew her look at any man save Anthony Crosse. And now it seems the only stain which tarnished her has been removed. For it was not a bastard that she bore him but his own true son.'

Pexton frowned. 'It is not that we are questioning your . . .'

'You had better think twice before you call a servant of the king a liar. I have done all that the sheriff instructed me to do. Now be off with you. If you would know more then see the sheriff.'

The beadle turned on his heels. The taller of his sons went with him. The bandaged one remained until sharply called for. Then he too turned away. Pexton remounted. He and Curteys exchanged glances then pulled on their bridles. Back on the road they discussed the interview.

'The man was frightened. There's no questioning it, he was afraid.' Richard glanced back at the manor house. 'You must have seen it.'

'I saw it,' William replied. 'The question is, what was he frightened of?'

'I don't know, but I intend to find out.'

'It'll be no easy matter.' William considered the implications of the beadle's uncooperative manner.

'We don't know who he spoke to. More to the point we have no idea where to find people who were in sound mind and body twenty years ago.' He sighed in an irritated way. 'We'll get nothing from those who were babes-in-arms while Tony was busy making babies in his father's haystacks.'

Richard would not be dissuaded. 'I've been often enough in these parts. I can't claim I know everyone – I spend more time in Boston. But I know a few names and faces . . .'

'And how many miles will we ride, or wade, to find these names and faces?' William glanced at the unwelcoming landscape. 'It could take a very long time.'

The retainers exchanged resigned glances as they listened to the conversation. It promised to be a long and miserable day. Unaware of the expressions of his men, Richard considered the issues raised by his companion. The horses stamped their feet and a kingfisher cut an emerald and blue arc through the misty air above the nearby creek.

'There are not so many as you might think,' he said musingly. 'We can ignore anyone who would have been younger than fifteen, twenty years ago. And few live to a ripe old age here. 'Tis a place for the young and fit, not the old in their dotage.'

Curteys looked a little more positive. 'And you know such families?'

'I know some at least. And so we can make a start. Who knows what memories we will stir up?'

Richard's determination was soon dented on the defences of the inhabitants of the scattered farmsteads that bordered the fen of Kirton Meeres. At each little habitation they were met with the same sullen hostility. It was as if a wall had been erected against them. And as every fisherman, or fowler, reluctantly replied, each taciturn word was watched by a couple of silent, wide-eyed children, or a pale wife . . .

'This is too much,' William commented as they rode away from the hut of yet another fenslodger. 'One or two ignorant, one or two hostile I can believe, but this is ridiculous. The entire fen is shut against us.'

'There's no question of it. Someone has put the fear of God into these people. And the way some of them talk of Edward's mother, I'm astonished she was not canonised. I've never heard of such virtue in a living soul. To hear those who were old enough to have known her, she was without sin of any kind.'

'I'll be honest with you, Pexton. When you first said about riding out here I thought it was a fool's errand. But now I'm not so sure. There's something wrong. Someone has primed these people and terrified the rest.'

'That's clear enough. But none of this will stand up in the shire court. We cannot use their tone of voice as evidence. Something is wrong here but we could never convey it to anybody else.'

William sighed. 'Now you are beginning to sound like me, Master Pexton!'

The two men laughed. It was the first time that they had ever done so in one another's company. The riding escort lolled in their saddles, bored and cold.

'Hah, but we have been fools!' Richard struck his palm with a clenched fist. 'And it's no wonder we've found nothing.'

'Pexton – spit it out. It's too cold for games.'

'I'm sorry.' Richard let go of his reins. He held up his open hands. 'How many fingers?'

'Pexton!'

Richard was grinning. 'How many?'

'Surprisingly there are ten. It seems that the cold which has gone to my backside has gone to your brain.'

'Ten: a "tithing". Think about it. The beadle is responsible for the law and order of the wapentake, yes?' Curteys nodded without humour. 'And how does he ensure that law and order is kept?'

'It's hardly a mystery, Pexton. He summons the regular meetings of the wapentake court and listens to whose dog has bitten off which cow's tail; which fisherman has built a weir in a drainage channel. It's an exciting job being a beadle. And if something really juicy turns up it's passed straight on to the sheriff to deal with at the shire court. So he gets all the real fun . . .'

'But who attends the wapentake courts?'

'The freemen of every tithing. You know as well as I do that every ten men are responsible for each other's good behaviour and must bring a wrongdoer to book.'

'Exactly. The beadle works through the tithings. Through the men. Now imagine you wanted to make sure that everyone called on to attend a jury told the same story. What would you do?' Before William could answer Richard said quietly: 'You would terrorise the beadle who in turn would pass on the fear to each tithing in the fen. But it would be the men of each tithing. And probably only those who were old enough to know something. But the men. Do you see it?'

Curteys was nodding now, and vigorously. 'You're

right, Richard. The person spreading the story would ignore the women because few if any would be empanelled. Just like we have. We have picked out only the men of the right age.'

'Which is exactly what he did. He targeted any men who might know and terrified them to silence.'

William smiled grimly. ' "He" being Edward or the beadle . . .'

'Which is the same difference if the fear of God has been put into the beadle. So when the sheriff orders a jury summoned, everyone who is old enough to have a story to tell will have been neutered.'

'By God, Pexton, if you are right, that bastard has put the whole fen in his pocket.' Then Curteys shook his head. 'Except the old women.'

'Exactly. They disregarded the women, but I did not forget them.' Richard's voice was defiant. It was as if he was making some form of public declaration that went beyond the terrorism of the marsh-dwellers. 'I remembered the women.'

'Yes,' said Curteys looking at him with sudden respect, 'you did, didn't you? And, as God is my judge, I would have forgotten them too.'

Pexton was thinking hard. 'There are not many either. Most marry in their late twenties and usually the husband is a little older. Those women will have been intimidated by the fear that has infected their menfolk.' Then his face was clouded with a look of sorrow. 'And so many die in childbirth that there are more widowers than widows . . .'

William had never heard the clerk so eloquent. And it had been a long time since he had heard such tenderness in the voice of a man. The incongruity touched him. He remembered how the clerk had seemed so close to Isabelle since her return. A slight twist of jealousy turned in his stomach.

'But I know a widow.' Pexton pointed towards the west. 'It's too damn close to Bicker but that's a risk we will have to take.'

'And you think she might know something?'

'I cannot tell, but she's in her late fifties, so is of the right age. Her first marriage was childless. The husband was drowned out fowling. That was before my time here. So she married again and the second husband died too. He was drowned also. I was at Bicker at the time. We found his body out beyond the sea-dyke. He had drowned in the mud as the sea returned. His mouth and nose were choked with it.' Pexton shuddered at the awful memory.

'Good God, I'll wager no men were battling for her suit a third time!'

'That's true enough. She has stayed a widow. But she has a son from the second marriage, and a daughter. She was late in the breeding of them: both cannot be much beyond their teens. Some people called her a witch what with the deaths of the husbands and the late births.'

'Then we should ride to speak with her. For if you are right she may be one of the few who fell through Edward's net.'

The matter was decided and in a more positive mood the two led the way westward. Richard was right about how close the little farmstead was to Edward's manor at Bicker. Across the head of the Bicker Haven the squat tower of the church rose above the grey mud of the creek and the breeze stirred willows.

371

'By Our Lady, this is under the bastard's very nose.' William turned to his retainers. 'Get those swords where you can use them,' he snapped.

A narrow, well-worn path led off from the causeway. It dropped down from the road and was flanked by reed beds and still water. A thin mist hung over the unreflecting dullness of the pools. A thicket of willows reduced the distance of the western horizon from for ever to a handful of yards.

'Fine place for an ambush,' William noted cheerlessly.

The track forced the riders to single file. A horse whinnied and the sound seemed to hang about the intruders. Another mount started as a dabchick splashed its way into cover. The escort were alert now, hands drifting to their sword hilts.

After about half a mile the track opened on to a clearing. A reed-thatched cottage leaned against a long, low barn. Nets hung drying and a boat was upturned in a corner of the muddy yard, its tarred belly black to the sky. Beyond the buildings an island of meadow was bounded by a protecting bank and drainage ditch. Beyond that, paths too narrow for horses wound out into the fen.

Richard turned to William. 'They make their way here by fowling and fishing. And the island of meadow is a godsend. Worth more than their other labours put together. Such as these owe labour service to no lord. They may take their loyalty where they will.' The affection in his voice was real. 'And perhaps even Edward's hand has not crushed their free voice.'

'I see someone has been busy.'

William was right. Large bundles of cut reeds lay

beside the barn. Richard dismounted and ran his hand over the damp fruit of the waterways. 'Good quality "lesch" this. Worth a few silver pennies. It'll make a fine thatch.' He pulled his glove back on. 'It's also illegal. These people may be free tenants with common rights in the fen but no one may exercise the right and cut reeds, rush or sedge from Michaelmas to Hokeday. Tony Crosse would have had their hide for this.'

While he was speaking a grey-haired woman appeared at the door of the little house. 'Oo are yer?' She waved a stick broom aggressively. 'Say oo yer are, or get out of 'ere.'

Richard came from behind the cut reeds with his hands up. A glimmer of recognition crossed the woman's face. 'Marster Pexton. What are yer 'ere for? Is the mestress back at the manor?'

Pexton ignored the question. 'We need your help. This man is William Curteys and he is a good friend of my mistress. May we come inside?'

The woman seemed surprised that anyone as high and mighty should want to come into her house, then surprise succumbed to pleasure at the honour. She beamed and waved them in with exaggerated movements. Inside the house the air was smoky and rancid with the smell of fish. Two ugly little dogs sniffed at the visitors. The woman kicked one and the other moved off of its own accord. A young girl was kneading dough in one corner. She stopped her work and turned to look at the strangers. A chair, the only furniture apart from a hand-carved box, was proudly put at the disposal of the visitors.

'You take it, Pexton. I'm happy to stand.' William

slapped at a flea that had fallen from the thatch on to his neck. 'No really, I am content to stand.' He threw the woman a false smile.

Richard spoke, trying to sound calm. 'We wondered if you might tell us about a girl who used to live hereabouts. She's been dead nigh on twenty years now.'

'Wos 'er name then?'

'Uhh, she was called Ellen Moyne. It may be that others have asked about her?'

The woman shook her head and Pexton threw a hopeful glance at his standing companion.

'Wos yer wanna know about 'er for?'

'So you remember her, then?'

The woman laughed. It was a loud and cackling noise of scorn. It was as if the question was plainly foolish. 'Hah, cors I calls 'er to mind. She was a fast un was that un!'

Pexton licked dry lips. Curteys leaned forward.

'A loose littul bit she wer. But the boys did luv it . . .' She cackled again. 'Mine oo I've know'd a few boys in the straw . . .'

She reached out a thin hand and stroked Pexton's knee. With an effort of will he controlled the urge to pull back. Instead he encouraged her to speak on. 'So she was not a retiring virgin then?'

The woman's hand slapped on the clerk's thigh.

'She had carnal knowledge of more than one man?' he persisted.

'Mine, as I tent's the fire . . .' She stirred the logs with a stick. 'Or 'twill slocken and the heat'll go . . .' She put down her makeshift poker. 'Oh, 'er did know a few men an' all. An' the lord's own son did 'ave 'is way weth 'er too . . .'

'That would be the late Tony Crosse?'

'Don know as 'ee was ever late whun she offered to drop 'er's kirtle for un . . .' She rubbed her hands with glee. Twenty years had not diminished the pleasure of the gossip. ' 'Ee was a keen un for 'er though. First time fer im I think. Gets un that way with the first un. Proper wudness.' She tapped her head and grinned at the thought of the folly of adolescent passion. 'An 'er knew 'ow to get a boy goin. Cors she got caught by 'is seed . . .'

Suddenly the light went from the doorway and Pexton turned as if stung. Two men entered, closely followed by the watchful retainers. The first was a young man whose face was still blotched red with acne. The other was a much older, heavily built man. He had a thick bull-neck and wore a long knife at his waist. There was a menacing aspect to the way he carried himself. William exchanged glances with Richard.

Richard stood up. 'We are just on our way. We needed to talk with your mother about a matter of some old history.'

William turned towards the door. He did not like the look of the bulky newcomer. He felt his hand stray towards the hilt of his sword, beneath his cloak.

The boy looked puzzled and glanced at his mother for some explanation.

'Anything interesting?' Bull-neck asked.

'No,' Pexton replied warily. 'Just a little private matter.'

The woman showed none of his caution. 'Ah, 'twas

just 'bout a loose bit lived 'ere once. Long time since. Ole man Moyne's kid. An she put ut about a bit . . . I was tellin Marster Pexton.'

'We must go.' Pexton was firm this time. 'We must get back to Boston before dark.' As he pushed past the heavily built man he added: 'You should mind that the lord doesn't see you cutting reeds this time of year.'

'Oh 'ee won' mine. 'Tis by 'is permis . . .'

Bull-neck stifled the boy's innocent communication. 'That's kind of you, sir. Now we must not keep you if you'll reach Boston before dark. It's a dangerous road as it gets into evening.'

Richard smiled a thin smile in response and re-mounted his horse and William did likewise. As they rode away from the buildings the bull-necked man ducked his head and went back inside.

'We really had better turn for home,' William suggested. 'The afternoon is well spent. I have no desire to get caught out here in the dark. And that bastard was a cut-throat if ever I've seen one.'

'You're right. We've got what we came here for. There would have been a time when I'd have suggested that we spent the night at Bicker . . .' Richard looked westward to where a smudge of smoke on the flat horizon betrayed the presence of the little village.

'I for one would rather not spend the night in the company of Edward Moyne . . .' William said quickly.

'Now there's a good sign.'

'What do you mean?'

'You called him Moyne. Edward Moyne. And you used to call him Edward Crosse. That's a move in the right direction.'

Curteys laughed. 'Well, from what that old crone said, Phillip Spayne must have known a different girl altogether. I'm going to ask him about that! I find it hard to believe that she had honour left to bargain with for a marriage.'

'But what's more important is that someone is doing all that he can to make people remember a very different girl. A girl who never existed. A girl like the one Spayne claimed he married to Tony Crosse.'

William ruffled his beard. 'The question is, will that old crone tell her tale to the sheriff? And will that puffed-up cockerel have the wit to see what it all means?'

'She will.' Richard sounded confident. 'And even he must sniff the stink of lies that floats over these marshes . . .'

By this time they had reached the causeway once more. William looked back towards the fowler's little assart in the wilderness. He did not look happy.

'I wonder, should we take the old woman away? I don't like the look of this place. It's too close to Bicker. And I didn't like the look of him . . .'

As he spoke a boat came into view amongst the reeds. It was a good way off but held a small crowd of men. Voices betrayed others deeper in the reeds.

'I think it is too late.' Pexton stood in his stirrups. 'There were never this many men in this part of the marsh. They must be Edward's. We cannot go back that way now.'

William slapped his hand on his saddle. 'Then we must leave her. Though I wish I had thought quicker when we were there.' There was genuine concern in his voice.

'Console yourself with this – she would never have come with us. This is her home. She has nothing else. We would never have persuaded her to leave it.'

'Yes, you are right. But it does not make me happier. There is something terribly wrong here. You were right about that too. The place stinks of it.' William pulled his horse's head around. 'Let's get back before the dark catches us here . . .'

The eight riders took the road home. It was indeed late. They had outstayed the day and evening caught them still on the lonely causeway. As a result they were forced to seek shelter in a little inn at the small village of Sutterton. Consequently they did not cover the remaining five miles into Boston. So the armed men who were waiting for them by the side of the causeway waited in vain. Evening turned to darkness and still the expected riders did not come along the deserted causeway. At last the footpads drifted away.

Just before dark a group of armed shadows descended on the manor of the beadle, coming along the road at a jog. The family were at a simple supper when the door of the hall was hammered on with the hilts of half a dozen swords.

'Open it,' the elderly official ordered his retainers. 'Open it before they have it off its hinges.'

Edward's bull-necked servant strode into the hall with an affected swagger. At his back were a band of toughs. One of them kicked over a stool. Another grabbed at a serving girl.

Bull-neck hawked and spat. 'I hear you entertained visitors today. Want to tell me about it?'

The old beadle pushed past his protective sons. 'It

was Isabelle Crosse's clerk. And another man.'

'Oh, we know who they were. What did you tell them?'

Something in the old man snapped. 'Damn you. You have no right to burst into my home at night. I am a servant of the king. Who do . . .'

Bull-neck kneed him in the groin. The old man gasped at the pain. As he doubled up the same knee caught him in the face.

'You are getting very rude aren't you?' Bull-neck said superciliously.

The two sons threw themselves at the man who had hurt their father. Before they could reach him they were brought down by his companions.

'Very naughty. Very, very naughty. You had better teach them some manners, my lads.'

As the old man was pulled up to watch, his two sons were systematically beaten up. In vain they struggled against the carefully placed blows and kicks, blood spurting from mouths and noses. The servants watched in terror but Bull-neck made no attempt to touch them. They were an important part of the game and would spread the word of what had happened far and wide.

'I told them nothing.' The old man was pleading. 'I told them only what you told me to tell the sheriff. As God is my judge I told them nothing more. Please make them stop . . . I told them nothing more . . . Nothing! Nothing!'

At last the beating was over. The two boys lay sobbing in their own blood. The beadle was released to kneel weeping beside his two children.

'There, there, no need to cry.'

The hired toughs laughed at their leader's wit.

'We believe you. You were a good boy and did as you were told. So just remember this. This is what happened to you when you did nothing. Just think what will happen to you if you try to be clever. And if I ever hear a sniff of news that my master's dear mother was a flighty little whore who would open her legs to anyone who parted the bushes it will be you who I come looking for. Bear it in mind whenever anyone asks again. And I hope your two sons feel better in the morning.'

As he turned to leave, Bull-neck saw the beadle's daughter crouched in a corner. He gave a broad grin. 'And should you ever forget what I've said, your daughter will learn just what a fine body of men we are.' The men with him hooted with laughter. 'We'll give her a night she won't forget in a hurry. So tell all your people to be good boys and girls.'

Out in the dark yard, Bull-neck rubbed his broad belly with pleasure. It had been a constructive evening's work. From the west a flickering glow rose from a lonely cottage fire. And where a reed lagoon lapped around a dark island of meadow, three corpses floated with their throats cut. One was a woman in her late fifties. Her long hair spread about her in the black water like a shifting weed.

Isabelle Crosse returned to Boston on the Friday before the November mart. She came in the company of the lay steward of the abbey of Ely and a party of lay brothers. The wherry on which they travelled was laden with produce for the coming week of trading. While the lay brothers unloaded the wherry, Ralph

Kymes escorted Isabelle to her home. There was a buzz of talk to mark her passage through the crowded streets.

In the sheds behind the hall, Richard Pexton was busy. Bales of woollen cloth were awaiting transportation across the Witham to be sold in the Fair of Holland and already that morning the clerk had supervised the movement of the furs promised to the Lincoln merchants. The whole affair had been carefully managed while the sheriff was dining with the Boston bailiff and while the king's and the manor's officials were taking tax and toll from a party of Hanseatic traders who had docked that morning. As a panting apprentice brought the news of Isabelle's arrival, Richard threw the ledger and tally sticks to a startled journeyman and half ran, half limped to greet his mistress.

Isabelle was already in the hall, Eve capering about her feet and excitedly pointing out everything that her vocabulary would stretch to. Eleanor was embracing Isabelle and both were crying.

Pexton gave Kymes a frosty look and knelt before his mistress. Taking his outstretched hands, Isabelle bid him stand.

'It is good to see you.', Richard chafed at the inadequacy of the words. 'I cannot say how we have all missed you.'

'And I have missed you. God knows I have missed you all. I still grieve at the manner of our parting, Richard. I know that you will have forgiven me. I can only hope that you can also understand.'

Isabelle could not quite look him in the eye. As he had greeted her she had seen the hunger there. She felt ashamed that she would never be able to satisfy the passion she had helped fuel. Never had she intended to hurt her clerk. Yet she could not undo what had passed between them on the banks of the river. She resolved somehow to make it up to him but did not know where to begin.

Richard held her hands tightly. 'It matters not. You did what you had to do and that is enough for me.' Inside he still ached at the manner of their parting. 'I have so much to tell you.' And then he added, because it was true: 'You look so much better. Before you were so tired and now you look refreshed and rested. I thank God for that.'

Eleanor put her hands on both their shoulders. 'Richard's right, Isabelle. You look your old self again.' Then she added: 'And if anything I did added to your burden or your pain, I apologise for it. As Richard will tell you we have not been inactive in your defence while you were away. There is no question but that Edward has conspired against you.'

Isabelle laughed. 'That I never doubted – but can we fight him and win?'

'Only God knows if we will win, but Richard, Will and I will fight him alongside you whatever the outcome.'

'William too?' Isabelle sounded surprised but very pleased. 'Then this is a joyful homecoming.' She let go of Richard's hands. 'We must go where we can talk. We have a lot to say to one another.' She beckoned to Ralph Kymes to accompany them.

When they were seated in the fire-warmed solar, Isabelle addressed her three allies.

'Eleanor, you have not met Ralph. He cares for the

abbey of Ely's lands in the fens. Like us they have suffered loss through the actions of Edward. You may speak openly before him. He is a friend and our cause is his cause too. He also has many contacts amongst the Boston guildsmen.'

Richard looked a little unhappy but said nothing. Instead he asked, 'Are you still determined to fight Edward?'

Isabelle smiled. 'Now I am. A month ago I would have not known what to say. There are not words to describe how desolate I felt.' She glanced at Richard who was watching her taut-lipped. 'It was as if my life was in ruins. God forgive me but I almost lost my faith in His providence. I think that had I remained here I would have given in.' Her eyes glistened but this time it was for pains recalled but conquered. 'I could scarcely eat, or sleep. I have never known such depths of despair.'

Richard clenched his fists, white-knuckled, tight. He could feel her pain as if it was his own. Eleanor was watching the younger woman's face intently.

'It was a shocking thing to stay behind at Ely,' Isabelle sighed. 'I could not explain it to you as I should have done but I could not come home either. I needed time; time and stillness. My spirit needed assurance of God's love once more.' She laughed. 'Perhaps assurance that He still recognised my existence. It is a dreadful thing to say, I know, but I was in the wilderness. But in the abbey I found the prayer and peace I needed. I have found the ointment for my soul. I do not know if I shall win but, as Eleanor said, I know that I shall not give in. I have found the peace to struggle and yet be obedient to what befalls. It is a sharper weapon than anger and a greater spur to action than wounded pride alone.'

Eleanor said softly, 'You have come to yourself. It was something no one else could do for you. Only you could go there; only you and God. And all else that came before this is passed away. It is a cleansing that you have received.'

Richard said nothing. His most treasured moments lay in that period of time which had been cleansed away. With solemn eyes he studied the warps and knots in the planks of the solar floor.

Isabelle regarded her faithful clerk. 'Before your arrival downstairs, Eleanor began to tell me of your adventures in the fen-country. Will you tell me yourself about all that you have discovered?'

Richard roused himself from his sombre contemplations. Cutting the tale to its bare essentials he recounted how he and Curteys had pursued the truth and found it tangled and corrupted by fear and intimidation. Then he described how the only witness he had found to tell the truth had, they soon discovered, been brutally murdered with no one apprehended for the crime.

'So we are back where we started,' he concluded. 'We must try to seek out another witness, only this time I doubt that anyone will speak to us. They would rather dance with the angel of death than chatter to us.'

'But it has not been wasted.' Isabelle was tender as she consoled her clerk. 'As you yourself said, before we thought they lied because we had to believe it, now we know that there is deceit and malice behind this tale of a pure girl secretly wed. And if there is such a depth of sin behind it then we no longer doubt that the whole story is a tissue of lies from beginning to end.'

Richard still looked downcast. 'I fear that the sheriff will be less impressed.'

'No doubt of it, Richard, but our own doubts have been dismissed. And when your mind is clear of doubts you can see other ways forward. Believe me for I know. I was blinded by self-doubts and fear. You have done a great service to us all in what you have found, even if it will not yet suffice to persuade a cynical sheriff.'

She might also have added 'and you have caused William to throw himself behind our cause' but instead she let it lie. She would talk with Curteys privately soon.

Ralph Kymes, who had been listening to all that was being said, at last made a contribution to the discussion. 'I play but a minor part in this. I happened to be at Ely when Isabelle came and there I was of some service to her, though I imparted little wisdom. I also know how the church has been hurt by the man who has set his face against you. After today I am sure that not only have we a common foe but that you are in the right.

'There is little that I can do, but I have friends in Boston and with them I will do what I can. But what I can assure you is that the prayers of God's house at Ely go with you, as does all the influence that we can muster. And though I carry little weight myself, the influence of Ely is much greater. And the weight of that is in the balance on your side of the scales.'

Isabelle broke open a bread roll. 'Now I have Richard Pexton, Eleanor de Bamville, William Curteys and the abbey of Ely on my side I feel that I can face Edward with more than just indignation and bravado.'

As she mentioned William's name she felt a leap of triumphant excitement. It was his support that she had desired for so long and at last it had come. She longed to speak to him but could not ignore the nervousness within herself. What was it that lay behind his decision? She had her hopes but no certain knowledge.

'Now,' Pexton added, 'all we need is a witness to uphold our story. One who can manage to stay alive until the tale is told.'

William Curteys was in the parish church as Isabelle celebrated her homecoming. He had resolved to have it out once and for all with Phillip Spayne. Whatever his secret hopes he could no longer be slow in Isabelle's defence. It shamed him to think that perhaps he had been so since the return from Riga, even though he had had his reasons. Now all his energies were concentrated on one thing. He would fight for her regardless of where it left his personal strategies. He had crossed the Rubicon and was glad of it.

Soon now he would talk to Isabelle. He had not yet fully resolved what he would say but knew that the time had indeed come to speak frankly with her. He was nervous, as a man might be at the approach of his first lover. The thought made him sigh. He was in this deeper than he had ever planned.

He found the priest in the guild chapel as usual. He was kneeling before the altar in the act of prayer. William waited until he had finished.

'Phillip, I need to speak with you.'

The tall priest turned at the voice. His tonsured red hair seemed to glow in the light from the altar candles. He bowed and genuflected before answering. 'I was praying for the soul of Adam Thymelby and for Anthony Crosse.'

William examined his nails. 'Tell me about Edward's mother.' His voice was very matter-of-fact.

The priest frowned. 'You heard all that I laid before the bailiff and the town. What else do you need to know?'

'Tell me again what kind of woman she was.' William sat on a convenient bench. 'Tell me about her.'

Spayne sat down beside him. 'She was a pure and good soul. Her honour was precious to her. That was why she would not lie with Anthony until he had married her. She was humble and meek, unlike many other daughters of Eve.'

'I know a person who tells another story, Phillip. One who says she was a harlot who cared nothing for her virginity . . .'

Spayne drew himself up in fury, 'God will damn the one who says such a thing for she was a pure . . .'

William ignored Spayne's outrage. 'I believe this person. I think Edward's mother was a slut.' Spayne's mouth dropped open. 'Furthermore I think Edward knows that she was a slut.' Spayne was scarlet. 'Now it is not a crime to be a slut and that does not mean she could not have married Tony. However, when one finds a thread of a lie and pulls it, the whole garment is apt to unravel . . .'

'You have listened to that Jezebel, to that proud woman Isabelle Crosse. God has seen fit to punish her pride and to humble her arrogance. No wonder she has fled the town. It is from judgement that she flees but she will not escape the judgement of God.' The priest's normally sunken eyes bulged with fury. 'She is a temptress, William, and you have fallen into the snare which she has set for you. Her body is a sink of depravity, a slime of sensuous . . .'

'That's enough, Phillip.' William's voice was ice-water on the fire of Spayne's anger. 'It is not the state of Isabelle's soul that we are discussing. Indeed there is no reason to fear for her. Rather the issue is whether your soul is in a state of grace.'

Phillip Spayne looked stunned. He had risen during his outburst. Now he sat down, his eyes fixed on William. The hooked nose quivered.

'I cannot prove that you did not marry them. Only you and Christ know that.' Curteys looked darkly at the priest. 'What I am sure of is that you have lied about the kind of woman that she was. I am also sure that Edward has terrified anyone who knew her into repeating the same lie.' William snapped his fingers. 'The woman I spoke to is dead – her throat cut. Very convenient, don't you think? So she cannot tell anyone where this unravelling lie begins.'

Spayne was pale. His tongue worked around the edges of his mouth. 'Then there is nothing that you can lay before the sheriff. You have no evidence at all.' In his eyes there was a glint of relief.

William's face showed contempt for the first time. If the priest had said anything else it might have kept alive a faint flicker of doubt in the guildsman. The hoarse retort had snuffed it out for ever.

'Sweet Jesus, what have you become?'

Spayne sneered. 'Don't you dare to lecture me. I am chantry priest of the guild.' The life was coming back into him again. 'I have spoken the truth at all times.'

'Edward is a lawless man who cares nothing for his soul, or for the lives of others. It is this person that you have yoked yourself to, Phillip. You have joined yourself with darkness. No – don't protest. Let me finish. I don't know why you have done this. But what I do know is that you have connived with Edward against Isabelle. You have committed yourself to a lie and all that you stand for – your soul itself – is in jeopardy.

'Edward has murdered and terrorised the fenfolk. You're right, I can't prove it, but it's true and it's a truth that you cannot escape. You are one with him, Phillip. It is this partner that you have taken. Never speak to me of prostitutes and Jezebels, for you have whored your very soul.'

William stood up and turned away. Spayne called after him. The voice was breathless and the words came fast. 'He married her. Anthony married her and no one can gainsay it. No one! Isabelle Crosse is finished. There is scarcely a merchant in the town who will not support Edward now. By Easter he shall have her out of her hall and out of this town. At the next shire court he will have her out.' The priest had followed Curteys to the door of the chapel. His voice was trembling. 'It's over, William. She is finished. She is finished.'

When William reached the pale sunlight he paused. In his heart he knew that Spayne was right. They could prove nothing. All they were defending was a sand-castle before the oncoming tide. But for once in his life he was absolutely content with the course of action that he had taken. He would have it no other way. He was on the side of Isabelle Crosse, come what may.

William paused as he crossed the expanse of Richmond Fee. Now that he had made his stand he could not ignore the consequences. When Edward finally had Isabelle's place, there would be war between Edward Crosse and the house of Curteys. Anthony Crosse's bastard would never forgive the man who had openly sided with his stepmother, and Edward would carry with him all of the guildsmen that he had bought. If that was the price of supporting Isabelle, so be it, but he knew it would be a heavy price. Ahead lay conflict and violence.

Chapter 12

Matthew Redman should have been attending to the last day of the mart. It would, at any other time, have been his prime occupation. However, he was not in his hall overflowing with goods, or out on the great stalls on Richmond Fee. Instead he was in his counting-house amidst piles of ledgers and sheets of vellum. He had left the sales in the hands of his experienced journeymen.

His clerk was reading through another pale cream sheet of parchment. Redman nodded as he took in the implications of what the younger man was saying.

'. . . so the cloth sold to the Gascons comes to fifty marks along with the raw wool deal we finalised yesterday with the merchants from Florence which adds one hundred marks to the total.' He rechecked his calculations. 'Yes, that's right.'

'Which still doesn't balance.'

'God willing the final figures for the mart and the orders we have secured for the spring should go a long way towards doing that.'

Redman raised his serious eyes. 'But we still have not made up the money lost when the land flooded last spring, and will not be in a position to repay the Crosse loan for at least a twelve-month.'

'That's right, sir.' The clerk blushed, as if the financial problems of the house were his fault instead of the result of some very bad luck. 'But we are working towards it. Isabelle Crosse has never put pressure on us.'

'No,' Redman agreed, 'she has never done that. Nor Tony Crosse before her.'

He was silent as he contemplated the implications of the morning's study of the accounts. The way things were he would stay in debt to the Crosse household for perhaps another two years. Then the improving trade would lift him back on to an even keel once more. If things stayed as they were.

He turned one of the ledgers. His eyes followed the columns of numbers to the base of the page. With one finger he traced one particular line of accounts. 'And the only outstanding loan is that which we made to Coppledyke.'

'That is so. Not that it would be enough to pay off the Crosse debts.'

'I know.'

Matthew looked at the figures once more as if they would supply him with the answer which eluded him. At last he glanced at his clerk and dismissed him. He had seen all that he needed to. There had been nothing new in the figures but he had to be absolutely sure.

Alone in the counting-house he leaned back against the wood panels. He had a lot on his mind. He closed his eyes as he weighed up his decision. A slow frown spread over his magisterial features. His hands slowly patted the table as he contemplated what he must do.

'Halve the debt . . .' He spoke the words aloud; the

words which had silently gone round in his head. 'Halve the debt . . .'

For a few moments more he thought over the issue. Whatever he did was fraught with difficulties. There was no easy solution. But the realist within him pushed the current all one way.

He opened his eyes and poured himself another goblet of wine. He sniffed at it and then sipped it slowly. The autumn sunlight caught the silver tonsure above his broad-boned eyebrows. He suddenly felt very old. He thought of how Curteys had come to him in September. He remembered his own words of advice. How easy it was to give advice to others. How hard to take it oneself.

Finally he made up his mind. His jaw tightened. He had to take the longer view. He could not allow himself to be bound by short-term visions and priorities. When all was said and done he had the safety of his own house to think of. There was no other way. The old guildsman sighed. Matthew Redman had finally made up his mind.

'Well, that's it then,' he murmured softly to himself. 'Now all I have to face is the doing of it.'

His jaw tightened again. For that would be even harder than the making of the decision in the first place. With a shake of his head he drained the last of the wine of Anjou.

Isabelle Crosse, watching an altercation between some traders and the Lincoln toll collectors on the Town Bridge over the Witham, was unaware of the decisions which were taxing the fatherly guildsman.

Eve, in Eleanor's arms, was intrigued by the procession of animals over the bridge.

''Orses . . . seeps . . . dows, dows . . .'

'Cows,' Isabelle corrected her, with a smile.

'Ess, ess,' Eve replied without tearing her glance away from the passing livestock. 'Ess, dows, dows . . .' Had it not been for the restraining arms of Eleanor she would have been down amongst the horses, sheep and cows that were being driven over the bridge.

'He'll have to pay in the end,' Eleanor grinned at her young friend. 'They always pay in the end. So the swearing is all for nothing.' A countryman from the south Holland fens was bitterly protesting at the cost of the toll being levied by the Lincoln men. It was a good little source of income which the merchants from the west bank of the Witham had traditionally been able to levy on goods and animals crossing the bridge.

'I know,' Isabelle replied. 'But the protest is part of the tradition. If he did not shout and swear so at the toll collectors the poor fellow would go home feeling cheated.'

Eleanor laughed out loud. 'I doubt that he would see it quite that way.' She adjusted her hold on the wriggling child. 'Of course, it's easy for you to be so philosophical. No one from the Honour of Richmond pays tolls to the Lincoln men.'

Isabelle tossed back her head. 'I know. It almost makes you want to buy a flock of sheep just to drive them to and fro over the bridge all day.'

It was good to hear Isabelle in more relaxed mood. She seemed a different woman since her return from Ely. Something of the brittle tension had gone out of her. Instead she appeared more relaxed and even more resilient. Eleanor decided that it was a good sign but as she enjoyed the smile on the face of the woman at her side she could not but wonder if the strength would be enough to face the trials which lay ahead of them all.

Across the busy market-place Edward's wife Ann was standing, half-concealed behind the awning of a haberdasher's stall, watching Isabelle Crosse. She knew now that her husband lusted after the woman for, one night, two weeks before, Edward had proved incapable of controlling his tongue when dreams loosened his hold on it. Distress twisted in Ann's stomach. She watched the innocent woman whom her husband delighted to destroy. Now, from the lewd and angry words Edward had muttered in his sleep, she knew beyond doubt that the lust belonged to Edward and not to Isabelle. She also knew that her husband had used her own love and insecurity as a pawn in his games. She longed to go over to the woman and pour out her shame and guilt. For she too had wronged her, had been made to seem foolish by her husband's own manipulation. Then, shaking her head, she slowly turned and walked away.

Richard Pexton limped through the milling crowds. He ducked to avoid the tray of a pie-woman and dodged about the hanging awnings of a haberdasher's stall. Finally he reached his mistress.

'Ichar . . . Ichar . . .' Eve turned from the cattle to the clerk. 'Ichar . . . dows, dows . . .'

Richard laughed shyly at the obvious affection that the child had for him. He reached out and stroked her head. She twisted like an eel to grab his hand.

'You deserve a rest, Richard. You have done so well this last week.' Isabelle tickled Eve and broke the grasp on the clerk's fingers. 'Leave poor Richard alone. He is working hard, you bully.'

Pexton smiled a rather reluctant smile at the compliment. Eleanor could not fail to notice the raw edge of longing in his dark eyes. She wondered if Isabelle saw it and she pondered on what had passed between mistress and clerk on the journey to Ely. Isabelle flushed a little and Eleanor had her answer. She had seen the look.

'Things are going better than we expected.' Pexton glanced at the threatening sky. 'The weather has held off, thank God. And I think will hold to the end of this day's trading at least. We've cleared almost all of the Russian furs from the warehouse.'

Isabelle nodded. She knew but made no attempt to deprive the clerk of the substance of his report.

'And it has sold for more silver than I've seen for a long time. The wool cloth will be almost cleared out by this evening and since it was all paid for, it will give a handsome profit.'

'It has been the best mart that I have ever attended. My husband would have been very proud.' Isabelle paused as she recalled the events of the last nine days. 'I think I've never seen more merchants here. We've never had such a fine choice of wine, spices and fish. Only this morning I purchased a loaf of sugar.' When the clerk looked shocked she added playfully: 'And I did worse too. I bought a pot of pickled lemons!'

Pexton laughed. 'Then it's a good thing that the furs

have sold as well as they have . . .'

For a moment there was a flash of intimacy between the clerk and his mistress. Then it was snuffed out by the raw look in his eyes. Isabelle glanced away.

'If you will excuse me, madam, I still need to make the purchases of ale and stockfish that you ordered.'

'Of course, of course.'

With a stiff little bow the clerk turned away. Isabelle watched him go and Eleanor observed the two of them with a feeling of sadness which quite disturbed her. Soon he had vanished amongst the throngs crossing the bridge over the Witham.

Richard Pexton pressed his way through the hordes of people. One hand clasped his purse and its silver coins. The other one warded off the pushing and shoving crowds. A few yards behind him his progress was being dogged by a figure careful to remain unobserved.

The trading on the west bank was almost as busy as that in the heart of the mart on Boston's Richmond Fee. Brightly coloured stalls displayed a staggering assortment of wares. Bricks and pantiles from Flanders lay cheek by jowl with pottery from Holland and spices from the Mediterranean. Cones of dirty brown sugar lay up against the pure white loaves of the type purchased by Isabelle. The pungent smell of the exotic spices seemed out of place under the low, grey sky of Lincolnshire.

Richard stopped for a moment beside a stall laden with dried and salted fish from the Baltic. He picked up a piece of board-hard stockfish and turned the dried cod over in his hands. It would suffice for the lower tables of the hall when the top table enjoyed this autumn's fresh eels.

After a few minutes of haggling he fixed a price acceptable to both himself and the German merchant, arranging to have the barrels of fish collected before the end of the day's trading. With only the ale now to purchase he pressed on deeper into the Fair of Holland, exchanging nods with the Lincoln merchants.

When the ale too had been purchased, Richard did not attempt to cross back into the town. Instead, he wandered away from the crowded market-place where the Lincoln men held sway. Drifting north he followed the bending bank of the river where the market-place gave way to another quayside. Richard sat down on a discarded barrel and watched the heavy waters in their endless flow. Soon he would have to go back but for the moment he shirked his responsibilities, needing to be alone with his pain.

Since Isabelle's return it was as if a veil had been drawn over the events of the journey to Ely. She had said nothing and he had dared not remind her of it and so the gulf had once again opened up between them. The gulf between a mistress and her man. It was as if the experience had been nothing more than a dream. He felt a sickening bitterness in the depth of his stomach. Picking up a pebble, he threw it far into the river. It splashed and was gone, like his hopes. Worse still the relationship between Isabelle and William seemed to be thawing like an icicle before the sun. Richard almost regretted enlisting the aid of the guildsman. As he thought over the matter he felt sick with frustration and jealousy.

Since William had confronted Spayne, he had become a regular visitor to the hall off Strait Bargate. Always there was a good reason: business arising from the trade in the Baltic; news of Edward and his schemes; a load of cloth newly brought from Lincoln to Boston. There was always a good reason for it but Richard recalled what William had said about marriage. Those words haunted him.

He felt that William's interest in his mistress was developing beyond the commercial. And, to make it worse, Isabelle seemed no longer to confide in her clerk. The brief moments of closeness had been snuffed out like a mutton-fat candle. All that remained of Richard's hopes was the wisp of smoke . . .

It was several minutes before he recognised that someone was calling his name. When he turned he was astonished to see Edward walking towards him. Richard leapt up as if stabbed. He had no wish to pass the time of day with Tony Crosse's bastard. The hatred was obvious on his face. Edward ignored it.

'Don't run away, Richard. I mean you no harm and a moment of your time will cost you nothing.'

'I've got nothing to say to you.'

'And nothing to say to the sheriff either it seems.'

Pexton turned scarlet. 'I've better things to do. Get out of my way you . . .'

'Running back to Isabelle? But she won't offer you any comfort, will she?'

Richard was stopped as if a tree had fallen before him. He turned a pale and angry face to his tormentor. 'What the hell do you mean by that?'

Edward made no rush to reply. Instead, he settled himself on the barrel which the clerk had so rapidly vacated.

'I'm at the market myself, selling wool and hides from the fen manors. And it's been a very good year for eels. We've salted down three hundred sticks . . .'

'What the hell did you mean by what you said just now?'

Edward's green-mottled blue eyes narrowed. 'You would not be the first clerk who fell in love with his mistress.' He paused. 'And a widow would be free to make a love choice . . .'

'You bastard . . .'

'I think I've made the point that you're not having much luck in proving that last accusation.' There was something so relaxed and confident in his tone that Richard was mesmerised. 'So let's talk about realities, shall we?'

'I don't know what you mean.'

'You love her and she doesn't love you. The best you can hope for is a smile now and then. Not much to have in bed with you, the memory of a smile.' Edward hesitated, watching the pain deepen on Pexton's face. 'So what do you owe her then, Richard? I'll tell you: damn all . . .'

'I'm going.'

Edward was on his feet. 'Before you go, just listen to this. Isabelle Crosse is finished. It doesn't matter what you think about it. She is finished. By Easter at the latest I shall have the entire Crosse inheritance. Minus her dower rights, of course. I have no intention of robbing a widow.' He looked straight at Pexton. 'All I want are my rights, and you know full well that I am going to get them, don't you?'

'You are a conniving son of a whore.'

Edward smiled a cruel smile. 'Now we both know that you're right on that point.' Richard gasped. 'You see, we have no need to play games. There are no witnesses here. I deserve the Crosse lands and only my damned father's infatuation with Isabelle stopped me from getting them.' The mask of coolness fell away a little; his voice was suddenly charged with intense anger. Then the glimpse was gone.

'Why are you telling me all this? What's to stop me going straight back . . .'

'Straight back to Isabelle? Well, firstly – so what? The sheriff will scarcely accord you the status of a neutral witness. Secondly, well, let's put it this way, why should you bother? What has she ever done for you?'

The knife twisted in Pexton's gut. He opened his mouth but the words of protest would not flow. The stream of his love had dried up.

Edward scratched his fox-red beard. 'I know that the juries in the fens will find for me. Furthermore I know that in the event of a contest here, there are many guildsmen who will side with me now.' He gave a confident smile. 'You would be amazed if I were to tell you the names of some of them . . .'

'What are you offering me?'

Richard's still voice made Edward pause a while to contemplate the man who stood before him. 'When she goes you will be finished too. As a clerk you will fall with her. Without her you have no future here. But with me you will have a fortune. I know you don't like me but that is not important. I don't ask you to love me.

I only ask that you recognise the way that the tide is turning. If you don't swim with it, Richard, you will drown. Believe me, you will drown.

'I can use a man of your proven ability. A man to look after my interests in Boston and the fens as competently as you did for my father. And, unlike Isabelle, I know how to reward those who serve me well.'

Richard turned away, his hands clenched by his side, his cheeks colourless.

'Think about it, Richard. You're no fool, whatever she thinks of you. Think about it . . .'

Edward picked up a pebble as Richard had done. Only instead of hurling it into the middle of the river, he casually tossed it in. It was the action of a man well pleased with his efforts and unwilling to exert himself. He yawned and watched the river flow by.

Richard got back to the hall in the late afternoon. The sun was low and the stalls were being dismantled in the market places on both sides of the river. He hurriedly dispatched some retainers to collect the barrels of fish and of ale that he had purchased that afternoon. Then he went to report to Isabelle.

He found her in the pantry examining the bread stocks. William Curteys was with her and both smiled warmly at the limping clerk's approach.

'You look very tired, Richard.' Isabelle seemed genuinely concerned. 'You have served me well these last nine days. Come and take some wine in the solar.'

The three retired to the privacy of the room where the butler and two servants waited on them.

'William has been telling me,' Isabelle confided in

Richard, 'that he has been to see Phillip Spayne again. However, nothing seems to move him . . .'

'I'd not put it quite like that. He's disturbed by what I've said to him. I suspect that no one has ever spoken to him like that before.'

'But he'll not change his story?' Richard's question forced them back to reality.

'No. He is adamant that there will be no changes on that front. He's boxed in tight. Like a pike with its head caught in a fish-pot.'

'I saw the sheriff today.' Isabelle pulled a pained face. 'He was at the Court of Piepowder, settling disputes in the market-place. He told me that he expects Edward to appear before the court of the shire in January. I shall be summoned too, of course. It seems Edward intends to charge me with holding the hall and goods in Boston without right.'

Richard recalled what Edward had said about the matter being settled by Easter. His silence prompted William to question him about his thoughts.

'Oh, nothing,' he lied, 'I was just thinking about the shire court. I expect Edward will put on quite a performance. He can turn on the charm when he wants to . . .'

'And the lies . . .' Isabelle added.

'Oh . . . yes,' Richard agreed slowly. 'And the lies . . .'

William interjected. 'We intend to ride out to see the beadle tomorrow. It may well be that the presence of Isabelle will shame him into acting the man after all. We can but hope.'

Richard agreed politely. 'If you'll excuse me, I have some matters to deal with, now that the mart is over.'

He bowed and left. As he shut the door he looked back. William had played the butler's part. He was pouring wine into Isabelle's goblet. She was smiling. Two good friends. Biting his lip he closed the door and dropped the latch.

Behind him William sipped at his wine and then sat down next to Isabelle. He was not sure exactly how to broach the subject. Nothing was ever simple with this woman. In the normal run of things there would at least be a father to negotiate with. That she stood alone was all too typical of the things that marked her out as different from other women. The things that challenged and disturbed a man and at the same time drew him on.

William Curteys was not used to being nervous. The disposition of spirit was alien to him. And he realised that whilst he had wealth and prestige, Isabelle was no shy teenager to be won by prosperity. Edward apart, she was a woman of means. She could choose and reject men without the iron hand of a father to guide her. Here was no dilemma to be resolved by a masculine cabal. A man needs must face a widow on ground of her own choosing. Words of a friend, who had once pursued such an heiress, came back to Curteys. All he could remember was one phrase which now echoed in his thoughts. It was a parody of the scriptures which summed up the powerful position of such a woman, wealthy and bereaved: 'the widow's might . . .'

The thought disquieted William. At least the only other time he had felt so exposed, love had followed on the heels of seemingly secure arrangements. This time his toes were on the edge of an unfathomable quicksand. He could not begin to explain to himself what drew him to such a disturbing woman; would dearly have liked to deny his heart – but he could not. It was because he was so unusually worried that he had planned out his strategy with such care. He was convinced that a woman like Isabelle Crosse required more than the outpouring of a man's heart.

'Isabelle,' he said slowly, 'I have a proposition to put before you.'

Isabelle looked intrigued. 'Go on . . .'

'Edward has homed in on you because you are a woman. And the men who back him think that they can intimidate you.' He put down his cup. 'They would think differently if you were married . . .'

Isabelle looked surprised. She opened her mouth to speak but William broke in before she could say a word. 'I am asking you to marry me. Your honour and your goods will be safe with me. He will not dare touch you if you are my wife. Many who prey on you now will back away if you are married to me. They will forget his claims. For they are only moved by the smell of easy pickings. Together we will forge a new alliance within the town. The united houses of Crosse and Curteys will not be intimidated by anyone.'

Isabelle's cheeks were a pale rose. 'Thank you, Will.' Her voice was tight. 'It would be, I am sure, a most prudent marriage.' She spoke the words as if she had vinegar on her tongue. 'A most prudent arrangement indeed. And it is most thoughtful of you. I shall think carefully about the proposition.'

William could feel the ground slipping away from him. He could not grasp what he had said wrong. 'There is no need to rush to a decision.' He was very conscious of the clipped sound of his own voice. 'We can talk of it again.' He downed his wine in one gulp. 'I must go now.' He stood up suddenly. 'Good day, Isabelle.'

'Good day, William.'

Once he was down in the hall William kicked savagely at a dog who wandered into his path, swore at his astonished retainers and strode out through the corridor. Out in the street he breathed in the cool air, gathering his thoughts. He had ruined it. He had explained it all carefully and yet he had clearly ruined everything. He had approached Isabelle prudently and in a manner designed to appeal to her grasp of the realities of the town and of trade. And yet the plan had collapsed before his eyes.

'What the hell did I do wrong?' he muttered as he pulled on the bridle of his horse. 'What more does she want? It must be obvious that I love her. Damnit but I have thrown over all reason to back her. What more does she want?'

He pulled himself up into the saddle and rode off down the busy street. His retainers kept a respectful distance behind him.

Back in the solar Isabelle leaned against the wall panel. Her heart was beating furiously. She did not know how to express her disappointment.

'A business transaction. Just a damned business transaction. What does he think that I am?'

A tear ran slowly over her cheek. She wiped it away with a clenched fist, thinking of Richard Pexton and his open love for her. She longed to love him too. To love him in defiance of William Curteys. But even that caused her the pain of guilt, for she knew that even as she had held on to Richard she had been thinking of William.

On Wednesday 9 December 1382 the weather finally broke. Torrential rain swept on to the east coast on a north-east wind. It rained solidly for a week. The days were dreary and bleak; the nights awash. On the following Monday it finally abated a little. On the Tuesday, Isabelle and William rode out into the fen country and through Kirton Meeres, their journey a tense one. With them went ten men, cloaked and armed, who seemed well aware of the chill between their respective master and mistress.

The waters were well up. On the seaward side of the causeway the salt marsh was flooded by surging sea water. On the landward side the silt fen was reduced to islands of low vegetation in a shifting, spreading lake.

'Apparently it's worse again in the southern fen country,' William observed, trying to break the icy silence. 'The Welland has been dammed back by the tide surges and some of southern Holland is two ells deep in floodwater.'

The horses slowed to a walk where part of the causeway had slipped away. A dense flock of knot lifted from the rippling salt marsh and flew in perfect unison over the water. They changed from white to mottled black as they wheeled and turned back again in their flight.

'I daresay 'tis not helped by the likes of Edward refusing to attend to the state of his drainage ditches and sea-dykes. Where one man reneges, a dozen of his fellows pay the price for his folly.'

William breathed a sigh of relief. Now at least they

were talking again. That was something. After the débâcle of his proposal he had had sleepless nights on the grounds that he had lost her for good. It was only then that he truly realised how much he wanted her.

'Too near the truth, Isabelle. Wohh, wohh . . .' William soothed his mount as it snorted with fear at the close-pressing edge of the causeway road. 'I've advised Ralph Kymes to report Edward to the Commission of Sewers. I dare say 'twill turn out that he has not even appointed a dyke reeve. At least they will fine him . . .'

'It will take more than a fine to get that one off my back, William.' Isabelle was riding side-saddle and glanced at her companion. 'I fear a fine will not reform him.'

'True enough, but every little helps. Who knows, if we are lucky he may refuse all summonses and they can wall him in a dyke. Now that would solve all our problems.'

Isabelle remembered a conversation that had taken place in another age. She fell silent as she recalled it. Looking ahead she could begin to guess the place where she and Richard had stopped and she had looked out to sea. It was ironic to pass the same spot this day when all that had begun that week seemed in jeopardy.

As she thought of her clerk, her feelings were once more at war within her. There was no denying the tenderness that she felt for him. No denying how much she valued him and trusted him. Yet it was tenderness that a woman might feel for a childhood sweetheart before childhood needs gave way to those of a woman. And only a few feet from her rode a man who stirred the needs of a woman, who angered her and yet challenged her. A man whom she desired to respect her as an equal and bed her as a woman . . .

The riders followed the same road as William and Richard had ridden in November. As they turned west towards the stolen manor of Bicker the rain began once more. It was light but was thrown against their backs by the wind.

'The sea-reach is well up.' A hooded William pointed to the left. The mud-flats were drowned and the water pushed against the sea-dyke. 'And from the depth of water in the fen the dyke between here and Bicker must have gone.'

Isabelle surveyed the scene. Kirton Meeres was badly flooded. Here and there an eddying channel showed where a flooded creak flowed deeper than the drowned land. 'It's getting worse, Will. If this continues it will flood right back to Boston.'

William was no longer listening. He was pointing ahead down the road. The curtain of rain lifted for a moment. Shadowy figures seemed to overflow the causeway. As they watched, one fell from the road and vanished into the sea-reach with its oozing mud. The rain closed down again and the picture blurred.

'There's something wrong. Stay here.'

Before Isabelle could protest, William had rallied half the riders and was spurring his horse down the dangerously narrow, raised road.

'I'm not just sitting here!' Isabelle dug her heels into her horse's flank. It leapt forward, followed by the remaining riders.

In the now driving rain William came upon a small battle being fought in the roadway and down in the water. Men were cursing and rolling in the mud. Some had fallen from the raised track and were floundering in the flood. At least two bodies were floating away on the grey water.

At the approach of the riders some of the men struggled to detach themselves and fled away down the track. Two others blocked the approach of the horses.

Curteys' mount immediately collided with a great bull-necked man who fell backwards. The horse slipped, tumbling from the dyke, but throwing William clear. He landed heavily and almost fell into the sea-reach but, digging his fingers into the dyke, he managed to pull himself back.

A heavy boot caught him on the shoulder. He collapsed over the dyke-side. Clawing at the earth he succeeded in saving himself from plunging into the swirling waters. The boot was jammed down on to his hands but the wet earth saved him. Even so blood oozed from his fingers. He looked up to a panting face. It was the face of the man at the old woman's cottage.

All along the causeway the road was a tangle of fighting bodies. There was no one to help Curteys. Desperately he cursed the man and tried to pull himself up. The boot fell again. Crack. His fingers broke and blood flowed from where William had bitten his own lip. The boot swung again. Curteys' swollen, crushed hands began to slide through the mud.

'Agghh . . .' A body crashed down on William and his face was rammed into the dirt. When he at last looked up, the man had vanished. In his place was the wide-eyed face of a horse, its teeth bared, its nostrils wide in flared fear.

410

Hands clutched William's cloak and he felt himself hauled from the dyke-edge. His own men were around him, their swords drawn, some smeared with blood.

Rushing forward, Isabelle threw her arms about the brown-haired guildsman. Exhausted, he leant against her shoulder, feeling her hair wet against his bruised cheek.

'What happened? Where's the whoreson who was killing me?'

'There.' Isabelle pointed out away from the bank.

William turned to see a head break surface ten yards into the channel. Arms flailed in a flurry of spray. The heavy head went under again. When it reappeared the mouth was just an open gash of terror. The current swept him further away. As William leant against Isabelle they watched the hands wave desperately one last time. Then they vanished beneath the restless surface.

Above the blood beating in his heart and temples, all William Curteys could hear was the cry of a curlew on the rain-sodden air. With his broken hand he hung on to Isabelle as tightly as he could. The rest of the footpads were either dead, or had fled, he was told as Isabelle wiped the filth away from his mouth. When he looked up he was surprised to see a pair of steely eyes and the moustached face of a prosperous-looking individual he had never seen before.

The man addressed himself to Isabelle. 'It must have been providence which brought you here, Mistress Crosse.' The ready smile broke out from amidst bruises. 'And if ever I did you a service, you more than repaid it today. You and your gallant companion.'

Isabelle laughed. 'Ralph Kymes, this is William

Curteys. You know I promised to introduce you?' The rain ran freely over her face. 'But I had rather hoped it could be in better circumstances.'

Then all three were laughing, although William's laughter came wincingly on account of the pain from his broken fingers and from the great bruises already shading his face and neck.

Phillip Spayne was pale as he faced the words of the lay steward of the abbey of Ely. He clearly had not anticipated any such embassy and was taken aback by it. On Kymes' suggestion Isabelle had not accompanied him to the church. Having enjoyed a comfortable night's sleep at Isabelle's hall, Kymes was rested from the attack on his party on the causeway and ready to speak to the chantry priest alone.

'So, as you are no doubt realising, the house of God at Ely has been sorely tried of late. Money owed to God has been denied His service and I myself have been set upon and nearly murdered.'

Spayne rested his head on his clasped hands as he listened to the steward's account of the assault which had come close to destroying him. 'But what has this attack to do with your complaints against Edward Crosse? And, more to the point, what has any of this got to do with me? I am a priest.'

Kymes appraised him coolly. 'I have no doubt that the attack was directly related to my desire to discover why the abbey has been denied its rights. Only the morning before I was set upon, I confronted this same Edward Crosse with the thefts he has perpetrated against the house of God. I have no doubt that I was attacked to silence a nuisance . . .'

'You have told the sheriff of this?'

'I have lodged a complaint but no doubt little will be done. I cannot prove that these footpads were sent by Crosse. They were lawless men, wolfheads who have no roots in this area. Few will recognise them. And the one who was recognised was swept away and drowned in the flood.

'But you must not mistake me. I do not lay evidence before you as before a court of the shire, or a judge of the king. I lay it before you as before a priest of Christ. You can see full well what manner of man you have allied yourself with.'

Spayne twitched. 'I spoke the truth. I spoke nothing but the truth.'

'So you say, and that is none of my business,' Kymes lied smoothly. 'But the abbey is my business. And there is a wolf loose in the fens who makes war on God's church. You have befriended that wolf. The abbey sees this and the abbey has a long memory.'

The priest started. 'You threaten me?' He was aghast. 'You are threatening me!'

'No, I'm warning you. God and His church will not forget a man who unites himself with such a one as you have. I have already spoken to the bailiff . . .'

Spayne was pale. 'It is that woman who has put you up to this. It is that woman . . .'

'Was it a woman who stole our fishing rights? Was it a woman who denied us "acre silver" and floods the fens? Was it a woman who tried to murder me?'

'You do not understand.' A sweat was breaking out on Spayne's brow. He had turned a grey colour about his cheeks. 'You do not see it as it is . . .'

Ralph Kymes leant towards the pale priest. 'I

suggest you examine your conscience. There is no church court in the land will accuse you of any crime. But there is a higher court which judges the hearts of men. Think about your motives, Phillip Spayne.'

Satisfied that he had done all he could, the steward got up to go. Spayne seized his arm. The cold fingers dug into his flesh, the deep-set eyes were wide, the pupils dilated. 'You don't understand what I've been through. You do not know how things are here. A priest must oppose sin and wickedness. Always . . . everywhere . . .'

Kymes stared at him in unblinking severity. 'I understand hate. I've known it eat a man up. Have you ever seen that?' Before Spayne could reply he added, 'And I understand lust.' The priest's grip intensified. 'And lust is any desire that feeds on the destruction of another. Examine your soul before God.'

Kymes prised off the grip and left Spayne standing before the altar. The priest was breathing hard, panting as if he had been running. 'You don't understand . . .' he muttered. He turned back to the altar. 'You don't understand . . .' This time he was staring at the crucifix itself. 'I have to. I must . . . You don't understand. That woman is a sink of sin . . .'

Isabelle was waiting outside in the cold air. William and Richard were with her. 'Well?' she inquired. 'What did he say?'

Kymes avoided her question. 'The man is eaten up. I know nothing of him but that. Something is eating him up.'

'But he said nothing to aid our cause?' Isabelle emphasised the word 'our'. She was anxious to bind Crosse and Ely closer together. Only that morning she had learned of more guildmasters who were pressurising the bailiff to recognise Edward's rights as a guildmaster in the town. The trap was closing about her and she felt the iron of its jaws.

'He said nothing to indicate that he repents of his support for Edward.'

Isabelle sighed. 'Pray God that something happens soon. If not, we are finished.' There was no panic in her voice, just the calm statement of the inevitable.

She led the way back across the market-place. William Curteys took her arm and Kymes and Pexton fell in behind them. Richard watched the pair ahead of him under hooded eyes. He was remembering what Edward had said on the afternoon of the last day of the November mart.

Richard Pexton was not the only man deeply troubled that morning. Phillip Spayne was hardly able to concentrate on his prayers before the altar. At noon he slipped out of the church. He made no response to passers-by who spoke to him. His thick black cloak was wrapped about his body and some invisible cloak seemed wrapped around his mind. Like a stooping raven he strode away from the place of prayer and worship. The dark figure, with the tonsured shock of red hair, made his way north, up Wormgate. The wind blew colder now and funnelled between the leaning timber buildings and though rain blew in his face he made no effort to protect himself from the cold, spitting drops.

Half-way up the street he paused before one of the tenement buildings. Behind him Nicholas Coppledyke was admiring a new reinforced gateway which lay across the access alley running from the street. While nervous apprentices held up a cloak to shelter him, he directed two men who were fixing a lock to the gate.

At the sight of the priest, Coppledyke called out a self-satisfied greeting. Spayne turned and looked at and through the stocky draper. It was as if he recognised the name called but could not quite remember to whom it belonged. He stared for a moment, then ignored the greeting and went into the opposite building. Coppledyke's choleric features flushed and he turned to abuse the men working on the security of his gate.

Spayne knew Edward was in Boston for the week and demanded admittance of the armed retainer who stood sheltering in the passageway into the building. For a couple of minutes he was kept waiting then he was escorted in.

Edward was at his noon-time dinner, his accompanying servants eating on long tables before him. It seemed to be an almost exclusively male gathering. Only Ann sat, conspicuous by her femininity, beside her husband.

Edward was in ebullient mood. He beckoned to the priest to come and join him. A member of the high table was dismissed without ceremony and went muttering to join the lower orders. Phillip Spayne sat down on the bench beside Edward, squeezed uncomfortably between husband and wife.

'What brings you here, Phillip? 'Tis a pleasure but something of a surprise.' Edward's voice carried the hint of disapproval.

Spayne seemed unaware of the note. Indeed he seemed unaware of the question. He stared out at the swearing, spitting crowd in front of him. Edward repeated the question in a louder voice. At last the priest came to.

'I need to speak to you.'

'Well, you've found me. What is it?'

Spayne stared at the table laden with food. ' 'Tis a fast day today . . .' He looked into the grinning face of his host. 'You know Holy Church commands fasts on a Wednesday. And this of all Wednesdays. Why 'tis the winter Ember Day fast . . .'

Edward exploded with mirth. 'Good God, man. Surely you did not come up here just to scold me over a fast missed? Is that the reason for this visit, against all sensible politics?' Suddenly he was no longer laughing. 'I take it you have chosen to be seen with me for some better reason?'

Spayne was frowning. 'Who are these men? They look like robbers. They have the faces of wolves . . .' A shadow fell across his features. 'Like ravening wolves . . .'

Edward was getting angry. 'Who they are is no concern of yours. What are you here for?'

'Did you order an attack on the lay steward of the abbey of Ely?'

Edward sneered. 'Who told you that?'

'Did you? I have to know.'

Edward put down his knife. 'You do not have to know anything.' The words were savage. 'Never forget that. You do not have to know a thing.'

'You did, didn't you . . . ?' Spayne's face was long and grey. 'And what of the woman murdered in the fens? Curteys says that you had her killed because she knew . . .'

'Shut up, you stupid fool.' Edward pushed against the priest. 'What the hell is the matter with you?'

Spayne's lips were trembling. 'I will not be party to murder. As God is my judge, I'll not be party to it. I won't . . .'

'You're not party to it, you fool. And I did not do it. It's all the lies of my enemies.' Spayne looked unconvinced so Edward did not pursue that tack. 'Besides, you are in too deep to get gutless now. The time for reflection is long past. You had a time to think about it. So don't bleat on about the judgement of God. We both did what we did with our eyes wide open so don't get holy with me now. Besides, if you don't hold your nerve you will soon realise that you have as much to lose as I do.'

'But the killing . . . For the sake of Christ, the killing . . .' Spayne's voice was pathetically strained. It was the voice of one who has woken from a nightmare to find that the horror continues. He gripped Edward's arm.

Unlike Kymes the red-bearded man was not gentle. He roughly broke the frenzied grip, bringing his face close to Spayne's ashen features. 'Listen to me.' The words were spoken slowly. 'Curteys and the whoreson from Ely are nothing to do with you. You just stick to your story. They have got no evidence which will break that – nothing. Do you understand me?'

Spayne licked his lips and nodded.

'Good. And they'll get nothing to break it either. That's why they are on to you. They want to make you feel guilty . . .'

'But the killing and the acts against God's house at Ely?'

'Shut up.' The command was like a bucket of water in the priest's face. 'Shut your mouth about all that. It's nothing to do with you. You just remember that you swore that you saw them marry. Nothing else concerns you. Leave the thinking to me. You can do the praying.' The contempt in Edward's voice was intense and he turned from the priest with a sneer.

Spayne rose from the table, his tall frame hanging over Edward for a moment like the shadow of some black bird of pray. Without a word he went.

Edward called to the sour-faced retainer who had been moved. The man laid down his trencher and answered the summons.

'Follow him,' Edward hissed, 'and I want to know the names of everyone that he speaks to. Understood?' The man grunted. 'Well, get out . . .'

Edward returned to his meal, drinking heavily from the jug of wine. He called for another which he drained too. The liquid stained his new wool tunic and he tore at his bread angrily.

'What did he mean?' Ann's voice quavered with fear.

Edward turned. 'What?'

'He said you killed people in the fens. You didn't? No, you could not have done. Tell me you did not do it.'

Ann was grey-cheeked. For so long she had lied to herself about the kind of man that she had been made to marry. She had clung to those lies the way that a drowning person clutches at twigs and branches. She had struggled to keep her love afloat. And in the name of that love she had swallowed indignities and tried to believe his lies. But more and more she had gagged as she forced herself to feed on his deceits. For years she had subjected the logic of her mind to the tyranny of her desperate heart but she could do it no longer.

'I didn't do it!' Edward poured more wine, waving off the attentions of his butler.

Ann's sea-green eyes were tearful. 'I don't believe you, Edward.' She was frightened and so the next sentence came quickly. 'You told him to "hold his nerve": you meant about the marriage, didn't you?'

Edward twisted her wrist until she cried out. He laughed at her fear and anguish, pulling her to him.

'He lied, didn't he?' She was crying now and the tears fell across her pretty rose cheeks. 'He lied about the marriage. Tell me the truth!'

'You stupid bitch.' Edward was dangerously drunk. 'You damned stupid bitch.' With his free hand he struck her in the face. 'Never say that, you whore.' He hit her again. 'You useless little bitch . . .'

Ann fell over the table. Pewter plates were swept off. Bread trenchers and wine cascaded off the board. In the hall the rowdy noise stopped. Ann was crying hysterically.

Edward rose and swayed. 'Don't ever say that again. Not ever, hear me?'

He called some of his men to help him. He had an important meeting later that day with the guildsmen who were supporting him. He would have to sleep off the wine if he was ever to be ready for it. As the men helped him to his chamber he ignored his weeping wife.

Edward slept until the wet December afternoon died away in darkening twilight. Then he rose and went out, speaking not a word to his bruised wife. Crossing the market-place he passed Matthew Redman riding home with an escort. Redman acknowledged the called greeting with a raised hand.

Edward caught him up. 'I've not heard from you, Matthew. Not since our talk. I felt we understood one another. I go before the sheriff in January,' he added. 'It'll all be settled by the spring. I look forward to hearing from you. You know we can work together; nothing has changed about my offer to my friends.'

Redman simply nodded noncommittally. He had made his decision but had put off the moment of committing his thoughts to paper, his resolution to words. Returning grim-faced to the hall he called for sheets of vellum, a quill and ink. Then he dismissed his attendants. What he was about to do he would accomplish alone. The words would be in his own hand; he would not use a clerk. Soon everyone would know what he had done. He paused to consider that. But for now, it would be known to him alone and to those who read the words in his own hand.

He ran his fingers over the smooth and expensive vellum. He hesitated before he wrote. 'But I have no choice.' He spoke to himself firmly. 'I have to take the long view. I have only one course open to me.' Finally resolved, he put pen to paper. 'My dear Edward, You were right when we met in the market-place. I should have acted sooner . . .'

Outside the closed shutters, the rain beat against the house. Alone with his task the silver-haired Matthew Redman wrote in silence, a block of red wax and his personal seal beside him. The only noise within the room came from the sputtering candle and the scratch of the nib on the smoothed vellum. When at last the deed was done, he scattered fine pumice over the sheets to dry the ink. Then he held the candle-flame to the little red block and sealed the document with hot drops of wax.

Matthew Redman was not the only person writing that night. In Richard Pexton's room a candle was also burning. With face tight with strain the clerk was painfully penning a letter of his own. After each word he stopped and gazed into the shadows. It was as if the exertion of writing was draining his strength. At one point a tear ran down his cheek and he wiped it away with the back of his hand. But still he wrote. Richard Pexton, like Matthew Redman, had also made the most difficult decision in his life.

When the deed was done, the clerk folded the letter and tucked it inside his tunic. He would deliver it by hand if the man to whom he was writing was not available. With his cloak wrapped about him he slipped out of the hall. In the shadows of Strait Bargate he almost ran into another hurrying figure. Both were cloaked against the rain and neither even looked at the other, each locked into their own private worlds.

Isabelle and Eleanor were sewing in the solar. It was late, almost nine o'clock. Soon they would retire to their shared room. Eve was asleep and the butler was waiting on them.

'I think that you have been very brave.' Eleanor paused from her embroidery. 'God knows this autumn has been hard on all of us. But on you . . .'

Isabelle laid down her needle. 'I don't know about brave. I only know that I could have done nothing without my friends.' She gave a sad smile to her companion. 'But now I truly fear that we have lost. Spayne will never side with me and, without that, all I can do is delay the inevitable.' She looked about the room. 'I shall miss this place.'

'William still thinks he may shake Spayne.'

'I never thought that he would come to support me so. Or I come to rely on him as I do. I fear that his words are a kindness designed to comfort the dying.'

She fell quiet. The thought of Will's proposal still pained her. Despite his welcome support she had hoped for so much more from him. So much more of himself. At last she continued. 'Two months ago this would have destroyed me. Now, though I will fight to the last, I can live with defeat. Is that fatalism?'

Eleanor considered. 'No, I don't think so. It's having come to find your own peace. There are many who are triumphant who never find it. You had little enough of it before this last year, did you?'

The gentle tease brought a smile to Isabelle's face. 'When I was doing well, you mean.' The two laughed.

'Neither were you helped this September when none of your friends saw your need. I shall always blame myself for that. Lord knows I thought I knew you better than anyone, but all I saw was pride when I should have seen pain.'

'That is behind us now. Besides, I was not alone.'

'Richard?'

Isabelle sighed. 'Yes, Richard. He alone understood my pain. We were two lonely souls together. I feel that I have done him a great wrong. It has tormented me since I returned from the abbey. Somehow I will make it up to him.'

'How have you wronged him?' Eleanor's heart sank. She suspected her fears about Richard had not been ill-founded. 'What have you done?'

'Not yet. I shall tell you soon but not yet. It is still too close and I have not yet resolved how to speak of it with him.' She paused. 'One thing is sure, I have put it off too long and must face it tomorrow.' Isabelle's face revealed the intensity of the pain that she felt for Richard. She doubted that she could ever really put it right now.

'He is a good man, Richard,' Eleanor concluded.

'I am surrounded by good friends. I do not know what I would do without you all.'

There was a soft rap on the door. The butler went to attend to it, returning to whisper into Isabelle's ear.

'I shall come down and speak with her directly.' Isabelle put aside her sewing frame. 'And she would not give her name?' The butler shook his head.

Isabelle and Eleanor descended into the hall. The trestle tables had been put to one side and the servants were playing 'hoodman blind' across the rush-strewn floor. They bowed at the presence of their mistress.

In the enclosed passageway which divided the hall from the buttery and pantry the visitor was waiting. A hood was drawn up to conceal her face, its features in deep shadow before the rush torch which illuminated her figure.

'Who are you? What message do you bring me in the dark of such a wild, wet night?'

Instead of answering, the visitor simply slipped back her hood. Wavy, mouse-coloured hair fell around a pretty face; a pretty face spoilt by a purple swelling about one eye and a full sensuous mouth bruised and split by a brutal blow.

'Ann Crosse!' The name came involuntarily to Isabelle. She started at both the identity and the evidence of violence. She did not know whether to be outraged or amazed that this woman had come to her home.

'No,' the visitor answered, 'I am not Ann Crosse; I am more properly called Ann Moyne.'

The next morning Edward was roused from a heavy sleep. Alcohol still bruised his eyes with hammer blows and he felt as if files had been rasped across his tongue. He had returned late to find two letters waiting for him, and his wife asleep in bed. Now he was not best pleased at being summoned from his bed, even though it was already seven o'clock and the town was about its business.

In the hall he found Nicholas Coppledyke pacing restlessly. The draper's little eyes glittered when he saw Edward. 'Look at this.' He was almost beside himself with rage. 'Look at what arrived before I took to my bed last night.'

Edward took the vellum sheet. He recognised the broken seal and turned it over to read. He scanned the closely written lines, tensing as he consumed the words.

'I can't believe that he would be such a fool.' Coppledyke was not only angry, he was stunned; even a little frightened. 'He must be mad to do such a thing at a time like this.'

Edward returned the letter. 'So, Redman is calling in all the money that you owe him . . .'

'Yes, and what am I to do?'

Edward ignored the fearful inquiry. '. . . Unless you remove your lock and allow Isabelle free access to her tenement yard. And support her in the guild assembly . . .'

'Damn him, damn him.' The draper's voice rose in pitch. 'He will ruin me. The filthy sod. He knows that I can't repay it yet. The miserable dog. It's all the fault of that bloody woman. God, she is poison!'

Edward had received his own personal missive from Redman. It had stunned him too. It did not seem possible that the guildsman could have thrown up the offer of his debts being cut. To do so at this late stage, when it was so clear that Edward would soon be in possession of his full rights, was unbelievable. The man was clearly a fool.

'Forget Redman.'

'Forget him? How can I forget him? I owe the bastard. If he calls the loan in it will cost me half my stock.'

Edward was about to assure Coppledyke that Redman could be dealt with but something stopped him. A sudden thought crossed his mind. 'You had best show this letter to the bailiff. 'Tis disgraceful that he should treat you so. The bailiff must see it. Only then will Isabelle's complicity be seen by everyone. Go and show him now.'

'But what about the money?' Coppledyke's voice was a whine. 'What about that? The bailiff won't advance me it, will he!'

Edward smiled. 'You show the bailiff. I will lend you the money.'

'Oh, my God, Edward, thank you.' He scratched at the mole on his cheek. 'I won't forget this. Between us we will do for that woman and her friends.'

'No question of it.' Edward nodded curtly and left the draper.

Coppledyke, caught unawares by the sudden termination of the interview, stood before the curious stares of Edward's retainers; then, mustering what dignity he could find, he marched out to seek out the bailiff.

On the stairs to his chamber Edward held a swift conversation with the man who had followed Spayne. '. . . Yes, that's right. I want a couple of them. Ones who have no connection with me. Try on the Lincoln side of the river. You know the type. And be discreet, you ape.'

As he ascended the stairs Edward felt for the second letter tucked inside his linen shirt. It had been a much more welcome letter.

Edward was not the only one up early that morning. Isabelle sought the presence of her clerk but in vain. He had been absent the night before and was still nowhere to be found. The servants reported that he had come back very late and arisen very early. As a result she was unable to tell him the momentous news brought to her by the tearful Ann. Instead she sent for William, who came in a hurry.

'You know that she cannot give evidence against her own husband?' William was excited but cautious. 'Even if we brought her before the sheriff informally, her evidence could be regarded as irrelevant. A wife cannot hang her husband. Besides, would she do it anyway? In the cold light of day she will have had plenty of time to consider what Edward will do to her.'

'I know,' Isabelle conceded, 'but at last we know that someone has the courage to speak out. God alone knows what that woman has suffered. To begin with I nearly had her thrown from the hall, after all that she has said against me. It was the marks of violence on her that stopped me . . . And then when she spoke it was as if she had suffered alongside me. God knows she confessed herself to me as if I was a priest.'

Isabelle blushed at what she had just said. And yet that had been how Ann had approached her – as if only Isabelle could absolve her of the guilty burden of slanders and lies.

'Yes, but I am very much afraid that Edward will silence her long before she can denounce him.' William considered the situation. 'My God, but he must have abused her to encourage such a betrayal.'

Isabelle looked at him strangely. She had not thought of that before. Ann was betraying her husband. How like a man to remind her of that. But anyway, William was right, they were far from saved.

'What does Richard think of all this?'

Isabelle was plainly troubled. 'I don't know where he is. He arose at first light . . .'

'Isabelle!' It was Eleanor, who had gone to look for the clerk. 'His horse is not in the stable. I've no idea where he can have gone.'

Behind her trotted Eve, crying, 'Ichar . . . Ichar . . .'

'It's all right my love,' Isabelle said comfortingly, 'Richard will be back soon.' She cast a worried glance at her two close friends. 'I'm sure that he will.'

Richard did not return all that day. After the noontime dinner a letter arrived from Matthew Redman

asking to see Isabelle and William during the afternoon. Isabelle readily agreed, but shortly after the
meal in the hall another Redman apprentice appeared
at Strait Bargate. He was bloody and dishevelled and
he brought horrific news.

'My master is dead,' he sobbed. 'Oh, sweet Jesus, he
has been murdered.'

Curteys pulled the man roughly from his knees.
'What in damnation do you mean?'

'We were on our way here. After dinner. By the fish
shambles two men attacked him. Attacked him with
knives . . .'

'And what the hell were you doing to protect him?'

The apprentice pulled roughly away. 'I took a blade
from one of the dogs . . .'

He groped at the sodden tabard. Only then did
William realise the extent of the man's injury. Blood
had soaked the layers of cloth and quite obscured the
device of Redman worked on it.

'We did what we could.' The apprentice was crying
openly. 'Never has the like happened here. They took
us by surprise. My master took a blade through his ribs.
We tried to staunch the flow.' His eyes were pleading.
'We did! We tried as best we could and carried him to
the porch of the church. He died there before Spayne
could confess him . . . God, even the priest seemed
half-mad to see my master killed . . .'

William had pulled on his cloak. 'And what of the
filth who did this?'

'Dead, both of them.'

'You killed the scum?'

'No.' The apprentice was white. 'As they ran from us

they met retainers of Edward Crosse.' He glanced at
Isabelle, unsure if he had used the right surname.
'They killed them. Cut them down as they ran for a
boat moored by the bridge. Both of the dogs are dead.'

Horrified and bewildered by the messenger's tale,
Isabelle spoke in a strained whisper. 'I do not believe
that this is possible.'

'But there is more, madam. As I came here from the
church I heard that the bailiff has seized Nick
Coppledyke for the killing.'

'What?' Isabelle and William spoke as one.

'It seems there was some row between him and my
master, only last night. Something about a loan. Now
Coppledyke is taken and accused of hiring lordless
men to kill my master.'

'And where is Edward?' William was sombre.
'Where is he?'

'I do not know, sir,' the apprentice replied.

The only person who knew where Edward would be
was at that moment standing in the wet grass on the
causeway road south-west of Boston. Richard Pexton
pulled his cloak about his shoulders and leant against
his mount. He watched the spiral descent of geese on to
the drowned land on the seaward side of the dyke. He
brooded on the melancholy of the winter scene.

He had stood there for a long time. What he was
about to do was more costly than he had ever
imagined. He of all people knew the bitter taste of
betrayal. As he pondered that, he thought once more
of the dyke-side near Ely. His heart broke within him
at the contemplation of what he had hoped for and how
transient his possession of it had been.

The feeling of pain woke him from his inactivity. He

fondled his horse's mane then put his boot in the stirrup and pulled himself up. He had a few more miles to ride before he met with Edward. He wanted to be there first.

He rode along a section of the causeway where the tide ran fast at its ebbing. Already the muddy waters were on the turn. Soon they would run as fast as a leat beside the sea-dyke. Richard pulled his reins and brought his horse to a stop. At this point an arm of the dyke swung higher than the road on the seaward side. He was in totally open countryside. There was no farmstead or cottage in sight. Only the dark waters of the flooded fen on one side and the sea on the other. A flock of wintering snow buntings were feeding on the coarse grasses of the dyke. They rose at Richard's approach with a flash of white wings.

He climbed from the road on to the dyke and limped along it for some distance. Seating himself on the wet grass he waited. Within the hour there was movement on the causeway. The riders kept a steady pace and rode two abreast.

'About time too,' Richard muttered.

Already the sun was well down in the west. There was only three hours of daylight left at the most, and that was a gift of the wind which had scattered the lowering clouds. The riders halted on the causeway, near where Richard's horse was grazing. The leader dismounted and climbed the dyke towards where Richard was seated some twenty yards along the dyke edge. The dismounted man walked the crest towards him.

'For God's sake, Richard, why was it necessary to meet out here?' But Edward was smiling. 'There are quiet spots closer to Boston.'

Richard stood up to meet the new arrival. He let his cloak fall away on to the dyke. 'You read my letter?'

'Of course! Why else would I be here?'

'Quite.'

'You are a wise man, Richard Pexton. I will reward your wisdom – and soon.'

Pexton was without expression. 'You will win against her, won't you?'

'There's no question about it. She can slander me but nothing can touch my right to what is mine.'

Richard nodded; he believed that too. Despite everything done in her defence, Isabelle had lost. Deceit had closed ranks against the truth.

'I have never betrayed before . . .' The clerk's voice was strained. 'This will not come easy to me. I shall miss her.' He paused. 'And I shall miss the child.'

Edward was cold and had no time to witness the clerk's heart-searching. Yet he held his impatience in check. The deed was worth the price. This would really hit Isabelle hard.

'Think of it not as betrayal. After all, what has she given you? Think on it, man. What has she given you?'

Pexton moved forward. 'But betrayal?'

'It is not so bad a thing. A man must look after his own.'

Richard offered his hand in a formal sign of friendship. Edward took it and laughed loudly. The clerk's grip tightened as a look of anguish and hatred spread across his features and suddenly he cried out, 'I love her. I shall look after my own. Here is the taste of betrayal . . .' He pulled Edward violently towards him, butting him in the face. Blood coursed from

Edward's nose as he grappled with his betrayer.

'You bastard . . .' Edward drove his knee into Richard's groin. Richard cried out in agony but did not let go. Edward twisted like a snake, butting Pexton again and again.

The men on the causeway were running towards them, slipping on the wet grass. One unslung a bow and notched an arrow. Regardless, Edward clawed at Richard's eyes, digging his nails into the edge of the socket. Blood ran into the grey-flecked beard. A hand was freed and Edward pulled a knife; plunging it into Pexton's chest. There was a grinding of metal and Richard fell back at the force of the blow. No blood spurted.

'You bastard . . . wearing mail . . . you son of a whore . . .' Edward leapt on Richard, who rolled and kicked. He was on his feet but made no attempt to escape Edward's knife. Instead he seized him in a hug. Digging in his heels he pushed the younger man to the dyke edge. The dark current swept below them.

'Madman. Bloody madman . . . kill us both . . .' Edward spat and tried to get away from the sea. 'Mad . . .'

Edward managed to turn Richard. The clerk's back was to the running retainers. For an instant he remained there then a longbow snapped and hissed. The arrow smashed into Richard, below his left shoulderblade. Through his heart and out of his chest it went, and into Edward's shoulder. The two men were pinned together; made one by the bloody shaft and steel head, the concentrated force of the blow throwing them both forward over the dyke edge and into the sea.

By the time the retainers reached the spot the current had carried the two men out into the sea-reach. One man was struggling but was riveted to a corpse. It was Edward who screamed and thrashed but the weight of mail and the dead man pulled him under. His fingers clawed at the air, seeking a grip on nothing. Then both were gone.

It was a clear spring day. Isabelle was watching as her men pulled a great bed out of the manor house at Bicker. They hauled it into the yard and broke it up until its wooden skeleton lay smashed amidst the dirt, straw and dung.

William Curteys came out of the house accompanied by Ann Moyne. She too watched as the bed was destroyed. Then both came over to Isabelle.

'You know that you are always welcome here.' Isabelle reached out and touched Ann's arm. 'Always.'

'Thank you.' She looked at the bed. 'There were good times too. He was not always . . .'

'No, I know.'

The two women stood awkwardly in one another's presence. So much united them and yet so much still stood between them. Only time would heal that wound, the wound that Edward had caused both of them.

'You have the manor at Swineshead and you will not want . . .'

'Save for a husband.' Ann stepped forward and kissed Isabelle. 'But that is not your fault.' Then she glanced away.

Isabelle wandered out of the stockade towards the church. The low sun lay across the squat tower. Behind her, Eve was running about the yard under Eleanor's supervision, a litter of puppies romping about them both. Between the church and the manor the stream ran down to the sea-reach. Isabelle sat on a stump and looked towards the haze above the water.

'He died to give me all this. You know that?'

'I know.' William Curteys knelt beside her. 'And all the time he never knew that Spayne had hanged himself.'

'Spayne guessed who it was had ordered Matthew killed. And he knew what lay behind it – his hate as much as Edward's greed. He had allowed Edward to feed, little knowing the monster that he would become.'

'It is always that way with hate.'

Isabelle looked at the guildsman with the hair of polished oak. Something more sensitive had grown out of the cynicism, something stronger; more precious.

'I only wish I could have talked to Richard . . .' Isabelle paused. 'I never told him I was sorry.' Then she added. 'It was an awful thing that he did. But it was done for love. God rest him, he faced the battlefield after all.'

As she thought of the clerk in his hour of decision she felt overwhelmed with grief. With what despairing love had he gone to his death? For she had left it too late to face up to what had happened to them both on the way to Ely. 'Tomorrow I will speak with him,' she had told Eleanor. And before she could do so he had

made his sacrifice. A gull flew in from the sea-reach of
Bicker Haven. For a moment she watched its swooping flight; watched the dip of the wings in the sunlight.

'He was not a bold man but he became a truly brave
man . . .' Her voice faltered as she recalled him, the
only person who had touched her in her agony, whom
she had needed and yet never desired in the way he so
clearly longed for her. If only she could have turned
back the shadow on the sundial she would have
travelled to Ely again and done it uncomforted rather
than cause that lonely man to embrace a love that was
but a phantom born of despair. If only . . .

'But I cannot go back . . .' She answered the query
which had existed only in her thoughts. 'I can only say
that I am sorry. And though it dies low, the flame of
that sorrow will always burn within me.'

William did not ask her for what she was sorry.
There would be a time for that. It was not now. Besides
which, he could guess a little of it. He too had known
Pexton for a long time and only lately come to value
him.

Kneeling beside her, he was overwhelmed with love
for this woman. 'Isabelle, this is not the place and
probably not the time either. Nevertheless I cannot
wait. I have come to love you. I think perhaps I always
did. Even when I was a burr under your saddle I think I
loved you. I hardly know why I tried you so. I suppose I
had never met a woman like you.' He laughed ruefully,
almost shyly. 'You can challenge a man, you know!
And disconcert him.' He grinned. 'And inspire him
too. And I was worried for you, though I suppose you
did not see concern in my words – only hostility . . .'

'William . . .' Isabelle reached out a hand and

touched his hair. 'William . . .'

'No, let me finish, or I will never have the courage to say it. It was in the Baltic that I slowly came to see what was happening to me. For years I have been unmoved by a woman. Deep down inside no one touched my heart in any way. I had cauterised old wounds and thought that my heart was dead. And then Tony Crosse's widow changed from a quiet beauty to a formidable guildmaster. You were the first woman in years to make me look twice and God knows it was in anger at first. But you quickened my passions and whilst at first all I saw was headstrong wilfulness, in time I saw courage and nobility and dignity.' He paused and looked down, biting his lip. 'There are times that you worry me still but I can live with that. Indeed, a woman like you will always mate love with worry in a man. For I have learnt that love is no quiet and cosy thing. Rather it is a gale that turns everything upside down and changes all things . . .'

Isabelle gave a shy smile. 'And all the time I longed to win your respect, though I would not dare admit it. My love too had a difficult birth.'

'Marry me, Isabelle. Marry me.'

'I have hurt too many men. One who served me well paid too high a price for love of me . . .'

'For God's sake, Isabelle, it is my right to choose the path I go along. I know that you are not as other women. You do not need to tell me that.'

Isabelle was silent. It seemed incredible that she should be holding back. How she had longed to hear these words, yet now she was holding his love away from her. She could hardly understand why.

It was more than guilt over Richard's death. It was

because it was all too comfortable, too safe. Pexton had died to protect her independence. All the struggles of the past year had been in order to prove that she could survive in the guildmaster's world. It was not easy to turn from all that, to give all that up, despite the longings of her heart. And yet she loved William Curteys. Isabelle was torn by the counter-currents of emotion.

'I love you, William. It is just that I need a little time to piece together my thoughts. A wild wind has run through them these past few months and I must settle them again. I must come to myself a little more. Can you understand that?'

William sighed. 'I should have known that the road to your heart could never run through peaceful lands.' He paused. 'And I suppose that you have plans for the passing of this time?'

'There is talk amongst the town guildsmen of another expedition to the Russias. I would like to go one more time . . .'

'Isabelle Crosse, I have never met a woman like you before, and there are days that I wish I never had.' He smiled the old, cynical smile. 'But I always repent of that wish, of course.'

Isabelle laid her hand upon his and he held it fast. 'Just a little time, William . . .'

The guildsman nodded as he held her hand. For a long while they just sat there, in the sunlight beside the church; with the light shimmering on the water.